Janet Evanovich's Stephanie Plum novels are:

"Suspenseful."
—*Los Angeles Times*

"Terrific."
—*San Francisco Chronicle*

"Irresistible."
—*Kirkus Reviews*

"Thrilling."
—*The Midwest Book Review*

"Hilariously funny."
—*USA Today*

"A blast of fresh air."
—*The Washington Post*

"Inventive and fast-paced."
—*San Diego Union-Tribune*

"Superb."
—*Detroit Free Press*

TWICE THE PLUM

TWO BOOKS IN ONE

PLUM SPOOKY

and

VISIONS OF SUGAR PLUMS

JANET EVANOVICH

St. Martin's Paperbacks

This is a work of fiction. All of the characters, organizations, and events portrayed in this novel are either products of the author's imagination or are used fictitiously.

TWICE THE PLUM: PLUM SPOOKY copyright © 2008 by Evanovich, Inc. and VISIONS OF SUGAR PLUMS copyright © 2002 by Evanovich, Inc.

For information address St. Martin's Press, 175 Fifth Avenue, New York, NY 10010.

ISBN: 978-1-250-16510-7

Our books may be purchased in bulk for promotional, educational, or business use. Please contact your local bookseller or the Macmillan Corporate and Premium Sales Department at 1-800-221-7945, ext. 5442, or by e-mail at MacmillanSpecialMarkets@macmillan.com.

Printed in the United States of America

St. Martin's Paperbacks edition / November 2017

St. Martin's Paperbacks are published by St. Martin's Press, 175 Fifth Avenue, New York, NY 10010.

10 9 8 7 6 5 4 3 2 1

PLUM
SPOOKY

I'd like to acknowledge the Unmentionable assistance of Alex Evanovich, Peter Evanovich, and my St. Martin's Press editor and friend, SuperJen Enderlin.

Chapter
ONE

Sometimes you get up in the morning and you know it's going to be *one of those days*. No toothpaste left in the tube, no toilet paper on the cardboard roll, hot water cuts out halfway through your shower, and someone's left a monkey on your doorstep.

My name is Stephanie Plum, and I'm a bail bonds enforcement agent for Vincent Plum Bail Bonds. I live in a one-bedroom, one-bath, unremarkable apartment in a three-story brick box of a building on the outskirts of Trenton, New Jersey. Usually I live alone with my hamster, Rex, but at eight-thirty this morning, my roommate list was enlarged to include Carl the Monkey. I opened my door to go to work, and there he was. Small brown monkey with long, curled tail, creepy little monkey fingers and toes, crazy, bright monkey eyes, and he was on a leash hooked to my doorknob. A note was attached to his collar.

HI! REMEMBER ME? I'M CARL AND I BELONG TO SUSAN STITCH. SUSAN IS ON HER HONEYMOON AND SHE KNOWS YOU'LL TAKE GOOD CARE OF ME UNTIL SHE RETURNS.

First, let me say that I've never wanted a monkey. Second, I barely know Susan Stitch. Third, what the heck am I supposed to do with the little bugger?

Twenty minutes later, I parked my Jeep Wrangler in front of the bonds office on Hamilton Avenue. At one time, the Wrangler had been red, but it had seen many lives before it fell into my hands, and now it was far from primo and the color was motley.

Carl followed me out of the car and into the office, hugging my pants leg like a two-year-old. Connie Rosolli, the office manager, peered around her computer. Connie had a lot of big Jersey hair, a freshly waxed upper lip, and breasts no amount of money could buy.

Lula stopped her filing and stood hands on hips. "That better not be what I think it is," Lula said, eyeballing Carl. "I *hate* monkeys. You *know* I hate monkeys."

"It's Carl," I told her. "Remember when we busted Susan Stitch for failing to appear? And remember her monkey, Carl?"

"Yeah?"

"Here he is."

"What are you doing with him?"

"He was attached to my doorknob with a note. Susan went on a honeymoon and left him with me."

"She got a lot of nerve," Lula said. "Where's he go to the bathroom? You ever think of that?"

I looked down at Carl. "Well?"

Carl blinked and shrugged. He looked at Lula and Connie, curled his lips back, and gave them a gummy monkey smile.

"I don't like the way he's lookin' at me," Lula said. "It's creepy. What kind of monkey you got here anyway?"

Lula is a former 'ho, and she's only moderately altered her wardrobe to suit her new job. Lula somehow manages to perform the miracle of squeezing her plus-size body into petite-size clothes. Her hair was blond this week, her skin was brown as always, her spandex tube dress was poison green, and her shoes were four-inch, spike-heeled, faux leopard Via Spigas. It came as no surprise that the monkey was staring at Lula. *Everyone* stared at Lula.

I didn't command that much attention in my jeans, girl-cut red T-shirt, gray sweatshirt, and inadequate swipe of lash-lengthening mascara. Not only did I feel like a bran muffin in a bakery case filled with eclairs, I was also the only one not packing a gun. My eyes are blue, my hair is brown, and my favorite word is *cake*. I was married for ten minutes in another life, and I'm not inclined to repeat the mistake anytime soon. There are a couple men in my life who tempt me . . . just not with marriage.

One of those tempting men is Joe Morelli. He's a Trenton cop with bedroom eyes, and bedroom hands, and everything else you'd want to find in your bedroom is top of the line. He's been my off-again, on-again boyfriend for as long as I can remember, and last night he was on-again.

The second guy in my life is Carlos Manoso, aka Ranger. Ranger's been my mentor, my employer, my guardian angel, and he's gotten as intimate with me as a man can get, but Ranger has never totally qualified as a boyfriend. Boyfriend might suggest an occasional date, and I can't see Ranger going there. Ranger is the sort of guy who slips uninvited into a girl's dreams and desires and refuses to leave.

"What's happening with Martin Munch?" Connie asked me. "Vinnie's in a rant over him. Munch is a big-ticket bond. If you don't drag his ass into court by the end of the month, our bottom line won't be good."

This is the way things work in the bail bonds business. A guy gets accused of a crime, and before he's released back into society, the court demands a security deposit. If the accused doesn't happen to have $50,000 under his mattress to give to the court, he goes to a bail bonds agent and that agent posts the bond for the accused for a fee. If the accused doesn't show up for his court date, the court gets to keep the bondsman's money until someone like me hauls the accused back to jail.

My ferret-faced cousin Vinnie owns the bonds office on paper, but he's backed by his father-in-law, Harry the Hammer. If Vinnie writes too many bad bonds and the office runs in the red, Harry isn't happy. And you don't want a guy with a name like Harry the Hammer to be unhappy.

"I've been looking for Munch all week," I said to Connie. "It's like he's dropped off the earth."

Martin Munch is a twenty-four-year-old genius with a doctorate in quantum physics. For whatever reason, Munch went postal on his project manager, riding him like Man O' War, breaking his nose with a Dunkin' Donuts coffee mug, knocking him cold. Moments later, Munch was caught on a security tape as he left the research lab cradling a one-of-a-kind monster cesium vapor magnetometer. Whatever the heck that is!

Munch was arrested and booked, but the magnetometer was never recovered. In a moment of insanity, Vinnie wrote a bond for Munch, and now Munch is playing hard to get with his contraption.

"This is a white-collar guy," Connie said. "He hasn't grown up in a crime culture. His friends and family are probably horrified. I can't see them hiding him."

"He hasn't got a lot of friends and family," I told her. "From what I can determine, he has neighbors who have never spoken to him, and the only family is a grandmother in a retirement home in Cadmount. He was employed at the research facility for two years, and he never socialized. Before that, he was a student at Princeton, where he never got his face out of a book.

"His neighbors tell me a couple months ago a guy started visiting Munch. The guy was a little over six feet tall, with an athletic build and expensive clothes. He drove a black Ferrari and had shoulder-length black hair and pale, almost white skin. Sometimes Munch would leave with him and not come back for several days. That's the whole enchilada."

"Sounds like Dracula," Lula said. "Was he wearing a cape? Did he have fangs?"

"No one said anything about a cape or fangs."

"Munch must have come in when I was out sick last week," Lula said. "I don't remember him."

"So what was it?" I asked her. "The flu?"

"I don't know what it was. My eyes were all swollen, and I was sneezing and wheezing, and I felt like I had a fever. I just stayed in my apartment, drinking medicinal whiskey and taking cold pills, and now I feel fine. What's this Munch look like?"

I took his file from my Prada knockoff messenger bag and showed Lula his mug shot, plus a photo.

"Good thing he's a genius," Lula said, "on account of he don't have much else going on."

At five-feet-two-inches tall, Munch looked more like fourteen than twenty-four. He was slim, with strawberry blond hair and pale freckled skin. The photo was taken outdoors, and Munch was squinting into the sun. He was wearing jeans and sneakers and a SpongeBob T-shirt, and it occurred to me that he probably shopped in the kids' department. I imagine you have to be pretty secure in your manhood to pull that one off.

"I'm feeling hot today," Lula said. "I bet I could find

that Munch. I bet he's sitting home in his Underoos playing with his whatchamacallit."

"I guess it wouldn't hurt for us to check out his house one more time," I said. "He's renting one of those little tiny row houses on Crocker Street, down by the button factory."

"What are you gonna do with the monkey?" Lula wanted to know.

I looked over at Connie.

"Forget it," Connie said. "I'm not babysitting a monkey. Especially not *that* monkey."

"Well, I don't let monkeys ride in my car," Lula said. "If that monkey's going with us, you're gonna have to drive *your* car. And I'm sitting in the back, so I can keep an eye on him. I don't want no monkey sneaking up behind me giving me monkey cooties."

"I've got two new skips," Connie said to me. "One of them, Gordo Bollo, ran over his ex-wife's brand-new husband with a pickup truck, twice. And the other, Denny Guzzi, robbed a convenience store and accidentally shot himself in the foot trying to make his getaway. Both idiots failed to show for their court appearances."

Connie shoved the paperwork to the edge of the desk. I signed the contract and took the files that contained a photo, the arrest sheet, and the bond agreement for each man.

"Shouldn't be hard to tag Denny Guzzi," Connie said. "He's got a big bandage on his foot, and he can't run."

"Yeah, but he's got a gun," I said to Connie.

"This is Jersey," Connie said. "Everyone's got a gun . . . except you."

We left the bonds office, and Lula stood looking at my car.

"I forgot you got this dumb Jeep," Lula said. "I can't get in the back of this thing. Only Romanian acrobats could get in the back of this. I guess the monkey's gotta ride in back, but I swear he makes a move on me, and I'm gonna shoot him."

I slid behind the wheel, Lula wedged herself into the passenger-side seat, and Carl hopped into the back. I adjusted my rearview mirror, locked onto Carl, and I swear it looked to me like Carl was making faces at Lula and giving her the finger.

"What?" Lula said to me. "You got a strange look on you."

"It's nothing," I said. "I just thought Carl was . . . never mind."

I drove across town, parked in front of Munch's house on Crocker Street, and we all piled out of the Jeep.

"This here's a boring-ass house," Lula said. "It looks like every other house on the street. If I came home after having two cosmopolitans, I wouldn't know which house was mine. Look at them. They're all redbrick. They all have the same stupid black door and black window trim. They don't even have no front yard. Just a stoop. And they all got the same stupid stoop."

I glanced at Lula. "Are you okay? That's a lot of hostility for a poor row house."

"It's the monkey. Monkeys give me the willies. And I might have a headache from all that medicinal whiskey."

I rang Munch's doorbell and looked through sheers that screened the front window. Beyond the sheers, the house was dark and still.

"I bet he's in there," Lula said. "I bet he's hiding under the bed. I think we should go around to the back and look."

There were fifteen row houses in all. All shared

common walls, and Munch's was almost dead middle. We returned to the Jeep, I rolled down the street, turned left at the corner, and took the alley that cut the block. I parked, and we all got out and walked through Munch's postage-stamp backyard. The rear of the house was similar to the front. A door and two windows. The door had a small swinging trapdoor at the bottom for a pet, and Carl instantly scurried inside.

I was dumbstruck. One minute, Carl was in the Jeep, and then, in an instant, he was inside the house.

"Holy macaroni," Lula said. "He's fast!"

We looked in a window and saw Carl in the kitchen, bouncing off counters, jumping up and down on the small kitchen table.

I pressed my nose to the glass. "I have to get him out."

"Like hell you do," Lula said. "This here's your lucky day. I say finders keepers."

"What if Munch never returns? Carl will starve to death."

"I don't think so," Lula said. "He just opened the refrigerator."

"There has to be a way to get in. Maybe Munch hid a key."

"Well, someone could accidentally break a window," Lula said. "And then someone else could crawl in and beat the living crap out of the monkey."

"No. We're not breaking or beating."

I rapped on the window, and Carl gave me the finger.

Lula sucked in some air. "That little fucker just flipped us the bird."

"It was probably accidental."

Lula glared in at Carl. "Accident this!" she said to him, middle finger extended.

Carl turned and mooned Lula, although it wasn't

much of a moon since he wasn't wearing clothes to begin with.

"Oh yeah?" Lula said. "You want to see a moon? I got a moon to show you."

"No!" I said to Lula. "No more moons. Bad enough I just looked at a monkey butt. I don't want your butt burned into my retinas."

"Hunh," Lula said. "Lotta people paid good money to see that butt."

Carl drank some milk out of a carton and put it back into the refrigerator. He opened the crisper drawer and pawed around in it but didn't find anything he wanted. He closed the refrigerator, scratched his stomach, and looked around.

"Let me in," I said to him. "Open the door."

"Yeah, right," Lula said. "As if his little pea brain could understand you."

Carl gave Lula the finger again. And then Carl threw the deadbolt, opened the door, and stuck his tongue out at Lula.

"If there's one thing I can't stand," Lula said, "it's a show-off monkey."

I did a fast walk-through of the house. Not much to see. Two small bedrooms, living room, single bath, small eat-in kitchen. These houses were built by the button factory after the war to entice cheap labor, and the button factory didn't waste money on frills. The houses had been sold many times over since then and were now occupied by an odd assortment of senior citizens, newly marrieds, and crazies. Seemed to me, Munch fit into the crazy category.

There were no clothes in the closet, no toiletries in the bathroom, no computer anywhere. Munch had cleared out, leaving a carton of milk, some sprouted onions, and a half-empty box of Rice Krispies behind.

"It's the strangest thing," Lula said. "I got this sudden craving for coffee cake. Do you smell cinnamon? It's like it's mixed up with Christmas trees and oranges."

I'd noticed the scent. And I was afraid I recognized it.

"How about you?" I asked Carl. "Do you smell cinnamon?"

Carl did another shrug and scratched his butt.

"Now all I can think of is cinnamon buns," Lula said. "I got buns on the brain. We gotta go find some. Or maybe a doughnut. I wouldn't mind a dozen doughnuts. I need a bakery. I got cravings."

Everyone vacated the kitchen, I closed the back door, and we all piled into the Jeep. I found my way to Hamilton and stopped at Tasty Pastry.

"What kind of doughnut do you want?" I asked Lula.

"Any kind. I want a Boston cream, a strawberry jelly, a chocolate-glazed, one of them with the white icing and pretty colorful sprinkles, and a blueberry. No, wait. I don't want the blueberry. I want a vanilla cream and a cinnamon stick."

"That's a lot of doughnuts."

"I'm a big girl," Lula said. "I got big appetites. I feel like I could eat a million doughnuts."

"How about you?" I asked Carl. "Do you need a doughnut?"

Carl vigorously shook his head *yes* and jumped up and down in his seat and made excited monkey noises.

"It's creepy that this monkey knows what we're saying," Lula said. "It's just not right. It's like he's a alien monkey or something."

"Sometimes Morelli's dog, Bob, knows what I'm saying. He knows *walk*, and *come*, and *meatball*."

"Yeah, Tank knows some words, too, but not as

many as this monkey," Lula said. "Of course, that's 'cause Tank's the big, strong, silent type."

Tank is Lula's fiancé, and his name says it all. He's Ranger's right-hand man, second in command at Ranger's security firm, Rangeman, and he's the guy Ranger trusts to guard his back. To say that Tank is the big, strong, silent type is a gross understatement on all accounts.

Fifteen minutes later, we were in the Jeep and we'd eaten all the doughnuts.

"I feel a lot better," Lula said. "Now what?"

I looked down at my shirt. It had powdered sugar and a big glob of jelly on it. "I'm going home to change my shirt."

"That don't sound real interesting," Lula said. "You could drop me at the office. I might have to take a nap."

Chapter

TWO

I parked my Jeep in the lot behind my apartment building, and Carl and I crossed the lot and pushed through the building's rear entrance. We took the elevator to the second floor, and Carl waited patiently while I opened my door.

"So," I said to him, "do you miss Susan?"

He shrugged.

"You do a lot of shrugging," I told him.

He studied me for a moment and gave me the finger. Okay, so it wasn't a shrug. And giving and getting the finger is a way of life in Jersey. Still, getting the finger from a monkey isn't normal even by Jersey standards.

My apartment consists of a small entrance foyer with hooks on the wall for coats and hats and handbags. The kitchen and living room open off the foyer, a dining area is tucked into an extension of the living room, and at the other end is a short hallway leading to my bedroom and bathroom. My décor is mostly whatever was discarded by relatives. This is okay by me because Aunt Betty's chair, Grandma Mazur's dining room set, and my cousin Tootsie's coffee table are comfortable. They come to me infused with family history, and they give off a kind of gentle energy that my life is sometimes lacking. Not to mention, I can't afford anything else.

I hung my tote on one of the hooks in the foyer and stared down at a pair of scruffy men's boots that had been kicked off and left in the middle of the floor. I was pretty sure I recognized the boots, plus the battered leather backpack that had been dumped on Tootsie's coffee table.

I walked into the living room and stared down at the backpack. I blew out a sigh and rolled my eyes. Why me? I thought. Isn't it enough that I have a monkey? Do I really need one more complication?

"Diesel?" I yelled.

I moved to the bedroom, and there he was, sprawled on my bed. Over six feet of gorgeous, hard-muscled, slightly tanned male. His eyes were brown and assessing, his hair was sandy blond, thick, and unruly. His eyebrows were fierce. Hard to tell his age. Young enough to be lots of trouble. Old enough to know what he was doing. He was wearing new gray sweatsocks, tattered jeans, and a faded T-shirt that advertised a dive shop in the Caicos.

He rolled onto his back and smiled up at me when I came into the room.

"Hey," he said.

I pointed stiff-armed to the door. "Out!"

"What, no kiss hello?"

"Get a grip."

He patted the bed next to him.

"No way," I said.

"Afraid?"

Of course I was afraid. He made the Big Bad Wolf look like chump change.

"How do you always manage to smell like Christmas?" I asked Diesel.

"I don't know. It's just one of those things." The smile widened, showing perfect white teeth, and crinkle lines appeared around his eyes. "It's part of my appeal," he said.

"You were in Martin Munch's house earlier today, weren't you?"

"Yeah. You came in the back door, and I went out the front. I would have hung around, but I was following someone."

"And?"

"I lost him."

"Hard to believe."

"Are you sure you don't want to roll around on the bed with me?"

"Rain check," I told him.

"Really?"

"No."

Here's the thing with Diesel. I'd be crazy not to want to take him for a test drive, but I've already got two men in my life, and that's actually one too many. Truth is, I'm a good Catholic girl. The faith has always been elusive, but the guilt is intractable. I'm not comfortable having simultaneous intimate relationships . . . even if it's only for a glorious ten minutes. And Diesel isn't a normal guy. At least, that's his story.

If Diesel is to be believed, there are people living among us with abilities beyond normal. They look just like anyone else, and most hold normal jobs and live relatively normal lives. They're called Unmentionables, and some are more unmentionable than others. From what I've seen, Diesel is about as unmentionable as a guy could get. Diesel travels the world tracking Unmentionables who've gone to the dark side, and then he pulls the power plug. I don't know how he accomplishes this. I'm not even sure I believe any of it. All I know is, one minute he's here, and then he's gone. And when he leaves, the barometric pressure improves.

Diesel stood and stretched, and when he stretched, there was a tantalizing flash of skin exposed between shirt and low-riding jeans. It was enough to make my eyes glaze over and my mouth go dry. I struggled to replace the image with thoughts of Morelli naked, but I was only partially successful.

"I'm hungry," Diesel said. "What time is it? Is it lunchtime?" He looked at his watch. "It's after noon in Greenland. Close enough."

He ambled out of the bedroom and into the kitchen, where Carl was sitting on the counter, staring into Rex's aquarium.

"What's with the monkey?" Diesel asked, his head in the refrigerator.

"I'm babysitting."

Diesel gathered up some cold cuts and sliced cheese and turned to me. "You don't strike me as especially maternal."

"I have my moments." Admittedly not very many, but probably they're just waiting for the right time to pop out.

Diesel found bread and made himself a sandwich. "He got a name?"

"Carl."

Diesel flipped Carl a slice of bread and Carl caught it and ate it.

"Are you a monkey man?" I asked Diesel.

"I can take 'em or leave 'em."

Carl shot Diesel the finger, and Diesel gave a bark of laughter. Diesel ate some sandwich and looked my way. "You two must get along great. You taught him that, right?"

"What are you doing here?" I asked.

"Visiting."

"You never just visit."

Diesel got a Bud Light from the fridge, chugged it, and wiped his mouth with the back of his hand. "I'm looking for a guy who has been known to hang with your friend Munch."

"Does this guy drive a black Ferrari and have long black hair?"

"Yes. Have you seen him?"

I shook my head. "No. I've talked to Munch's neighbors, and apparently he was Munch's only visitor. Munch didn't have much of a social life."

"What kind of leads do you have?" Diesel asked.

"The usual. Nothing. And you?"

"I tracked my man to Munch's house but missed him by minutes. I've been trying to tag him for over a year. He can sense my approach, and he moves on before I get too close."

"He's afraid of you."

"No. He's enjoying the game."

"His name?"

"Gerwulf Grimoire," Diesel said.

"Wow, that's a really bad name."

"This is a really bad, really powerful guy. Somehow he connected with Munch, and now they're palling around together with Munch's magnetometer."

"Why was Whatshisname in Munch's house?" I asked Diesel.

"Gerwulf Grimoire, but he goes by Wulf. I suppose he went back to get something. Or maybe he was playing with me. The house was clean when I got there. I followed Wulf's breadcrumbs to Broad Street, and then they disappeared."

"Breadcrumbs?"

"Cosmic debris. Hard to explain."

"Do I leave cosmic debris?"

"Everyone leaves it. Some people leave more than others. Wulf and I leave a lot because we're dense. We both carry high energy."

"That's weird."

"Tell me about it," Diesel said. "You should walk in *my* shoes." He crossed to the foyer, took my bag off its hook, and stuck his hand in.

"Hey!" I said. "What are you doing?"

"I want to read your case file on Munch."

"How do you know it's in there?"

"I know. Just like I know you're wearing a pink lace thong, and you think I'm hot."

"How? What?" I said.

"Lucky guess," Diesel said, pulling the file out of my bag, scanning the pages.

"I do *not* think you're hot."

"That's a big fib," Diesel said.

"I can save you some time," I told him. "There isn't anything in Munch's file. Only a grandmother."

"Then let's talk to the grandmother."

"I've already talked to her."

Diesel shoved his feet into his boots and laced up. "Let's talk to her again."

I changed my shirt, and we headed out.

"Your car or mine?" I asked him when we got to the lot.

"What are you driving?"

"The Jeep that used to be red."

"I like it," Diesel said.

"What are *you* driving?"

"The hog."

I looked over at the black Harley. No room for Carl, and it would wreck my hair. "Probably it's easier to follow cosmic dust when you're on a bike," I said.

Diesel settled himself into the Jeep's passenger-side seat and grinned at me. "You don't really think there's cosmic dust, do you?"

I plugged the key into the ignition. "Of course not. Cosmic dust would be . . . ridiculous."

Diesel hooked an arm around my neck, pulled me to him, and kissed me on the top of my head. "This is going to be fun," he said.

Chapter
THREE

Cadmount is a sleepy little town on the Delaware River a few miles north of Trenton. It looks quaintly historic—a bunch of big, white, clapboard houses with black shutters and yards shaded by oak and maple trees. Lydia Munch's retirement home was a sprawling single-story redbrick structure. The architect had enhanced the entrance with a portico and four white columns in an attempt to make it look less like a retirement home. The result was that it looked a lot more like a funeral parlor.

I parked in the visitor lot, and we shuffled into the lobby. The walls were a pleasant pale peach, and the floor was covered in dove gray industrial pile carpet. It was a relatively small area, large enough to accommodate the reception desk manned by two green-smocked women, a uniformed security guard old enough to be a resident, and a couple wingback chairs for tired guests.

I asked for Lydia Munch and was directed to a lounge in her wing. I'd already done this drill twice before, but no one seemed to remember me, and the rules and directions were precisely repeated. They would tell Lydia she had a visitor, and Lydia would meet us in the lounge. Diesel and I moved toward the corridor leading to the lounge, and one of the green-smocked women called after us.

"Excuse me," she said. "There's a monkey following you."

We turned and looked down at Carl. We'd forgotten he was with us.

"Go back to the car," I said to Carl.

Carl looked at me with his bright monkey eyes. The eyes dimmed down a notch, and he blinked.

"Don't play dumb," I said to him. "I know you understand."

Another blink.

"We don't allow monkeys," the woman said.

Carl flipped her the finger and took off down the corridor toward the lounge.

"Security!" the woman shouted, waving her hand at the old man at the door. "Expel that monkey."

The security guard looked around. "What monkey? I don't see no monkey."

Carl scampered down the length of the hall and swung through the door to the lounge. A murmur went up from the room when Carl entered, a woman screamed, and something crashed to the floor.

Diesel and I followed Carl into the lounge and found a little old lady who looked like Mother Goose pressing herself into a corner. A little old man with his pants hiked up to his armpits was scrabbling after Carl. The little old man was trying to smack Carl with his cane, but Carl was too fast. Carl was scurrying around, avoiding the cane, jumping on tables, knocking lamps to the floor, climbing up the drapes. He jumped onto Mother Goose's head, leaned over into her face, and gave her a kiss on the lips.

"He Frenched me!" Mother Goose said. "I've been Frenched by a monkey."

Diesel grabbed Carl by the tail, lifted him off Mother Goose, and held him at arm's length, where Carl meekly dangled like a dead opossum. The old man took a swipe at Carl with the cane but missed and tagged Diesel. Diesel held Carl with one hand, and with the other, he snatched the cane away from the man and snapped it in half.

"I need mouthwash," Mother Goose said. "I need a tetanus shot. I need a Tic Tac."

"I'm looking for Lydia Munch," Diesel said.

"Two doors down on the right," the man told him. "Apartment 103."

Diesel thanked him, and we trooped out of the lounge with Carl riding on Diesel's shoulder. Several residents were in the hall. Lydia Munch was among them. Easy to recognize Lydia. She was five-foot-nothing and had the same curly strawberry blond hair and freckled skin as her grandson.

"What's the ruckus in the lounge?" she asked. Her eyes focused on Carl. "Is that a real monkey?"

"Yep, it's a real monkey," I told her. "And this big guy is Diesel. He'd like to talk to you about your grandson."

"Martin? I don't know what to say about him. I haven't seen him since Christmas. I know he's accused of stealing something where he worked, but it's hard to believe. He's such a nice young man."

"I need to find him," Diesel said. "Do you have any idea where he might be staying?"

"He has a house in Trenton. Other than that, I don't know. There's not a lot of family left. His mother and father were killed in a car wreck five years ago. He doesn't have any brothers or sisters. The rest of the family is in Wisconsin. He was never close to any of them."

"Friends?" Diesel asked.

"He never mentioned any. It was always hard for him, being so smart. He didn't go through school with kids his own age. And then he had that whole *Star Trek* thing where he dressed up like Mr. Spock. I told my daughter to get him help, but she said it was just a phase. And when he took the job at the research center, he was working on something secret that he couldn't talk about. He was real excited about it. He worked all the time on it. Weekends and nights. I thought he should be going out with girls, making some friends, but he said everyone he met was boring."

"Did he ever mention someone named Wulf?" Diesel asked.

"No," she said. "I would have remembered."

Diesel gave Lydia a business card. "I'd appreciate a call if you hear from Martin."

I looked over at the card. It said DIESEL, and below that was a phone number.

"Very professional," I told him.

Diesel nodded adios to Lydia, took my hand, and pulled me down the hall toward the back door. "They were a Christmas present from one of my handlers. He said I had to stop writing my phone number on people's foreheads."

"Handlers?"

"The guys who move me around."

"So you can follow the cosmic dust?"

Diesel opened the back door and pushed me through. "Very funny. Keep in mind not everything I say is bullshit."

"What would you say is the bullshit percentage? Twenty? Thirty?"

"Thirty might be low."

We circled the building and jumped into my Jeep. I

cranked the engine over, and an animal control van rolled into the lot just as we were leaving.

"Now what?" I asked Diesel.

"Did you thoroughly search Munch's house?"

"Lula and I walked through the rooms and looked in closets and drawers. There wasn't much to see. The house was empty. No clothes, no food, no toothbrush in the bathroom."

"Maybe we should take a second look."

I made the trip back to Trenton in less than thirty minutes. Traffic was nonexistent at midday, and I didn't get a single red light. Diesel took credit for this, but I thought his claim might register a ten on the bullshit-o-meter. Then again, maybe not.

I turned onto Crocker and immediately saw two cop cars and an EMT truck angled into the curb in front of Munch's house. I did a slow drive-by, turned at the corner, and stopped at the entrance to the alley. There were two more cop cars parked with lights flashing halfway down, plus a crime lab truck, an unmarked cop car, and what looked like the medical examiner's meat wagon.

"This doesn't look good," I said to Diesel.

Diesel stared down the alley. "Call your boyfriend and find out what happened."

I crept forward, parked just past the alley, and dialed Morelli.

"Is there something going on in Martin Munch's house on Crocker Street?" I asked him.

"A call came in reporting two women and a monkey doing a B&E," Morelli said. "One of the women was fat and black and stuffed into not nearly enough green spandex, and the other was wearing jeans and a red T-shirt. I don't suppose you were in the area?"

"Who, me?"

"Shit," Morelli said. "Where'd you get the monkey?"

"What monkey?"

"Fine. I don't actually want to know. Fortunately, it's not my case. I have a nice, sane, multiple gang-slaying to work on."

"What happened?"

"The usual. A bunch of kids shot each other."

"No. What happened at Munch's house?"

"A uniform responded to the call. He looked in the windows and tried the doors and was on his way back to his car parked in the alley when his attention was caught by a pack of vultures sitting on a white '91 Cadillac. The car was parked one house down from Munch's. Long story short, there was a body in the trunk."

"And?"

"Unidentified male. Not Munch. No bullet holes or stab wounds. Bucky Burlew pulled the case, and since the guy's head was facing in the wrong direction, Bucky's thinking his neck was broken. Ordinarily, I wouldn't know any of this, but I was supposed to meet Bucky at Pino's for lunch. This is half-price day for meatball subs."

"Did you get a sub anyway?"

"Yeah. I went with Joe Zelock. He's in town with those naked male dancers. He's their token heterosexual."

Zelock used to be a Trenton cop. He rose in the ranks, went politico, and got busted for acting in a porno film. Somehow, he got himself onto one of those reality talent shows. He didn't win, but he got a gig with a traveling Chippendales-style dance troupe. Word on the street is that he's making okay money. Of course, some of it gets stuffed into some pretty strange places, but I guess a little disinfectant spray, and the money's as good as any other.

I disconnected and told Diesel about the dead guy.

"Did Morelli say there was anything unusual about the victim?"

"Like what?"

"I've seen Wulf's handiwork. He likes to break his victim's neck. Nice and neat. Doesn't get blood on his clothes. He uses an ancient Chinese technique that only a few men have ever mastered. In fact, it's said you have to be born with the Dragon Claw."

"What's a Dragon Claw?"

"Wulf can channel energy to his hands and use them to burn a brand into flesh. When he uses his hands to kill, he also inflicts a perfect print of his hand on the victim's neck."

I felt the blood drain out of my brain, my vision went cobwebby, and bells clanged in my head.

Diesel reached over and put his hand to the back of my neck. "Breathe," he said.

His hand was warm, and the warmth radiated out to my fingertips and toes and everyplace in between.

"Are you okay?" he asked me. "Your face turned white, and I felt your blood pressure drop."

"Too much information. I didn't need to know about the Dragon Claw."

Diesel smiled wide. "You're such a girl."

"I'm going to take that as a compliment."

"I need to crash," Diesel said. "I was brought in from Moscow last night and I'm beat."

"Where do you want me to drop you?"

"Take me home."

"You have a home?"

"Take me to *your* home. I'm staying with you."

"Oh no. No, no, no."

"Give it up," Diesel said. "It's not like you can kick me out."

"You are *not* staying in my apartment. Where will you sleep?"

"I'll sleep with you."

"Never happen. No way. Forget about it."

"You'll come around. Anyway, I want your bed, not your body."

"Really?"

"No. That was a flat-out lie."

"Get out."

"Honey, kicking me out of your car won't change anything."

I pointed stiff-armed. "Out!"

Diesel heaved himself out of the Jeep. "Do you want me to take the monkey?"

"Yes."

Carl hopped out of the backseat onto Diesel's shoulder. I suspected they'd both be in my apartment waiting for me when I returned tonight, but at least I wouldn't have driven them there. Sort of a hollow victory, but it was the best I could manage. I took off, and from my rearview mirror I could see Carl give me the finger.

I reached the corner and blew out a sigh. I couldn't do it. I couldn't abandon Carl. I hooked a U-turn to retrieve the little guy, but Diesel and Carl had disappeared. *Poof.*

Chapter
FOUR

Forty minutes and twelve red lights later, I rolled to a stop in front of the bail bonds office.

"You look confused," Lula said when I pushed through the front door. "You got that what-the-heck-just-happened look to your face."

"Remember Diesel? He's back."

"I wouldn't be lookin' confused at that," Lula said. "I'd be lookin' *Hello, hotstuff*."

"He's not normal," I said to Lula.

"Don't I know it. He was at the head of the line when God was handing out the good stuff. I bet he got a great big power tool, too."

I had enough problems without dwelling on Diesel's power tool. I was fifty dollars short on my rent, my mother expected me for dinner, and I had a monkey.

"I'm at a dead end with Martin Munch," I said. "I thought I'd go after one of the new guys."

"I guess I could help you with that," Lula said. "So long as I don't have to chase some fool all the hell over the place. I'm wearing my Via Spigas today, and I don't do that shit in my Via Spigas. So I'm voting we go clap the cuffs on the idiot with the shot-up foot."

"Works for me," I said. I was wearing sneakers, but

I didn't want to chase some fool all the hell over the place, either.

"Where's the monkey?" Lula asked. "You still got the monkey?"

"The monkey went with Diesel."

"That monkey's a lucky duck," Lula said. "I wouldn't mind going with Diesel."

I pulled the case file out of my bag. "Denny Guzzi lives in an apartment on Laurel Street."

"That's not such a good neighborhood," Lula said. "That's off Stark. Probably Guzzi was robbing stores trying to get himself a better way of life."

"Probably he was robbing stores so he could buy dope," Connie said.

"See, now that's uncharitable," Lula said. "You're judging him without knowing the circumstances. He could have had a reason. He could have a sick mama who needed medicine."

Connie didn't look convinced. "Would you rob a store at gunpoint if your mother needed medicine?" she asked Lula.

"I didn't need to," Lula said. "I had skills. I had a honest profession."

"You were a hooker."

"Exactly," Lula said, taking her purse out of a bottom file drawer and poking around in it, looking for her car keys. "I'll drive on account of you probably still got monkey cooties in your car."

Lula drives a red Firebird with a pimped-out sound system. She had her radio tuned to rap, and by the time we reached Guzzi's house on Laurel, I was afraid my fillings had been rattled loose from the bass vibration. Lula parked, we got out of the car, and we stood looking at the building. It was originally yellow brick, but at the present moment, it was solid graffiti.

"This here's a good example of urban art," Lula said. "Denny Guzzi's probably a sensitive guy to live in this building."

I cut my eyes to her. "It's graffiti. A bunch of loser gang members marked their territory on this building."

"Yeah, but they did a good job of expressing themselves. I got a better point of view than you because I've been taking a course at the community college on positive thinking. I'm a glass-is-half-full person now, and your sorry ass is still in half-empty country. I'm willing to give people the benefit of the doubt, and all you got is the doubt."

I opened the front door and stepped into the dimly lit foyer. "Your glass wasn't half full when you saw I had a monkey."

"He took me by surprise. And anyway, monkeys don't count."

A row of mailboxes lined one wall. Twelve mailboxes in all. No names on any of the mailboxes. No elevator. This was a three-story walk-up. Four apartments to a floor. The building wasn't large. Probably, the apartments were all studios with kitchenettes. Denny Guzzi lived in 3B.

Lula and I hiked up two flights of stairs, and I listened at the door to 3B. The door was wood, without a security peephole. The veneer was cracked and stained. The area around the doorknob was grimy. I could hear a television droning inside the apartment. Lula stood to one side, and I stood to the other. I reached out and knocked on the door.

"What?" someone yelled from inside the apartment.

The voice was male. Probably Guzzi.

"It's Lula, honey," Lula called out. "I got somethin' for you, sugah. Open the door."

"Go fuck yourself," came back at her.

"He must be a man of high moral fiber," Lula whispered to me.

I did an eye roll and knocked again. No answer.

"Hunh," Lula said to me. "I guess you're gonna have to kick the door down."

Kicking down doors wasn't a skill I had ever actually mastered. The men in my life could put the heel of their boot to a lock and destroy it. The best I could do was scuff up the finish.

"Bond enforcement," I yelled. "Open the door."

Over the background noise of the television, there was the unmistakable sound of a shotgun ratchet. Lula and I jumped back, and the jerk in the apartment blasted a two-foot hole in his door.

Lula and I looked through the hole at Denny Guzzi, holding a shotgun, sitting in a chair with his foot propped on a couple cases of beer.

"What the devil was that?" Lula said to Guzzi. "Are you friggin' nuts? You don't go around shooting at people like that. And after I was real nice to you, giving you an invitation and all. How the hell is that to treat a woman?"

Guzzi ratcheted and aimed, and Lula and I dove away from the door. *Boom!* Guzzi took out a good-sized chunk of wallboard on the other side of the hall. I looked over at Lula, and she was on her ass, holding the spike heel to her shoe.

"Sonovabitch," Lula said, eyes narrowed, face scrunched up. "That worthless piece of pig shit made me break the heel on my Via Spiga. That's it for me. That's the end of my charitable ways. He's going down. He's gonna die." Lula got to her feet, pulled a nickel-plated Glock out of her purse, and fired off about ten rounds at the door.

"Jeez," I yelled at Lula. "You can't just shoot at the guy like that."

"Sure I can," Lula said. "I got lots more ammo in my purse."

"If you kill him, there's a mountain of paperwork."

Lula stopped shooting. "I hate paperwork."

BAM! Guzzi fired through the door again, and Lula and I took off down the stairs. We got to the second landing, and Lula stumbled on her broken shoe. She knocked into me, and we both went head over teakettles down the last flight of stairs. We sprawled spread-eagle on our backs on the filthy foyer floor and sucked air.

"Been here, done this," I said. More than once.

"I need to go to Macy's," Lula said. "They're having a shoe sale. I got a big date tonight, and now I need replacement hot shoes."

I got to my feet and limped out onto the sidewalk, where two scrawny guys in baggy pants and wall-to-wall tattoos were standing by Lula's Firebird, trying to jimmy the door.

"Get away from my baby," Lula shouted. And she opened fire on the two guys.

"Stop shooting," I said. "You can't kill them, either."

"You got a lot of rules," Lula said to me. "To hear you talk, I can't kill *anybody.*"

The two guys peeked out from behind the Firebird.

"Crazy bitch," the one said. "We were just gonna steal your car. It's not like it's a big deal. You park a car here, it gets stolen. Everyone knows that."

"I just broke my Via Spigas, and I'm in no mood," Lula said. "I'm giving you two seconds to get invisible, and then I'm putting a cap in your ass."

The two guys grabbed hold of their pants and walked away, swaying as they walked on feet encased in unlaced basketball shoes that seemed way too big for their stick bodies.

"Between the pants and the shoes, it's a wonder they can walk at all," Lula said.

This coming from a woman in four-inch heels and a dress that fit her like a condom.

Lula checked her car over to make sure it wasn't scratched, and we got in and motored back to the bonds office.

"So what's this big date?" I asked her.

"Me and Tank are gonna talk about the wedding. You know, we didn't have enough time to do the June wedding, what with Tank needing a special-made tuxedo and all, so now I'm thinking a Christmas wedding would be okay."

"Does Tank want a Christmas wedding?"

"Hard to tell. He don't say. He starts to sweat soon as I talk about it. I swear, sometimes I wonder if I want to spend eternity with a man who sweats like that. He's gonna sweat all over my wedding gown. I'm gonna have to treat it with one of them water-repellent chemicals before I wear it. I'm gonna have to wear a raincoat when we dance."

"Tank dances?"

"He don't now, but I signed him up for lessons."

"No wonder he's sweating."

Lula pulled to the curb in front of the office. "Tell Connie I got a shopping emergency, and I'll see her tomorrow."

I waved Lula off and went in to see Connie.

"Anything on the police bands about the body in the car on Crocker?" I asked her.

"Not much. I heard the call go in. At first, I thought it was just another body in a car, but then I caught a conversation from one of the EMS guys. He said the victim's neck was broken, and he had two handprints burned into his neck."

Crap. Diesel was right.

"Has the dead guy been identified?"

"I haven't heard anything."

I told Connie about Guzzi and Lula's shopping emergency. I took a couple candies from the jar on Connie's desk and speed-dialed Morelli's number on my cell phone.

"Yeah?" Morelli said.

When Morelli left my apartment at five-thirty this morning, he was in jeans and an oversize blue-and-white striped shirt from the Gap. His black hair was still damp from the shower, a month overdue for a cut, curling around his ears and down the nape of his neck. The memory was warm and sexy down low in my stomach, resurrected by the sound of his voice.

"I want to know the latest on the guy in the trunk," I said to Morelli.

"I'll get back to you."

I was halfway through Connie's candy jar when Morelli called back.

"We have a tentative ID on the guy in the trunk. His name is Eugene Scanlon, and he was Munch's immediate boss. Scanlon ran the project at the lab. Something to do with ions and magnets."

"Who owned the car?"

"It was Scanlon's car."

"Any suspects?"

"Only Munch at this point. Personally, I can't see Munch breaking Scanlon's neck. Munch is a lightweight, and his background shows no martial arts training. I know he smashed a coffee mug into Scanlon's face, but I think if he wanted to kill Scanlon, he would have shot him."

"Anything else?"

"Yeah, but you don't want to know."

"The handprints on his neck? Connie heard about it over the radio."

"The ME has no idea how the burn was inflicted. He thinks it's probably torture."

"Speaking of torture, we're supposed to go to my parents' house for dinner tonight."

"I have to beg off. My brother Anthony got kicked out of the house again, and he's moved in with me for a couple days. He's all bummed, so I said I'd go bowling with him."

"You're kidding!"

"Last time he got kicked out of the house, he went on a six-day drinking binge and got arrested for attempting to bribe a female traffic cop, Shaneeka Brown. Anthony said he was just trying to get a ride home. Shaneeka said the barn door was open and the horse was out to pasture, looking to get ridden."

With the exception of Joe, the Morelli men were a sad lot of drunken bar-brawlers who cheated and lied and gambled away every cent they made. They were also drop-dead gorgeous and charming and managed to marry women who stuck with them.

"Anyway, I promised my mom I'd keep a lid on Anthony until his wife decides to take him back," Morelli said.

"Why did she kick him out?"

"I think it had something to do with the horse."

"Maybe you need to take him to a vet."

"I'll add that to the short list of fun shit to do. Gotta go."

"The dead guy's name is Eugene Scanlon," I said to Connie. "Munch's supervisor. The one he took out with the coffee mug. Let's run a profile on him. Maybe it'll lead me to Munch."

Connie punched Scanlon into her computer, and twenty minutes later, I had seven pages of information.

"I can go deeper," Connie said, "but it'll take a day or two."

"This is a start," I told her. "Thanks."

I drove back to my apartment and blew out a sigh at the sight of Diesel's bike still in my lot. It wasn't that I didn't *like* Diesel. It was that he always created large problems. And honestly, I had no idea who he was or if he was crazy. He made Ranger look normal by comparison. And Ranger wasn't nearly normal.

I skipped the elevator and trudged up the stairs in penance for eating doughnuts. I paused for a moment outside my door and listened. The television was on inside. This generated a second sigh on my part. I plugged my key into the door and walked in on Diesel and Carl sitting side by side on the couch watching a war movie. Men were dying all over the screen, arms and legs exploded off bodies, blood and guts everywhere.

"That's disgusting," I said to Diesel. "What on earth are you watching? I don't get the allure of war movies."

"It's a guy thing," Diesel said.

"Apparently, it's also a monkey thing."

Diesel remoted the television off. "Yeah. Guys and monkeys have a lot in common."

"You were right about the branded handprint. The victim's name is Eugene Scanlon, and he was Munch's boss. He was found in his own car." I handed Diesel the seven pages Connie had printed out for me. "Here's some background on Scanlon."

Diesel read through the pages and returned them to

me. "Fifty-six years old. Single. Living alone. No arrest history. Some credit problems. Originally from Baltimore. Graduated from BU and got his doctorate at Stanford. Nothing in there about his research."

"Connie's still digging."

"I'd like to look at his apartment, but for the next couple hours it'll be crawling with police. We'll go in tonight."

"*You* will go in tonight."

"*We* will go in tonight."

"You can't make me."

"Of course I can."

"You don't scare me. I know you'd never hurt me."

"True, but I have ways."

"Magic?"

"Muscle," Diesel said.

"You'd physically force me to go with you?"

"Yeah."

"Why?"

"It's more fun when you're along. And you make it difficult for Wulf to zero in on me."

"Let me guess. This is about cosmic dust, right? Our dust mingles together, and Wulf gets confused."

Carl gave me the finger.

"Carl's tired of hearing about cosmic dust," Diesel said. "It's getting old."

"Then maybe you want to explain the whole zeroing-in phenomenon to me."

"It's not a big deal. You know how sometimes you walk into a room and get a creepy feeling that you're not alone? Or maybe you're looking for a guy, and you get this feeling that he's in the coat closet, so you open the door, and there he is? It's like that . . . but Wulf and I operate at a higher level."

"Why do I make it difficult for Wulf?"

"When I'm with you, some of my chemistry changes, and it becomes more difficult to trace my sensory imprint. At least, that's the theory. I'm told it has to do with sexual attraction and expanding blood vessels. There's more, but the expanding blood vessels is the good part."

I'd never actually seen Diesel's blood vessels in all their expanded glory. I had a feeling it was a spectacular sight. And just the thought of it scared the bejeezus out of me.

"As long as they don't expand too much," I said to Diesel.

"Your loss," Diesel said.

"Anyway, I can't go with you tonight because I promised my mom I'd be over for dinner."

"Sounds good. We'll eat dinner with your parents, and then we'll check out Scanlon's apartment."

History was repeating itself. As always with Diesel, I was going down as the big loser in the power struggle.

Chapter
FIVE

Pot roast, spaghetti with red sauce, roast chicken, kiel-basa and sauerkraut, meat loaf, minestrone, stuffed manicotti, baked ham, pork chops with applesauce, la-sagna, chicken paprikash, and stuffed cabbage stretch in a time line from my birth to this afternoon, pulling together my Hungarian and Italian genes, forever bind-ing together food and parental love.

Dinner at my parents' house is always at six, it's al-ways served at the dining room table, and it's always good. To my mother's dismay, my current lifestyle isn't nearly so civilized. Left to my own devices, I eat stand-ing over my kitchen sink when I get hungry, and my culinary expertise relies heavily on peanut butter and white bread.

My parents live in the Chambersburg section of Trenton. Their house is small and narrow, cojoined on one side with an identical twin differing only in paint color. There's a minuscule front yard, a slightly longer backyard, and in between is a small foyer off the front door, living room, dining room, and kitchen, with three tiny bedrooms and a bathroom upstairs. The bath is far from luxurious, but it has a window that opens to the roof over the kitchen. This window was my escape route all through high school whenever I was grounded. And I was grounded a lot.

We were all seated at the dining room table—Diesel, Carl, my mother, my father, and my Grandma Mazur. My Grandma Mazur moved in with my parents when Grandpa Mazur bought a one-way ticket to God's big theme park in the sky. Grandma buys her clothes at the Gap, her sneakers at Payless, and her Metamucil at the supermarket. She has short gray hair, and more skin than she needs.

"Isn't this nice," Grandma Mazur said, setting the green bean casserole in the middle of the table, taking her place opposite me. "This feels just like a party. Can't hardly remember the last time Diesel was here. It feels like ages. And anyway, it's always a treat to have a handsome man in the house."

My father stopped shoveling slabs of pot roast onto his plate, his lips compressed, and his eyes fixed on his knife as if he was contemplating carving something other than cow. He mumbled a few unintelligible words, his color returned to normal, and he moved on to the mashed potatoes. This happened at least five times during a normal evening meal with my father and grandmother. He thought my grandmother was a trial.

I was sitting to my father's left, and Diesel was next to me. My grandmother was to my father's right and Carl was next to her. My mother was at the other end of the table. My father looked up in search of gravy and for the first time spotted Carl.

My sister, Valerie, has a flock of kids who regularly visit with my parents, and as it turns out, size-wise it's a fairly easy transition to go from kids to a monkey. Carl was sitting in my niece's booster chair with a white napkin tied around his neck.

"There's a monkey at the table," my father said.

My mother looked at my father and looked at Carl, and then she belted back something I suspected was straight whiskey cleverly disguised as ice tea.

Grandma spooned some green beans and applesauce onto Carl's plate. "Stephanie's babysitting the little guy," she told my father. "His name is Carl."

Carl's attention was fixed on his beans. He picked one up, smelled it, and ate it.

"Do you want pot roast?" Grandma asked Carl.

Carl shrugged.

Grandma put a slice of pot roast on Carl's plate and added mashed potatoes. Carl's eyes lit up at the sight of the mashed potatoes. He grabbed a handful and shoved them into his mouth.

"We don't eat mashed potatoes with our hands," Grandma said to Carl.

Carl stopped eating and looked around. Confused. He rolled his lips back and did a forced monkey smile at Grandma.

"We use our fork," Grandma said, holding her fork for Carl to see.

Carl picked his fork up and looked at it. He smelled it and touched a prong with his boney monkey finger.

Grandma scooped some potatoes up with her fork and ate them. "Yum," Grandma said to Carl. "Good potatoes."

Carl stuck his fork into his potatoes, raised a glob to his mouth, and the potatoes slid off the fork onto the floor. "Eeee!" Carl said.

"Don't worry about it," Grandma said to Carl. "It happens to me all the time."

Carl took a second shot at it with the same result.

"Maybe you want to skip the potatoes," Grandma said.

Carl's mouth dropped open, and his eyes went wide

with horror. He shook his head *no*. He wanted his potatoes. He very carefully, very deliberately raised a forkful of potatoes to his mouth and at the last minute . . . disaster. The potatoes dropped onto the floor. Carl threw the fork across the room, jumped onto the table, and ran off with the bowl of mashed potatoes.

There was a collective gasp from everyone but Diesel, who obviously required more than a monkey stealing potatoes to make him suck air.

Diesel scraped his chair back and stood. "I'm on it."

Moments later, Diesel returned with Carl and the empty potato bowl.

"Who would have thought a monkey could eat all those potatoes," Grandma said.

Carl stuck his tongue out and gave Grandma the raspberries. "Brrrrp!" And then he gave her the finger.

My grandmother gave Carl the finger back. My mother took another belt of whatever amber-colored liquid was in her water glass. My father had his head bent over his food, but I think he was smiling.

"Carl needs a time-out," I told Diesel. "Put him in the bathroom upstairs."

Grandma watched Diesel leave the room. "He's a big one," she said. "He's a real looker, too. And he has a way with monkeys."

It was almost eight when I finished helping my mom with the dishes. Diesel was in the living room with my dad, slouched in a chair, watching a ball game. Carl was still in the bathroom.

"Time to go," I said to Diesel. "If we stay any longer, I'll eat more pineapple upside-down cake."

"Will that be a bad thing?"

"It will be tomorrow when I can't zip my jeans."

Diesel smiled and looked down at my jeans, and it was clear he wouldn't mind if I couldn't zip them.

"One of us has to get Carl," I said.

Diesel hauled himself out of the chair. "I guess that would be me."

He ambled off, and moments later, he called from upstairs. "Got a problem here."

I found Diesel standing in the doorway to an empty bathroom.

"Where's Carl?" I asked.

"Don't know," Diesel said, "but the window is open. It was closed and locked when I put Carl in here."

I went to the window and looked out. No Carl.

"I used to escape through this window all the time when I was in high school," I said. "What are we going to do?"

"We're going to check out Scanlon's apartment."

"What about Carl?"

"Easy come, easy go," Diesel said.

"Maybe you can sniff him out. Look for his ecto-plasm or something. Follow his sensory imprint."

"Sorry. I don't do monkeys."

"Well, that's just peachy. That's fine." I threw my hands into the air and stomped off to the stairs. "Don't help. Who needs you anyway? I'll look for him myself."

Diesel followed after me. "I didn't say I wouldn't help. I just said I didn't think I could tune in to monkey ectoplasm."

I stopped at the front door and yelled that I was leaving. "Thanks for dinner," I said.

My mother came to the door with a bag of leftovers. "Here's for lunch."

My grandmother was with her. "Where's Carl?"

"He went on ahead," I told her. "We're going to catch up with him later."

We slowly drove around the block but didn't see Carl.

We parked and walked a four-block grid, including alleyways. No Carl.

"Are you getting anything?" I asked Diesel.

"Yeah, I'm getting tired of walking around looking for a wiseass monkey."

"I feel responsible. Susan trusted me to take care of Carl until she came home."

"Honey, Susan's never coming home. She just dumped her monkey on you."

"You don't know that for sure."

"True. I was putting myself in Susan's place." He draped an arm around my shoulders and pulled me into him. "Here's my deal. If you snoop around Scanlon's apartment with me, I'll come back and look for Carl in the morning."

"Deal."

Connie had listed Scanlon's address as 2206 Niley Circle in Hamilton Township. I was familiar with Niley Circle. It was part of a large town house condo complex off Klockner Boulevard. I found the complex and parked in the lot. Diesel and I got out and studied the cluster of narrow town houses in front of us. Easy to find Scanlon's, since the door was sealed with yellow crime-scene tape.

Diesel ripped the tape off and opened the door.

"How did you do that?" I asked him. "How did you just turn the knob and open the door?"

"I don't know. It's a gift. I can flush a toilet without touching the little lever, too."

"Really?"

Diesel grinned down at me. "You are so gullible."

I narrowed my eyes at him. "You're scum."

"It's okay," Diesel said, planting a kiss on the top of my head. "It's cute."

We were standing in a small foyer in the dark. This was a two-story town house, so presumably, there were stairs somewhere, plus furniture and a kitchen and all the things one ordinarily finds in a home. Unfortunately, I couldn't see any of them because it was pitch black. I felt Diesel leave my side, and I could hear him moving around the room.

"Can you see where you're going?" I asked him.

"Yep. Can't you?"

I blew out a sigh. "No."

"Maybe you need to eat more carrots or blueberries or something."

I took a couple steps forward and fell over a large unseen object. Diesel crossed the room, picked me up, and set me on my feet.

"Stand here, and don't move, and let me look around," Diesel said.

I listened to him search the condo for what seemed like forever and a day. My eyes adjusted to the absence of light enough to see a few large shapes but never enough to make out detail. From time to time, I'd see a penlight flick on, and moments later, it would flick off. Diesel could see in the dark, but not perfectly.

"This is boring," I said to him.

"I'm almost done."

"Are you finding anything helpful?"

"He was planning on leaving the country. He had a suitcase packed, and his passport is out on his dresser. No travel itinerary. There are computer connections but no computer. And Wulf's been here. The place reeks of him."

"The crime lab might have taken the computer."

"It's possible. Or Wulf might have taken it."

Diesel wrapped an arm around me and steered me to the foyer and out the front door. We made a half-hearted attempt to reattach the crime-scene tape, but it had lost most of its sticking power, so we left it on the ground and scuttled back to my car.

Halfway home my phone rang.

"Carl's here," Grandma Mazur said. "I went to answer the doorbell, and there he was on the porch looking all dejected."

"Where is he now?"

"He's here in the kitchen, eating cookies."

"I'll be right there."

Thirty minutes later, Diesel walked into my apartment, went straight to the couch, and flipped the ball game on. Carl scampered up beside him.

"Make yourself at home," I said.

"I'm going to pretend that wasn't sarcasm," Diesel said. "I don't suppose you have any chips?"

I brought him a bag of corn chips and a jar of salsa. I took a chip for Rex and dropped it into his cage, along with a baby carrot. I put my mother's leftover bag in the fridge, and I shuffled back to the couch.

"I'm going to bed," I said to Diesel. "Alone. And I expect to wake up alone."

"You bet."

I looked down at Carl. "And I expect you to behave yourself."

Carl did a palms-up and shrugged.

Chapter
SIX

I woke up with a heavy arm across my chest. Diesel. I knew from past experiences that Diesel didn't fit on my couch and wasn't the sort of guy to tough it out on the floor, so I'd taken the precaution of going to bed dressed in T-shirt and running shorts.

Diesel shifted next to me and half-opened his eyes. "Coffee," he murmured.

I slithered out from under him, rolled out of bed, and stepped over the clothes he'd left on the floor, including seafoam green boxers with palm trees and hula girls.

I used the bathroom and shuffled into the living room, where Carl was watching the news on television. I got the coffee going and fed Rex. I wasn't sure what monkeys ate in the morning, so I gave Carl a box of Froot Loops. Diesel ambled into the kitchen and poured himself a mug of coffee.

"What have we got to eat?" he asked.

"Carl's eating the Froot Loops, so that leaves leftovers from last night, peanut butter, hamster crunchies, and half a jar of salsa. Looks like you ate all the chips."

"I shared with Carl." He retrieved the leftover bag from the refrigerator and dumped it on the counter. Pot roast, gravy, green bean casserole. No mashed potatoes. He put it all on a plate and nuked it. "There's enough here for two."

I sipped my coffee. "I'll pass."

Diesel dug into the mountain of food and ate it all.

"It's not fair," I said. "You eat tons of food. Why aren't you fat?"

"High rate of metabolism and clean living."

"What are you doing today?"

"I thought I'd hang out," Diesel said.

"You and Carl?"

"Yeah."

Carl gave Diesel a thumbs-up.

"Well, I'm a working girl," I told him. "I'm going to take a shower and go catch a bad guy."

"Knock yourself out," Diesel said. "If you get a line on Munch, let me know."

Lula was on the couch in the bonds office when I walked in. She was wearing a pink sweat suit and sneakers, and she was holding a box of tissues. She didn't have any makeup on, and her hair was somewhere between rat's nest and exploded canary.

"What's up?" I asked.

"I'm dying is what's up," Lula said. "I got the flu back. I woke up this morning, and I couldn't stop sneezing. And my eyes are all puffy. And I feel like crap."

"Maybe it's an allergy," I said to her.

"I don't get allergies. I never been allergic to anything."

"How'd it go with Tank last night? Did you set a new date for the wedding?"

"I decided December first is a good time on account of it'll be easy to remember for anniversaries."

"That was okay with Tank?"

"Yeah. He had his eyes closed when I told him, but I'm pretty sure he was listening."

Lula sneezed and blew her nose. "I swear, this just came on me. One minute, I'm doing the nasty, and then next thing, I got the flu again."

"Maybe you're allergic to Tank," Connie said.

"I gotta get my numbers done," Lula said. "I think there's something wrong with my juju. I'm gonna call Miss Gloria. This just isn't right."

I pulled Gordo Bollo's file out of my bag. "I'm going to look in on Mr. Bollo. According to his file, he works for Greenblat Produce on Water Street."

"I'll go with you," Lula said. "I heard about Greenblat. That's a big fruit distributor. I could get an orange or a grapefruit for my bad juju while we're there. And I'll call Miss Gloria from the car."

We piled into the Jeep and I took Hamilton, driving toward Broad Street. I had my top up but none of the windows zipped in. It was the end of September, and Trenton was enjoying a last-ditch warm spell.

"Hello," Lula said into her phone. "This here's Lula, and I need to talk to Miss Gloria. It's an emergency. I'm sick, and I think it's my juju, and I need my numbers done right away before I might die or something." Lula disconnected and dropped her phone into her purse. "I hate being sick. No one should ever be sick. And if they do have to be sick, there should never be mucus involved."

I didn't want to hear any more about mucus, so I punched the radio on, found a rap station for Lula, and blasted it out. By the time I rolled to a stop in front of Greenblat Produce, Lula was on a rant over my radio.

"You can't play rap on this cheap-ass radio," she said. "There's no bass. This is like Alvin and the Chipmunks do Jay-Z. On the other hand, your open-air car got my head cleared out. I can breathe. I don't even feel a sneeze coming on."

Greenblat Produce was housed in a large cement-block warehouse with a loading dock in the rear and a small windowless office in the front. There were four desks in the office, and they were occupied by women who looked like Connie clones.

"What?" one of them said to me.

"I'm looking for Gordo Bollo."

"Oh damn, what'd he do now?"

"He forgot his court date. I represent his bail bonds-man, and I need to get him rescheduled."

"I guess it could be worse," she said.

"Oh boy," Lula said to me. "This guy's in deep doo-doo when he got worse visitors than us."

"He's in the back," the woman said. "Go through this door behind me. He's probably sorting tomatoes."

Lula and I entered the warehouse, and I showed her a photo of Gordo.

"He looks real familiar," Lula said. "I know him from somewhere. Maybe I knew him in a professional manner from when I was a 'ho. No wait, that's not it. Now, that's gonna drive me nuts. I hate when this happens. Okay, I got it. He looks like Curly from the Three Stooges. Same bowling ball head and everything. No wonder his wife divorced him. Who'd want to be married to a man with a head like a bowling ball?"

"Have you been taking cold medicine?"

"Maybe I had a couple hits this morning for medicinal purposes," Lula said.

"I think you should wait in the car."

"What? I'm not waiting in no car. I want to see the guy with the bowling ball head."

"Fine, but don't say anything."

"My lips are sealed. See what I'm doing? I'm zipping

them and locking them. And look at this. I'm throwing away the key."

Lula sneezed and farted.

"Oops, excuse me," Lula said. "I thought I was done sneezing. Good thing we're in this big warehouse with all this rotting fruit."

I took a giant step away from Lula and scanned the room. I walked down an aisle formed from crates of iceberg lettuce, turned the corner, and found Bollo offloading a pallet of tomatoes.

"Gordo Bollo?" I asked.

"Who wants to know?"

"We want to know," Lula said. "Who the heck do you think?"

I gave Bollo my card. "I represent your bail bondsman," I told him. "You missed your court date, and you need to reschedule."

"The whole thing is bogus," he said. "My foot got stuck on the accelerator."

"You run over that guy twice," Lula said.

"Yeah, my foot got stuck twice. It was an accident."

"It really doesn't matter," I said to him. "You'll have a chance to explain all that if you'll just come with me to get a new date."

"I can't go now. I'm working."

"These look like real nice tomatoes," Lula said.

And then she sneezed and farted again.

"Cripes, lady," Bollo said. "You just cut the cheese on the tomatoes."

"I didn't do no such thing," Lula said. "I was facing the other direction." She turned and looked behind her. "I laid one on these grapefruits from Guatemala. And anyways, it's not my fault. I got bad juju going. I'm waitin' on a call from Miss Gloria."

"This won't take long," I said to Bollo.

"I'm not coming with you. Go away. Leave me alone."

"I gotta get out of here," Lula said. "There's something in here making my nose twitch."

"Go out to the car. I'll be there in a minute."

"You sure you don't need me?" Lula asked.

"I'm sure!"

Bollo went back to sorting tomatoes.

"Listen up," I said to him. "You are required by law to return to the court, and I'm authorized to use force if necessary."

"Oh yeah? Force this," he said.

And he hit me square in the forehead with a tomato. I turned and *SPLAT*—I took another in the back of the head. By the time I reached the door, I'd taken at least three more tomatoes.

"Uh-oh," a Connie clone said when I staggered into the office. "Looks like you pissed Gordo off. That man could use some anger management."

"I'll be back," I told her. "How late does he work?"

"He'll be here until four."

I left the office and settled myself behind the wheel of the Jeep.

"What the Sam Hill happened to you?" Lula wanted to know.

"Bollo needs anger management."

"I'd go shoot him or something for you, but I'm waiting on Miss Gloria."

I wheeled out of the lot, turned onto Broad, and Miss Gloria called Lula back.

"Yeah?" Lula said to Miss Gloria. "Un-hunh, un-hunh, un-hunh."

"Well?" I asked her when she disconnected.

"It's my moons. Miss Gloria ran my numbers, and they didn't look so good, so then she did my chart, and it turns out my moons are all screwed up."

"So?"

"I just gotta wait it out. She said I need to be extra careful during this time and not make any big decisions on account of they could be life changing and I could decide the wrong thing."

"Because of your moons?"

"Yeah, and we're on the cusp of something right now, but cell reception wasn't good, so I didn't get it all."

I parked curbside at the office and followed Lula through the front door.

"Omigod," Connie said. "What happened? Is that blood?"

"Tomatoes."

"Gordo Bollo had issues with takin' a ride with us," Lula said.

"I need cuffs and pepper spray and a stun gun," I told Connie.

"You haven't got any?"

"She lost them when someone stole her purse at the mall last week," Lula said. "I was with her. One minute, we were in the food court, eating pizza, and next thing, she didn't have no purse. Lucky she just paid for the pizza, and she had her wallet in her pocket, or she wouldn't have no credit cards."

"Take whatever you need," Connie said.

I got myself outfitted, and walked outside into the midday sunshine. A black Porsche turbo slid to a stop behind my Jeep, and Ranger angled out from behind the wheel and stood hands on hips, looking me over.

"Babe," Ranger said. And he almost smiled.

Ranger dresses in black. The rest of him comes in varying shades of brown. Silky dark brown hair, light brown skin, and brown eyes that are more often than not hidden behind mirrored sunglasses. He's two months older than I am and years ahead in life experience. He's a security expert and part owner of Rangeman, a protective services company located in a stealth town house in center city.

"Tomatoes," I said by way of explanation.

"Do you need help?"

"No. But thanks for asking."

"Diesel is back," Ranger said.

"Yes. How did you know?"

"I woke up with a migraine this morning." Ranger picked a chunk of tomato out of my hair. "Word on the street is that you're looking for Munch, and Munch is looking for pure barium. And he's willing to pay serious money. There are a couple vendors who deal in this sort of thing. Solomon Cuddles and Doc Weiner. If you watch one of these guys, you might run into Munch. You can find Cuddles at the mall somewhere between the food court and the Gap. Weiner operates out of the Sky Social Club on Stark. Don't go in there alone. In fact, don't go in there at all."

"Why would Munch want barium?"

"I don't know. It's commonly used in X-ray imaging. And it's useful in making certain kinds of superconductors. I'm sure it has other uses, but I'm not a barium expert."

A shiny black SUV rolled to a stop behind Ranger's Porsche. Tank was in Rangeman black fatigues behind the wheel, and Hal was next to him.

"I have to go," Ranger said. "Try not to stand too close to Diesel. He has some bad enemies. You don't want to get caught in the cross fire."

Chapter
SEVEN

Diesel opened the door to my apartment before I had a chance to plug my key in.

"Did you feel my sensory imprint approaching?" I asked him.

"No. I was looking out the window, and I saw you pull into the parking lot. What's with the tomatoes?"

"Uncooperative FTA. I tried to take him down in a produce warehouse."

"If we put some mayo on you, I could eat you for lunch. Which reminds me . . . there's no food here."

"That's because you and your monkey have eaten it all."

"Hey, he's not *my* monkey," Diesel said.

"Speaking of the monkey, where is he?"

"I think he's in the bathroom."

I heard the toilet flush, the bathroom door banged open, and Carl walked into the living room. He waved at me, climbed onto the couch, and remoted the television on.

"Did you wash your hands?" I asked him.

He held his hands above his head and gave me the finger.

"He's not normal," I said to Diesel.

"And?"

"I need to take a shower."

"I'm going to use your Jeep to do some shopping. Do you want anything special for lunch?"

"Anything but tomatoes. My keys are in my bag in the foyer."

"Thanks, but I don't need keys."

A half hour later, I pulled my clean hair into a ponytail and dressed in jeans and a black V-neck stretchy T-shirt. Diesel was still out, so I checked in with Morelli.

"How's it going?" I asked.

"Would you consider getting married and moving far away from my family? Maybe France or Phoenix?"

"Not working out with your brother?"

"I'm locking my gun in my car when I get home so I'm not tempted to shoot him. He's an even bigger slob than I am. I've got empty beer cans all over the house, and he's only been with me for twenty-four hours. Last night, I took him bowling, and he hit on everything that moved and was remotely female. And by the time we got home, he was crying because he missed his wife. *Crying!* Then he watched television until three in the morning and charged two porn films on my cable account."

"You need to talk to him."

"My brother? Are you kidding?"

"Is his wife showing any signs of reconciliation?"

"Not so far, but my mother said she'd make me a tray of lasagna and come over to clean my house if I kept him another day."

"Are you going to keep him?"

"Yeah, he's my brother."

"Call me when he leaves."

"You'll be the first to know."

The locks tumbled on my front door, and Diesel pushed his way in, arms wrapped around bags of food.

"Food shopping isn't my favorite thing," Diesel said. "I wouldn't do it for anyone but you."

"How do you eat if you don't shop?"

"People feed me." He pulled a couple subs out of a bag and tossed one to me. "Women think I'm adorable."

"Adorable?"

"Maybe adorable is a stretch."

I unwrapped my sub and took a bite. "I have a line on Munch. He's looking for barium, and there are only two vendors in the area. Solomon Cuddles and Doc Weiner."

"What would Munch want with barium?"

"I don't know," I said. "I don't know anything about barium."

"It's a heavy metal. Hard to find in pure form because it oxidizes when it's exposed to air. That's all I remember from Chemistry 101."

Carl walked into the kitchen and did a gesture that said, *What about me?*

Diesel handed Carl a bag with apples, oranges, bananas, and grapes. "I got you fruit."

Carl looked at the fruit and gave Diesel the finger.

"Dude," Diesel said. "I've spent a lot of time in southeast Asia. Monkeys eat fruit."

Carl jumped onto the counter and pawed through the remaining food bags. He found a box of cookies and took it back to the couch.

"You'll rot your teeth," I told Carl. "You'll get diabetes."

"Do you know where to find Weiner and Cuddles?" Diesel asked.

"Yes."

He finished his sub and grabbed a banana. "Let's roll."

"What about Carl?"

Diesel looked in on Carl. "Are you okay here by yourself?"

Carl vigorously nodded his head and gave Diesel a thumbs-up.

We chose to watch Doc Weiner because the mall felt unwieldy. Too many people. Too much space, plus I couldn't see myself looking for a guy named Cuddles who was walking around dealing heavy chemicals out of a briefcase.

Not that I was excited about staking out Stark Street. It was affectionately known as the combat zone, and it lived up to its name on a daily basis. In order to better fit in with the local atmosphere, Diesel was driving a black Cadillac Escalade with titanium wheel covers, dark tinted windows, and multiple antennae. I didn't ask where he got it. We were parked half a block down and across the street from the Sky Social Club, and we looked like your average contract killer/neighborhood drug dealer in our badass gas-guzzler.

"Do you know what Doc Weiner looks like?" Diesel asked.

"No. Does it matter?"

Diesel pushed his seat back and stretched his legs. "Just curious."

"What do you think goes on inside this social club?"

Diesel looked across the street. "Business transactions, card games, prostitution. The usual."

"Have you ever been in a social club like this?"

Diesel nodded. "They're the same the world over. They're grungy hangouts for crime families and their retinue of suck-ups and stooges."

"There are a couple social clubs in the Burg, but most of the men are recovering from hip replacements and are on oxygen."

"The golden years," Diesel said.

The Sky Social Club was housed in a narrow three-story building, squished between a butcher shop and a coin-op Laundromat. The front door to the club was wooden and weathered. The windows had blackout shades drawn. Overall, the appearance was grim.

Two young guys went into the club. Minutes later, one came out with a folding chair. He set the chair by the door, lit up, and sat down. An hour later, we were still watching, but nothing was happening. No one was going in, and no one was coming out.

"We don't need two people to do this. I should take off and watch the guy at the mall," I said to Diesel.

"Give me a break. You just want to go shopping."

I rolled my eyes so far into the top of my head I almost went unconscious, and I did a huge snort of indignation. This all in spite of the fact that he was right.

"You are so annoying," I said.

"I try my best."

"Tell me again why I need to sit here with you."

"If I stay here alone and Wulf shows up instead of Munch, he'll sniff me out and vanish. And then he might not come back, and we'll have lost our lead. The real question is why do I have to sit here with *you*. I could be taking a nap in your nice, comfy bed right now."

"Good grief."

"Don't you want to know why I'm here?" Diesel asked.

"No."

He grinned at me and tugged at my ponytail. "I'm here to protect you so you don't get hurt in this bad neighborhood."

I didn't know how to react to this. I was sort of offended but at the same time grateful. And deep down inside, I knew it was bullshit. He was here hoping Wulf would show up.

"Did you buy that?" Diesel asked.

"Partially."

I slouched lower in my seat and watched the sidewalk across the street. A man came out of the bar at the end of the block and walked toward us, head down. His hair was braided and shoulder length. He looked to be in his late twenties. Slim. Average height. He was wearing work boots and jeans and a dirt-smudged T-shirt. He got even with us and picked his head up to check out a passing car. Holy cow. It was Hector Mendez. He was in my dead file. He failed to appear for court six months ago, and I was never able to find him. And then someone said he was dead. Shot in a gang thing.

"I know that guy," I said to Diesel. "I looked for him for months and finally gave up."

I grabbed cuffs and pepper spray out of my bag, shoved them into my jeans pockets, and bolted from the car. Diesel asked if I needed help, but I hit the ground running. No time for small talk. I knew the instant Mendez saw me he'd take off. He was a small-time drug pusher who was constantly in and out of jail, and this wasn't the first time I'd chased him down.

I was halfway across the street, running flat out, when he spotted me. His eyes went wide, and it was easy to read his lips.

"Oh fuck," Mendez said.

"Stop!" I yelled. "I want to talk to you."

"Sorry," he said. "I gotta go. I'm in a hurry."

I never broke stride, and I had momentum, but he was a better runner. He had long legs and a lot of motivation. We rounded the corner, and he turned down a service road that intersected the block. There were cars parked behind businesses and rooming houses. I saw a sign for the rear entrance to the Laundromat, and suddenly Mendez stopped short. I didn't bother to question his reason. I took a flying leap and tackled him, taking him down to the ground. We rolled around cussing and clawing, my knee connected with his gonads, and that was the end of the rolling around. I cuffed him and sprang to my feet, feeling like I'd just won the calf-roping competition at the county fair.

"I'm gonna sue," Mendez said. "My privates are injured. This here's some kind of brutality."

I was breathing heavy, trying to get a grip, and then I saw the reason Mendez had stopped running. He'd come face-to-face with Wulf. At least, I was pretty sure it was Wulf. He was almost as tall as Diesel but not quite as solid. His hair was black and shoulder length, swept away from his face in waves. His skin was pale and unearthly, like moonlight reflecting off still water. He was shockingly handsome, and his face was disturbingly devoid of expression. He was wearing black dress boots, black slacks, and a lightweight black cashmere sweater with the sleeves pushed up to his elbows. He had an expensive watch on his left wrist. And he had a narrow black metal bracelet on his right wrist. He was standing beside a black Ferrari, and he was looking past me.

I glanced over my shoulder and saw Diesel standing about twenty feet behind me, relaxed, looking amused.

"Walk away," Wulf said to Diesel.

Diesel shook his head no. His mouth still held the very small smile, but his eyes were hard.

Wulf moved close to me, wrapped his hand around

my arm, and I felt a buzz of electricity run from his hand to my fingertips.

"Get in the car," he said.

"No."

"I could snap your neck."

"And I could shove your nuts into your small intestine with my knee."

This was absolute bravado on my part. It was one thing to sort of accidentally on purpose connect with Hector Mendez. Kneeing Gerwulf Grimoire would be a whole other ball game. He was flat-out scary, and he radiated power. And I was pretty much frozen to the spot. What I knew for sure was that it would be a huge mistake to get into the car. I was guessing women went into his car in a lot better shape than they came out.

"Release her," Diesel said.

Wulf's voice was low and silky. Wind whispering in the trees. "I won't tolerate interference in my business. If necessary, I'll destroy you and everyone associated with you."

Diesel's posture was relaxed. No fear visible. "I have a job to do. Nothing personal, but I *will* do it."

"We'll take this up some other day," Wulf said.

He released my arm and stepped away from me. There was a blast of heat and a flash of fire, and when the smoke cleared, Wulf was gone. The car was still there.

Diesel was hands on hips, looking disgusted. He gave his head a small shake. "Mr. Hollywood."

"I didn't see nothing," Mendez said, still on the ground. "I don't know what just happened, and I didn't see it."

I made a move to the car, and Diesel pulled me back.

"You don't want to touch Wulf's car," he said. "You never know what might happen."

I processed Mendez and returned to Diesel. He was parked in the public lot across the street from the court, and he was zoned out behind the wheel. I slid onto the seat next to him and buckled myself in.

"You look deep in thought," I said to him.

"I should have known Wulf was in the building."

"Maybe his blood vessels were expanded."

Diesel grimaced.

"Or maybe he wasn't *in* the building. Maybe we caught him going in. Maybe he'd just got there," I said.

"That's a happy idea. That would make me feel much better, because the possibility that I might have lost my ability to sense Wulf depresses the crap out of me."

"How did he disappear in a flash of fire?"

"The fire and smoke is right out of the *Magic for Dummies* book. Any nine-year-old kid can do it. And it creates a diversion for his exit." Diesel rolled the engine over. "Now what?"

"Back to the office so I can collect my capture money."

We got to the office in less than ten minutes, due to the fact that every light was green and traffic was nonexistent.

Diesel parked at the curb and grinned at me.

"That was pure luck," I said to him. "I don't for one instant believe you can control traffic lights."

"I didn't say anything."

"You grinned."

"We could make a bet," Diesel said.

"Can I set the stakes?"

He shook his head. "No. It's my ability that's called into question. I think it's fair that I set the stakes."

"No way."

"Afraid you'll lose?"

"Not willing to take a chance."

"This isn't doing a lot for my ego," Diesel said.

"Your ego doesn't seem especially fragile."

"That doesn't mean I can't be crushed. I'm only human . . . sort of."

I did a mental eye roll and got out of the car. "If you said that to a health care professional, they'd shoot you full of Thorazine."

"Hey, look who's here," Connie said, eyeballing Diesel. "Long time, no see."

Vinnie stuck his head out of his inner office. "Who's here?"

There are many members of my family tree who would like to take an axe to Vinnie's limb. He's a decent judge of people, and that makes him a good bail bondsman. Unfortunately, he's also oily, addicted to every vice possible, and sees nothing wrong with being a sexual deviant, so his score as a human being isn't all that great.

"It's Diesel," Connie said. "Stephanie's friend."

"So what are you doing here?" Vinnie asked Diesel. "Are you porking her?"

"Not yet," Diesel said.

"Why aren't you working? What do you do?"

"I work for the power company. I'm the guy who pushes the disconnect button."

"That sounds like fun," Vinnie said.

"It has its moments."

I gave Connie my body receipt. "You'll never guess. Purely by accident, I ran into Hector Mendez."

"I thought he was dead."

"Nope. He's alive and kicking."

"He's alive, but he wasn't doing much kicking after Kung Fu Princess here got done with him," Diesel said.

"Ha!" Vinnie said. "I bet she got him in the ol' casabas."

"Gave my boys the creepy crawlies just looking at it," Diesel told him.

"Gives *my* boys the creepy crawlies thinking she's wasting her time on Mendez," Vinnie said. "Mendez is penny-ante. I need to see Munch get his shrimp ass hauled back to the slammer. I don't have Munch by the end of the month, and I'm gonna have to move to South America. I'm out Munch money, and I'm in the red. And Harry don't like the color red unless it's blood."

"Harry?" Diesel asked.

"Harry the Hammer. His financial backer who also happens to be his father-in-law," I told him.

Diesel smiled, and Vinnie gave his head a shake, as if even after all these years he still didn't believe it.

I took my capture check from Connie and dropped it into my bag. "See you all tomorrow."

"Yeah," Vinnie said, "and make sure you have Munch's body receipt next time you waltz in here."

Diesel and I left the office, and Diesel beeped the Escalade unlocked. "And you're working for him, why?"

"It annoys my mother. I don't have to wear pantyhose. And I'm not sure anyone else would hire me."

"All good reasons."

Diesel drove us back to my apartment, and when we walked in, Carl was still watching television.

"I was hoping he'd made dinner," Diesel said.

"Do you cook?"

"No. Do you?"

"No. I can open a jar of marinara sauce, dial pizza, and I can make a sandwich."

"Works for me," Diesel said. "What's your choice for tonight?"

"Sandwich."

We worked our way through ham-and-cheese sand-wiches, a tub of macaroni salad, and half an apple pie. We'd just finished the pie when Diesel's phone rang. This was cause for concern because in the short time I'd known Diesel, his phone had never rung for anything good. He didn't get social calls, family calls, or dinner invitations. It looked to me like only a few people had his number, and their calls were always work related.

"Yeah?" he said into the phone. He listened for a moment, told the caller he was on his way, and discon-nected. "We have to hustle," he said to me. "Flash is on Wulf's tail."

I grabbed my bag, and we rushed out of the apart-ment and ran to the Escalade. Diesel took us out of the lot to Hamilton and headed for Broad.

"I had Flash watch the Ferrari," Diesel said. "I knew Wulf would come back for it."

I was familiar with Flash from previous Diesel visits. From what I could tell, Flash was a nice guy who did odd jobs and had no special talents other than the ability to tolerate Diesel. He was five feet ten, with spiked red hair and multiple piercings in his ears. He was slim and at first glance looked younger than his actual age, which I thought was probably early thirties.

We picked up South Broad and Flash called in.

"I'm on the outskirts of Bordentown. I'm betting he's going for the Turnpike," Flash said and disconnected.

"He always goes south," Diesel said to me. "I got hung up in traffic on Broad Street when I was follow-ing him, and I suspected he went to the Turnpike, but I couldn't catch him."

Another call came in from Flash. "We're on the

Turnpike going south. I can't imagine how fast he's going, but if I go any faster, my fenders will fall off."

"You can go home," Diesel said. "Appreciate the effort. I'm a couple miles behind you. I'll take the Turnpike and ride for a while to see if I pick up on him."

"To infinity and beyond," Flash said.

We stayed at it for another twenty minutes before Diesel gave up and turned around.

"Wulf could be going to Atlantic City or any point in between," Diesel said. "There are some goofball Unmentionables in the Pine Barrens, but I can't see Wulf getting cozy with any of them. We have two people working together in the scientific community, and one of them is dead and the other missing. I'd like to know if either of them had property in south Jersey."

"I don't remember seeing anything about property in south Jersey in either file."

"Did Connie run Munch and Scanlon through all the programs?"

"No. Some of those investigations take days."

"Then let's go to the bonds office and see if anything else came in."

"The bonds office is closed."

"We'll open it."

"I hate this idea. You'll trip the alarm, and we'll get arrested, and I'll get fired."

"To begin with, I won't trip the alarm. And even if I did trip it, the bonds office is armed with Rangeman security. Ranger isn't going to send you to jail."

True, Ranger wouldn't send me to jail, but Ranger wouldn't be happy to find me engaged in breaking and entering with Diesel. And I suspected a face-off between Diesel and Ranger would be ugly.

"Okay, but it'll be boring," I said. "We could wait

and ask Connie in the morning, and we could go back to my apartment and watch television with the monkey."

"No," Diesel said.

"That's it? No? What about my vote?"

"This is why I'm not married," Diesel said. "Women make everything so friggin' complicated. And stop rolling your eyes at me."

"You're staring straight ahead at the road. How do you know I'm rolling my eyes?"

Diesel did a full-on smile. "I don't have to look at you to know when you're rolling your eyes. You roll your eyes every time I act like a jerk."

Chapter
EIGHT

It was a dark, moonless night, and we were lost in shadow when Diesel parked the Escalade in the small lot behind the bail bonds office.

"I'll wait here," I told him.

"This could take some time. You'll be more comfortable inside."

"Are you going to be a jerk again and make me come in?"

"No. Are you going to drive off without me?"

I hadn't intended to, but it wasn't a bad idea now that he'd planted the seed.

"Well?" he asked.

"I'm trying to decide."

He pulled the key out of the ignition and pocketed it. "Lock yourself in and lean on the horn if someone tries to steal you."

I watched him go to the back door and open it as if it hadn't been locked. He just put his hand to the doorknob and opened the door. No alarm sounded. The door closed behind Diesel, and I settled in. An hour ticked by, and the police didn't show. No Rangeman goons arrived in SWAT gear. I reclined my seat and closed my eyes.

* * *

I was suffocating. I was struggling to come out of a deep sleep, and I was desperate for air. I forced my eyes open and saw the problem. I was in bed, and Diesel had his arm draped across my chest again. Diesel was a big guy with a lot of muscle, and his arm weighed a ton. I thought back to the night before and vaguely remembered falling asleep in the car, and next thing, Diesel was shuffling me into my building and into the elevator. After that, it was fuzzy. I checked around and discovered I was wearing panties and Diesel's T-shirt. That was it. Diesel was wearing less.

I squirmed around, trying to slide away from Diesel, but he tightened his grip and drew me closer.

"Hey," I said. "Hey!"

He half opened his eyes and looked at me. "What?"

"You've got me in a death grip. I can't breathe. And what's with my clothes? I'm wearing your T-shirt."

"Yeah, I didn't know what to put on you. You looked uncomfortable sleeping in your jeans and sweater and stuff."

"Did you undress me?"

His eyes slid closed.

"Wake up," I yelled at him.

"Now what?" he said.

"I don't remember a lot about last night. We didn't . . . I mean, you didn't . . ."

"Honey, being intimate with me is not a forgettable experience."

"I guess that's good to know."

"Yeah, file it for future reference. What time is it?"

"It's almost eight o'clock."

Diesel sighed and rolled away from me. "I hate mornings. They start so early."

I left the bed and gathered my clothes up from the

floor. "Did you get anything useful last night at the bonds office?"

"I printed out a copy of Munch's doctoral thesis, but didn't get a chance to read it. I'm hoping it'll tell me something about the theft at the research center. I'd like to know why he took the magnetometer. Nothing else local turned up on Munch. It's like he has no life. Scanlon shows some promise. His sister, Roberta Scanlon, has a house in north Philadelphia. He had a second sister, Gail, but she's like smoke. Eugene Scanlon was also heavily in debt. He defaulted on a car loan and had two credit cards in collection. His research isn't published, but he was Munch's project supervisor, so they had to be working in similar areas."

I carted my clothes into the bathroom and locked the door, not that it would make a difference. I took a shower, gave my hair a two-minute blast with the dryer, and got dressed. Diesel was sleeping when I came out. I took a moment to study him, thinking he was heart-stoppingly handsome in a rugged, outdoorsy kind of way. His initial appearance was beach bum, but I'd come to decide that was a façade. Diesel was driven by his job. The job itself was open for discussion. If he was to be believed, he was a kind of paranormal bounty hunter. I thought it was just as possible he was a contract killer or a career nutcase.

I went to the kitchen and fed Rex and Carl and got coffee brewing. I dropped a bagel into the toaster and took a tub of cream cheese out of my fridge. Diesel might not be much of a cook, but he sure as heck knew how to stock a kitchen.

I heard the shower running in the bathroom, and minutes later, Diesel strolled in looking for coffee. He poured himself a mug and ate half my bagel.

"I want to take the morning to wade through Munch's thesis," Diesel said. "When I'm done with the thesis, I thought we could visit Roberta Scanlon."

Carl came into the kitchen and handed me his empty cereal box. He jumped onto the counter, got a mug out of the cupboard, and helped himself to coffee.

"This apartment smells like a monkey," Diesel said.

Carl gave him the finger and went back to the television.

"I'm out of here," I said to Diesel. "I'm taking another shot at Gordo Bollo today. This time, I'm ready. I've got a stun gun, pepper spray, and cuffs."

"Kick ass," Diesel said. "If you aren't home by noon, I'll have you teleported back here."

I must have looked horrified because he burst out laughing.

"I'm falling in love," Diesel said. "You're the only one on this earth who believes everything I say."

I tried really hard not to roll my eyes, but I couldn't help myself and rolled them anyway. I grabbed my bag and flounced out of the apartment. It wasn't so much that I *believed* what Diesel said. It was more that I was terrified it might be true.

Lula was filing when I swung into the office.

"What are you doing?" I asked her.

"I'm filing. What does it look like I'm doing? It's my job, you know."

"You never file."

"Your ass," Lula said.

"I'm paying a visit to Greenblat Produce this morning," I said. "Anyone need fruit?"

"Hell yeah," Lula said. "I'm not missing that. I was in the car when all the action went down last time."

I could happily do without that kind of action. Still, we took my Jeep, just in case there was another tomato incident. Lula didn't want to veg up her Firebird.

I drove to Greenblat and parked in the lot. I got out of the Jeep and transferred the pepper spray, stun gun, and cuffs from my bag to my jeans for easier access.

"Don't you worry," Lula said. "If he starts something this time, you gonna have Lula there. I'll sit on Bowling Ball Head and squash him into a pancake."

"Fine. Just don't shoot him."

"Did I say I was gonna shoot him? Did you hear me say that?"

"I was only reminding you."

"You got a thing about shooting people. I bet Diesel shoots lots of people."

"Diesel doesn't carry a gun."

"Get out of town!"

I entered the office, said hello to the Connie clones, and went straight to the door leading to the warehouse. I walked up and down aisles formed by stacks of crates and found Bollo putting little stickers on apples.

"Look who's here," Bollo said, spotting me. "Come back for more tomatoes?"

"You need to come with me to get rescheduled."

Bollo palmed an apple. "No."

"If you hit me with that apple, I'm going to let Lula shoot you," I said.

Bollo looked past me. "I don't see no Lula."

I turned and scanned the aisle. He was right. No Lula.

"She was here a minute ago," I said.

"Well, she ain't here now."

I shouted her name, and she rounded a stack of crated oranges at the end of the aisle.

"You looking for me?" Lula said, her arms filled with fruit and vegetables.

"Yes, I'm looking for you. You're supposed to be my backup. What are you doing?"

"I'm shopping. This place got really good produce. I got some grapefruit and a eggplant, and look at these red pears. And I got a dozen eggs. They even got fresh eggs here."

"We don't *sell* produce here, fatso," Bollo said. "We only distribute to stores. Put them back."

Lula's eyes bugged out of her head. "Did you just call me fatso? Did I hear that right?"

"Yeah," Bollo said. "What of it?"

"That's a mean thing to say. And it isn't even true. I'm just a big and beautiful woman. I got more of all the good stuff than most other women. And people who have heads like bowling balls should watch what they say about other people. You're lucky I'm not a vicious person, because if I was vicious, I'd call you Coconut Head. Or Gordo Gourdhead."

And then Lula bounced a grapefruit off Coconut Head's forehead. And Coconut Head tagged her with the apple he'd been holding. And what happened after that was a blur of flying fruit and eggs. I had my stun gun in my hand, but it was hard to get to Bollo and dodge the fruit at the same time. I finally managed to get the prongs on him, I hit the go button, and nothing happened. No juice.

Bollo shoved me away, and I lost my footing, sliding on fruit slime. I grabbed a fistful of his shirt and took him down with me. I was hanging on to him, and he was trying to get away, and Lula fired off a shot to the ceiling.

"Next bullet's gonna be up your ass," Lula said to Bollo.

Bollo paused to consider that, and a rat dropped from an overhead rafter and landed inches from Lula in her red patent-leather stilettos.

"Damn rats are all over the place," Bollo said.

Lula just about went white. "I hate rats," she said. "I hate rats more than I hate monkeys."

The rat twitched, its beady black eyes blinked open, and it got to its feet.

"You just stunned him," Bollo said to Lula. "Shoot him again."

Lula took aim and the rat charged at her. Personally, I think the rat didn't know what the heck it was doing, but Lula freaked.

"Eeeeeeee," Lula shrieked, dancing around in her heels, arms in the air, completely apeshit.

The rat scurried across Lula's foot and kept going past boxes of potatoes and beans. It took a left and headed for Pennyslvania. Bollo did the same. By the time I got to my feet, and Lula stopped freaking, Bollo was long gone.

A bunch of guys had gathered around us. They were throwing out comments in Spanish and laughing.

"What are they saying?" Lula wanted to know.

"I don't know," I told her. "I don't speak Spanish. The only thing I could pick out was loco."

"What are you looking at?" Lula said to the men. "Don't you have anything better to do? This place should be shut down. I'm calling the health inspector. I'm gonna report this place to the fruit police." Lula turned to me. "And what's with you and the dud stun gun? Let me take a look at that thing."

I handed Lula the stun gun, and she tested it out on the guy next to her, who immediately collapsed into a heap on the floor and wet his pants.

"Seems to be working now," Lula said, handing the stun gun back to me.

I dropped the stun gun into my bag, Lula pocketed her Glock, and we hotfooted it out of there. We chose to leave through the loading dock exit and walk around the building rather than drip egg and melon guts onto the office floor. We wiped off as best we could and climbed into my Jeep.

"You see, this is what Miss Gloria's talking about," Lula said. "I got bad juju. How else could you explain it?"

"It's not our juju," I told Lula. "It's our skill level. We're incompetent."

"I got a high skill level," Lula said. "I just shot a rat off a rafter."

"You weren't aiming for it."

"Yeah. My skill level is so high I do things I don't even try to do."

Chapter
NINE

I dropped Lula at the office, drove myself home, and dragged myself through my front door. The egg-and-fruit gunk had dried en route and was matted in my hair and plastered to my jeans and T-shirt.

Diesel looked me up and down. "Another issue at the produce warehouse?"

"I don't want to talk about it. It involved a rat."

"What's in your hair?"

I felt around. "I think it's mostly egg."

"Do you need help? Do you want me to hose you off in the parking lot?"

"Jeez Louise," I said. "I had a really crumby morning and I've got egg in my hair. Could I get a little sensitivity here?"

Diesel smiled. "I could take a shot at it." He gathered me into his arms, held me close, and leaned his head against mine. "You smell nice," he said. "Like fruit salad."

An hour later, we were all in the Escalade. Carl had pitched a fit about being left alone, so we'd brought him along. He was in the backseat, strapped in by a seat belt, his hands folded in his lap, looking as if at any moment he was going to ask if we were there yet.

"Is it me, or is this whole monkey thing getting a little Twilight Zone?" Diesel asked, checking Carl out in the rearview mirror.

"You think it's just *getting* Twilight Zone? You don't think it's *always* been Twilight Zone?"

"Have you heard anything from his mother?"

"No. Not a word."

"It's like we've adopted a hairy little kid," Diesel said. "There's something about him sitting in the backseat that's friggin' spooky."

I looked over my shoulder at Carl, and he sent me a finger wave.

"So if I wasn't along for the ride, would you just pop yourself over to Philadelphia?" I asked Diesel.

"No. It's not that easy to get *popped* someplace."

"Wulf didn't seem to have a lot of trouble with it. Is he more powerful than you?"

"No. He's just different."

"How so?"

"For starters, he kills people."

Diesel crossed the Delaware River into Pennsylvania.

"Do you know Wulf?"

"Yes."

"Have you known him for a long time?"

"I've known him forever," Diesel said. "He's my cousin."

That took my breath away. His cousin. He was hunting down a family member!

"This must be hard on you," I said to Diesel. "I would hate to be in that position." And my mother would be in a state.

"Someone has to disable Wulf, and I've been tapped. Even if it wasn't my job, I would probably feel compelled to stop him."

"Has he always been bad?"

"He's always been different. Intense, melancholy, angry, obsessed with his power. And brilliant."

Diesel looked normal. He was the embodiment of the all-American charismatic oaf. But he was from a gene pool closely related to Wulf. And Wulf wasn't nearly normal. Wulf dominated his airspace and radiated unnatural energy. And God knows what else Wulf could do. So I had a few thoughts here about Diesel and his abilities that went beyond normal. Or heck, maybe I've just seen so much weird stuff since I became a bounty hunter that I'll believe anything.

Carl was making sounds in the backseat. "Puh, puh, puh."

Diesel looked at him in the rearview mirror. "What's with the monkey?"

"I think he's amusing himself."

"Puh, puh, puh, puh, puh," Carl said.

Diesel turned the radio on and Carl made the sounds louder.

"PUH, PUH, PUH, PUH."

Diesel shut the radio off and shot a black look at Carl. "If you keep making that sound, I'm going to set you out at the side of the road and not come back for you."

Carl blew out a sigh and went silent.

"Feeling cranky?" I asked Diesel.

"Not until a couple minutes ago."

"Chirrup," Carl said. "Chirrup, chirrup, chirrup."

"Do you have your gun with you?" Diesel asked me.

"Yeah, but there aren't any bullets in it."

"Probably a good thing," Diesel said.

"Chirrup, chirrup, chirrup, chirrup, chirrup," Carl said.

Diesel exited the highway and hooked a right.

"You aren't really going to leave him on the side of the road, are you?" I asked him.

"No. I saw a sign for Walmart. I'm making a pit stop."

He pulled into the lot and parked. "Stay here. I'll be right back."

Carl sat up straight and looked out the window. "Eeee?"

"No," I said. "We're not there yet. Pit stop."

Carl looked confused. He didn't know pit stop.

"Just go with it," I told him. "Diesel will be back in a couple minutes."

"Chirrup."

Ten minutes later, Diesel jogged back to the SUV. Carl had gone from chirrup, to choo choo choo, to buh-buhbuhbuh, and I was on the verge of gonzo. Diesel angled behind the wheel, handed me a bag, and tossed a bag into the backseat.

"Knock yourself out," Diesel said to Carl.

"What's in his bag?"

"Food and an electronic game. I got them to sell me the demo that was already charged."

"What's in my bag?"

"Food."

Carl selected a bag of chips, and I did the same.

"That was pretty smart," I said to Diesel.

Diesel stuck his hand into the chip bag and took a fistful. "I have a highly developed sense of self-preservation, and a low tolerance for monkey business."

"What do you expect to get from Scanlon's sister?"

"I don't know. You throw the net out and see what you pull in."

"I hate intruding at a time like this. She just found out someone killed her brother."

"She'll want that person brought to justice. And I'm sure you're good at talking to a grieving woman."

"Me? What about you?"

"I suck at it."

"You're kidding! You're going to make me do the interrogation?"

"Yeah. This is one of those girl skills."

"That's so sexist."

"And?"

"What do you want me to ask her?"

"I'm looking for real estate. I'm guessing Wulf and Munch are holed up somewhere in south Jersey within commuting distance to Trenton. I did property searches on Munch and Scanlon and nothing turned up. I looked for Wulf using known aliases and holding companies and got zero. I guess they could be under assumed names in a high-roller suite at Caesars, but it would be impractical. Especially if they're working with illegal technology. Munch was a complete loner with no Jersey ties that we know of. That leaves Scanlon. Ask about the missing sister."

"There could also be a third person involved. Someone we haven't discovered yet."

"It's possible."

Carl was examining the handheld game. He shook it and smelled it. He bit it. He looked forward to me. I leaned over the seat and showed Carl how to turn the game on and push the buttons.

A castle appeared on the screen. Blue sky. Clouds. Music. Birds flying. A little man ran into the center of the screen. The little man was joined by a pretty girl in a pink gown. Lightning struck the castle. The castle exploded.

"Eep," Carl said.

The man and the pink-gowned girl returned and Carl hunkered in, eyes narrowed, concentrating.

Diesel was back on the road, the big Escalade rolling south like a cruise ship under full power. Farms flew by the window, and in the backseat Carl was barely breathing as his fingers twitched on the game buttons and the happy sounds of Super Mario Bros. drifted up to us.

Roberta Scanlon lived in a brick row house in a blue-collar section of north Philadelphia. According to Diesel's research, she had never married, and she worked out of her house doing Web site design and maintenance. We sat at the curb for a couple minutes, watching the house, getting a sense of the neighborhood. It was quiet at this time of the day. No traffic. No kids playing outdoors. No dogs barking. Only Carl the Monkey making Mario music in the backseat.

"Okay, cutie-pie," Diesel said to me. "Go do your thing."

I blew out a sigh and heaved myself out of the SUV. I hated this part of my job. I hated prying into people's private lives and intruding on their grief. I understood that it was sometimes necessary, but that didn't make it any more palatable. I trudged up the sidewalk and rang the bell, thinking I wouldn't mind if Roberta wasn't home. No such luck. Roberta Scanlon opened the door and looked out at me.

"Yes?" Roberta said.

I apologized for the intrusion, introduced myself, and asked if I could speak with her.

"I suppose," she said, "but I've already spoken to the police. I just don't know what more I can tell you."

"Did your brother own property in south Jersey?"

"Not that I know about, but he didn't tell me much. It's not like we were a close family. I couldn't even tell you when I talked to him last."

Roberta was in her forties but looked older. Her brown hair was shot with gray; her face was lined and makeup-free. Her clothes were shapeless, designed for comfort and not for fashion.

"I couldn't find any information on your sister, Gail," I said to Roberta. "I couldn't find an address."

"Gail's a free spirit. She doesn't exactly have an address, although she obviously lives somewhere. Everyone lives *somewhere*, right? Even street people live somewhere."

"How do you get in touch with her? Does she have a cell phone?"

"She has a post office box in Marbury. I sent her a letter about Eugene, but I haven't heard anything back."

"When was the last time you saw her?"

"Years ago. She came for our father's funeral. She flitted in and flitted out. She said she had to get back to her animals. I don't know what kind of animals she was talking about. Gail always has some sort of cause. She left home after she graduated from high school so she could live in a tree and save a habitat for owls. After that it was wood ducks. And I think at one time she had a collection of rabbits that she'd rescued from a cosmetics lab."

"But she always gets her mail in Marbury?"

"So far as I know. I guess she could have it forwarded somewhere."

"And what's her last name?"

"Scanlon. She never married. None of us ever married."

I left my card with Roberta and asked her to call if she heard from Gail.

"Well?" Diesel wanted to know when I buckled myself in next to him.

"Not much. Her sister doesn't have an address, but she has a post office box in Marbury. And it sounds like she's made a career of saving owl habitats and rabbit eyelids."

"That's it? That's all you got?"

"Yep."

"Where's Marbury?" he asked.

I got a map out of the side-door pocket and found Marbury. "It's on the way to Atlantic City," I said. "Give or take a bunch of miles."

Carl tapped me on the shoulder. "Eep."

"What?"

"Eep."

"I don't speak monkey," I told him. "I don't know *eep*."

He pointed to his crotch and crossed his legs.

"I think he has to go to the bathroom," I said to Diesel.

Diesel powered a back window down. "Go to it," he said to Carl.

Carl looked out the window and looked up and down the street and shook his head.

Diesel cut his eyes to Carl. "Dude, you're a monkey. You can do it anywhere."

Carl shrugged.

"I think he might have some species confusion," I said to Diesel.

Diesel put the car into gear and drove back to the main street. He cruised two blocks, found a McDonald's, and parked. Carl jumped out the window and scampered to the door to McDonald's. He grabbed the handle with both hands, but he couldn't get the door to open.

"I'll get it," I said to Diesel. "I could use a milk shake. Do you want anything?"

"Double cheeseburger, fries, Coke."

I opened the door for Carl, and he rushed off. I put my order in, paid the cashier, and was about to leave with my food when there was a muffled scream from the ladies' restroom. A door banged open, and a woman stormed out with Carl in tow.

"Who owns this monkey?" she asked. "It was in the ladies' room, looking under all the stall doors."

Carl pointed to me.

"You need to teach your monkey some manners," the woman said.

I looked down at Carl. "Are you done?" I asked him.

He shrugged, and we quickly walked back to the SUV. I sucked down my milk shake, Diesel ate his burger, and Carl ate his box of cookies.

"Your monkey was looking under the stall doors in the ladies' room," I told Diesel.

"That's my boy," Diesel said.

Chapter
TEN

It was almost four o'clock when we rolled into Marbury. Diesel nosed the SUV into a parking space in front of the post office and unbuckled his seat belt.

"My turn," he said. "This shouldn't take long. It sounds like Gail Scanlon's had a post office box here for years. I'm hoping someone knows her."

I watched Diesel walk away, and I enjoyed the view. I had no intention of getting involved, but that didn't mean I was blind to the masterpiece in front of me. Diesel was a big, solid guy who moved with seemingly effortless efficiency. Everything about him was in perfect proportion. And from where I was sitting, his ass looked like Little Bear's bed . . . not too hard, and not too soft, but *just right.*

Diesel disappeared into the building, and I turned to Carl. "So," I said, "how's it going?"

Carl looked at me, shrugged, and went back to his game. A pickup rumbled past us. An old man shuffled out of the post office and walked down the street. I went to my cell phone to call Morelli, but we were in the middle of the Jersey Pine Barrens, and there wasn't cell service.

The Pine Barrens is a heavily forested area covering a little over a million acres of coastal plain across south Jersey. The soil is sandy and the trees are pine mixed with oaks that have managed to survive the occasional fire. Hundreds of acres are uninhabited, unless you count blueberries, and cranberries, and the stubborn, hardscrabble folks known as Pineys who live and work there. There are also hundreds of antique shops, bed and breakfasts of varying quality, and dirt roads that go nowhere. Plus, there's the Jersey Devil. The Pacific Northwest has Sasquatch. Loch Ness has Nessie. And the Pine Barrens has the Jersey Devil.

Diesel left the post office, walked to the car, and slid in behind the wheel.

"Well?" I asked.

"Gail Scanlon comes in on no fixed schedule and gets her mail. Sometimes she's in once a week. Sometimes they don't see her for six months. Her box was emptied yesterday, but no one saw her come in. The post office boxes are around a corner from the counter."

"Did you get a description?"

"Slim, average height, long black hair, early forties, eccentric."

"What does 'eccentric' mean?"

"They didn't elaborate. But she must really be out there for them to call her eccentric. This isn't exactly the center of sane."

"Did they know where she lived?"

"No. One of the guys said she was a citizen of the world. And the woman next to him said she was a nymphomaniac."

"Sounds like your kind of woman."

"Yeah, she has potential."

"Now what?" I asked.

"Now we go home and regroup."

* * *

Diesel was regrouping on the couch, watching *Seinfeld* reruns, and Carl was sitting beside him.

"This is going too slow," I said to Diesel. "You're supposed to be the big-deal super bounty hunter. Why aren't you doing something?"

"I am doing something. I'm waiting."

"Waiting isn't good. I hate waiting. Waiting feels like doing nothing."

"I have Flash watching the Sky Social Club. And every ten minutes, I go to the window to see if the cloud of doom has rolled over Trenton, signifying Wulf's presence."

"Nothing personal, but I don't care about Wulf. I need to find Martin Munch."

"I know how Wulf works. Right now, he's involved in a project that involves Munch, and they're joined at the hip. If we find one of them, we'll find both of them. If we don't find them until after Munch has served his purpose, we'll find Munch with his head screwed on backwards."

I cracked my knuckles and gnawed on my lower lip. I didn't want to find Munch with his head screwed on backwards. I felt my cell phone buzz at my hip, and I checked the readout. Morelli.

"I have a problem," Morelli said.

"No kidding."

"More than that. I just got home, and Anthony is missing, and there's a naked woman in my bed."

"And?"

"I don't want to talk about this on the phone. Can you get over here? I need help."

"I'm on my way." I disconnected and grabbed my bag. "Gotta go," I said to Diesel. "Morelli needs help with a naked woman."

"I didn't know you were into that," Diesel said.

"It's not a party. It's a problem. I'll be on my cell if you notice the cloud of doom hanging over my apartment building."

Ten minutes later, I walked into the disaster area that used to be Morelli's living room. It was littered with empty beer cans, fast-food wrappers, and discarded socks, shoes, and underwear. Crumpled pages ripped off a yellow lined pad were scattered across the floor. A rumpled pillow and balled-up quilt were pushed to one end of the couch.

Morelli smiled when he saw me, and I got warm inside and smiled back. He was still in work clothes. Dark jeans and boots. Cream-colored sweater with the sleeves pushed to his elbows. Gun on his hip. He had a garbage bag in one hand and a can of air freshener in the other.

"I thought your mother was coming over to clean?" I said to him.

"She was here this morning. This is afternoon trash."

"What's with all the crumpled pieces of lined paper?"

"Anthony decided he should write a book about his life."

"Because why?" I asked Morelli.

"He thinks his life is fascinating. He's calling his book 'Love Your Inner Jerk.'"

"What does that mean?"

"I don't know," Morelli said, "but it can't be good."

I helped gather beer cans and food wrappers and stuffed them into the garbage bag. I left the underwear for Morelli. I wouldn't touch the underwear with a big stick.

"Doesn't Anthony have a job?" I asked.

"Not this week. He took the week off to get his act together."

"Looks to me like he's spreading his act all over your house."

"This is nothing. You should see what I've got upstairs."

"The naked woman?"

"Yeah. She won't leave. She says she's waiting for Anthony to come back with pizza."

"So when he comes back she'll leave, right?"

"He's been gone for almost two hours. For all I know, he could be gone for two days. It's happened."

"Did you try telling her to leave?"

"Yeah. She told me to take a hike."

"You're a cop. You probably drag naked women out of bedrooms all the time."

"Almost never. And this is *my* bedroom. And this woman was brought here by *my* married brother. I'm supposed to be keeping him in line. If this gets back to my sister-in-law and my mother, I'm in big trouble. And even worse, if I lay a hand on this bimbo, she could scream rape or police brutality or God knows what."

"So you want me to get rid of her for you."

"Yeah." Morelli grinned at me again. "If you did that one thing for me, I'd be nice to you. *Really* nice."

"And then what? Would I have to be really nice to you?"

"No. You could walk away. Adios. Sayonara. Good night."

I'd heard this before. Once Morelli got rolling, no one walked away. No one ever *wanted* to walk away. Morelli naked was a force of nature. Of course, I could have him keep his clothes on, but that might feel weird.

"What about your brother?"

"I'll lock the doors."

"Hasn't he got a key?"

Morelli dropped the garbage bag onto the floor and stuffed his hands onto his hips. "Are you going to do this for me, or what?"

"Sure. Do you know her name?"

"All I know is she's naked, and mean as a snake."

I climbed the stairs, knocked on Morelli's closed bedroom door, and pushed it open. There was a naked woman in his bed all right, and she was mad. She was sitting up with her arms crossed over her huge breasts and her eyes narrowed. She had a lot of overprocessed blond hair in a teased-up rat's nest. She was early forties, with tanning-bed skin one step away from a carcinoma epidemic. Her lips had been inflated by someone not especially good at it. And she had a spider tattooed on her arm.

"Now what?" she said.

"You're in my boyfriend's bed."

"He said he wasn't attached. Are you some crazy bitch jilted girlfriend?"

"Nope. I'm the current girlfriend. This house belongs to Joe Morelli, and you're waiting for his worthless married brother, Anthony."

"Are you kidding me? Anthony told me this was his house."

"Anthony's house is about a quarter mile away, and his wife is living in it."

"How do I know you're telling me the truth? And what's Anthony doing here anyway? He had a key and everything."

"His wife kicked him out, and he's stuck here until she decides to take him back."

"So he sort of *isn't* attached," she said.

"He's married! And he has five kids."

"Yeah, but she kicked him out."

I had the feeling this was going nowhere. Time to improvise.

"Truth is, his wife would be better off if you took him off her hands," I told her. "He comes home drunk all the time and beats her and the kids with a gravy ladle."

"Jeez," she said. "That's awful."

"And he can't keep a job, so his wife has to work nights at the button factory," I said.

"I didn't know they made buttons at night."

"She cleans up. Washes floors and toilets and stuff."

"Ick. That's even worse than my job."

"What do you do?"

"I work for a construction company. They're all a bunch of assholes."

"You didn't give him any money, did you?"

"I gave him money for the pizza and more beer," she said.

"Bad move. He probably bought a hooker with the money."

"I don't know. He didn't look all that lively when I was done with him."

"Yeah, but he's a sex addict. Got a bunch of diseases. He wore a condom, right? I mean, you didn't touch him or anything, did you?"

That got her out of bed, hunting for her clothes. "I do *not* need any more diseases," she said. She yanked black stretch pants over her ass and tugged a sweater over her head. "That prick had a lot of nerve misrepresenting himself. The more I'm thinking about it, the more steamed I'm getting." She rammed her feet into four-inch stilettos and grabbed her purse off the dresser. "He hasn't heard the last of it from me, either."

She stormed out of the bedroom, stomped down the stairs, swept past Morelli and out the front door.

"I'm impressed," Morelli said to me. "How did you do it?"

"We just had a heart-to-heart. You know, girl talk."

"Do I get to be nice to you now?"

"No. Now you put on a pair of rubber gloves and take all the sheets off your bed and throw them away."

Morelli went upstairs with a new garbage bag, and I continued to pick up the downstairs.

"Where's Bob?" I called up to Morelli.

"He's tied out back. I had him at work with me, and I didn't want him snarfing around in the living room until I cleaned up."

Bob is Morelli's dog. He's mostly golden retriever, with a touch of Sasquatch. He's big and goofy, entirely lovable, and he eats everything . . . chairs, table legs, whole hams stolen from the table.

I let Bob in, and Bob rushed through the house, excited to be home, jumping around me like a rabbit. I filled his bowl with fresh water, and another bowl with dog crunchies, and Bob dug in. I tied off my garbage bag and set it by the back door. I was starting up the stairs to help Morelli when Anthony walked in.

"Hey, beautiful," Anthony said to me. "Haven't seen you in too long."

Anthony, for all his faults, can be charming and hideously likable. He was carrying a large pizza box and had his fingers hooked around a six-pack of Bud.

"Charlene," he yelled up the stairs. "Come get your pizza."

"Jeez," I said. "Bad news. Charlene took off."

"No big deal," Anthony said, not missing a beat. "More pizza for us, right? Where's Joe?"

"Upstairs."

The front door banged open, and Charlene stormed

in and pointed a nail gun at Anthony. Anthony partially turned to look at her, and she shot him in the ass. *Bang, bang, bang.*

"That's for the gravy ladle," she said. "You should be ashamed of yourself." And she left, slamming the door shut behind her.

Anthony and I were momentarily stunned, mouths open, bug-eyed.

"Fuck," Anthony finally said. He dropped the pizza, and Bob galloped in and ate it.

Morelli appeared at the head of the stairs. "Were those gunshots?"

"Charlene came back and shot Anthony in the ass with a nail gun. She works for a construction company."

"Where is she now?" Morelli asked.

"Gone."

Morelli jogged down the stairs and looked at Anthony's backside. Blood was seeping through his jeans.

"Shit," Morelli said. "Why'd she shoot you?"

"I don't know," Anthony said. "Something about a gravy ladle."

I ran to the kitchen and got a couple towels. By the time I got back to the living room, Morelli was dragging Anthony out the door to the car.

Morelli owns an SUV, so Bob has a safe, comfy place to ride, but he keeps a Ducati in his garage for times when he needs to take his wild side for a drive. We loaded Anthony into the back of Morelli's SUV and Morelli drove the short distance to St. Francis Hospital. The pain was setting in when we off-loaded Anthony. He was white-faced and sweating, and he was swearing in two languages. Morelli dragged him into the emergency entrance, and I parked the car in the parking garage.

Okay, so I felt a little bad, but how was I to know Charlene would shoot Anthony over the gravy ladle? I mean, who would even believe it? A gravy ladle, for crying out loud. I had no idea where gravy ladle had come from. Baseball bat and tennis racket had horrified me, and then gravy ladle popped into my head. Maybe I was hungry.

Morelli was slouched in a chair in the waiting room when I walked in. I took the seat beside him and sat with my bag hugged to my chest.

"Will he be okay?" I asked Morelli.

"That's a complicated question. There's a lot more wrong with him than a nail in the ass."

An hour later, Anthony got wheeled out facedown on a gurney, ready to go home. He was wearing baggy hospital pajamas, and one side of his butt had a big bulge where he was bandaged.

"He's full of local anesthesia and happy juice," the nurse told Morelli, "so he should be okay for the ride home. And he's got a prescription for painkiller and antibiotic. And he's got directions for changing the dressing once a day. Bring him back in ten days to get the sutures removed." She handed Morelli a little bag. "Here's his nails in case he wants to frame them."

I ran for the SUV and hustled it around to the emergency entrance. Morelli and a male nurse loaded Anthony into the back, and I drove us to Morelli's house. Morelli dragged Anthony into the house and got him facedown on the couch.

"Women," Anthony said. "Can't live with them, can't live without them."

Bob sniffed Anthony and ran away. I was in pretty much the same frame of mind as Bob.

"Gotta go," I said. "Things to do."

Morelli walked me to my Jeep. He wrapped his arms

around me and kissed me with a lot of tongue and desperation.

"You're leaving a sinking ship," he said.

"Think of this as a bonding time. And keep him tranqued."

Chapter
ELEVEN

Diesel was at the dining room table working on my computer when I walked in. "What's the word on the naked woman?" he asked.

"I managed to get her out of Morelli's bed, but she came back and shot his brother in the ass with a nail gun."

Diesel pushed back in his chair and smiled wide. "I'd ask for details, but they might be disappointing compared to what I'm thinking."

"It was a fiasco." I got a beer out of the fridge and chugged half of it. "What are you doing?"

"Prowling around on the Net. Trying to learn something about electromagnetic fields. Munch's doctoral thesis was specific to atmospheric ionization, a subject about which I know zip."

I couldn't see Carl, but I could hear Super Mario Bros. coming from the couch.

"Has he been playing that all night?" I asked Diesel.

Diesel stood and stretched. "Yep."

"And you're okay with it?"

"Yep."

"Boy, I'm impressed. That's so mellow."

"Actually, I'm only hanging on until the battery runs

down. I figure he's got about two minutes left. And he doesn't know how to recharge the thing."

And at that moment there was silence in the room.

"Eep?" Carl said. He stood and looked over the back of the couch at us. He held the game player up for us to see. "Eeep."

"It's dead," Diesel said.

Carl's eyes went wide and his mouth dropped open. He shook the game player and examined it.

"Jeez," I said to Diesel. "That's tough."

"Easy for you to say. You spent the night with a naked woman, and I spent it with this monkey."

Carl threw the game at Diesel and tagged him in the back of the head.

"This is getting old," Diesel said, picking the game up off the floor. "I'm not as nice as I look. If I hear one more *eeep* I'm gonna open a can of whoop-ass on the monkey."

"You're frustrated because you can't get to Wulf."

"That's part of it." His phone rang, and he answered and listened. "Be right there," he said and disconnected.

"Flash?" I asked.

"Yeah. Wulf returned to the Sky Social Club. He's inside. Let's roll."

"What about Carl?"

"What about him?"

"I don't want to just leave him here in this mood."

Diesel pulled a charger out of his pack and plugged it into the game. "I'm recharging this," he said to Carl. "I'm going to plug it in, and when the red light turns green it's good to go. Do you understand?"

Carl shrugged.

Diesel grabbed my hand and pulled me to the door. "We need to move."

* * *

Flash was parked halfway down the alley. We slid to a stop behind him, cut our lights, and we all got out and stood looking in the direction of the Sky building.

"He's still in there," Flash said. "His car is parked behind the building, and it hasn't moved."

"Do you have any idea who's in there with him?" Diesel asked.

"I have my girlfriend watching the front, and from what we can tell, Doc Weiner is there with two lieutenants. Mostly, the club runs during the day and empties out at night."

The back door to the club opened, and Wulf walked out. Too dark for me to see more than his outline. There was the sound of his car door opening and closing. The Ferrari engine turned over, and Wulf backed out and drove away from us. We all scrambled to get into our cars.

Diesel wheeled around Flash, and just as he approached the Sky building, there was an explosion that blew out the building windows and doors and rocked the Escalade. I looked behind us and saw Flash put his car into reverse and tear down the alley. Diesel did the same. Flaming debris blocked the narrow road directly behind the club.

It took me a couple minutes to catch my breath and get my heart to stop racing. "What was that?" I asked Diesel. My voice was an octave higher than normal, and my eyes felt like they'd been popped out of their sockets.

"My guess is Wulf burned a bridge," Diesel said.

Diesel and Flash circled the block but couldn't pick up the Ferrari. Diesel continued to drive south without success. The trail was cold.

"I'm hungry, and I want beer," Diesel said. "Where do I go?"

"Pino's will be open. It's just off Broad."

Ten minutes later, we parked on the street several houses down from Pino's. It was a dark, starless, moonless night that had turned too cold for my sweatshirt. I power-walked the distance from the car to Pino's entrance and pushed into the heat and noise of the crowded bar. The place was filled with cops and nurses gone off shift, and my phone rang minutes after Diesel and I took a table and ordered food.

"What's up?" Morelli asked. "I just got four calls telling me you're out with a guy who looks like he could kick my ass."

"It's Diesel."

Silence on Morelli's end. I figured he was counting his fingers and toes, trying to get a grip.

"Diesel," he finally said. "My life isn't bad enough, now I have to worry about Diesel."

"You don't have to worry."

"Where's he sleeping?"

"Wherever he wants. Can we change the subject? How's Anthony's ass?"

"He's in your bed, right? Maybe I should just shoot him and be done with it," Morelli said.

"I think he might be hard to kill. Anyway, you're supposed to trust me."

"Hah!" Diesel said. And he chugged half a bottle of beer.

"I trust *you*," Morelli said. "I just don't trust *him*."

"He'll be gone soon. Hang in there."

More silence. This wasn't a good time for Morelli.

"Okay, here's the deal," I said. "He's gay, but he's only halfway out of the closet."

"What?"

"Yeah. I'm not his type."

"He doesn't look gay," Morelli said.

"How can someone look gay?"

"They're usually neat."

"Well, he's a gay slob, what can I say? And on top of that, he can't get it up. Some sort of war injury. Blew his nuts off."

Diesel had eyebrows raised.

"I have to go," Morelli said. "Anthony is moaning for pie. I have a Mrs. Smith's in the oven."

"You're a good brother."

"I'm an idiot."

And he disconnected.

"That sucks," Diesel said. "I could have managed gay, but I really hate not having nuts."

"It's a temporary thing. Next week, you'll be in Spain or Malaysia, and you'll have your nuts back."

"True. Call Ranger and see if he knows anything about the Sky explosion. He monitors the police band."

I punched Ranger's number, and he immediately came on the line.

"Babe," Ranger said.

"Sky Social Club had an issue tonight."

"That's what I'm told."

"It wasn't my fault."

"It's never your fault," Ranger said. "So far, no bodies found, but I don't think they've been able to get into the building yet."

"I was watching the club when it blew. My man Munch is hanging out with a creepy guy named Wulf. Wulf left the club and *BLAM!*"

"You want to stay far away from Wulf," Ranger said.

"You know him?"

"I know *about* him."

"That's a relief. I thought maybe you were related."

"Not nearly. Diesel and Wulf are Swiss."

"Swiss!"

Diesel had been watching the television behind the bar, but that brought his attention back to me.

"You know where I keep the key if you need a safe haven," Ranger said. And he disconnected.

I looked at Diesel. "You're Swiss?"

"Origin of birth."

"You seem so American."

"I've spent a lot of time here."

I awoke alone in my bed. Diesel's side was rumpled, but Diesel was missing. Daylight halfheartedly peeped from the edge of my curtains, and I could smell coffee brewing. I dragged myself out of bed and into the kitchen.

Diesel handed me a mug and filled it with coffee. "It lives," he said.

"You're up early. What's the occasion?"

"It's not that early. It's almost eight o'clock, and we need to be on the road. My sources tell me there's going to be a memorial service for Eugene Scanlon today. It's being held in a church in north Philly. I'm hoping his long-lost sister will show. Or his killer."

"I hate memorial services."

"Maybe they'll have doughnuts," Diesel said. "You have thirty-five minutes to get memorial-ready."

"What about the monkey?"

"He's had breakfast, his game is charged, and the television remote is within reach."

The church was two blocks from Roberta Scanlon's house. It was gray stone, with the standard bell tower and carved oak door. It was moderate size, and all parking was on the street. We arrived ten minutes ahead of the service, and there were only a handful of cars at the curb. I was wearing my black suit with the short pencil skirt, three-inch heels, and a white silk sweater. Diesel had selected for the occasion his jeans without a rip in the knee.

Roberta was at the door when we entered.

"Thank you for coming," Roberta said to Diesel and me. "We'll have doughnuts after the service."

I felt Diesel smile behind me.

"Have you heard from your sister?" I asked Roberta.

Roberta motioned to the inside of the church. "Third pew from the altar on the left. She's the woman with the pink streaks in her hair."

We sat three rows behind Gail Scanlon, and her sister sat next to her for the short eulogy. I counted thirteen other people present. All but two were women. All were Roberta's age. Eugene Scanlon was not in attendance. He was in Trenton awaiting his autopsy.

After the service, the Scanlon sisters stood and filed out to the vestibule, where the buffet had been set. They were both stoic. Roberta was in a shapeless black dress. Gail was wearing a bright rainbow-colored tunic top and flowing ankle-length skirt. Neither touched the food. Roberta spoke to the few mourners who approached her, and Gail quietly stood to the side.

Gail looked at her watch and twisted the tunic hem in her fingers.

"She's getting ready to bolt," Diesel said, pushing me forward. "Talk to her."

"I don't know her, and this is so private. What will I say?"

"Tell her the blouse she's wearing is pretty."

"What?"

"Look at her," Diesel said. "She's chosen to wear something colorful. I'm sure it was deliberate. But now she's feeling uncomfortable because she's made herself even more of a misfit. A compliment would go a long way here."

"That's shockingly sensitive."

"That's me," Diesel said. "Mr. Sensitivity."

I crossed the room to Gail Scanlon. "That's a beautiful tunic," I said. "Is it handmade?"

Scanlon looked surprised, obviously astonished that someone would speak to her, much less compliment her clothes.

"There's a woman in the Barrens who makes these," she said, smoothing a wrinkle away. "I think they have positive energy."

"Do you live in the Barrens?"

"Yes. Usually. Sometimes I travel."

"I haven't spent much time in the Barrens. People tell me they're interesting."

"They're wonderful. My life work is in the Barrens."

"What do you do?"

"I'm a soul guardian."

That caught me off guard. A soul guardian. I liked it, but I didn't know what it meant. It sounded a little wacko.

"I protect endangered trees and animals," Gail said. "Someone has to speak for those who have no voice."

"Like a tree."

She smiled. "Exactly."

And then it slipped out. The required statement I didn't really want to make. "Sorry about your brother."

"You're in the minority," Gail said. "He was a miserable human being."

Whoa. I hadn't seen that coming. "Excuse me?"

"You probably are shocked, but you didn't know Eugene. He was a self-centered troublemaker all his life. Even when I was a kid. I know I shouldn't speak bad of the dead, but that's how I feel." She stuffed her arms into a heavy knit sweater she'd been carrying. "What I know is that Eugene caused his own death. He did something bad one time too many, and it caught up with him. He was a real smart man, but he wasn't a *nice* man."

"I should introduce myself," I said. And I handed her my card.

Gail checked her watch. "Roberta said she spoke to you. Unfortunately, I have to get home. I have a lot of mouths to feed."

"Where's home?"

"I've got a patch of land in the Barrens."

"Do you know Martin Munch?" I asked her. "Do you know a man called Wulf?"

"No," she said. "I have to go. I can't talk anymore."

"One more thing," I said, but she waved me off and hurried away.

Diesel moved next to me. "Well?"

"Nothing. She said she had to get home."

Diesel and I went to the door and watched Gail get into an old Army surplus Jeep and ease into traffic.

Diesel grabbed my hand and pulled me to the Escalade. "Let's see where she goes." He took the wheel and jumped from the curb. "She's going to be easy to follow in that Jeep. She hasn't looked in her mirror once to see if she has a tail."

"She's anxious to get home."

"And home would be where?" Diesel asked.

"Down a dirt road."

"Good to know. In case by some freak chance I lose her, all I have to do is look for a dirt road."

"Hey, don't blame me. That's all she said."

"Nothing else?"

"She said her brother was a miserable person. And

had always been a miserable person. And that he probably deserved what he got."

Diesel shook his head. "Man, that's severe. Imagine what she would have said if it wasn't his memorial service."

Gail hit the 95 and went south to the Tacony-Palmyra Bridge. We were a couple car lengths back, rolling at the speed limit. Gail wasn't a rule breaker on the highway. Diesel was relaxed at the wheel. I was thinking about the doughnut I didn't get at the service, wishing I'd been quicker at the buffet.

I was raised in the Burg, where death is more a social opportunity than a tragic event. Viewings and wakes hold the potential for a decent food spread and free-flowing alcohol. It's one of the few occasions when throwing back whiskey at ten in the morning is in good form. It's guaranteed that on occasion grief won't be easily set aside by a plateful of meatballs, but no reason to let that unhappy thought ruin a perfectly good time at the viewing for a distant acquaintance. Personally, I'd rather be at a mall.

"What do you think about death?" I asked Diesel.

"I like the buffet. After that, it's not my favorite thing." He looked over at me. "What do *you* think about death?"

"I think carnations should be banned from funeral parlors."

We rode in silence after that. I mean, what was left to say? Gail still showed no sign of noticing our behemoth black SUV close on her tail. She sailed over the bridge and took 73 south. Miles later, I was thinking I was on the road to nowhere. And then Gail slowed and hooked a left off 73. She wound around some, and after a while the road turned to dirt and narrowed. We dropped back as far as possible, although I doubt we could be seen through the dust cloud Gail was kicking up. There were scrubby bushes on either side, and the rutted road twisted around trees and chunks of rock.

Diesel powered forward, into a stand of scruffy pines, and *BAM!* Something bounced off the front bumper, and we were blinded by a blizzard of feathers and blood.

"Omigod," I said, my heart beating in my throat. "What was that?"

Diesel stopped the car and looked at the windshield, which was plastered with what could only be bird guts.

"That had to be the biggest bird on the planet," he said, unbuckling his seat belt, getting out to take a look.

I stayed buckled. I didn't want to see any more than I was seeing. I was glad I didn't have a memorial service doughnut to spew.

Diesel kicked at something on the ground and examined the front of the Escalade. He swiped a finger through the red stuff on the windshield and looked at it up close.

"Fake blood," he said. "I think we hit the Pine Barrens version of a booby-trap piñata."

"The feathers?"

"Real. But the bird who gave his all for them is long gone."

"Why would someone booby-trap this road with a feather bomb?"

"I'm guessing Gail did it. Stops people from going forward. Makes a statement of sorts. Doesn't really hurt anyone. This is probably what war would look like if women were in charge."

Diesel got behind the wheel and flipped the windshield washers on. The fake blood mixed with the washer fluid and feathers and gummed up the wiper blades.

"What have you got in your bag?" Diesel asked.
"Tissues?"

He took the tissues, got out of the car, and tried cleaning the blades. No good. The tissues were now mixed with the blood and feathers and washer fluid. The whole windshield was a disgusting red smear.

"I'm not happy," Diesel said.

I was still pawing through the junk in my bag, and I found a travel-size nail polish remover pad. "This should do something," I said. "I only have one, so don't waste it." I tore the foil envelope open and gave the saturated pad to Diesel.

Diesel looked at the two-inch square. "You're kidding."

"Do you have anything better?"

"No. I'd stand on the hood and piss on the windshield, but I'm empty."

"Some superhero."

Diesel flipped me the bird and went to work with the polish remover. Moments later, he had a small piece of window exposed in front of the steering wheel. He cranked the car over, wheeled it around, and carefully picked his way down the dirt road, turning right when he reached the paved road. He followed signs to the Atlantic City Expressway, and found a gas station just before the Expressway entrance.

We were watching the attendant pump gas and scrub the windshield when the Ferrari sped by the gas station and took the Expressway, heading west to the Turnpike.

"Too bad you can't fly," I said to Diesel.

"Yeah, rub it in. All through high school I took it for that."

"Do you want to go back to the dirt road?"

"No. I want to get on a computer and do some research first. We could ride around for days on that road and never find anything. And we're not even sure Gail means anything to us."

I washed down a sandwich with a soda and fed the last bite of bread to Rex. Better a late lunch than no lunch at all. Diesel was on my computer, looking at aerial views of the Barrens.

"This was taken several months ago," Diesel said, "but I see a clearing and a house and a fairly large out-building at the end of the road we were on. There are a lot of narrow roads intersecting and going off in all directions from that dirt road, but there's really only one house that can be reached by Jeep."

"Are you going back now?"

"No. I want to look at more aerial views, and I have a call in to Scanlon's supervisor."

"That's okay by me. I'd like to take another stab at Gordo Bollo."

"As long as you don't go out of cell range . . . and you take the monkey."

"Why can't Carl stay here?"

"He's annoying. It's non-negotiable."

"Okay, fine, but you owe me."

"Lookin' forward to settling the score," Diesel said.

"Boy, you never give up, do you?"

"I wouldn't be me if I gave up."

I got Carl settled in the back of the Jeep and I drove to the office.

"I'll go with you," Lula said, "but I'm not going in-side. I'm not having no more rat experiences."

"What good are you if you won't go inside?"

"I can guard the Jeep. Suppose by dumb luck or something you snag Melon Head. You want to make sure the Jeep is still there when you come out, right?"

Twenty minutes later, I left Lula and Carl in the park-

ing lot, put on my game face, and walked into Greenblat Produce.

"If you're looking for Gordo, you're out of luck today," one of the women said. "He called in sick."

"That was fast," Lula said when I climbed behind the
wheel.

I pulled Bollo's file out of my bag. "He called in
sick." I thumbed through pages and found his home address. "He lives in Bordentown."

"I'm cool with that," Lula said. "Let's go to Bordentown and root him out."

The day had started out warm, but clouds had rolled
in and the temperature was dropping. Not winter-quality
dropping, but enough to notice when there were no windows in your car. I turned the heater on full blast and
hunkered down.

"Where's your windows?" Lula wanted to know.

"They need to get zipped in."

"Well, zip them in. I'm freezing my ass off."

I'd bought the Jeep a month before, when it was hot
and I didn't need windows. I'd tried to zip them in once
when it rained and had partial success. I was willing to
try again. I pulled to the side of the road, and Lula and
I grunted and tugged and cussed at the plastic windows.
We finally got most of them secure, with the exception
of the back window. The back window would zip only
halfway.

"Good enough," Lula said. "We need ventilation
anyway since the monkey's back there."

Carl gave her the finger.

"That all you got?" Lula asked Carl.

Carl grabbed his crotch and hiked it up.

"That's disgusting on a monkey," Lula said. "You
been letting him watch MTV? You want to monitor his
television viewing."

I checked Carl out in my rearview mirror. He was back to playing with his game.

"Get the map out and find 656 Ward Street in Bordentown," I told Lula.

Lula opened the map and traced a line with her finger. "You gotta get off Route 206 in about half a mile."

Ten minutes later, we were on Ward Street, but we couldn't find Bollo's house. There was no 656 on Ward Street. The only thing on Ward Street was a cemetery on one side and a ceramic pipe factory on the other.

I called Bollo's home phone. No answer. No machine picked up. I called his cell phone.

"Yeah?" Bollo said.

"This is UPS. I have a delivery for Gordo Bollo, and I need a correct address."

"Eat me," Bollo said. And he hung up.

"I think he knew it was me," I said to Lula.

"Should have let the monkey make the call."

I called Connie. "I got a bogus home address for Gordo Bollo."

"I'll get back to you," Connie said.

"You know what?" Lula said. "We're halfway to Atlantic City. We could go to Atlantic City and make a killing on the slots."

"Tempting, but I told Diesel I'd be available."

"Available for what?"

"For bounty hunter stuff."

My phone rang and I heard labored breathing and a whispered *hello*.

"Yes?" I said.

"Is this the bounty hunter?"

"Yes."

"Thank God. I had your card in my pocket, and I didn't know who to call. They think I'm still unconscious. I couldn't call the police. I'm afraid they'd take my animals. But you find people, right?"

"Gail?"

"You have to help me. Please. They're taking me somewhere." It was clear she was struggling to talk, trying not to cry, but a sob escaped before she reined herself in. "I'm in terrible trouble," she whispered. "You have to find me. And take care of my poor animals. Oh God," she moaned. "It's Wulf. He's coming back. He's coming to get me." And the line went dead.

"You don't look good," Lula said to me. "You just turned white. What was that call about?"

"It was Gail Scanlon. It sounded like Wulf has kidnapped her."

I dialed Diesel's cell. No answer. I left a message to call me, and I called my home phone. No answer there, either. I put the Jeep in gear and called Ranger.

"Do you have my Jeep bugged?"

"Bugged?"

"You know, the gizmo you always put on my cars so you can find me."

"Yeah."

"Can you find me anywhere?"

"Pretty much. Where are you going?"

"I'm heading for the Pine Barrens to check out a woman in trouble, and I'm afraid I'll get lost."

"Babe," Ranger said.

"There isn't cell service in some spots, so if you don't hear back from me for a couple days, you should come get me."

"I'll make a memo on my calendar."

I hung up, and Lula was shaking her head. "I swear, if I was gonna ask a favor of Ranger, it wouldn't be to come rescue my ass. And I don't believe he's got a tracking device on your junk of a car. What's that about?"

"He has them on all his fleet vehicles, and he puts one on mine because I sometimes work for him." And because he cares for me . . . a lot. The caring is mutual, but Ranger, like Diesel, is out of my relationship comfort zone.

"So now what? Are we gonna go after Gail Scanlon?" Lula wanted to know.

"Yeah. I have a pretty good idea where she lives. We'll start there."

Lula had the map in front of her again. "You got an address?"

"Yup. It's follow the dirt road."

I took Route 206 to Marbury Road and turned left. Route 206 was a slower road than the Turnpike but more direct. Carl was happy in the backseat with a bucket of fried chicken parts. Lula had a bag of burgers and fries. I had a vanilla milk shake. I left Marbury Road, and my confidence level dropped. I was going as much on instinct as memory, relieved when something looked familiar. I reached the dirt road and slowed. I didn't want to create a dust cloud announcing my approach.

Lula peered through the Jeep's small windshield. "Are you sure we're in Jersey? This don't look like Jersey to me. This don't even look like America."

"How much of America have you seen?" I asked her.

"In person or on television?"

I crept around a stand of pines and saw the massacred faux bird bomb on the ground in front of me. Hooray. I was on the right path.

"This is as far as I got with Diesel," I said to Lula. "We lost Gail Scanlon here."

"You know how to get out of this hellhole, right?"

"Piece of cake."

"I don't like all these trees and no strip malls. It don't seem normal."

I followed the dirt road for a half mile and came to a fork. Both sides of the fork looked exactly the same. I got out of the car and examined the dirt like I was Tonto running point for the Lone Ranger.

"Well?" Lula asked.

I got back into the Jeep. I hadn't a clue. "Left," I said.

"Boy, you're good," Lula said. "I didn't see nothing in that dirt."

Carl was on his feet in the backseat, peering over my shoulder, looking worried.

"What do you think?" I asked Carl. "Left?"

"Eeep," Carl said.

I took the left fork, and after a while, I came to another fork in the road. And then another.

"All I can see is trees and sand," Lula said. "It's like the end of the world. There's no sidewalks. Where's the cement? And I haven't got no bars on my cell phone. What's with that? I don't like being without bars."

I looked at my phone. She was right. No bars. I hoped Diesel wasn't trying to reach me.

"Maybe we should turn around," Lula said. "I'm freaking. These trees are closing in on me. I need bars on my phone."

"The road's too narrow to make a U-turn. I'll turn as soon as it widens."

"What if it don't widen?"

"It'll widen!"

Truth is I had no confidence it would widen. And I had no idea where I was. I was lost beyond being lost. My plan was to go forward and keep turning left, and eventually I thought it had to take me somewhere.

"I gotta go to the bathroom," Lula said. "I shouldn't

of had that super-size soda. You need to find a gas station or McDonald's or something."

An hour later, I was still creeping along in the Barrens. No golden arches in sight.

"I'm gonna burst," Lula said. "I gotta go."

I came to a stop. "Pick a tree," I said.

"What?"

"This is as good as it's going to get. We're lost, and we're out of gas."

"I don't want to hear that," Lula said. "It's gonna get dark. I don't like the idea of being here in the dark. It's creepy. And the Jersey Devil comes out at night."

"There's no Jersey Devil."

"I heard about it. It got wings. *Big* wings."

Carl had climbed over the seat and was sitting hunched on the gearshift. Carl didn't like talk of the Jersey Devil.

"Are you sure we're out of gas?" Lula asked.

I turned the key, but the engine didn't kick over.

"I can't believe you got me into a situation where we're out of gas and there's no restroom," Lula said. "I'm going down this road, and I'm finding a place on my own."

Lula heaved herself out of the car and set off down the road.

"That's not a good idea," I yelled after her. "You'll get even more lost."

"Roads don't just go nowhere. Roads go somewhere. I'm following this road."

I slid from behind the wheel and ran to catch up to her. I thought walking off was a dumb idea, but she had the gun with bullets in it. I didn't get into a cold sweat over the Jersey Devil, but I wasn't crazy about the idea of Wulf finding me unprotected in the Jeep.

We walked for a half hour, and we were definitely

losing light. Carl was close on my heels, wide-eyed and silent. Lula was two steps in front of me, huffing along. She suddenly stopped and cocked her head.

"Did you hear that?" she asked.

"What?"

"That flapping sound. Like something flying through the trees."

"I didn't hear anything."

"I'm pretty sure it was the Devil," Lula said.

"The Jersey Devil is folklore. It's a bedtime story. And it's not even scary. It's supposed to look like a pot-bellied horse with wings."

"Yeah, but I heard that the Devil likes to eat plus-sized, beautiful brown-skinned women."

"That's ridiculous. Horses are herbivores."

"This is a devil horse. There's no telling what it eats. And it could stomp you with its hooves. Or it could put a spell on you."

The Jersey Devil was starting to sound like Morelli's crazy Italian grandmother.

"What we really want to worry about is the whine of a Ferrari engine."

"Not gonna be a Ferrari on this road," Lula said. "It's full of big ruts. A Ferrari'd bottom out."

She was right. This was both good news and bad news. Good news because I didn't want to get run over by Wulf. Bad news because I was on the wrong road.

"I see something through those trees," Lula said, heading off into a stand of pines. "I bet there's a house over there. I bet it's got a bathroom."

"Be careful. Even if it is a house, you don't know who lives in it. It could be a crazy person." Like Wulf.

"I don't care if they're crazy so long as they have a bathroom."

Ten minutes later, we were still walking through the pines, following a beam of light.

"This is like the enchanted forest," Lula said. "I always think we're getting somewhere, and then we get nowhere. Remember in *The Wizard of Oz* they had to walk through that forest and the trees were reaching out and grabbing at Dorothy? Or was that Harry Potter? Anyway, that's how I feel. It's like the trees got eyes and mouths, and they're whispering about us. And their limbs are moving around like arms, and they're clutching at us with hideous tree fingers." Lula did a whole body shiver. "I'm telling you it's like ghost trees. Like we're in a ghost forest."

"It's the wind!"

"It don't sound like wind. I know wind when I hear it. This is talkin'. The trees are watching us and saying things. I got a feeling going down the back of my neck that's like a death crawl. If I had gonads they'd be so far up in my body they might never find their way back down."

I didn't need this. I was already freaked out on my own. I didn't want to hear about trees talking. Bad enough we were lost beyond anything I could have imagined. The road was a distant memory behind us, and I was having flashbacks of news stories involving stupid hikers and skiers who'd wandered off the trail and were never seen again. And now she had me imagining talking trees. And the worst part was that the trees really did sound like they were talking.

Chapter
TWELVE

We skirted a boggy area and stopped at the edge of a clearing. Not too far from us was a small, weathered house with a tin roof. A garden taken over by pumpkins sat to one side of the house. Beyond the house was a large caged habitat filled with monkeys. A long low shed was attached to the habitat. Carl wrapped his arms around my leg and wouldn't let go.

"What's with him?" Lula asked.

"I think he's afraid of the monkeys."

"No shit. There must be twenty monkeys in there."

"I have a feeling this is Gail Scanlon's latest cause. She probably rescued these monkeys from a lab or a zoo."

"Don't look like anybody is here," Lula said.

We cautiously moved into the clearing and looked around.

"Those monkeys are wearing hats," Lula said.

I moved closer and looked at the monkeys. Lula was right. They were wearing hats. Metal helmets held on by chin straps. A small antenna stuck up from the top of each helmet. They looked like some German monkey army left over from WWI.

There were no cars in the yard. No lights on in the

house. Power lines ran through the woods to the house and monkey shed. It looked like there was a road leading out of the compound, just past the caged habitat.

"I don't care about monkeys," Lula said. "I care about a restroom. I don't know who owns this place, but I'm using the facilities."

She knocked on the front door to the house, and when no one answered, she tried the doorknob. Unlocked. We stepped inside and looked around.

"Anyone home?" I yelled.

No answer.

Lula used the bathroom, and I prowled through the kitchen and living area. The colors inside the house were bright, reminding me of Gail Scanlon's clothes. There were lots of books lining the walls but no television or phone. No computer. Basic pots and pans. Her appliances were old but serviceable. A stack of mail addressed to Gail had been placed on a small desk. Notice of her brother's death was on a kitchen counter. I didn't see anything that would tie her to Munch or Wulf.

"I feel better," Lula said, coming into the kitchen. "I feel like a new woman. I'll feel even better when we get out of the enchanted forest. I'm gonna hotfoot it down the road on the other side of the monkey cage before it gets *really* dark and the Jersey Devil goes on a rant."

Sounded okay to me. The alternative was to go back the way we'd come, and I wasn't sure I could retrace our steps.

"I don't suppose you found a phone," Lula said. "We could call a taxi if we had a phone."

"No phone. And I still haven't got service on mine."

We walked out of the house and froze. There were monkeys everywhere. The yard was lousy with monkeys in monkey helmets. They were shrieking and

running in circles and jumping up and down. I heard
Lula suck in air behind me.

"This here's a monkey nightmare," she said. "This
is like that movie where birds were swarming all over
the houses and crashing through windows and attack-
ing people, only this is monkeys."

Not exactly. These monkeys weren't interested in at-
tacking or swarming. They were interested in getting
the heck away from the habitat. One by one the monkeys ran off into the woods. Only Carl was left, looking worried, standing by the open door to the empty
cage. He had one hand on the door handle, and it was
pretty obvious how the monkeys had gotten out.

"Think this is one of them *born free* things," Lula
said.

I thought it was more like one of those *good thing I
don't have a loaded gun because I'd shoot myself*
things. I was supposed to look out for Gail's animals,
and now they were running loose in the woods. How
was I ever going to get all those monkeys back?

Lula took off for the road. "I'm getting out of here
before the monkey keeper shows up. I'm not paying for
no runaway monkeys. I just used the restroom. I'm not
responsible for this."

Carl looked at Lula, and then he looked into the
woods, where the monkeys had disappeared.

"Don't even think about it," I said to Carl. "Susan
expects you to be waiting for her when she comes back."

Carl gave me a thumbs-up and took off.

"Carl!"

"Maybe he needs a girl monkey," Lula said.

I looked overhead. The sun was about to set. I didn't
have a lot of time to find my way out, but I didn't
want to leave without Carl. It wasn't just that he was

my responsibility. I liked Carl. Okay, so he was a pain in the ass sometimes, but he was *my* pain in the ass.

"I can't leave Carl," I said to Lula.

"Yeah, but you can't stay, either. It's gonna get dark, and we gotta get out of here. We haven't got any phone service, and there's kidnappers and who knows what kind of lunatics in these woods."

She was right, of course, but I had a sad stomach at the thought of Carl left all by himself in the woods. I called Carl one more time, and when he didn't show, I reluctantly followed Lula down the road.

After ten minutes, Lula dropped the pace. "I can hardly see where we're going. If it gets any darker, I won't know if I'm on the road. Lordy, I don't want to wander off the road and have the Tree People get me."

"If we can find our way back to the Jeep, we'll be okay."

"The Jeep's out of gas."

"Ranger will find us if we stay by the Jeep."

"Yeah, but when?"

Knowing Ranger, he already had someone on the road looking for me.

"Hold on," Lula said, voice low, eyes wide. "I hear that flapping again. Good golly, it's the Jersey Devil. I just know it's him. He's coming to get us."

I heard it, too, but it didn't sound like flapping. It sounded more like someone walking through the woods. The steps were evenly spaced, muffled by the dropped pine needles. *Smosh, smosh, smosh, smosh.* The walker was moving toward us.

There wasn't a lot of cover. Our only option was some scrub brush bordering the narrow dirt road. I pulled Lula into the bushes, and we crouched and held our breath. Lula had her gun in her hand. The reality of Lula shooting is that she couldn't hit the side of a barn if it was ten feet away. That's not to say she couldn't get lucky some day and actually nail someone. My biggest fear was that it would accidentally be me.

There was some weak light filtering onto the road. The *smosh, smosh, smosh* came closer, and a kid stepped out of the pines, onto the road. And then I realized it wasn't a kid. It was Martin Munch dressed in baggy jeans, a gray sweatshirt zipped to his neck, and looking like a fourteen-year-old Opie Taylor from *The Andy Griffith Show*. He was alone, appeared unarmed, and he was smaller than me. I liked the odds. I waited a moment longer, hoping he'd get closer, but he suddenly stopped and looked directly at me. He turned without a word and took off into the woods, running flat-out the way he'd come.

I ran after him, crashing through the scrubby underbrush, following his zigzag path around trees. He was fast for a little guy, clearly familiar with this patch of woods. I could hear him panting in front of me, and I could hear Lula thundering behind me. I saw light ahead. If it was a road, and he chose to take it, I could run him down. I wasn't an athlete, but I was in better shape than Martin Munch.

He broke out of the woods, and I momentarily lost him. I reached the road and looked right. Munch was on an ATV. He hit the start button and roared away.

Lula burst out of the woods and bent at the waist. "I'm dying. I'm a dead woman. I need something. Oxygen. A lung. Legal drugs. Hell, any kind of drugs."

I pulled her back into the pines. "Catch your breath while we walk. We don't want to be here when he comes back with his partner."

"Was that Martin Munch?" Lula asked.

"I think so."

"Where are we going?"

"I don't know where we're going. I just know we can't stay on the road."

"What do you mean you don't know where we're going?"

"Look around. What do you see?"

"Nothing," Lula said. "It's black as a witch's tit in here."

"Exactly."

"We could be walking in circles. We could be easy prey for the Jersey Devil and the Tree People."

Or worse.

"I don't want to alarm you or nothing," Lula said. "But I'm gonna have a freak-out. I'm feelin' a freak-out coming on. I'm not a woods person. I need cement under my feet. I need a streetlight. I need a burger."

"Don't panic. This isn't Alaska. This is Jersey. We'll be fine. We have to just keep walking, and we'll get somewhere."

"Shush. Do you hear that?"

"What?"

"They're talking again. I hear the Tree People talking. Feet, don't fail me. I'm getting out of here."

Lula took off in the dark and didn't run more than ten steps when *SPLASH*.

"They got me," she shrieked. "Help. I'm drowning. I'm a goner."

Lula was floundering around at the edge of what looked like a cranberry bog. I squinted into the dark and reached out to her. "Grab my hand."

"I got it," Lula said. "Get me out."

I planted my foot, the mud oozed over my shoe, and I went into the soup with Lula.

"I'm getting sucked away," Lula said. "I'm gonna die. This is the end. The swamp monster got me."

"You're only in two feet of water," I told her. "You're

not going to die. Not unless I choke you because you won't shut up."

I tried to stand, but the ground gave way, and I went down again. Hands grabbed me from behind and lifted me out of the muck. It was Ranger. He was up to his knees in swamp water.

"Babe," Ranger said.

"How did you find me?"

He set me on solid ground and waded out of the water. "I heard Lula yelling. Half the state heard her."

Two of Ranger's men had slogged over to Lula and had her by the armpits, dragging her out.

Ranger took my hand and tugged me through the woods. "Talk to me."

"Gail Scanlon called me and said Wulf had her locked away somewhere. She didn't know where she was, and she was terrified. She asked me to help. I tried to get in touch with Diesel, but he wasn't answering, so I called you, and I came looking for her."

"Did you find her?"

"No. She wasn't in her house."

"What would Wulf want with Gail Scanlon?"

"I don't know, but he killed her brother."

We reached the road, and Ranger continued to lead me.

"Your Jeep is parked just around the curve in the road. I'm parked behind you," Ranger said.

"I ran out of gas."

"I noticed. Is anything else wrong with the Jeep?"

"Only everything."

Ranger paused. "There's a monkey sitting in the middle of the road."

It was all dark shadow to me. "Are you sure it's a monkey?"

"Yeah."

"Is it wearing a hat?"

"Yeah."

"Bummer." I was really wishing it was Carl.

The men behind us were using flashlights. The beam swept across the monkey, and it ran off into the woods. We reached my Jeep and moved past it to the Rangeman SUV.

"I'll send someone to get your car in the morning," Ranger said, remoting the SUV doors unlocked.

Lula and I were dripping wet with mud and water plants stuck in our hair, caked onto our shoes. The temperature had dropped, and I was so cold my teeth were chattering.

Ranger wrapped me in his jacket and trundled me onto the Rangeman front seat. Lula and Ranger's two men got in the back. Ranger climbed behind the wheel, blasted heat at me, and backed out.

We reached the Atlantic City Expressway, and four messages popped up on my phone. All from Diesel. All the same. *Where are you? Call me.*

I dialed his cell and told him about Gail Scanlon.

"Where are you now?" he asked.

"We're on the Expressway. My Jeep ran out of gas in the woods, and Ranger rescued Lula and me."

"Tell him I appreciate the help. And try to get him to pick up some dinner on the way home. A rotisserie chicken would be good."

"That's not going to fly."

"Worth a shot," Diesel said.

I unlocked my apartment door, stepped inside, and kicked my shoes off in the kitchen.

Diesel sauntered in and looked me over. "Am I allowed to smile?"

"As long as you don't laugh out loud."

"What happened?"

"It was dark under the pines, and Lula and I sort of fell into a swamp."

"Where's Carl?"

"He ran away after he turned all the other monkeys loose. And you were right about Gail's house. It was the one you picked out from the aerial view of the Barrens. It was empty when I got there. I didn't see any sign of struggle. Nothing to indicate where Wulf took Gail. Or why he took her."

"Back up. Other monkeys?"

"About twenty of them in a habitat next to Gail's house. They were wearing little helmets with antennae on the tops. Carl opened the door, and they all ran off into the woods."

"Anything else?"

I told him about Martin Munch.

"Where were you?" I asked Diesel. "I tried to reach you when Gail first called me, but you weren't picking up."

"I had to solve a problem in Panama."

"Do I want to know about the problem?"

"No."

I carefully walked to the bathroom, trying not to dislodge any mud clods, and I took a shower. I blasted my hair with the dryer and put on some clean sweats. I went to the kitchen and looked for food.

"Have you eaten?" I asked Diesel.

"When?"

"Recently."

"No."

I considered my choices. Cereal, peanut butter, scrambled eggs, grilled cheese. Hands down, it was grilled cheese. I got everything going in the fry pan and

Diesel stood pressed to my back, looking over my shoulder. "Is that for me?"

"Do you want it?"

"Badly," Diesel said.

"I'm talking about the cheese."

"That, too."

Diesel ate two grilled-cheese sandwiches, and I ate one. I was debating cleaning the fry pan or just throwing it away, and Morelli called.

"Just shoot me," Morelli said. "Put me out of my misery. His wife doesn't want him back. I don't blame her. I don't want him, either, but I'm stuck with him. I can't get him out of my house. He can barely walk. I'm waiting on him hand and foot. The only thing he can do is work the channel changer. I've got a full-scale gang war going in the projects, and seventeen times a day I get a phone call from Anthony adding things to his gimme list. He wants lip balm. He wants bananas. He wants a *TV Guide*. He wants beer."

"I'm really sorry. I wish there was something I could do to help."

"There is. I hate to ask you to do this, but I'm desperate. Can I have the gimme phone calls transferred to you for just one day? I have meetings up my ass tomorrow. I can't keep taking these phone calls."

"Sure. Have him call me. Do you know anything about the explosion at the Sky Social Club? Did they find any bodies inside?"

"One. Tentative identification is Doc Weiner. His two stooges were out front and were blown across the street but didn't get hurt."

I hung up and told Diesel about Doc Weiner.

"Why would Wulf blow up the building?" I asked Diesel. "If he wanted to get rid of Weiner, why didn't he just kill him like Scanlon?"

"Hard to say with Wulf. He sees himself as a sort of avenging angel, but then, he has a playful side."

"Blowing up a building is playful?"

"It is if you're Wulf."

Diesel went to the dining room, retrieved my laptop, and took it to the couch. He turned the computer on and brought up the satellite map of the Pine Barrens. It showed a bird's-eye view of trees, lakes, dirt roads, and houses dotted throughout the area.

"Here's Marbury Road," he said. "We turned off the paved road and eventually we took this dirt road. The road gets difficult to see on this screen because it narrows and becomes obscured by trees."

I traced my route and was able to pick out Gail's animal rescue compound. It was easy to see the exit road on the screen. I found the boggy area that tried to swallow up Lula and me, and the road Munch took on his ATV. The ATV road fed into a crazy quilt of dirt paths that crisscrossed and connected to about a hundred other dirt roads.

"Martin Munch could be living anywhere in the Barrens," Diesel said. "There are single-room camps, junker Airstreams, and small ranch-style houses stuck everywhere. Some are legal and some are squatters. From what I know about Munch, he doesn't require a lot. Electric for his computer and some basic amenities. Wulf, on the other hand, isn't the type to rough it."

"Don't these guys need an evil laboratory somewhere? A lair where they conduct their dastardly experiments and measure magneto-type stuff with their stolen magnetometer?"

"I don't know. It depends what they're doing. One thing we know is that they have Gail Scanlon locked away, and she was able to use a phone."

Chapter

THIRTEEN

I was on my second cup of coffee and the caffeine wasn't kicking in. Diesel, on the other hand, was bright-eyed and bushy-tailed.

"What's with you?" he asked.

"You kept me awake all night. You're big and hot and you kept squishing me. I can't sleep when you're laying on top of me."

"No problemo. Tonight, you can take the top. And here's a thought. If you didn't go to bed wearing everything in your closet, you might not be so hot. The only thing missing is body armor."

If I had it, I'd wear it, I thought. I dragged myself out of the kitchen and went to my living room window to see if my car was in the parking lot. I got to the window and my cell phone rang. Anthony.

"Hey, gorgeous," he said. "Joe tells me I'm supposed to call you if I need something."

"Yep. What's up?"

"I want Halloween candy. I want a couple bags of that sugar candy that's shaped like pumpkins and bats and corn. And I need more M&Ms."

"You called to tell me you want candy?"

"Yeah. I know it's unreasonable, but I feel so crappy. I'm depressed, and I think I'm running a fever, and the nail holes sort of ooze blood when I walk around."

I felt my upper lip curl back. I didn't want to hear about his nail holes oozing blood. Better to get him the candy than to hear about the nail holes. I disconnected and searched the lot for my car. No luck. Rangeman hadn't delivered it yet. Anthony would have to wait for his pumpkins. Diesel's Escalade was still in the lot, but the Harley had disappeared.

I looked back at Diesel. "What happened to your bike?"

"I gave it to Flash. I wasn't using it."

Two Rangeman cars pulled into my lot and parked. Rangeman cars are always new, black, and immaculate. Their origin is a mystery, but there seems to be an inexhaustible supply. Hal got out of the second car. He was dressed in the usual black Rangeman fatigues, and he was carrying a small plastic bag. I watched him disappear into my building, and minutes later, he was at my door.

"I have some good news and some bad news," Hal said. "The bad news is there was a back window open on your Jeep, and when we got there this morning the Jeep was full of raccoons. It looked like they were originally after a bucket of fried chicken, but they pretty much tore up everything when they were done with the chicken. And then they relieved themselves." Hal shook his head. "I've never seen anything like it. It was like every raccoon in the state came in there to . . . you know. We had to get it towed. They ate the driver's seat." He handed me the plastic bag. "We found this game in the back. It still looks okay. And we took the registration and insurance papers out of the glove compartment.

They're in the bag, too. Ranger got rid of the wrecked Jeep and told me to loan you the one we just drove into your lot." Hal handed me a set of keys.

I thanked Hal and went to the window to see my new car. It was a shiny black Jeep Cherokee.

"I get the feeling this happens a lot," Diesel said.

"I have bad car juju."

My phone rang, and I knew from the ringtone it was Lula.

"I'm at the Shop and Bag. I figured I'd pick some stuff up before I went to work, and who do you think is here? It's the guy who shot himself in the foot. Whatshisname. He's got his foot in one of them boot things, and he's driving a motorized shopping cart. I wouldn't mind going over and beating on him, but I thought you might want first crack."

"I'll be right there." I ran to the foyer and grabbed my jacket and bag. "Gotta go," I said to Diesel. "Lula's spotted one of my FTAs."

"Make sure you're back here by noon at the latest," Diesel said.

I sprinted down the hall, down the stairs, crossed the lot to the new Jeep, and looked inside. Oh boy, leather seats. I slid behind the wheel and sucked in the new-car smell. I missed Carl, but I had to admit this smelled better than monkey.

Ten minutes later, I was at Shop and Bag. I had cuffs stuck into the back pocket of my jeans, pepper spray clipped to my waistband, and a stun gun that might or might not work shoved into my jacket pocket. I jogged to the entrance and called Lula on her cell.

"He just went down the cereal aisle," she said. "He's heading for dairy. I'm hiding out in personal products."

I turned down condiments and had him in sight. Lula was right. He was heading for dairy. Lula joined me and we followed him past the cheese and approached him in front of yogurt.

"Denny Guzzi?" I asked.

"Yeah," he said, turning his vehicle to face me. "Oh shit."

"You missed your court date," I said. "You need to reschedule."

"Forget it. There wasn't a crime. I'm not doing the time."

"You robbed a store."

"I didn't get to keep the money. It doesn't count."

"That's true," Lula said.

"It's not true!" I told her.

"Well, there does seem to be some injustice."

"Have you been hitting the medicinal whiskey again?"

"I was a little congested this morning," Lula said.

I reached for Guzzi with the cuffs, and he wheeled his cart around, clipped me with the basket, and took off down condiments.

"Help," he yelled. "Crazy lady."

He was grabbing jars off the shelves, throwing them at me, smashing them on the floor. Ketchup. *Crash.* All over the floor. Dill pickles. *Crash.* All over the floor. Giant-size mayonnaise. *Crash.* All over the floor. Lula and I were sliding in glop, picking our way around glass shards, pickles, olives, sliced beets.

"Cleanup in aisle nine," came over the public address system.

Lula and I turned and backtracked in an effort to outflank Guzzi. We ran down aisle ten, rounded the endcap, and blocked his forward progress.

"This is not a big deal," I said to him. "It'll only take a few minutes to get a new court date, and then I'll bring you back so you can finish your shopping."

This was a huge lie, of course, but I was desperate. I needed the money, and besides, I didn't like him. Call me crazy, but I don't like people who shoot at me and hit me with their motorized shopping carts.

"Okay, how about this," Lula said to Guzzi. "How about I root your crippled ass out of that rent-a-wreck and kick your butt all the way across the parking lot."

"What'd I ever do to you?" he asked.

"You shot at me," Lula said.

"You disturbed me when I was in my home."

"I guess that's true," Lula said. "I wasn't thinking about it like that."

Another motorized shopper buzzed up to us. "What's going on?" she wanted to know. "Is this a mugging? We got rights to be in these things. I got a handicap sticker on my car and everything."

"Oh yeah?" Lula said. "What's wrong with you?"

"None of your beeswax," the old lady said.

"I bet you're fibbing," Lula said. "I bet you don't got no sticker. I bet you're a big liar."

"Go get the car and bring it around to the door," I said to Lula. "I don't want to drag this guy any further than is necessary."

"You and who else?" he said.

And that was when I juiced him with the stun gun. He sort of slumped in his seat, and Lula took off.

"It's okay," I said to the people gathering around. "He's my brother. This happens all the time. He just needs to take a nap. He'll be fine."

I could have said I was a fugitive apprehension agent, but that always freaks people out. The store rent-a-cops muscle in, and the police are called, and then I have to drag out all my paperwork. Better to lie and make a fast getaway.

"He pissed his pants," an old guy looking on said. "What's the matter with him?"

"War injury," I said. "You should stand back. He could get violent when he comes around."

I grabbed two bags of Halloween candy from a display by the register and gave the checker a ten-dollar bill. I got my change, snagged Guzzi by the front of his jacket, and wrestled him out of the cart. He was sort of floppy and twitchy, but I managed to back my way out of the store entrance with him in tow. Lula skidded to a stop in front of me and jumped out to help me get Guzzi into the backseat. I cuffed him, thanked Lula, and drove my catch to the police station.

I off-loaded Guzzi at the back door to the station and dragged his uncooperative body all the way to the docket lieutenant. I turned him over and my phone rang.

"Where are my pumpkins?" Anthony wanted to know.

"Keep your shirt on. I've got them."

"And the M&Ms?"

Dammit, I forgot about the M&Ms.

"It's almost lunchtime," Anthony said. "Maybe you could get me a sub from Pino's."

Maybe I could add poison to the sub, shoot you with a real gun, and throw you into the Delaware River, I thought. Okay, Stephanie, take a deep breath. Remember, his butt got nailed, and it's partly your fault.

"Sure," I said. "I'll get you a sub."

I got my body receipt for Guzzi and ran to my car. I checked my watch. I had a half hour to get the sub and M&Ms, drop everything off at Morelli's house, and get back to my apartment.

I pulled up to Morelli's house and my phone rang.

"Mrs. Ardenowski saw you at Shop and Bag, and she

said you were abusing a handicapped man," my mother said.

"He wasn't handicapped. He shot himself in the foot while he was robbing a store."

"Mrs. Ardenowski said he was in one of those motorized shopping carts."

"Yeah, because he shot himself in the foot."

"They don't give those carts to just anybody. If he had a cart, he had to be handicapped. And what are you doing arresting people in supermarkets? Florence Molnar's daughter doesn't do that. She has a good job at the bank."

"I've gotta go," I said to my mother. And I disconnected.

I used my key to get into Morelli's house. I gave Anthony his candy and sub. I took Bob out for a short walk. Bob pooped on Mr. Fratelli's lawn, and Mr. Fratelli came out and yelled at me to pick the poop up, but I didn't have any bags with me.

"I'll send Morelli over for it when he gets off from work," I told Mr. Fratelli.

I was ten minutes late getting home, which was pretty good, all things considered.

"Hey," Diesel said.

"Hey to you."

"Did you get your guy?"

"I did! I took him down at Shop and Bag."

Diesel grinned. He grabbed me and kissed me on the lips. "Congratulations."

It was like a mild electric shock running from my lips to my toes. "Jeez," I said, "my lips are tingling."

"Yeah, if I'd Frenched you, your sneakers would be smoking."

He was kidding again, right?

"What's next?" I asked him.

"Road trip."

Diesel had a mud-splattered Subaru SUV parked in my lot. A cart had been hitched to the Subaru, and the cart held two ATVs.

"I thought the ATVs would give us a lower profile and more flexibility," Diesel said.

We took the Turnpike to the Atlantic City Expressway. My phone rang just as we got on the Expressway, and I cringed at the display. It was Anthony.

"Yes?" I said by way of greeting.

"I need ice cream, and it's all the way in the kitchen."

"And?"

"I was hoping you could get it for me."

"I can't help you right now. I'm in south Jersey."

"But Joe said—"

"Anthony," I yelled into the phone. "Walk your broken ass into the kitchen and get your own stupid ice cream."

And I hung up.

"Sounds like that went well," Diesel said.

"Morelli comes from a scary gene pool."

We reached the dirt road leading to Gail Scanlon's compound and we off-loaded the ATVs.

"Do you have a plan?" I asked Diesel.

"I thought we'd start with Gail Scanlon's house. I'd like to see it for myself. After that, we'll play it by ear. Ride around and see what happens. And in case my instincts fail, I have a handheld GPS. Do you feel comfortable with this ATV?"

Sure, aside from the fact I'd never been on one. "It looks pretty straightforward." Like a big Tonka toy. Four wheels with aggressive tread tires, steering wheel, gas pedal, brake, some buttons.

We had no trouble finding Gail Scanlon's compound. The booby trap hadn't been reset, but some of the remains were still on the ground. We turned right at the fork and followed the road to the monkey farm.

We drove into the yard and got off the ATVs. Not a monkey in sight. No other cars in the yard.

"Feels like a ghost town," Diesel said.

We went into the house and snooped around, finding nothing of interest. After the house, we went to the monkey shed. I'd expected to find cages, but the shed was actually an indoor habitat with heat and electric and running water. Only thing missing was the monkey horde.

I left the shed and stood in the middle of the yard and called Carl, but Carl didn't appear.

"Boy," I said, "after all I did for him. And this is the thanks I get."

"You're freaking me out," Diesel said. "You sound like my mother."

"You have a mother?"

"If you're going to be mean to me, I'm not going to let you make me any more grilled cheese."

"You *let* me make the grilled cheese?"

Diesel smiled wide enough for his dimples to show.

I shook my finger at him. "Don't you dare use those dimples on me."

Diesel rocked back on his heels, still smiling wide. "I can't help it if I have dimples."

"Yes, you can. I know all about you and those dimples."

"Most women like them."

"I'm not most women."

"No shit," Diesel said. "Get on the ATV."

We took the road leading out of the compound until we came to the fork, and then we turned right. After several yards, a rough path cut off into the pines, and I assumed this was the path Munch took when I chased him through the woods. I followed Diesel along the path, and we began working our way through a labyrinth of ATV tracks.

Stephanie Plum, off-road warrior. Now, this was the way it should be, I thought. Taking action. Hauling ass in the woods behind Diesel. Well, okay—truthfully, I wanted to be in *front* of Diesel. I wanted to ride point, lead the charge, be the big kahuna. Unfortunately, Diesel was the one who'd memorized the aerial map. And he was supposedly the one with super senses.

"Big whoop-de-do, super senses," I said.

"I heard that," Diesel yelled back at me.

"No, you didn't."

"Yes, I did."

Every now and then I'd catch a glimpse of a monkey with a hat, sitting in a tree or running across the path, but I didn't see Carl. We skirted a boggy area and came on a rusted-out trailer set up on cinder blocks. An equally rusted-out pickup truck was parked not far off, and an old man sat smoking and drinking beer in front of the trailer. His face and hands were weathered by the sun and the years. Everything else was hidden away in a pink bunny suit that had seen much better days. The bunny ears hung limp alongside the old guy's head, and the fur was moth-eaten and matted. A monkey with a helmet hunkered on the hood of the pickup, watching us.

"What the hell?" I mouthed to Diesel.

"Easter Bunny," Diesel said. "Retired."

We got off the ATVs and walked over to him.

"Why is the monkey wearing a hat?" I asked.

"Not my monkey. And I don't know. Just one of the many weird-ass things happening in the Barrens. Are you folks tourists?"

"No," I said. "We're bounty hunters."

He gave a hoot of laughter, and I was able to count his teeth. He had two. They were big buckteeth in the front of his mouth, and they weren't in such good shape.

"Bounty hunters," he said. "I like that. We got a bunch of characters here, but I think you're the first bounty hunters."

"What other characters are here?" Diesel asked.

"Sasquatch has a place up the road a ways. And Elmer the Fire Farter is there, too."

"Does he really fart fire?" Diesel asked.

"Fuckin' A," Easter Bunny said. "I've seen it. He has to be real careful what he eats or else he farts in his sleep and burns his house down. And then there's the Jersey Devil. I don't know where he lives, but he flies over my yard sometimes."

"Anyone else?"

"We got a monkey horde. A bunch of them showed up to watch me make dinner last night. And they were all wearing hats. And there's someone in the woods to the north, shooting lights into the sky at night. Damn lights mess up my television reception. I got a dish on the roof of my mobile home. It's not cheap running that dish, and now my reception is crap. And sometimes when the reception is crap, all my fur stands on end. And then it rains. But it only rains next to my truck. You see that big mud puddle? That's where it rains."

"I can't help noticing you're wearing a rabbit suit," I said to him.

"Seemed a shame to throw them all away just 'cause I retired," the guy said. "And anyways, the zipper's stuck on this one. I can't get it off."

"I'm looking for Wulf," Diesel said. "Have you seen him?"

The Easter Bunny made the sign of the cross and

hugged his beer bottle to his chest. "No. And I don't never *want* to see him."

"Why am I the only one who never heard of Wulf before?" I asked Diesel.

"You're not an Unmentionable. You don't get the newsletter."

"There's a newsletter?"

Diesel gave a snort of laughter and tried to grab me, but I jumped away.

"You're scum," I said to him.

"I know," Diesel said. "I can't help myself."

We got back on the ATVs, and I followed Diesel down the Easter Bunny's driveway and along the road that presumably ran past Sasquatch and the Fire Farter. We saw no sign of Sasquatch or his house, but we passed a patch of scorched earth and two charred remnants of small mobile homes. We paused for a moment and looked at the ruins.

"I bet it was chili," Diesel said.

Chapter
FOURTEEN

It was dusk when we returned to the Subaru. We hadn't encountered any more people or habitable houses. We'd ridden around for hours, but we covered only a very small portion of the Barrens. Diesel secured the ATVs and locked the back gate on the trailer. He pulled onto the paved road and headed toward Marbury.

"This isn't the way home," I said.

"I'm looking for a place we can hang for a while. I'd like to see the lights."

Five miles down the road, we found a soft-serve stand, closed for the season. The small parking lot was empty and dark. No ambient light for miles. Diesel positioned the Subaru so we were looking north, and we settled in.

"What about food?" I asked Diesel. "I'm hungry."

"Sorry," Diesel said, "you're going to have to live off your fat for a few hours."

I gave him a shot in the arm.

Diesel grinned. "Let me rephrase that."

"Too late," I told him. "You're in big trouble."

There was a flash of light in the sky, and then it was gone. We sat perfectly still, and two more flashes shot out of the pine forest.

"Those weren't beams of light," Diesel said. "They were tails from a rocket."

We had our windows rolled down, listening for rain or the crackle of electricity. Nothing carried to us.

"Hard to tell exactly where the rocket originated," Diesel said, "but I have an idea of the general area. I'll go over the aerial maps again when we get home, and tomorrow we'll do more off-road."

We found fast food just outside of Hammonton and collected bags of burgers, fries, onion rings, fried chicken, and doughnuts. Diesel took the Atlantic City Expressway and connected with the Jersey Turnpike, eating while he drove. Who says men can't multitask?

I woke up with a start. The phone was ringing. It was still dark. Someone must be dead, I thought. My grand-mother or my father. Heart attack while they slept.

Diesel reached across me and got the phone.

"Yeah?" he said to the caller, listened for a moment, and handed the phone to me. "It's Lula."

"Lula? What time is it?"

Diesel looked at his watch. "It's five A.M."

"I'm a sick person," Lula said. "I got the flu back. I can't stop sneezing. And I can hardly breathe. I'm just about breaking out in a rash. And I haven't got any of my meds. Tank and I went out last night, and I left my purse in his car. He got everything. He got my decon-gestant and my antihistamine and my car keys."

"And?"

"And he isn't answering his phone. He sleeps like a dead man. I need a ride over there so I can get my purse. Or else I need to find some store open so I can buy drugs."

"Why don't you just call the Rangeman control room?"

"He don't live in a Rangeman apartment anymore. He's got his own place. It's brand new. I haven't even seen it yet."

"Give me a couple minutes to wake up, and I'll be right over."

"You could call her a cab," Diesel said. "And then you could stay in bed with me."

If there was an argument that would get me on my feet, that was it. I rolled out of bed, stumbled into the bathroom, got dressed, and stumbled out to the lot. I stood for a moment inhaling the cold air, willing it to go to my brain. I sat my ass behind the wheel and drove on autopilot to Lula's house.

Lula rented the top floor of a very small house. Small living room, bedroom, bathroom, and a kitchenette. Lula fit the apartment like she fit her clothes. It was all a tight squeeze. She was sitting on the stoop, waiting for me, when I stopped at the curb.

"You could just drive me to the cemetery," she said, slumping into the passenger seat. "It would save time."

"I can't believe you left your purse in his car. That purse is practically attached to your shoulder."

"He picked me up, and we were gonna get some Chinese takeout and bring it back to his house on account of I've never been in his house. And we didn't even get to Chang's and I started getting sick. Came on me like *BANG*. So I told Tank I wanted to go home. By the time we got to my place, I was sneezing my head off, and I wasn't thinking good. I don't even remember getting out of the car."

"This comes on you every time you see Tank."

"It never used to."

Lula's hard-working, low-income neighborhood was bordered by a slackard, *no*-income neighborhood. Since there were no legal drugs to be had in the no-income neighborhood, I drove back toward Hamilton and Broad, where there were a couple all-night convenience stores. I stopped at the first store with lights blazing, and Lula lurched out of the Jeep and went inside.

Lula was wearing big, pink, fluffy slippers, pink sweatpants, and a white down-filled quilted coat. A red flannel nightgown hung two inches under the coat. Her hairstyle was *yikes*.

It was almost six A.M. Morelli and Ranger would be up. Diesel was most likely still asleep. Diesel wasn't a morning person. I dialed Morelli's cell phone while I waited for Lula.

"Yo," Morelli said. "What's up?"

"Just calling to say hello."

"That's a relief. I was afraid your apartment was fire-bombed again. You're not usually up this early."

"Lula is sick, and I had to take her out on a drug run."

"Maybe you can bring some over for me. I'm ready to start taking Anthony's happy pills."

"Is he feeling any better?"

"He's bitching less when he goes to the can. Did you really tell him to get his broken ass out to the kitchen and get his own ice cream?"

"Yeah."

"You're my hero," Morelli said.

"Do you want me to take phone calls again today?"

"Thanks, but no. I can manage Anthony today. I do have another huge favor though. Do you suppose you could talk to his wife? Maybe you can get her to take him back."

"You're kidding. What on earth would I say? He's a womanizing, cheating, perverted idiot. My advice to her is to run like hell and don't look back."

"Cripes, Stephanie, I'm trying to get rid of this guy.

Help me out here. Lie. You do it all the time on your job. You're good at it."

"You want me to lie to your sister-in-law?"

"Hell, yes!"

"Okay, I'll try to find time to talk to her."

Lula wrenched the door open, and I said good-bye to Morelli.

"I got a bag full of stuff," Lula said, holding the bag open for me to see. "Pick one for me."

I chose one that was for allergies.

"Tank is probably up by now," I said. "Do you want to stop in and get your purse?"

"Yeah, that would be great. I need my car keys."

"Where does Tank live?"

"He's in a house on Howard Street, two blocks from Cluck-in-a-Bucket."

Good deal. There was a Dunkin' Donuts alongside Cluck-in-a-Bucket. I was ready to kill for coffee, and I wouldn't mind a couple dozen doughnuts, either.

I pointed the Jeep in the right direction and drove with renewed motivation. Lula took a pill from the box I picked and then sampled a couple more meds.

"You should go easy on that," I said. "I don't think it's good to mix and match."

"I figure I'll keep taking them until I find one that works."

"They don't work right away. You have to give them a chance."

"I don't have all day for some dumb pill. I got things to do. I got no patience for this."

"If you stop taking pills, I'll get you a bag of doughnuts and a nice greasy breakfast sandwich."

"I like the sound of that. And we could get some of them home fries, too."

"Right. Home fries. And coffee. Lots of coffee."

"I feel better already," Lula said.

I drove to Tank's house first. It was a small yellow-and-white Cape Cod. Far from what I would imagine for Tank. It had a tiny front yard and a front porch with a white railing. It was a total little-old-lady house.

"You sure this is the right house?" Lula asked. "This don't look like no Tank house."

"This is the address you gave me."

Lula set her bag of cold aids on the floor, got out of the Jeep, and walked to the front door. She rang the bell and looked in the front window. She rang the bell a second time, and Tank opened the door. He was dressed in Rangeman black, ready to go to work. Hard to see his expression from where I sat, but he had to be surprised. Not only was Lula on his doorstep unannounced, she looked like she'd just escaped from the electroshock room of the loony bin.

Lula went into his house, and he closed the door. Minutes later, the door banged open, and Lula stormed out. She had her purse in her hand, and she was wasting no time getting to the Jeep. She ripped the door open and rammed herself into the car.

"I need food," she said. "A lot of it."

Hard to tell what that meant. Lula ate when she was pissed off, happy, sad, tired, or bored. Food solved it all for Lula.

"Dunkin' Donuts okay?" I asked.

"It's perfect. I love Dunkin' Donuts." And then she sneezed and farted. "Excuse me," she said.

"Well?" I asked her. "Was Tank responsible for that sneeze?"

"He's got cats! Three of them. Suzy, Miss Kitty, and Applepuff. It's no wonder I'm dying here. I'm allergic to cats."

"I thought you said you weren't allergic to anything."

"Yeah, except for cats."

"I didn't know Tank had cats."

"He said that's why he moved. He adopted this family of cats, and he couldn't keep them at Rangeman. So I told him I was allergic to cats, and he was gonna have to make a choice."

"And then what happened?"

"He said he couldn't get rid of the cats on account of they didn't have any other home. He said I should get allergy shots."

"And?"

"I'm not getting no allergy shots for a man who chooses a cat over me."

"What are you going to do? Is the wedding off?"

"I don't know. I gotta call Miss Gloria. She always said my numbers weren't so good with Tank's anyway. And our moons didn't line up, either. I should have listened to her right from the start."

I pulled into the Dunkin' Donuts lot and parked.

"Maybe you should go in and get the stuff," Lula said. "Tank wasn't real complimentary about my appearance."

"What did he say?"

"He said I was scarin' his cats."

"Shouldn't you be crying or something?"

"I guess, but I don't feel like crying. I feel like eating," Lula said.

"What do you want?"

"Everything."

"You got it."

I gave my order in and waited while the food and coffee were gathered together and bagged.

"Office party?" the girl behind the counter asked.

"No," I told her. "Pity party."

Lula was on the phone with Miss Gloria when I got back to the Jeep.

"Okay," she said to Miss Gloria. "I appreciate your taking the time for me like this."

I set the coffee out and unpacked the sausage-and-egg sandwiches first.

"I feel much better," Lula said. "Turns out it wasn't nobody's fault. It was just to do with me being on the cusp of something, and Tank being in the wrong quadrant. Miss Gloria said it was good the cats came because me and Tank were on a collision course with our moons and shit."

"Does this mean the wedding is off?"

"Yeah. I was thinking I might not want to spend eternity with Tank anyway. I can't sleep with that man. He snores, and he sweats. Is that something I want to look forward to for the rest of my life? I don't think so." Lula polished off her sandwich and went to the doughnut box. "You can count on Dunkin' Donuts," she said. "I'll take a doughnut over a man any day of the week."

"Your allergy sounds better."

"Yeah. I think one of them pills did the trick."

I dropped Lula off at her house and headed for home. Lights were on in the bonds office when I drove by, so I made a U-turn and parked. Connie was booting up her computer when I walked in. I gave her the body receipt for Denny Guzzi, and I looked through the new FTA files on her desk.

"Nothing interesting," she said. "Domestic violence, grand theft auto, destruction of personal property."

"Did you get an address on Gordo Bollo?"

"His employer has him residing at 656 Ward Street in Bordentown. I verified it with his sister. She posted the bond."

"I was on Ward. There's nothing there. A cemetery and a ceramic pipe factory."

"You must be missing something. Or maybe there are two Ward Streets. Are you feeling okay? You look sort of green."

"I had breakfast with Lula, and it's not sitting well."

"What did you eat?"

"Everything."

I shoved the new FTAs in my bag and left the bonds office. Might as well get the lying and begging out of the way first thing, I thought. Visit Anthony's wife and get it over and done. It wasn't a long drive to his house. He lived in the Burg in a house similar to my parents' house. The sun was weak in the sky, the sky was gray with a thick cloud cover, and the air felt raw.

Anthony's wife is named Angelina. Angie for short. I think Stephanie Plum is an okay name, but Angelina Morelli is a symphony. If I was named Angelina, I'd marry a Morelli just for the name alone.

Angie opened the door as soon as I rang the bell. We went to the same schools but never knew each other until we both hooked up with a Morelli. She was two years younger than me, and she was really pretty. Classic Italian. Olive skin, brown eyes, lush body, and lustrous black hair. She also had a splotch of baby barf on her shirt.

"Omigod," she said. "Let me guess. They sent you over to talk me into taking him back."

"Yep."

"Come on in. I'm feeding little Anthony."

Little Anthony was in one of those baby-chair contraptions. Hard to say how old he was. All babies sort of look alike to me. He had a lot of orange glop on his pajamas, and he didn't smell all that good. I was thinking I was smart to have a hamster.

Angie sat opposite Barfman, and I took a chair as far away as possible. She spooned some green stuff into him, and he gummed it around.

"So," I said. "Are you going to take him back?"

"Do you think I should?"

"No."

Angie laughed out loud. "You're not supposed to say that. Didn't they give you a rehearsal?"

"You have a nice house. It's cozy. It's a family house."

"I feel like the lady in the shoe who had so many kids she didn't know what to do. We're bursting at the seams."

"Yes, but it feels good in here."

Except for the kid with the spewed mush on his clothes. It was Saturday morning, and the rest of her pack was in front of the television in the small living room. They were all eating cereal out of a box, not saying anything, mesmerized by whatever was on the screen.

"Is it easier without Anthony?" I asked her. "One less mouth to feed."

"No. He's great with the kids. Not like his father. His father was a mean, abusive drunk. Anthony is sweet. He's just got too much machismo. All dick and no brain."

"You love him."

"Yeah. Stupid, huh?"

"Yes, but in a good way. God knows, someone has to love him. He's pathetic. Did they tell you he got shot with a nail gun?"

Angie pressed her lips together. "He is such a *jerk*. He deserved to get shot. And I'm not letting him back in this house until the stitches come out. He's horrible when he's sick. He expects to be waited on hand and foot. A head cold is a major catastrophe for him."

"So, you're taking him back?"

"Probably. Someone has to haul the garbage out to the curb and shovel the walk, and it's not going to be me. And maybe someday he'll grow up, or get a prostate condition. He'd be terrific if he didn't have gonads."

"I guess my work here is done," I said. "I have to go catch some felons now."

Angie stood and walked me to the door. "It was nice to see you. Stop in anytime."

I gave her a hug, walked to the Jeep, wedged myself behind the wheel, and called Morelli. "I talked to Angie," I said.

"And?"

"There's some good news, and there's some bad news."

"I hate this good news, bad news shit," Morelli said.

"How about this. There's bad news, and there's bad news. Do you like that any better?"

"No."

"She's taking him back, but not until the stitches come out."

"I don't suppose you'd want to come over for dinner tonight?"

"You suppose right. Anyway, I'm trying to find Martin Munch. Vinnie's in a rant over him. Anything new on your end?"

"No," Morelli said. "But we found eight other unsolved murders spread all over the country with the same MO."

"Rotated neck and a burn that looks like a handprint?"

"Yes."

"It's creepy. Is that Anthony yelling in the background?"

"He wants breakfast. He can't find clean socks. He needs batteries in the television remote. It's endless."

"You're being an enabler. He can do all those things for himself, but he has no incentive if you do them for him. And he has no incentive to want to shape up and go home to his wife as long as you're taking her place. The only thing missing in your relationship is sex. And that might not be a big selling point, since I suspect the sex scene in his house is going to be very frosty for a long time."

"You're right," Morelli said. "Let him find his own damn socks. I'm done."

"Gotta go. Things to do."

Chapter

FIFTEEN

Diesel was on the phone when I walked into my apartment. His hair was damp, and he was freshly shaved, which meant he'd used my razor. Diesel traveled light. He hung up and wrapped an arm around me.

"You smell like doughnuts," he said.

"I bought Lula breakfast."

"I have a guy flying in to a small airport just north of Hammonton. He's going to take us over the Barrens. I'm hoping we can spot the rocket-launch site from the air."

"How small is this plane?"

"It's not a plane. It's a helicopter."

"Oh boy."

"Something wrong with that?"

"I've never been in a helicopter. I've never *wanted* to be in a helicopter. They don't look safe."

"Sweetie, nothing that flies looks safe, including birds."

He lifted my bag off the hook on the wall and draped it over my shoulder. "Time to roll."

We took the Subaru with the trailered ATVs. If we found the launch site, we'd use the ATVs to get back to it. If we didn't find the launch site, we'd ride around and hope we got lucky. I had mixed feelings about getting lucky. I wanted to snag Munch, but I didn't especially want to see Diesel in action, shutting Wulf down.

At the best of times, Trenton isn't especially pretty. And this wasn't the best of times. The sky was the color and texture of wet cement, and everything under it felt like doom. I looked up at the sky, and I prayed for rain. I was pretty sure helicopters didn't fly in the rain.

By the time we found Hammonton Airport, the sky had lightened a little, and I knew I wasn't going to be saved by rain. The helicopter was sitting on a stretch of blacktop, waiting for us. It was blue and white, had a clear bubble nose, and looked like a big dragonfly. It seated four.

"Oh God," I said on a moan.

"Think of this as an adventure," Diesel said.

"I'm from Jersey. I get my adventure on the Turn-pike. I only fly if there's a beach or a casino involved. And then it's in a big plane serving alcohol."

We parked and crossed the blacktop to the pilot. He was average height, average weight, and covered head to toe with tattoos. His graying blond hair was pulled back in a ponytail.

"This is Boon," Diesel said. "I've known Boon for about a hundred years."

I nodded a numb acknowledgment and stood in a catatonic stupor.

"She thinks helicopters aren't safe," Diesel said to Boon.

"Hah. If everything we did was safe, we'd never do anything, would we?" Boon said.

I inadvertently whimpered, and Diesel scooped me up and set me in the backseat of the helicopter. He took the seat next to Boon and passed me a headset with a microphone.

"Buckle up and put the headset on so we can talk to each other," Diesel said.

Boon fired the bird, we lifted off the ground, and my heart rate went to stroke level. I closed my eyes and chanted the rosary. This from a woman who hadn't been to church in three years, and then it was just for Christmas Mass because my mother had made me.

"Open your eyes," Diesel said over the headset. "Help me look for a clearing where someone could launch a rocket."

We'd been in the air for five minutes and hadn't plummeted to the ground in a smoking fireball, so I dredged up some courage, held my breath, and peeked out the window.

Diesel's voice was in my ear again. "You have to breathe. And stop thinking about flaming, twisted debris and body parts spread over the Barrens."

"Are you reading my mind?"

"Yeah, and it's creepy."

Boon was flying grids, high enough for us to see a large area, low enough to pick out details. We passed over Gail Scanlon's house and the monkey habitat. It looked untouched. The door to the habitat was still open. No vehicles in the yard. No monkeys. No Carl. The thought made my heart constrict. It was much easier to understand the Barrens from our bird's-eye view. We could get a better picture of how the paths connected and led to campsites and abandoned homesteads. There were plenty of clearings, but none that held any real interest. We didn't see any rocket launchpads. We saw a number of cabins and double-wides that looked occupied. A car in the driveway of one. Smoke curling from the chimney of another. Not a lot of activity. A truck bounced along a rutted road leading to a little house with chickens scratching around in the front yard.

"Fly over this area again," Diesel said to Boon. "I know it's here, and somehow we're missing it."

"Maybe it's not in this area," Boon said. "Maybe the rockets get trucked in. Remember when we were in Columbia?"

"I hate that idea," Diesel said. "That makes my life much more complicated. They could truck them in from anywhere."

"I don't think they're that far away," I said. "Munch was in Gail Scanlon's neighborhood on his ATV."

"What exactly are we looking for?" Boon asked Diesel.

"Wulf is hanging with a guy named Martin Munch, a genius working with electromagnetic waves. All of a sudden Munch's project manager is dead . . ."

"Twisted neck?" Boon asked.

"Yeah. And now Wulf's got the manager's sister. I'm guessing Munch made some sort of discovery, and Wulf is intrigued by it."

"Had to be some badass discovery to get Wulf into the Pine Barrens. Wulf is more Vienna, Paris, Dubai," Boon said.

"I think they must be using the Barrens for research," Diesel said. "There's lots of space here, and it's close to areas where Munch has sources for materials."

"How much space does Munch need to do research?"

"I don't know," Diesel said. "Could be as small as a room or as large as a barn. He'd need a source of electric. Maybe a generator. If he didn't want to be picked up by helicopter surveillance, he'd need a garage for his ATV. He'd need a decent road to truck stuff in."

"We haven't seen anything as big as a barn," Boon

said. "A generator could be hidden under tree cover. There was a ranch house with an attached garage. There was a double-wide with a couple outbuildings. Both had dirt roads connecting them to civilization."

"Enlarge the grid," Diesel said. "Fly us around a little more, then we'll head back to the airport."

We were in the Subaru, watching Boon lift off and head for Atlantic City. Lucky him, I thought. Boon was going to the land of the endless buffet, and I was still stuck in the Barrens. It was early afternoon, and I knew Diesel was itching to mount up and check out some houses.

"I'm not doing anything until you feed me," I said.

"How elaborate does this meal have to be?"

"Just get me some food."

Ten minutes later, Diesel pulled into a gas station and handed me a twenty. "See what you can find inside."

"Boy, you really know how to treat a girl right."

"Now what? Would you rather watch the guy pump the gas?"

I played the vending machines and came away with a couple granola bars, a couple snack packs of peanuts, two Little Debbie cakes, Reese's Peanut Butter Cups, an assortment of gummi bears, and two bottles of water.

I got back into the SUV and put the bag between the two front seats. Diesel looked in the bag and took one of the Reese's.

"I thought for sure you'd go for the granola bar," I said.

"No way."

"Ranger would take the granola bar."

"And Morelli?"

"The peanuts."

"And what about you?" Diesel asked.

"The cake."

He put the SUV in gear and turned onto the road. "I knew it would be the cake."

I ate one of the cakes, the remaining Reese's, and the peanuts while Diesel drove. He'd picked out five houses he thought deserved a closer look, and he was searching for the best road in to the properties. We were in the heart of the Barrens, and I was bleary-eyed with the monotony. Scrub pines, sand, and some high-bush cranberries. I couldn't imagine how Diesel was finding his way without a Taco Bell to serve as a landmark. Remembering to turn right at the large pine wasn't going to do it for me.

"Here we go," he said, swerving off the paved road onto hard-packed dirt.

He drove for a quarter mile on the dirt road and parked in a small clearing. We got out of the SUV and off-loaded the ATVs. The sky was growing darker by the minute, hanging just above the treetops.

I tipped my head back and studied the cloud cover. "This doesn't look good."

"No, but I can't let rain stop me. I'm running out of time. I can't see Wulf hanging in the Barrens much longer. Even with the proximity of Atlantic City, it's not going to hold his attention. If the technology is worth something to him, he'll move Munch to a more obscure location and lock him down. And then Wulf will find a more entertaining environment."

"Then let's do it. Neither rain, nor sleet, nor lack of a bathroom will stop me."

I followed Diesel's ATV down the dirt road. There were several forks, but Diesel knew his route. He slowed just before he came to the first house and went off-road into the pines. We parked the ATVs and moved in on foot. The house was more decrepit than it had appeared from the air. The yellow paint was faded and peeling. The small front porch sagged. Its step had been replaced by a cinder block. A tricked-out Ford pickup was parked in the yard not far from the front door to the house.

We skirted the house and looked in the garage window. The garage was wall-to-wall junk. A rusted washing machine, stacks of newspapers, a bed mattress with the innards spilling out from a huge rip in the middle. There was a mountain of big plastic bags, which I suspected from the smell leaking out of the garage contained garbage. We walked around back and looked in the kitchen window. The kitchen looked a lot like the garage.

A skinny young guy in jeans and a wifebeater shuffled into the kitchen and threw an empty beer can into the sink. The sink was already full of beer cans, and the can rolled off the pile and fell onto the floor.

Diesel rapped on the back door and opened it, and the skinny guy looked at Diesel blank-faced, too trashed to be surprised.

"I'm looking for a friend of mine," Diesel said.

"He ain't here, man. I'm the only one here."

"Yeah, but maybe you've seen him around. Red hair, short guy, about your age or a little older."

"No, sorry. Haven't seen the little dude."

"How about a guy with shoulder-length black hair and really pale skin."

"The vampire. Shit, he almost ran me off the road twice."

"Where did you see him?"

"He was on the road that goes to the monkey lady. He was in a big, black, jacked-up truck. I mean, it was bad, dude."

"Does that road connect to your road here?"

"No. I got a friend who grows some primo shit back there. I was on a shopping trip."

A monkey with a hat ran out of the woods and stopped inches from us.

"Whoa," the skinny guy said. "Do you see a monkey wearing a hat?"

"Yeah," Diesel said.

"Shit, that's a relief," the skinny guy said.

We returned to the ATVs.

"I'm thinking he was Unmentionable," I said to Diesel.

"Not in a good way," Diesel said.

We backtracked to a road that led to the second house on Diesel's list. It had started to drizzle, and I was wishing I had a hat. It wasn't bad when the dirt road narrowed and the pines gave us some cover. It was a misery when the pines parted and the rain soaked into my sweatshirt and jeans.

By the time we got to the second house, it was pouring. My hair was plastered to my face, I was squinting to see through the sheets of wind-driven rain, and I was cold clear to the bone. The dirt road was mud. The mud clung to the wheels of the ATV and splattered everything in its path, including Diesel and me.

We got off the ATVs, slogged to the house, and looked in the front window. The house was empty. No furniture. The inhabitants had moved on. Diesel went inside, did a fast pass-through, and came out.

"Zero on this one," he said. "We can cross it off the list."

"It looks dry in there," I said wistfully.

"Yeah, it would be perfect, except for the dead raccoon in the kitchen and the forty rats trying to figure out what to do with it."

The yard in front of the house was a quagmire, and on the way back to the ATV I lost my shoe in the mud. It sucked it off me. I took a step, and next thing, I was wearing only one shoe.

"Fuck!"

Diesel turned and looked at me. "I don't hear you using that word a lot."

"I lost my fucking shoe! The fucking mud fucking sucked it off my fucking foot."

Diesel gave a bark of laughter and retrieved my shoe. We were both ankle-deep in mud, the difference being he was wearing his beat-up boots, and I was wearing sneakers. He swept me off my feet and carried me to the ATV. He set me on the seat, knocked most of the mud off my sneaker, and laced it back on my foot.

"Follow me," he said. "We're going to the Subaru."

It was slow going in the mud and rain. If it had been warm, it might have been fun sliding around on the slick, rutted road, but it wasn't warm, and I wasn't having fun. We reached the car, and I dragged myself off my ATV.

"I lied about neither sleet nor snow, blah, blah, blah," I said to Diesel.

"You gave up your shoe for the cause," he said. "You can't ask for much more than that." He released the hitch on the ATV trailer and handed the car keys to me. "You're going home, and I'm staying here. Call Flash when you get cell-phone reception and tell him to meet you somewhere and swap out the Subaru. And then send him back here to wait for me."

"I feel like a wimp."

"Yeah, but you're a cute wimp. And I'm an awesome superdude. Just don't forget to send Flash."

He took my phone and programmed Flash's number

in. Then he reached into the SUV and took a granola bar and the gummi bears.

"See you tonight," he said.

"What about Wulf? Don't you need me to disguise your bread crumbs?"

"I'll manage."

So I'm a wimp. Better a warm, dry wimp than a dead, hypothermic idiot. And when I got the chance, I'd do something nice for Diesel.

I was on the Atlantic City Expressway, en route to the Turnpike, and Martin Munch blew past me. He was doing ninety in the rain, driving a mud-splattered Audi. I would never have noticed, but he cut out around me, and I caught a flash of red hair and a vision of him hunched up on the wheel. I put my foot to the floor, and the Subaru lurched forward.

After a mile, Munch pulled right, took the exit, and I followed. It was Saturday afternoon, we were in the middle of a monsoon, and Martin Munch felt compelled to drive two exits down the Expressway to a junk shop masquerading as a crafts and antiques fair. The parking lot was vast and empty. The building was a renovated, industrial-size chicken coop. The walls were cement block, and the roof was tin. Inside the chicken coop, the rain on the roof was deafening.

I'd stealthily squished across the lot and entered the building several steps behind Munch. I was wet and disgusting and not feeling at my best, but getting passed by Munch on the highway was an act of God I couldn't ignore. He cruised the corncob dolls and miniature wooden hand-painted cranberry buckets that said PINE BARRENS, USA and, on the bottom in small letters, MADE IN CHINA. He meandered into an aisle of dented lunch boxes from the 1950s and Howdy Doody puppets. He paused to heft an antique Etch A Sketch, and I thought, Come to mama.

"Martin Munch?" I asked him.

He turned and looked at me. "Yes."

Clink. I clapped the cuffs on him.

"Do I know you?" he asked.

"I work for your bail bondsman. You missed your court appearance. And I chased you through the woods yesterday."

"Jeez. You scared the heck out of me. I thought you were one of those crazy Pine People. There's an old guy who thinks he's the Easter Bunny. And the worst of all is the Jersey Devil. You can hear him flying around at night, and his eyes glow in the dark. I saw something big and black with glittery eyes in the bush, and I started running."

"What were you doing in the woods?"

"I was going to check on a house, and I didn't want to take the ATV through the bog in the dark."

"Gail Scanlon's house?" I asked.

I never heard his answer because there was pain. It went through me like lightning. I went to my hands and knees and saw a pair of expensive black boots and black slacks with a razor-sharp crease step into my field of vision. I looked up and saw Wulf staring down at me. He was even more impressive and frightening in daylight. He was big and ghostly pale. His eyes were black, shaded by thick black lashes. He reached out to me, and when he touched me, there was more pain, and then nothing.

Chapter
SIXTEEN

My mind came awake before my body. I was thinking, and then I was hearing. I opened my eyes, and I could see, but I couldn't move. I was stretched out on a bed, and Munch was poking me like I was a yeast roll and he was testing my freshness.

"Stop it," I said. "What the heck are you doing?"

"I wanted to see if you were awake."

"What hit me?"

"Wulf. He's awesome. It's like he's not even human or something. It's like he's some sort of dark titan."

I could feel tingling in my fingers and toes. The tingling moved along my arms and legs, and there was a rush of heat throughout my body.

"He's not a titan," I said. "He's just a big, scary, creepy guy in expensive clothes. What are you doing with him?"

"We're partners. We're going to take over the world."

"Get real."

"Actually, I don't really care about that," Munch said. "I just want to be able to do my experiments. And I want to get chicks."

"Excuse me?"

"You know, girls. Pussy. Wulf said he'd make sure they were all over me."

"You need Wulf to get you girls?"

"No way. I can get all the girls I want. It's just that I'm busy, you know? I don't have time to do the whole bar scene. Anyway, I think the bar scene is old. I mean, who does that anymore anyway, right?"

"What, do they check your ID?"

"Yeah. It's humiliating."

I pushed myself up to a sitting position and swung my legs over the side of the bed.

"So how's Wulf going to get you girls?" I asked him.

"He brings them in to me. Like you. You're my first. We have the monkey lady, but she's kind of old and Wulf is using her for other stuff. Anyway, Wulf said I could practice on you. You're kind of a mess, but you're nice and soft."

"Soft?"

"Yeah. Your breasts are soft."

"You touched my breasts?"

"I would have done more, but you're all muddy. I figure we'll put you in the shower now that you're awake, and then I'll have a go at you."

"How about if I have a go at *you*," I said. And I kicked him in his Munchkins.

He crashed to the floor and rolled around in a fetal position, gasping for breath. The door to the little bedroom opened, and Wulf looked in at us.

"I see it's going well," Wulf said.

I wanted to say something clever, do a kung fu move on him and run like the wind, but truth is, my brain was numb with fear. Wulf scared the crap out of me. There was something about him. The lack of facial expression. The black eyes. The perfect clothes over the body that exuded evil power. He was the dark side of Diesel.

"I need to move you," Wulf said. "You can walk with me, or I can incapacitate you and drag you out."

"I'll walk."

He stepped aside and motioned me out the door. We were in a small but comfortable ranch-style house from the seventies. He led me out the door and across the yard to an outbuilding. It had stopped raining, but the air was raw and the ground was oversaturated. The outbuilding was nothing more than a shed. Maybe five by five. A door and no windows.

"I'll be back," he said. "And when I come back, you're going to have to be nicer to Martin."

He closed and locked the door with a padlock, and I was in total blackness. Not a hint of light. No furniture. No bathroom facilities. Just a metal shed. I felt my way around the shed, but there were no weak seams. I still had my cell phone clipped to my jeans, but there was no reception.

I was in a terrible position. My Jeep was in my parking lot, and Ranger had no idea I was in trouble. Diesel was rambling around in the woods, oblivious to my predicament. When he finally returned to rendezvous with Flash, Flash wouldn't be there. Bottom line, I was on my own, locked in a shed, waiting for a madman to return and give me over to a geek who wanted to get laid.

A half hour passed, and I heard a car drive away. A couple more minutes, and it sounded like someone was clunking the padlock against the shed exterior. There was silence and then more of the clunking and some scratching. The padlock clicked, the handle turned, and the door opened a crack. I cautiously peeked out. The sun had set below the trees, but the sky still held some light. No one was in the yard. I pushed the door fully open, and that was when I saw him. It was Carl!

I picked him up and hugged him to me.

"Eeep," Carl said.

The padlock was on the ground, the key still stuck in the lock.

"Is anyone else here?" I asked him. "Gail Scanlon or Martin Munch?"

Carl shrugged his shoulders.

This wasn't one of the properties Diesel had tagged for further investigation on his first sweep. The little ranch-style house sat in the middle of a cleared patch of ground. No garage. No generator. Just the toolshed, which was big enough to hold a lawn mower and not much else.

I crept to the house and looked in a window. Lights were off. No activity. I tried the front door. Locked. I worked my way around the house, looking in all the windows. No one was in the house. There was a yellow pad on the kitchen counter. Dishes in the sink. Some clothes on the floor in the second bedroom. Looked like jeans and boxer shorts.

A window was broken in the kitchen, the glass cleared out with a stick that was left on the counter. I looked down at Carl.

"I imagine that's how you got the key to the padlock."

Carl scratched the top of his head.

I reached through the window, got the stick, and used it to break a window in the back door. I opened the door, and we stepped inside. My search was fast. I didn't want to be there when Wulf returned. No phone that I could find. There was a power cord for a computer in the kitchen but no computer. Milk and a couple cans of soda in the fridge. A jar of peanut butter, half a loaf of white bread, and an opened box of cereal had been left on the kitchen counter. Minimum clothes in the dresser.

A couple T-shirts and a pair of Power Rangers briefs. A down jacket in the closet.

Munch was living in the house, but it looked more like a stopover than a residence. And he was working someplace else.

I dropped my wet sweatshirt onto the kitchen floor and zipped myself into Munch's down jacket. The yellow pad on the counter caught my eye. It looked like Munch had a grocery list going. The first item was HTPB. The second was APCP. He also listed a transmitter, barium, and BlueBec rockets. I ripped the page off the pad and stuffed it into my jacket pocket.

I left through the back door with Carl tagging after me, clutching the cereal box. I guess life in the woods lacked amenities like cookies and cereal. We crossed the yard and followed the road. After a half hour, I heard a car approaching and saw headlights shining through the trees. Carl and I ducked into the woods, crouching low, hiding in the shadows. The headlights swept around a curve and the Audi passed us on its way to the house.

As soon as the lights disappeared around the next curve, I took off running. In a matter of minutes, Wulf would be hunting me down. It was dark, and the road was slippery and pocked with potholes. I went down twice, scrambled to my feet, and stumbled forward. The dirt road widened slightly, and a short driveway to my right led to a double-wide. There was a pickup parked in the drive. I ran to the pickup and looked in the window. Keys in the ignition. Pineys are trusting people.

I jumped into the pickup, Carl scampered over me and sat in the passenger seat, and I turned the key. I backed it out to the dirt road, and the door to the double-wide opened and a big guy, more Wookiee than human being, filled the doorway. He had to be over seven feet, wearing a T-shirt and shorts, and he had hair *everywhere*.

He roared, there was a shotgun blast, and the windshield was peppered with birdshot that didn't completely penetrate.

"Eep," Carl said, eyes big and bugged out.

I whipped the truck around and took off down the dirt road in Sasquatch's broken-down heap that reeked of giant prehistoric wet dog. In seconds, I was able to turn onto pavement. I had no idea where I was. I didn't recognize anything. I was in a stolen truck with half a tank of gas, no identification, no credit cards, no money, and a monkey. I stuck to the paved road, and after ten miles, I came to an intersection with signs. The signs meant nothing to me, but just ahead I could see the glow of overhead lights to a parking lot. The lot was empty except for one car. The Subaru. Somehow I'd found the junk store.

I had the SUV keys in my jeans pocket. I swapped out the truck for the Subaru and laid down rubber, wasting no time getting the heck onto the Expressway. I called Diesel while I drove. No answer. Diesel was probably waiting for Flash and had no reception. I needed to go back and get Diesel. Crap. I really didn't want to do that. I was afraid I'd run into Wulf.

"What do you think I should do?" I asked Carl.

Carl didn't answer. Carl had discovered Super Mario stashed in the console and was beyond happy, eating his cereal and making Mario jump around.

I made a U-turn at the next interchange and headed back for Diesel. If I got to the pickup point and he wasn't standing there with the two ATVs, I'd turn around and not stop driving until I pulled into my apartment building parking lot.

My heart started skipping beats a quarter mile away.

I wanted Diesel to be waiting for me, unharmed. I wanted to get him in the car and make a safe retreat. And as far as I was concerned, Munch could stay in the wind forever. Vinnie would just have to deal with it. My rent was due, but better to be evicted than be dead . . . or even worse, be a Munch toy.

I was the only car on the road. I switched to my high beams and slowed to almost a crawl, looking for the dirt road, afraid I wouldn't recognize it. Fortunately, it wasn't an issue, because Diesel was at the edge of the road. He was standing hands on hips, mud splattered and wet through to his skin. I stopped, he opened the passenger-side door, and Carl gave him a thumbs-up.

"I get the feeling I missed something," Diesel said, shooing Carl into the backseat and sliding in next to me.

I gave him the short version of my evening adventures.

"Take me to the house," Diesel said.

"What, are you nuts? There's one road in and one road out. And there are homicidal maniacs there."

"I can only hope," Diesel said. "I need to catch Wulf by surprise, preferably with his back to a wall. I'm sure they'll abandon the house, but we might be able to get them in the process."

The only way I knew to find the house was to go back to the junk shop and retrace my route.

"This all looks the same to me," I said to Diesel. "If you hadn't been standing out in the open, I probably would never have found you."

Headlights swung onto the road in front of me, and a police cruiser passed me going in the opposite direction. I took the road the cruiser had just left, and *hooray*, there was the double-wide. No doubt the police had been responding to the stolen-truck report.

I felt kind of bad about taking Sasquatch's truck, but it wasn't far away, and I'd left it in good shape.

I swapped seats with Diesel, and he cut the lights and drove the muddy road in the dark. He parked the Subaru just short of the clearing, and we got out. Carl stayed in the Subaru with his game.

There were no cars in the yard. This meant I was relieved, and Diesel was unhappy. We crossed to the house and looked inside. It seemed empty.

"Are you going in?" I asked.

"Maybe." Diesel prowled the yard and found a large rock. "Get back," he said. "Stand by those trees."

He hefted the rock and pitched it through a front window. Seconds after the window shattered, the house was literally blown apart by an explosion.

"No need to go in," Diesel said.

"What the heck was that?"

"Motion bomb. Remember the Sky Social Club? Classic Wulf. He loves that crap." He took my hand and pulled me to the car. "We need to get out of here before the police and fire trucks clog the road."

"But the house is on fire!"

"It'll burn itself out. There's no wind, and the woods are wet from the rain. There's a large enough patch of cleared ground around the house, so the fire won't spread. I'm sure there's no one inside, and if there is, it's too late to help them."

We ran to the Subaru. Diesel opened the door and groaned. The SUV was full of monkeys. Six of them in all, plus Carl. They were all sitting in a row in the backseat. All but Carl were wearing hats.

"Get out," Diesel said.

The monkeys sat tight and exchanged nervous glances.

"I know you understand me," Diesel said.

I looked at the monkeys. "They must be Carl's friends."

"I don't care if they're members of Congress. They have to go."

"Carl *did* save my life," I said.

Diesel rammed himself behind the wheel. "I don't have time for this."

He drove into the clearing, turned the Subaru around, and drove out. He hooked a right at the end of the road and headed for the Expressway. We could see the flashing lights of emergency vehicles in our rearview mirror.

"We can leave the trailer and the ATVs here," he said. "I have to get out of these clothes. I'm starting to mildew."

We stopped on the way home and got four large pizzas and a six-pack of beer. Diesel parked the Subaru in my lot, then we all got out and trooped into my apartment building and into the elevator.

"I feel like I married into the Brady Bunch," Diesel said, monkeys hanging on to his pants legs.

I hit the button for the second floor and got my key out of my bag. "Last time you came to town, I ended up with a horse in this elevator. These things don't happen when you're not around."

"I don't believe that for a second," Diesel said.

I opened the door to my apartment, and we all rushed inside. Diesel put two pizza boxes on the floor for the monkeys, and we ate ours off the counter. Who says I'm not civilized? I just hoped my mother never found out about this.

Diesel ate an entire pizza and chugged two bottles of beer. He kicked his boots off in the hall and dropped his still-wet jeans on the floor.

"I need a shower," he said.

I was relieved to see he was wearing underwear and that his T-shirt covered almost all the good stuff.

"I could strip down further," Diesel said.

"Not in front of the monkeys."

He grinned, ruffled my hair, and sauntered off to the bathroom.

I cleaned up the monkey mess, sat them all in front of the television, and tuned to the Cartoon Network. I nibbled on one last piece of pizza and called Morelli.

"How's it going?" Morelli wanted to know.

"It's average. Stole a truck. Blew up a house. Brought seven monkeys home with me. And now I have a naked man in my shower."

"Yeah, same ol', same ol'," Morelli said.

"What's new with you?"

"Pulled a double homicide. Shoveled dog shit off old man Fratelli's lawn. Started drinking at three o'clock."

"I assume Anthony is still with you."

"He's like a boil on my ass."

I took a shower when Diesel was done. When I came out, he was in the kitchen. He'd removed all the monkey helmets and was studying them.

"I don't get it," he said. "It looks like a little antenna on the top, but I have no idea what it's supposed to do."

"Gail Scanlon rescued animals from labs. Hard to believe she would turn around and use them for experimentation."

"She was a woman living alone in a secluded area. She didn't have a phone. I don't think she had a gun. She kept intruders away with a piñata. If she had something Wulf wanted, like land or monkeys, she'd be an easy target."

"Why would Wulf want monkeys?"

"Don't know the answer to that."

"Wulf has Gail. Munch said they had her locked away and that she was serving a purpose."

"Maybe she's wearing a helmet," Diesel said. "What are we going to do with the monkeys?"

"They're watching television."

"They're used to living in a habitat without flush toilets, and you just fed them pizza. It's going to get ugly in here."

"You have a point. We need something temporary until we find Gail. We can't put them in a fenced yard because they'll climb out. If we call animal control, they'll put them in a cage."

"Maybe they'll put them in a *big* cage," Diesel said.

Carl glared at him and gave him the finger.

"Carl doesn't like that idea," I said.

"How do you know which one is Carl? They all look alike."

"Carl is wearing a collar."

"Maybe we should give Carl a credit card and let him find a hotel room," Diesel said.

"I have a better idea. I have a *genius* idea. We'll put them in Munch's house. He isn't living there."

"That's really rotten," Diesel said. "I wish I'd thought of it."

We put all the boxes of cereal, cookies, and crackers in a bag and led the monkeys out of my apartment and down the hall. We herded them into the elevator and into the Subaru and drove them across town. Diesel walked through Munch's house to make sure it wasn't being used, and then we turned the monkeys loose.

I gave Carl the bag of food. "This should last you until tomorrow morning. The television remote is on the coffee table in the living room. You're in charge. Everyone's housebroken, right?"

Carl looked around and scratched his armpit.

I could feel Diesel smiling behind me.

"I'm not coming back here," he said. "I'm never setting foot in this house again. And I'll swear on a Bible I didn't put these monkeys here."

Chapter
SEVENTEEN

The first thoughts in my head when I woke up were about Gail Scanlon and her monkeys. The next thoughts were about the big guy sprawled on top of me.

"Hey!" I said to Diesel.

"Mmmm."

"You're on top of me again."

"Life is good."

"It's *not* good. I can't breathe."

"If you couldn't breathe, you'd be dead."

"If you don't get off me, *you're* going to be dead."

Diesel rolled to the other side of the bed and settled in with a sigh.

"I'm going to take a shower and go check on the monkeys," I told him.

No answer. Diesel was already asleep.

A half hour later, I had my hair fluffed out and my eyelashes gunked up, and I was anxious to start my day. Diesel was still sleeping, so I called Lula while I drank my coffee.

"How are you feeling?" I asked Lula.

"I'm feeling fine, but I have a craving for another one of them breakfast sandwiches."

"I have to check on Munch's house on Crocker Street.

I could pick you up on the way, and we could stop somewhere."

"I'll be outside waiting for you."

I finished my coffee, took my bag from the hook in
the hall, and saw Munch's jacket still lying on the floor.
I remembered the grocery list I'd taken from the yellow pad and pulled the crumpled piece of paper out of
the jacket pocket. It was soggy but legible.

"Diesel!" I yelled. "Get out here."

Nothing. No sound of man getting out of bed.

I stomped into the bedroom and yelled at him up
close. "Diesel!"

"Jeez," he said. "Now what?"

"I ripped this page off a pad in Munch's house. So
much happened last night, I forgot about it. It looks like
a shopping list."

Diesel looked at the list. "Barium, rockets, HTPB."

"I have to go," I said. "I told Lula I'd pick her up."

Twenty minutes and ten traffic lights later, I pulled to
the curb in front of Lula's house and Lula got into the car.

"Why are you going to Munch's house?"

"I have groceries for the monkeys."

"Say what?"

"Long story short is we found some of Gail Scanlon's
monkeys yesterday, and we stashed them in Munch's
house."

"That's just wrong," Lula said. "They're gonna poop
all over."

"It was me or Munch."

"Okay, I could see that then."

After a fast-food drive-through experience and five
more traffic lights, I reached Crocker Street. I parked
in the alley and took a bag of what I hoped was appropriate monkey food to the back door. I opened the un-

locked door, we let ourselves in, and I set the bag on the kitchen counter.

"So far, so good," Lula said. "No monkey poop in the kitchen. No monkeys, either, for that matter."

I poked my head into the living room, where Carl was watching television.

"Where are the rest of the monkeys?" I asked him.

Carl put his hands over his ears and stared at the television.

I walked through the house, looking in all the rooms. No monkeys.

"Did someone take the monkeys?" I asked Carl.

Carl hopped off the couch, walked into the kitchen, and pointed to the pet hatch in the back door.

I was stunned. I'd forgotten about the hatch.

"The monkeys escaped," I said to Lula.

"How many monkeys we talking about?"

"Six."

Somewhere not far off, a woman's scream pierced the air.

"There's one monkey," Lula said.

I ran outside, and two doors down, a woman was standing in her backyard. I took a box of cookies from the grocery bag and went to investigate.

"Is something wrong?" I asked her.

"I opened the door to take the garbage out and a monkey ran into my house."

"Don't worry," Lula said. "That monkey escaped from Monkey Control, and we're here to catch the little bugger. Just step aside and we'll take care of this." Lula looked at me. "Go ahead. Go get the monkey."

"You aren't going to help?"

"Hell no. You know how I feel about monkeys."

I went into the house and found the monkey drinking out of the toilet bowl.

I held a cookie out to him. "Yum," I said.

The monkey's eyes got bright, and he followed me out of the house. I gave him two cookies and locked him in the Jeep.

"One down," I said to Lula.

We walked through the neighborhood rattling the cookie box, and we captured two more monkeys.

"These cookies are good," Lula said, her hand in the box. "It's no wonder monkeys come to get them."

"We've been around the block twice," I said as we completed another loop, "and we're still missing three monkeys."

"Maybe Gail won't notice," Lula said.

"That's not the point. I can't just let monkeys loose in Trenton."

"Why not? There's all kinds of crazy shit loose in Trenton."

We returned to the car, and a monkey was sitting on the hood looking in at the other monkeys. I gave him a cookie and added him to the collection. I retrieved Carl from Munch's house, set a box of Pop-Tarts on the floor as monkey bait, took the rest of the monkey food, and closed the door. We all piled into the Jeep, and I slowly drove down the alley and did a couple laps around the block. We didn't see the remaining two monkeys.

"My eyes are watering," Lula said. "These monkeys need some hygiene lessons. What are you gonna do with them, anyway?"

A monkey darted across the road. I stopped the car, grabbed the cookie box, and took off after him. I chased him for half a block and cornered him against a chain-link fence that ran along the button factory parking lot.

"Want a cookie?" I asked him.

He took the cookie and followed me back to the car. Do I know how to catch monkeys, or what?

"Now I'm only missing one monkey," I said.

"This is a nightmare. Next time, I'm the one chasing the monkey, because I'm not sitting in the monkey Jeep."

"I'm giving it one more try," I said. "I'm going back to Munch's house to see if my monkey bait worked."

"Monkey bait?"

"Pop-Tarts in Munch's kitchen."

I returned to the alley and parked the car. Lula, Carl, and I got out and went to the back door and looked in the kitchen. Sure enough, there was my monkey. I went in, confiscated what was left of the Pop-Tarts, and we all marched back to the car.

The car was locked.

"Did you lock the car?" I asked Lula.

"No way."

I looked inside. The key was in the ignition. The monkeys had somehow managed to lock the car.

"You got a problem," Lula said. "You better hope they don't drive away. Where's your extra key?"

"I don't have an extra key."

It was a little after ten. I called Diesel, but he didn't pick up. I could call a locksmith, break a window, or call Ranger. Since it was Ranger's car, the choice was obvious.

"I'm locked out of the Jeep," I told him. "The key is in the ignition, and the doors are locked."

"Where are you?"

"In the alley behind Munch's house on Crocker Street."

Ten minutes later, a black Rangeman SUV eased to a stop behind the Jeep. Ranger got out of the SUV, walked over to me, and looked in the Jeep.

"Babe," he said.

I blew out a sigh. I had five monkeys in the Jeep and two sitting on the roof.

Hal was left at the wheel of the Rangeman SUV, and I could see he was turning red, making an effort not to laugh. Hal is one of Ranger's younger guys. He keeps his blond hair cut short in a buzz cut, he has a personality like a St. Bernard puppy, and he's built like a stegosaurus.

Ranger's life is mostly made up of serious business, and it's not often you see Ranger laughing, but I guess a car full of monkeys was the tipping point because Ranger was smiling.

He took a key out of his pocket and opened the car door. "Do you want the two on the roof inside? Or do you want the five inside to get out of the car?"

"I want the two on the roof inside," I said.

I rattled the cookie box and threw it into the back-seat. Gail's monkey jumped into the car, and all the monkeys attacked the cookie box. Carl didn't want any part of it. Ranger had regained his calm, and I thought he was probably calculating the depreciation on his Jeep. Not that this was unusual. I'd done worse to his cars.

"I know I'm going to regret asking," Ranger said, "but where are you going with the monkeys?"

"I don't know. Originally, they were in a habitat in the Barrens, but Carl opened the door and they all escaped."

"Carl?"

"Eep," Carl said.

Ranger looked at Carl, and Carl gave him a thumbs-up.

"Anyway, a lot happened in between," I told Ranger, "but last night, Diesel and I were in the Barrens looking for Wulf and Martin Munch, and we ended up with all these monkeys in the car."

"Diesel's been driving these monkeys around?"

"More or less."

Ranger looked like he might burst out laughing again, but he squelched it.

"It's not like they're bad monkeys," I said. "It's just that I don't know what to do with them. Except for Carl, they belong to Gail Scanlon, but Wulf has her locked away somewhere. I can't bring them back to the habitat and leave them there all alone."

Ranger cut his eyes to the monkeys. They were fighting over the cookies, shoving them into their mouths, cookies flying everywhere.

"I can put a man at the habitat until this sorts itself out," Ranger said.

"I don't know if that's safe with Wulf prowling the Barrens."

"Wulf won't go after my man."

Ranger motioned to Hal. Hal left the SUV and approached the Jeep.

"You're going to follow me in the Jeep," Ranger said to Hal.

Hal's mouth dropped open and he went white.

"The Jeep's full of monkeys," Hal said.

Ranger clapped him on the back. "You'll be fine. Just don't touch the cookies."

We dropped Lula off at her house, and Hal followed behind in the Jeep.

"Hal looks terrified," I said to Ranger.

Ranger checked him out in the rearview mirror. "This is going to cost me. I'm going to have to give him hazard pay for this trip."

We took the Turnpike and the Atlantic City Expressway. We exited the Expressway, and Ranger wound his way around the Barrens to Gail Scanlon's compound. He drove the SUV into the habitat yard and parked. Hal parked behind him, and we all got out. Four monkeys had returned to the habitat and were huddled together on an outside table. They were still wearing their helmets.

"We took the helmets off the monkeys I had in the Jeep," I told Ranger. "We couldn't figure out why they were wearing them."

"Did Gail Scanlon put these helmets on?"

"I doubt it. I think it must have been Munch or Wulf."

Ranger approached the huddled monkeys, removed the helmets, and gave them to Hal.

"Put these in my SUV," he said. "If Wulf wants them back, he can talk to me."

We wrangled the remaining monkeys into the compound. We set food out and made sure there was fresh water. We closed and locked the door.

"Eep," Carl said, monkey fingers curled around the chain-link fence, looking out at me.

I opened the door, let Carl out, and relocked the door.

"He doesn't belong with the rest of the monkeys," I said to Ranger.

"No doubt," Ranger said.

We went into Gail Scanlon's house and took stock. It seemed exactly as I'd left it.

"I'm going to leave you here," Ranger said to Hal. "Make sure the monkeys have food and water. As soon as I get phone reception, I'll dispatch someone to bring in a couple days' supplies and communication."

Hal seemed okay with that. He was out of the monkey truck. Life was sweet again.

Ranger, Carl, and I left the compound. Ranger stopped when he got to the paved road.

"Do you want to look for Munch or Gail Scanlon?" Ranger asked.

"I wouldn't know where to begin. They're here some-where, but I have absolutely no direction. We did aerial surveillance and couldn't find anything." I pulled Gordo Bollo's file out of my bag. "This is the guy who threw the tomatoes at me. He lives in Bordentown, and since it's a weekend, he might be home. I'd love to catch him."

Ranger looked at the file and punched the address into his navigation system.

"What's the charge on this guy?"

"His ex-wife remarried, and I guess he had unre-solved marital issues because he ran over the new groom with his pickup truck, twice."

A half hour down the road, Carl was squirmy in the backseat.

"Puh," Carl said. "Puh, puh, puh."

Ranger's eyes flicked to Carl in the rearview mirror.

"Does he want to live?" Ranger asked.

"Eep," Carl said.

The nav system got us to Ward Street, and it didn't look any more promising this time than it had last time. A cemetery ran down one side, and on the other was scrub field and the ceramic pipe factory. Ranger drove the length of it, turned, and drove back. He stopped at the entrance to the cemetery.

"Babe, there aren't any houses here."

"Connie double-checked this address."

Ranger called in to his office and asked them to run Gordo Bollo. Minutes later, the same address came back.

"I'm sitting here, and there's no house," Ranger said. "It's a field next to a ceramic pipe factory. Go into the tax records and see who owns this land."

Ranger waited for the answer, and when it came, he disconnected.

"Gordo Bollo owns 656 Ward, but it's a lot. No house."

Diesel was at the dining room table with coffee and my computer when Carl and I walked in.

"Every time I call you for help, you don't answer your phone," I said. "Where were you this time? Peru? Madagascar?"

"I was in the shower. You didn't say to call back. I figured you were pulling on rubber gloves and decontaminating Munch's house."

"The monkeys all escaped through the pet door."

"There's a pet door?"

"Anyway, I found them and took them back to the habitat. Ranger has one of his men staying there until we find Gail."

"It looks like you didn't take them *all* back to the habitat."

"I guess Carl had enough of the nuts and berries thing. What are you doing on the computer?"

"HTPB stands for hydroxyl-terminated polybutadiene. It's a clear, thick liquid used for rocket fuel. APCP is ammonium perchlorate composite propellant, an oxidizing agent that helps burn the fuel. BlueBec rockets are sounding rockets. They're about eighteen feet in length, and they carry instruments designed to take measurements and perform experiments in the suborbital area of the Earth's atmosphere. They're Canadian made, and they've been around a long time. It would be fairly easy for Wulf to get his hands on some."

"Do you think this is what made the rocket tails we saw when we were in the Barrens?"

"No. I think we saw something smaller."

Diesel punched a number into his cell phone.

"I need a favor," he said to whoever was on the other end. "Eugene Scanlon was project manager at a research lab in Trenton, Brytlin Technologies. I need the names and addresses of everyone on his team."

Diesel shut down the computer and went to the kitchen for fresh coffee. "Your rat is awake," he said.

"He's a hamster."

"Whatever."

I gave Rex fresh water and dropped half a walnut and a baby carrot into his bowl.

"How will your contact get the names and addresses?"

"I don't know. He has ways. I imagine he'll hack into the company computer."

"That's illegal."

"You have a problem with that?"

"Just saying. Where will Wulf go to get the rocket fuel?"

"I'd guess whoever had the barium also had the ability to get the fuel components."

"Yeah, but Wulf blew one of those guys to smithereens."

Diesel answered his phone and wrote three names and addresses on the back of Munch's shopping list. He hung up and shoved the list into his pocket.

"I want to talk to these people."

"It would go faster if we divided them up. It's Sunday, and Gail has been missing since Thursday. We have no idea what Wulf intended to do with her, but it can't be good. Maybe we should bring the police in."

"Give me one more day. If Wulf learns the police are combing the Barrens, he'll pack up and leave. And he'll take Munch and Gail Scanlon with him . . . or worse. There were two other people working under Scanlon.

Lu Kim Rule and Vladimir Strunchek. The third name
I have is his supervisor. Barry Berman. Berman lives
in north Trenton, Rule lives not far from here on Becker,
and Strunchek was Eugene Scanlon's neighbor. You
take Rule, I'll talk to Berman, and we'll meet back here
and do Strunchek together."

The Subaru was in the parking lot, but the Jeep that
Ranger had loaned me was with Hal in the Barrens.

"Drive me to my parents' house," I said to Diesel. "I
can borrow my Great-Uncle Sandor's car."

When Sandor went into assisted living, he gave my
Grandma Mazur his car. Since Grandma has had her
license revoked, the behemoth '53 powder blue and
white Buick Roadmaster is mine to use in emergency
situations. It's not my favorite car, but it's free.

Diesel dropped me off, and I ran inside to get the
keys from my mother.

"What happened to *your* car?" my mother wanted to
know.

I didn't know where to begin. Was she talking about
the car that was destroyed by raccoons or the car that
was filled with monkeys?

"It's getting serviced," I said. "Oil change, spark
plugs, the works."

I grabbed a couple chocolate chip cookies from the
cookie jar and ran to the garage. I backed the Buick
out and hoped no one was green in the neighborhood.
The V-8 engine could be heard a block away, and the
trip down the driveway alone sucked up a quarter tank
of gas.

Lu Kim Rule lived less than a half mile away. It was
a solid working-class neighborhood with mom-and-pop
businesses mixed with two-story, residential row houses.
A kid answered the door and yelled *"Mom"* when I
asked for Lu Kim.

Lu Kim was slim and of mixed cultures, with al-
mond eyes and straight black hair. I introduced myself
and asked if I could talk to her about Eugene Scanlon.
Lu Kim stepped onto her porch and closed the door behind her.

"What do you want to know?"

"I'm looking for Martin Munch," I told her. "I think
he might be with Eugene's sister, and I think they might
be in the Pine Barrens. Did either Eugene or Martin
ever mention property in the Barrens?"

"No. They never mentioned property anywhere."

"Tell me about Martin Munch."

Lu Kim rolled her eyes. "Martin Munch. A brilliant
guy but creepy weird. I never had a conversation with
him that his eyes ever went above my breasts. And in
the two years we worked together, he never said anything that wasn't work related. It was as if he'd gotten
dropped from another planet."

"And Scanlon?"

"My job for the group was more clerical than scientific. Eugene gave me professional papers to file, ex-
pense reports, equipment requisitions, that sort of
thing, but he never talked to me. I worked for him for a
year before I found out he wasn't married. Mostly, Eugene talked to Martin. He thought Martin was the re-
incarnation of Einstein. He had his eye on everything
Martin did."

"Do you know why Munch stole the magnetometer?"

"I figured he just grabbed something and ran out of
the building. He wasn't exactly with the program all the
time. I'd find his coffee mug in the file cabinet. And
once he lost his car keys, and a week later I found them
in the freezer."

"What about the research the group was doing?"

"I wasn't involved in that end of things, but it seemed

like it was routine. We were subcontractors for a much larger project. It always looked to me like we were working with minutia, but I guess that's the way it is in the scientific community."

I left my card with Lu Kim and chugged home in the Buick. I pulled into my lot and looked for the Subaru. I wasn't surprised to find it missing. Even with Diesel rigging the traffic lights, he had a longer drive than I did. I parked and debated waiting in the lot for him. I checked my watch and thought about Carl. We'd left him alone in the apartment. It wasn't a big deal. We'd left him alone before. Still, I felt uneasy. I took the elevator to my floor. I plugged my key in, opened the door, and stepped inside.

I looked left and saw Carl on the kitchen counter, his back pressed against the hamster cage. Carl's eyes were huge, and his monkey fur was standing on end. I looked right and saw Wulf.

"It looks like my cousin has found a playmate," Wulf said. "Too bad I'm going to have to ruin his fun."

I turned and put my hand on the doorknob, but the door was locked and wouldn't open.

"Martin is very depressed," Wulf said. "He was looking forward to spending time with you, but you managed to escape, and he's been moping ever since. As it turns out, when Martin is depressed, he's not productive. And I need Martin to be productive. So you're going to have to come with me."

"I'm sure there are lots of women who would be overjoyed to spend time with Martin."

"Unfortunately, he wants you. And since I can't count on your cooperation, I'm going to have to scramble a few neurons."

"Is that the touchy, painful thing? I hate that."

Wulf reached out for me, and I jumped off into the

kitchen, grabbed the still-unwashed fry pan off the stove, and threw it at him. He batted it away, and I whacked him with the spatula. Still no expression on his face. He ripped the spatula out of my hand, grabbed my wrist, and it was good night. The last thing I heard was Carl.

"Eep!"

Chapter

EIGHTEEN

I came awake tired. Flat-out exhausted to the point of being barely able to breathe. Too tired to open my eyes. Someone was talking to me, but it sounded like they were underwater.

"Just let me sleep," I said.

"Steph!"

I opened my eyes and looked at Diesel.

"Are you okay?" he asked me.

"No. I feel like death. Where am I?"

"In your apartment."

"Oh yeah. I knew that."

I was stretched out on my bed, Carl was watching from the dresser, and Diesel had his hand wrapped around my wrist.

"What are you doing?" I asked him. "My wrist burns."

"I've got a cold pack on it," Diesel said.

He took his hand away, and I saw he'd been holding a facecloth filled with crushed ice on my wrist. Under the facecloth was a red welt in the shape of a hand. Wulf's hand.

"He burned me!"

Diesel put the ice pack back on my wrist. "It's not a bad burn. It'll fade in a couple weeks. Leave the ice on for a little while longer, and then rub some Bactine on the burn."

"I think I missed a chunk of action. The last thing I remember, I was in my kitchen, and Wulf zapped me. I'm getting fed up with the zapping thing. That was the third time. How does he do it?"

"It's not difficult. It's a parlor trick. Like bending spoons."

"Can you do it?"

"Yes. And you can, too, with a stun gun."

"How long was I out?"

"Probably ten to fifteen minutes. He had you over his shoulder like a sack of flour when I pulled into the parking lot. He dropped you when he saw me, and he vanished behind a flash of light. I have to admit, I don't know how he does the vanishing thing. It's new. I think it's a little over the top with the light and the smoke, but that's Wulf. He's always loved the dramatic."

"He said Munch was moping around, thinking about me, and wasn't productive, so he came to get me for Munch."

"That makes my skin crawl. I don't want you out of my sight until we resolve this."

"Oh great."

"You're supposed to be relieved because big bad Diesel is going to protect you."

"I appreciate the thought, but I like to think I can protect myself."

Diesel pulled me to my feet. "Don't get carried away with the strong female thing. Wulf isn't normal. And I don't know how to break this to you, but you have no self-defense skills beyond kicking a guy in the nuts."

I was standing, but I wasn't feeling especially stable. "I can't feel my legs," I said to Diesel.

"You'll come back faster if you walk around."

I took a step forward and went down to my knees. Diesel scooped me up and carried me to the foyer, with Carl scuttling behind him. Diesel shifted me to his shoulder, grabbed my bag, and opened the front door.

He looked down at Carl. "Stay here and keep away from the pay-per-view stations."

"If you'd give me a moment, I could walk on my own," I said.

"We don't have a moment. By the time we get to Strunchek, you'll be fine."

He carried me to the elevator, across the lot, and loaded me into the Subaru. I had feeling in my hands and feet, but my ass was pins and needles.

"What did you find out from Eugene's supervisor?" I asked Diesel.

He took the wheel and drove out of the lot. "Not much. He wouldn't talk about the project. Said Eugene never talked about property in the Barrens. He knew Eugene had a sister in Philadelphia and a sister some-where else, but that was all. He knew even less about Munch. He said Munch was brilliant but hard to keep focused. It sounded like Munch might have been on his way out. What about Lu Kim?"

"I got even less from her."

All traffic lights were green, so we made Strunchek's condo complex in record time. I swung my legs out of the Subaru and walked a few steps. My ass had stopped tingling, and everything seemed to be in working order.

Strunchek answered the door with a can of beer in his hand. He was in his midthirties, had badly cut brown hair, a body gone soft, and bloodshot blue eyes. I was guessing that before starting on the beer he'd done some preliminary weed.

"Getting ready for the ball game," he said. "What can I do you for?"

Diesel gave him a business card that just said DIESEL. Nothing else. Not even a phone number. Strunchek took the card and looked confused. Probably wondering what the heck DIESEL meant.

"We'd like to talk to you about Eugene Scanlon and Martin Munch," Diesel said.

"Martin Munch. It's always about Martin Munch. I hate him. The only good thing he ever did was break Scanlon's nose with his coffee mug."

Diesel and I exchanged glances and stepped inside.

"You want a beer?" Strunchek asked.

"Sure," Diesel said. "What's the deal with Munch?"

"Lousy prima donna. Boy genius. Big whoopitydo. We're supposed to be working on a sensor for the gizmo."

"Magnetometer?" Diesel asked.

"Yeah. I do all the grunt work, and Munch is all the hell all over the place. He's designing grids and he's researching wavestrengths. Has nothing to do with our end of the project. Our end of the project is too boring, too small for the boy genius."

Diesel took his beer and chugged it. "What about Scanlon? Didn't he keep Munch's feet to the fire?"

"Scanlon's loving it. Scanlon's encouraging Munch. And then, like this isn't insulting enough, all of a sudden only Scanlon can see Munch's research."

"Do you know what that research involved?" Diesel asked.

Strunchek gave Diesel another beer. "Not entirely. We were part of HAARP, and Munch was pulling in data from them. In the beginning, he was just looking at it, saying it was interesting, and then he got into it.

He was generating computer models of the power grid, and half the time I didn't know what the heck he was talking about. I'm an engineer. Munch is Fred MacMurray inventing flubber."

"Do you know what the fight was about between Scanlon and Munch?"

"I know this sounds crazy, but it was like they were arguing over a wolf. I only caught the end of it. It was after work hours, and I came back for my wallet. I'd got to the gas station and realized I left my wallet on my desk. I walked in and heard them yelling. I don't think they knew I was there. Scanlon said the land was his, and there was no place for the wolf. He said the wolf was overstepping his bounds and would ruin everything. He told Munch the wolf was out, and if Munch didn't like it, his runty little ass would be out of a job." Strunchek drained his beer can and got another. "That was when Munch clocked Scanlon with the coffee mug and left. Munch was sensitive about his runty little ass. You could call Munch an asshole and a whoremonger, but you didn't make cracks about his size."

"Do you know where Scanlon's land was located?" I asked Strunchek.

"No. That was the first I'd heard of it. I didn't talk to Scanlon any more than I had to. And he didn't show a lot of interest in talking to me."

"Munch was caught leaving with the magnetometer," Diesel said.

"Yeah, that was a lot of nerve. It was a prototype. It had the sensor in it that I redesigned."

"What about his computer?" Diesel asked. "Did he clean out his desk?"

"No. He never came back. Scanlon went through the desk and had the computer wiped clean."

"Thanks," Diesel said. "We appreciate your help."

"You sure you don't want to stay for the game? I got a lot more beer."

"Some other time," Diesel said.

We buckled ourselves into the Subaru, and Diesel made a phone call.

"I want to talk to someone about HAARP," he said. "I'll be back at the apartment in ten to fifteen minutes."

He disconnected and looked over at me. "I could get the information off the computer, but I'm Googled out and this will be faster."

Fifteen minutes later, we stepped out of the elevator and I saw a young guy standing in front of my door. He was cute, with brown hair that needed a cut, ratty sneakers, and baggy jeans. I put his age at twenty-five. No wedding band. Five inches shorter than Diesel.

He stared up at Diesel, smiled, and extended his hand. "Ivan. And you must be Diesel. I've heard a lot about you."

"This won't take long," Diesel said, opening my door, ushering Ivan into my apartment.

"No problem. I was in the area."

"Tell me about HAARP."

"HAARP stands for High-Frequency Active Auroral Research Program. The HAARP facility in Alaska has a high-frequency transmitter system that stimulates and controls ionospheric processes that alter the performance of communications systems. In other words, it transmits radio waves into the Earth's atmosphere to heat and temporarily modify the ionosphere. At least, in theory."

"Walk me through it," Diesel said.

"A signal is generated by a transmitter. The signal is delivered to an antenna array. In the case of the Alaskan station, there are one hundred and eighty antennae requiring thirty-six hundred kilowatts of transmitter power. The antenna array directs the signal into the atmosphere, where it's absorbed at an altitude between twenty to sixty miles. The ionosphere is heated, causing changes that can be measured with a magnetometer."

"What's the purpose?"

"It allows the scientific community to study atmospheric phenomena."

"Why would Wulf be interested?"

"The Chinese have been experimenting with generating Very Low Frequency Waves in the ionosphere, hoping to control weather. So far as I know, they haven't been very successful. If you could actually *create* weather, it would be worth something."

"What role would barium play in this?"

"I suppose if you seeded the ionosphere with barium, you could increase the cold plasma density and accelerate the process of manipulating atmospheric conditions."

"Like weather," Diesel said.

"Yeah. Like weather."

"Jeez," I said. "Do you think Wulf is making an Evil Weather Machine?"

Ivan looked over at me and smiled. "Civilians," he said. "You gotta love 'em."

Diesel grinned and tugged at my hair. "She makes a mean grilled cheese."

"Hey," Ivan said. "You don't want to underestimate a good grilled cheese."

Diesel opened the door for him. "Thanks for taking the time to talk to me. I appreciate it. This was helpful."

"Anytime," Ivan said.

Diesel closed the door, and I narrowed my eyes at him. "Grilled cheese?"

"Now what?"

"You could have said I was smart or brave or trustworthy."

"I was going to tell him you were hot, but I was afraid you'd think it was sexist and kick me in the nuts."

"Grilled cheese is sexist!"

"I don't suppose you want to make me some lunch. All this talk about grilled cheese is making me hungry."

"I'll only make you lunch because you're so pathetic."

I slapped together three peanut butter and olive sandwiches. I kept one and I gave one to Diesel and one to Carl.

"So is this a pity peanut butter sandwich?" Diesel asked.

"You have a problem with that?"

"Nope." He looked at his sandwich. "It's lumpy."

"It's the olives."

"No shit." He took a bite and sent me the smile with the dimples. "I like it. It's a sandwich with a sense of humor."

"Do you think Wulf is trying to control weather? Munch said Wulf was going to take over the world."

"Sounds ambitious." Diesel pulled the shopping list out of his pocket. "Ranger monitors the police bands. Ask him if WINK radio has had any transmitters stolen. I want to know how much of this list has been fulfilled. I'm going to the mall to see if I can find Solomon Cuddles. I'd like you to stay here and do some research on the list. See if you can identify local sources for the rockets and rocket fuel. Do *not* go out of the apartment. Do *not* let anyone in. If Wulf shows up, call me immediately, and keep your door locked."

"What if he *pops* in?"

"He can't *pop* in, but he's good with locks, so stay alert."

I called Ranger and asked him to check on the transmitter, and I looked in the Yellow Pages for rocket fuel. None listed. I called Ranger back and asked him where I'd find rocket fuel.

"Solomon Cuddles would be the underground source for anything out of the box, rocket fuel included. There are a couple chemical plants in the Bayonne area that might also produce the components. I can check for you. I have the answer to your transmitter question. WINK hasn't reported anything stolen. We called to double-check, and they said nothing had been stolen, but one of their transmitters was damaged by freak lightning last night, and it's being repaired."

"Thanks."

I couldn't remember hearing rain last night. And everything seemed dry when I went out this morning. I wouldn't have questioned the lightning strike, but the weather-control seed had been planted in my head.

I dialed Lula. "I want to check something out at WINK, and I don't want to go alone."

"You called the right person. I'm bored to death."

Chapter
NINETEEN

WINK was in a rattrap, cement bunker–type building in a part of the downtown business district that hadn't been included in the beautification package. The parking lot was surrounded by chain-link fence, the gate controlled by a security guard. There was a dish and a couple antennae on the roof and a sign on the front of the building telling people they were at WINK.

I parked the Buick at the curb across the street from the lot, and we sat there for a half hour watching the building.

"What are we doing?" Lula said.

"Watching."

"For what?"

"There's a flatbed truck backed up to the building at the far side of the parking lot. It looks like there's someone in the truck, behind the wheel, but I can't see him. Two men in khaki uniforms are walking from the truck to the building, doing something. I'm pretty sure they're supposed to be repairing a transmitter, but I think they might be stealing it."

"No way. How would you know that?"

I gave Lula the sanitized version of Wulf and the Evil

Weather Machine. And I told her about the shopping list.

"Double no way," she said.

I looked in my mirror and saw a black Rangeman SUV pull in behind me. Tank was at the wheel. I didn't recognize his partner. We all got out and stood hands on hips.

"Ranger saw you parked in front of the radio station and sent me to make sure everything is okay," Tank said.

"It was okay before you showed up," Lula said. "Now I'm not so sure. Do you still have those cats?"

"Yeah. You want to see pictures?"

Tank pulled his wallet out of his back pocket and showed us a picture of three cats sitting, looking at the camera.

"This one's Miss Kitty, and this is Suzy, and this is Applepuff."

"You're carrying around pictures of your cats?" Lula said. "You never had a picture of me in your wallet, and we were engaged."

"I have big news about Applepuff," Tank said. "I think she's pregnant. I'm going to have kittens!"

"Kittens! Are you prepared to have kittens? That's a responsibility. Does Ranger know about this? I have a mind to tell Ranger."

"I'm going to find good homes for them," Tank said.

Lula sneezed and farted. "See what you do to me. Get away from me. You're full of cat cooties."

"I can't get away," Tank said. "Ranger wants me to stay with Stephanie."

"You're too late," Lula said. "I'm already here. This could be a dangerous mission, and Stephanie needs me. And there's no car big enough for the both of us."

"There would be if you'd lay off the fried chicken," Tank said.

Tank's partner sucked in some air and took a step back.

Lula leaned forward. "Did you just say what I think you said?"

"No," Tank said. "I didn't say that. I don't know where that came from. You make me crazy. Look at me. I'm sweating. You scare the heck out of me."

"It's unnatural the way you sweat," Lula said. "You should have it looked into."

Tank's partner was making a big show of looking at his watch. "I should be getting back to Rangeman," he said. "I'm supposed to do something."

Tank turned to me. "Ranger wants Jim to bring the Buick back to your lot, and I'm supposed to drive you around."

Good deal. I had Tank to protect me from Wulf. I gave Jim the car keys, and Jim smiled wide.

"Cool car," he said. "I'll take real good care of it."

Men love the Buick. Truth is, it reminds me of Lula. A lot of rumble, you have to muscle it around, and it's got great big headlights.

The flatbed truck was still parked, and I hadn't seen the uniformed men in a while. I was beginning to worry I might be wrong. I mean, what are the chances that someone could actually control weather? Zero? And what are the chances that these uniformed guys were sent by Wulf to steal a radio-station transmitter? It was preposterous.

"You guys stay here and wait for me," I said to Tank and Lula. "I'm going inside to snoop around."

"I gotta go with you," Tank said. "Ranger will kill me if anything happens to you."

"Me, too," Lula said. "I'm sticking to you like glue."

"I'm going across the street to a radio station. Nothing's going to happen to me."

"I'll be real discreet," Tank said.

As discreet as a six-foot-six, no-neck guy weighing three hundred and fifty pounds, all dressed in black SWAT clothes, with a Glock holstered at his side could be.

"Me, too," Lula said. "I'll discreet your ass off."

Tank and I looked at her. She was wearing a traffic-stopping, orange fake fur jacket, a poison green spandex skirt that stopped just short of her ass, green ankle boots that matched the skirt, and her hair was sunflower yellow.

I allowed myself a small sigh of defeat, and I crossed the street with Tank and Lula on my heels. I pushed through the front door into a small, dark lobby with a tattered rug and sad, worn-out furniture. No money in radio, I thought. A woman behind a receptionist desk focused on us.

"Can I help you?" she said.

"I'm from the *Trenton Times*," I said. "We're doing a feature story on WINK, and I'm doing some preliminary work, scouting out a front-page photo op."

"I didn't hear anything about it," she said. "You're not on my schedule."

"Well, how about us?" Lula said. "Are we on your schedule?"

"Who are you?"

"I'm Lula. Who the heck do you think? And this here's Tank."

The woman scanned her list of names.

"Jelly bean counting contest," I told the receptionist. "They're part of the photo shoot."

Lula sneezed and farted. "Excuse me," she said to the receptionist. "It's not my fault. I'm allergic to the *cat lady* here."

"That's mean," Tank said. "Men can have cats, too. Cats guarded royal houses back in Egypt."

"If they guarded my house, I'd be dead," Lula said. "I'd sneeze myself into the grave. And a lot you care. You picked a *cat* over *me*."

"It was one of those fate things," Tank said. "It's just these cats came along. It wasn't like I was looking for them."

"I should have known. Right from the beginning, Miss Gloria said our moons were incompatible."

The receptionist perked up at that. "I know Miss Gloria. Miss Gloria does my charts."

"Get out," Lula said. "Don't you love her? You couldn't live without her, right?"

"I don't make a move without Miss Gloria's say-so. One time, I was driving to work, and I was on the phone with her, and she told me I was gonna be in an accident, and next thing you know, I rear-ended a guy."

"That's scary amazin'," Lula said.

"I thought we might want a shot of the behind-the-scenes workings of a radio station," I said to the receptionist. "Where's your transmitter?"

"They're down that hallway all the way, and to the right, and out the door, but there are people working on the main. We're on backup right now."

"I never saw a radio-station transmitter before," Lula said. And she took off down the hall, opening doors, looking inside the rooms.

"You can't do that!" the receptionist yelled after Lula.

"I'll go get her," I said. "She's just excited. Miss Gloria told her this was going to be her big break."

"Is that a real gun?" the receptionist asked Tank. "You can't bring a gun in here."

"Bean counters don't carry real guns," I said. "They shoot blanks."

"Do you want to see a picture of my cats?" Tank asked the receptionist. "I'm pretty sure Applepuff is pregnant."

Lula got to the end of the hall and waved at me to follow. I ran after Lula, and Tank stayed behind to show the receptionist his cats. Lula and I pushed through the door marked NO ADMITTANCE and found the two uniformed men winching a huge machine onto the flatbed.

"Is that a transmitter?" I asked them.

"No hablo ingles," the one man said.

The flatbed engine cranked over, and the truck idled while the two men strapped the machine down and secured clamps.

"They're taking off with the transmitter," I said to Lula. "We need to get Tank. We need to follow them."

Lula and I ran down the hall, snagged Tank, and we all ran across the street and jumped into the Rangeman SUV. The flatbed swung around in the lot and rolled to the gate. The gate opened, and the truck made a wide turn onto the street. The driver of the truck looked directly at me when he made the turn. His eyes went wide, and red spots instantly appeared on his cheeks. It was Munch.

"That's Munch!" I said. "That's my man."

Munch put his foot to the floor and the flatbed took off down the street. Tank was close behind. Lula was in the backseat with her head out the window and her Glock in her hand.

"Pull alongside him!" Lula yelled. "I'll shoot out his tires. I'll bust a cap up his ass."

"Got it," Tank said, easing up beside the truck on a two-lane city street.

"Drop back!" I told him. "You'll get us killed."

Munch swerved away from the SUV and took out three parked cars and a light post. The flatbed surged ahead, jumped the curb, and cut a corner, sending two people screaming into a Starbucks.

"The little guy at the wheel can't drive," Tank said. "He's all over the road."

"You're scaring him," I said. "Back off."

"Don't listen to her," Lula said. "I got this bad boy in my sights."

Lula squeezed off two rounds and shattered the rear window of a parked car. The flatbed ran a light, and cars swerved to avoid it, horns blaring. Tank slowed and crept through the intersection. Six people gave him the finger.

"He's heading for Broad," I said to Tank. "He's going to the Pine Barrens."

Tank turned onto Broad with the flatbed in sight. Several cars were between us and the truck. The flatbed took the orange light at Hamilton, and everyone behind him stopped for the red.

"Don't you have no flashy lights or anything?" Lula asked Tank. "Aren't we an emergency vehicle?"

"Ranger doesn't let us use them," Tank said.

"Ranger this and Ranger that," Lula said. "Don't none of you people think for yourself? I bet you can't wipe yourself without Ranger telling you."

Tank looked at her in the rearview mirror. "I'm telling him you said that."

"I might have misspoke," Lula said.

We couldn't see the truck anymore, but we could measure its progress by the destruction on the side of the road. Four more trashed cars, a flattened mailbox, two demolished street signs.

We reached Bordentown and approached the Turnpike entrance.

"I haven't seen any wrecked cars for over a mile now," Lula said. "Do you think he took another road?"

"Maybe he's learning how to drive his rig," Tank said. "What should I do here?"

"Take the Turnpike," I told him.

It was a gamble. There were three main roads going south from Bordentown. The Turnpike was the fastest. Tank took the Turnpike south, and after a few miles, I was feeling insecure. The road stretched like an endless ribbon in front of us, and I didn't see the flatbed. We passed Burlington and Cherry Hill and came to the Atlantic City Expressway exit.

"Now what?" Tank asked.

"Take the exit to Atlantic City," I told him. "We've gone this far. We might as well look around the Marbury area."

This was depressing. I'd come so close to capturing Munch, only to have him slip through my fingers. A whole bunch of *what ifs* was running through my head. What if I'd gone out and looked at the driver when the truck was idling at the radio station? What if I'd called Ranger for help with the car chase? What if I was smarter, faster, braver, thinner . . . It was endless.

Tank drove through Marbury and doubled back along the road to the gift shop. He passed the gift shop and went north on a secondary road. It was a two-lane, blacktop road running through pinewoods, dotted here and there with small ranch houses. Every house had a mailbox set at the edge of the road. Single-lane gravel and dirt roads shot off the blacktop road into the outback of the Barrens.

Tank stopped the SUV, and we all stared at the dirt road and pale green bungalow in front of us. The mailbox to the bungalow was demolished and heavy-tread tire tracks were cut deep into the bungalow's front yard. The tire tracks ran over the smashed mailbox and swung onto the single-lane road, where they almost entirely disappeared on the hard-packed dirt.

"Bingo," Lula said.

Tank turned onto the dirt road and followed it through the forest for almost a mile into a cleared area that reminded me of a small landing strip for a plane. The flatbed was parked in front of us, but it was missing the transmitter, Munch, and his uniformed crew.

A rutted path large enough for an ATV led into the woods at the end of the cleared strip. Tank drove to the path, and we got out to take a look.

"I can't get the SUV down this path," Tank said. "Do you want me to walk it to see where it goes?"

"We'll all walk it," I said.

I had no desire to lag behind and run up against Wulf all by my lonesome. I still had his hand imprinted on my wrist. Call me chickenshit, but if I came across Wulf, I wanted to be hiding behind Tank.

Tank led the way and Lula and I followed. It was twilight, and Tank had taken a flashlight from the SUV. The path obviously served a purpose, because the scrub had been worn away at the edge and there were some recently broken branches kicked to the side. We trudged through a thick stand of pines and stepped into a woodland fuel depot. There were rows of tanks that were the size you might use for a gas grill. Neatly placed in front of the tanks were some steel drums. Maybe twenty feet away, stacked like cordwood under the roof of a three-sided shed, were rockets. Not BlueBec. These were smaller. From what Diesel had told me, I knew the BlueBecs were about eighteen feet long. These were closer to six and narrower in diameter.

"You could have a barbecue here," Lula said. "Only thing missing is the ribs."

It would seem logical that if fuel and some rockets were here, then the command center and Gail and Munch shouldn't be far away. Problem was, there were no other paths. And no buildings. There was only one way in to the tank farm, and we'd just walked it. Beyond the flatbed and what looked like a landing strip, there were no roads, no buildings, no ATV trails.

Tank tipped his head back and looked at one of the pines by the shed. "There's a camera stuck into that tree," he said. "This area is under surveillance." He looked around. "There are two more cameras that I can see."

Total panic attack. I felt like someone was squeezing my heart. "We have to get out of here."

"Only one way to go," Tank said.

We turned and started to head out, and four ATVs driven by guys in khaki uniforms powered in at us.

"Am I getting punked?" Lula said. "Is this real? This shit don't happen in real life."

My eyes were rolling around in my head, looking for an escape route.

"Through the woods," Tank said, grabbing my hand, shoving Lula.

"Stop!" one of the men shouted. "Stop, or I'll shoot." And he fired off a couple rounds.

"Damn," Lula said. "Those are real bullets." She pulled her Glock out of her bag and fired back. Her round missed the guy in the uniform and zinged into one of the tanks. The cylinder exploded into a fireball and flew forty feet into the air. It hit the ground and ignited every other cylinder and steel drum. Cylinders were shooting into the air like firecrackers, and the fire spread to the rockets. It was the Fourth of July, Chinese New Year, and Armageddon.

"Oops," Lula said. "My bad."

"Run!" Tank yelled in my ear. "Now! Run back to the SUV."

Lula and I took off, and Tank ran behind us. I went down twice, and Tank dragged me to my feet. Lula never once went down. Lula was haulin' ass. We had the SUV in sight when there was a sound like *whoosh*, and *BANG*—the SUV was toast.

"Rocket," Tank said. "Ranger's gonna hate this."

We turned and ran through the woods, keeping the dirt road in sight, heading for the paved road. A pickup barreled down the dirt road. The back of the pickup was filled with guys in the khaki uniforms. We crouched low until they were past, and then we ran some more. We were almost to the road when lightning cut across the sky, and it started to rain. A mist at first, and then, within minutes, we were in the middle of a torrential downpour.

"I'm gonna drown," Lula said. "I've never been in a rain like this. This is unnatural."

Headlights appeared on the dirt road, an SUV going slow in the rain, sliding on the road that was fast turning to mud. Tank recognized it first. It was Hal in Ranger's Jeep Cherokee.

We stumbled out of the woods and climbed into the Jeep.

"Get us out of here," Tank said to Hal. "Fast."

Hal threw the Jeep into reverse and ground his way through the mud to the pavement. It probably only took him five minutes, but it was the longest five minutes I could remember. My heart was pounding in my chest, and I couldn't breathe. I was in the backseat with Lula, and I had a death grip on the sleeve of her soaking-wet, fake fur jacket. Lula was rigid alongside me, breathing like a freight train.

The instant we were on pavement, the rain stopped. We looked back into the pine forest, and it was still raining, the rain dampening the thick, black smoke rising from the fuel depot and Ranger's Cherokee.

"I swear," Hal said, "this place is like the Bermuda Triangle. It's friggin' spooky. I went out to feed the monkeys last night, and I saw the Easter Bunny walking down the road with Sasquatch. And now there are rockets shooting into the sky from nowhere."

"Don't think you'll be seeing any more rockets anytime soon," Lula said.

"What were you doing on that road?" Tank asked Hal.

"The control room followed your blip to the Barrens and saw you parked. They told me to take a look and make sure everything was okay. I'm a couple miles away babysitting monkeys."

"I knew I smelled monkey," Lula said. "Now I recognize this car."

Chapter

TWENTY

I stood in front of my door and said a prayer. Please, God, don't let Diesel be home yet. I held my breath, opened the door, and looked up at Diesel. Darn.

Diesel grabbed the front of my wet jacket, hauled me inside, and held me three inches off the floor in front of him.

"I told you not to go out," he said, giving me a shake for emphasis. "I told you to keep the door locked."

"You were worried about me," I said.

"Yes. And I'm not used to worrying at that level. I had to take some of your Pepto-Bismol. I was feeling like the fire farter."

He set me down and looked at me. "You're wet again. And you smell like campfire."

I sniffed at my jacket. "I think it's rocket fuel. Lula accidentally blew up Wulf's fuel depot. At least, I'm pretty sure that's what it was. And then it rained on us, which was a good thing because it probably put out the fire. Otherwise, the whole Barrens would have gone up in smoke." I dropped my jacket on the floor and kicked my shoes off. "Did you find Cuddles?"

"Yes. And Wulf hasn't completed the deal with him

yet. I'm waiting for Cuddles to call me back and let me know when the meeting will take place."

"Bad news. Being that we blew up all Wulf's rockets, he might not be needing barium anytime soon. Although, it's possible the rockets we blew up weren't the barium carriers."

"Anything else I should know?"

"Munch has his transmitter. And he absolutely can't drive a truck."

"Have you eaten dinner?" Diesel asked me. "Do you want a grilled-cheese sandwich?"

"Yes."

"Make one for me, too," he said. "Do you have bacon? I want bacon on mine."

"Nice try, but no. And I don't have bacon."

I squished to the bedroom, took a quick shower, and dressed in dry clothes. I took the laundry basket from my closet, put my wet clothes in it, and carried it to the foyer. There was a huge pile of damp, discarded clothes in the foyer. Part mine. Part Diesel's. I needed to do laundry.

I left the basket by the door and went to the kitchen and watched Diesel. He was making grilled cheese. He slid one out of the pan onto a plate and handed it to me.

"Thanks," I said. "This looks great."

My cell phone rang, and I looked at the screen.

"It's all zeros," I said to Diesel.

"It's Wulf," Diesel said.

"Ms. Plum," Wulf said. "It has been brought to my attention that you were responsible for a fire that destroyed twenty-three of my X-12 King rockets. I'm afraid I must demand that you replace them in twenty-four hours, or I will have to sacrifice Gail Scanlon."

"Sacrifice?"

"I'm sure you are familiar with the term. You may call this number when you are ready to deliver my rockets."

"It was all zeros."

"Just do it," Wulf said. And he disconnected.

"Boy, he's kind of cranky," I said to Diesel.

"He's not used to having his rockets blown up."

I ate some of my sandwich. "He said they were X-12 King rockets, and I had to replace them by this time tomorrow, or he'd kill Gail. Where am I going to get twenty-three rockets?"

Diesel finished his sandwich.

"Cuddles might have a source. We'll hit the mall first thing tomorrow. If the mall is open, Cuddles is there. Turns out he's not too crazy about Mrs. Cuddles. Likes to spend as much time as possible at the office."

Since the mall didn't open until ten o'clock, I took the luxury of sleeping late. I straggled into the kitchen at nine-thirty A.M., ate a strawberry Pop-Tart, and polished off a mug of coffee. Diesel was already up, slouched against the counter, watching.

"Ready to rock and roll?" he asked.

I put my coffee mug in the dishwasher, went to the foyer to grab my bag, and realized I didn't have any clean sweatshirts. My denim jacket was in the laundry basket soaking wet. Munch's jacket was in the laundry basket. My only remaining jacket was a black wool peacoat.

"What?" Diesel said.

"I haven't got a sweatshirt to wear."

His backpack was sitting on the floor in the foyer. He pulled a black sweatshirt out of the pack and tugged the sweatshirt over my head. I had an extra six inches on the sleeves, and the bottom of the sweatshirt almost came to my knees. Diesel pushed the sleeves up to my elbows.

"Perfect," he said. "Let's go to the mall."

A half hour later, we found Cuddles in the food court sucking down a chocolate milk shake. He was in his fifties, average height, glasses, extra-curly brown hair that blossomed out in a white man's Afro. Bald on top. Baggy tan pants. Red plaid shirt. He was the last person in the mall I'd pick out to be selling contraband rockets and barium. He looked like Woody Allen all swollen up.

Diesel and I sat down at Cuddles's table, and Cuddles didn't look happy to see us.

"This table is for paying customers," Cuddles said.

"We might be paying," Diesel told him.

"Oh?"

"We need some X-12 King rockets."

"You and everybody else. Those are very popular rockets. Very versatile. How many?"

"Twenty-three," Diesel said.

Cuddles worked his straw around, trying to get the last dregs of milk shake into his gut. "How soon?"

"Now."

"Hah, that's funny. It'll take a week, minimum."

"I haven't got a week," Diesel said. "Where do I go to get them now?"

"How about Canada?"

"Do you remember the conversation we had earlier today?"

"The one about breaking every bone in my body and then sucking my fat out with a Shop-Vac and shoving it up my ass?"

"Yeah, that one."

"Eeuw," I said.

"Brytlin Technologies might have some Kings. They design some of the payload for the BlueBec sounding rocket, and the King is essentially a miniature Blue-Bec. It can be used to do more economical preliminary testing."

Diesel stood. "You're going to call me when you hear from Wulf."

"Yes."

I didn't say anything until we got back to the Subaru. I buckled myself in and looked at Diesel.

"Suck his fat out with a Shop-Vac and shove it up his ass?"

"It was one of those inspired thoughts."

"How are we going to get the rockets from Brytlin?" I asked Diesel. "It's Monday morning. It's not like we can waltz in and buy them."

"We're not going to buy them."

I felt my eyebrows go up to my hairline. "Oh no. No, no, no. I'm not going to steal rockets. And the whole place is on camera. Remember when Munch left with the magnetometer, and they got him on tape?"

"Don't worry. I have a plan."

"Oh boy. A plan."

Diesel cruised the mall lot. "The first thing we have to do is steal a car."

"What?"

"The Subaru can be traced to Flash, so we don't want to park it in the Brytlin lot." He pulled in next to an old Econoline van. "This'll work. It'll be easy to load the rockets into this."

"We're going to jail," I said. "I'm going to have to use one of those steel toilets without a seat."

Diesel was out of the Subaru. "I wouldn't let that

happen," he said. "I'd make sure you got a good toilet." He opened the driver's side door, got behind the wheel, and turned the engine over.

"How did you do that?" I asked him.

"They left the key in the ignition. Get in."

I moped around to the passenger seat. "I'm going to be really mad at you if I get arrested."

"It could be worse," Diesel said. "You could be Gail Scanlon."

I looked at the ignition. No key.

"There's no key in the ignition," I said. "How did you start the van?"

Diesel held his finger up.

"You started the car with your finger?"

"Yep. And that's nothing. You should see what this finger can do on a G-spot."

"Good grief."

Diesel backed out of the parking space and took the exit to Route 1. "Put the hood up on the sweatshirt and pull the drawstring tight so no one can see your face."

"What about you?"

"I don't photograph."

"How is that possible?"

"I don't know. It's just one of those weird things."

"Like your finger?"

"Sweetie, my finger isn't *weird*. It's *magic*."

Brytlin occupies a seven-acre campus just off Route 1 and is centrally located in a sprawling corridor of technology companies. Diesel wound his way through the parking lots, looking at the redbrick buildings, scoping it all out.

"Ordnance wouldn't be kept in the main office building," he said. "They have two buildings on the perimeter of their campus that look to me like maintenance facilities. I'm guessing our rockets are kept in one of them."

Both buildings had a regular door in the front and garage doors in the rear. Diesel backed the van up to one of the garage doors.

"Stay here," he said. "I'll be right back."

"Are you insane? You can't just walk in and steal rockets during business hours!"

"No one's over here."

"Yeah, but there could be someone inside."

"Then I'll deal with it."

He opened a garage door, slipped into the building, and minutes later, he reappeared with an armful of rockets. I jumped out of the van and opened the back door for him. He slid the rockets into the van and ran back for more. He loaded a total of twelve rockets into the van and closed the garage door.

"That's all they had," he said. "Get in the van. I'm going to check out the other building." Diesel drove to the other building, parked, ran inside, and instantly returned. "Just lawn mowers and snowblowers in there."

We returned to Route 1, and Diesel called Flash.

"I'm looking for eleven X-12 King rockets. See if any of the research labs on the tech corridor bordering Princeton have anything. If you can't find any there, try north Jersey."

Diesel drove the van back to the mall, and immediately we saw the flashing lights. A single cop car was parked in the lane behind Diesel's Subaru. We were two lanes over, and we could see a scruffy young guy talking to a cop, gesturing to the empty parking space where his van used to be parked.

Diesel slid from behind the wheel. "Drive the van to the other side of the mall by the food court. I'll get the Subaru and meet you there."

I climbed behind the wheel and drove to the food court entrance. I found a parking spot with an empty space next to it and parked the van but left it at idle. If I turned it off, I wouldn't be able to get it back on without Diesel. I tied the hood tighter around my face and gripped the wheel. It wouldn't be an exaggeration to say that at any moment I might throw up. I was sitting in a hot van with twelve stolen rockets.

A few minutes later, Diesel eased the Subaru into the spot next to the van. We transferred the rockets from the van to the Subaru, cut the engine on the van, locked its doors, and drove away in the Subaru. The perfect crime.

"Are you okay?" Diesel asked me.

"Sure. I'm peachy. And you?"

"I'm good."

He stopped the SUV at the edge of the lot, untied the hood, and pushed it back off my face.

"You look like you're going to faint," he said. "Your face is white and your eyes are glassy."

"I've never stolen rockets before. I'm pretty sure it's against the law. And what if they explode?"

"They aren't going to explode. They're just shells. No fuel. No payload. No explosive device."

We sat for a few more minutes, waiting to hear back from Flash. When the call came in, it was negative. He hadn't been able to locate any companies that might have X-12 Kings.

"Call Wulf back and tell him you have his rockets," Diesel said.

I punched Wulf's callback, and he answered on the first ring.

"I have your rockets," I said. "Now what?"

"Do you have all twenty-three?"

"No. I could only find twelve."

Silence.

"This is as good as it's going to get," I said. "There are no more in the area."

"There's an envelope in locker 2712 at the train station. Get the envelope and read the instructions."

"Do I need a key?"

"No. You need Diesel to open the locker."

The Trenton train station is to the south of center city. As with most of Trenton, it's a mixed neighborhood where busy commuters can mingle with hookers and muggers and various interesting bag people. It was just past noon, and traffic was slow around the station.

Rather than chance sitting in short-term parking with a car full of rockets, Diesel had me drive around the block while he ran into the station and retrieved the instructions. I picked him up after two laps, and I drove us to Cluck-in-a-Bucket. We got a bucket of extra-crispy, extra-spicy fried chicken and opened the envelope.

The first instruction was that Diesel was not allowed to participate, that I had to run through the directions without him. I would be directed to five different locations and closely watched. The fifth location would be the drop where I would exchange the rockets for Gail Scanlon.

"I know Wulf. He doesn't care about the rockets," Diesel said. "This is a way to get you. He's going to lead you around, and in the end, you're going to have to deliver the rockets to him. And when you deliver the rockets, he's going to turn you over to Munch."

"Do you think he'll really kill Gail if I don't cooperate?"

"Hard to say. Wulf doesn't usually kill innocent people, but he'll kill if it's justified in his mind."

"Is there a way you can watch me without Wulf detecting you?"

"No. I flunked invisibility."

"I'll be okay until I get to the fifth location. I'll take Lula with me, since he didn't say anything about Lula. And I'll use the Buick, so Ranger can track me. I can keep in phone contact with you. And we can reevaluate after the fourth location."

Diesel dumped his half-eaten chicken breast back into the bucket, wiped his hands on his jeans, and cranked the engine.

"Let's get this over with," he said. "It's ruining my appetite."

Chapter
TWENTY-ONE

I had the twelve rockets rammed into the Buick's trunk. Problem was, they didn't entirely fit.

"Should I tie a red flag on one of them?" I asked Diesel. "I don't want to get stopped by the police."

"You need more than a red flag. You've got stolen rockets hanging out of the back of a Buick. We need to wrap them."

Ten minutes later, I had the rockets wrapped in my only quilt.

"I've got an open line to Rangeman control room," Diesel said. "And I've got another line open for you. I'll be on the road, following you from a safe distance."

Lula's Firebird swung into my lot and parked next to the Buick.

"Is that the rockets all wrapped up in the quilt?" Lula asked. "That's real pretty. No one would guess they're rockets."

That was true. Most people would guess dead body. Lula and I got into the Buick, and I drove out of my lot to Hamilton.

"I'm supposed to go to the corner of Broad and Third to get directions," I told Lula.

"I know that block. The corner of Broad and Third is a 7-Eleven."

I turned onto Broad, and two blocks later, I was at the 7-Eleven on Third. A man in a khaki uniform was waiting in the lot. I pulled up to him and identified myself. He looked in the Buick, then he gave me another envelope.

"I need one of them big pretzels and a drink," Lula said. "You want anything?"

"No."

"Just park over there by the post," Lula said. "I'll only be a minute."

"I don't think I fit in that spot."

"Sure you do. Back up real slow."

A '53 Buick is a whale. There's no real beginning and no end. It's like parking a giant sub sandwich. I inched back and *crunch*.

"Uh-oh," Lula said, turning in her seat, looking out the rear window. "I think you dented one of Mr. Wulf's rockets. Maybe you need to pull forward a little. Do you want me to go around and take a look?"

"No! I want you to get your pretzel so we can get on with it."

I called Diesel and told him the next address. It was a motel on the outskirts of Bordentown.

"He's taking you south," Diesel said. "He's going to bring you to the Barrens."

"Okay," Lula said, back in the Buick with her drink and her pretzel. "I'm ready to go. You always need food like this on a road trip."

"This isn't a road trip," I told her. "We're ransoming Gail Scanlon from a scary maniac."

"Yeah, but I need to keep my strength up in case we need to kick ass."

Another uniformed man was waiting for me at the

motel. He got into the back of the Buick and directed me to a light industrial park just off Interstate 295. I couldn't call Diesel, but I knew I was a blip on Ranger's screen, and I suspected Diesel was close. I wound through the industrial park to a warehouse. A bay door rolled up, and I was told to drive in.

"I don't think so," Lula said to the guy in the backseat. "We don't do none of this drive into a warehouse shit. Someone wants to see us, they gonna have to come out."

The uniform got on his phone and relayed the message. There was an entire conversation in Spanish. A man peeked out from the warehouse, looked us over, and retreated. More Spanish. Finally, a shiny black van pulled out of the warehouse and drove up next to us.

Four men got out of the black van, removed the rockets from the Buick, and loaded them into the van.

"This was easy," Lula said to me. "We didn't have to worry after all. We didn't even have to go to all five locations. I might need to get another pretzel on the way home."

I wasn't that optimistic. I saw five uniformed guys with guns strapped to their sides. Two of them had assault rifles hanging on their shoulders.

"Now you will get out," the one uniform said to me.

"No way," Lula said. "You got your rockets. We're gonna go get more pretzels now."

Everyone aimed a sidearm at me.

"Okay," Lula said. "We don't need more pretzels, anyway."

"You can stay with this car," the uniform said to Lula. "This other one will go with us."

Okay, I said to myself, so I go with these guys, they take me to the Pine Barrens, and Wulf gives me over to Martin Munch. How bad could it be? He probably isn't operating at peak efficiency after that shot I gave him in the nuts. Maybe he'd be happy watching *Star Trek* reruns. Maybe he's just lonely.

"It's okay," I said to Lula. "I'll be fine. Take the Buick back to my apartment."

I was guided into the back of the van and sat between two of the armed men. No one spoke for the duration of the ride. There were no side windows. No windows in the rear doors. It was difficult to see the route through the windshield from where I sat. Once we were in the Barrens, it was all trees.

The ugly truth is that I've had my share of terrible moments since I've become a bounty hunter. I've managed to survive them, and while I wish none of them had ever happened, I have to admit there are things I've learned. I've learned that one of my best traits is that I'm resilient. And I've learned that fear is a normal reaction to danger. And I know for certain that panic is the enemy. So I sat in the truck and I tried to keep it together.

I felt the road change from smooth pavement to rutted dirt. Occasionally, I would hear the scrape of brush on the side of the van. I checked my watch. We'd been on the dirt road for ten minutes. The van took a right turn, and after a couple minutes, we entered a cleared area and stopped.

We all got out of the van, and I looked around. The clearing was small. Nothing that would attract attention from aerial surveillance. A crude, one-story, cinderblock building had been erected at the edge of the clearing. Maybe 1,500 square feet. The size of my apartment. It looked like new construction. Nothing fancy. Utilitarian windows and doors. Tin roof. Single metal pipe chimney sticking up out of the roof. The land around the building was raw. No grass, no flowers, no shrubs to soften the landscape. Gravel had been dumped and graded to make a drive court and walkway to the building.

"What is this?" I asked one of the uniforms.

"House," he said.

Kind of grim for a house, I thought. The Easter Bunny's trailer was more appealing than this.

A black SUV with dark tinted windows drove into the clearing and parked behind the van. Wulf and Munch got out and made their way over to me. Wulf was wearing Armani black, dressed more for Monaco than the Pine Barrens. Munch was wearing jeans with the cuffs turned up and a *Star Trek* shirt.

Munch was practically vibrating with excitement. Wulf, as always, showed no emotion. His face was as cool and smooth as alabaster, his eyes were obsidian.

"We will try this one more time," Wulf said to me. "I've brought you here so you can be nice to Martin. If you kick him, bite him, spit on him, or break his nose, you will answer to me. Do you understand?"

"Yes."

"Take her into the house," Wulf said to the uniform standing next to me. "Restrain her and leave two men to watch the house." He turned to Munch. "We have everything we need to go forward."

"We don't have enough barium."

"The barium is in transit. The progress of this operation is delayed by your sulking. You have an hour to satisfy yourself, and then I expect you to return to work."

"I've only got an hour with her?"

"We need to put a rocket up tonight. And you need to finish your calculations. When the rocket is successfully launched and we've retrieved the data, you may return to your toy. Ms. Plum will not be leaving us so long as you wish her to stay."

Munch looked at me and grinned ear to ear. I was Christmas morning. Lucky me.

The interior of the house wasn't much better than the exterior. The smell of fresh paint mingled with the smell of new carpet. The furniture was tasteful but bland. Marriott meets college dorm. There was a living room with a couch, two club chairs, a coffee table, and a television. Two small bedrooms with queen-size beds. A bath and a half. An eat-in kitchen that opened to a family room that ordinarily would have had a television and a comfortable couch, but in this house was set up as an office and lab. This was Munch's house, I thought. Hastily finished when the ranch-style house burned down.

Munch, the English-speaking uniform, and three other uniforms with guns drawn led me to the kitchen. A uniform pulled a wooden kitchen chair to the middle of the room, sat me down, and secured my hands behind the chair back with cuffs. He cuffed my right ankle to a chair leg, my left ankle to another chair leg, and he took a step back and set the key on the kitchen counter.

"Is that okay?" he said to Munch.

"Yeah," Munch said. "That's great, except she's got all her clothes on."

The uniform opened a couple kitchen drawers, found a pair of scissors, and handed them to Munch.

"Have fun," the uniform said.

The four henchmen left, locking the front door on their way out. There was the sound of two vehicles moving on the gravel surface, and then it was quiet. Just Munch and me left in the cement-block house.

"So," I said to Munch, "see any good *Star Trek* re-runs lately?"

"Yeah. All the time. I have the whole collection. All the seasons. And all the movies."

"Wow, that's amazing. Do you want to watch some?"

"Maybe later. I only have an hour to have fun with you."

"What does fun involve?"

"You know . . . fun."

"It looks like you work here. That's a serious-looking computer."

"It's okay. Mostly, I work at the main facility."

"Where is that located? Is it far away?"

"It's through the woods. Everything is through the woods here."

"Wulf said you were sending a rocket up tonight. That's pretty exciting. I wish I could see it."

"It's not that exciting. It's just a small X-12 King. When we get the barium, we'll fly the big bird, the BlueBec. It holds twenty-three hundred pounds of propellant, and it's got a full payload. It'll be the first real test. If it works, we'll go global."

"Global? What does that mean?"

"It means we'll be able to control weather. Well, not entirely. I can't do everything with the waves. At least, not yet."

"What *can* you do?"

"I can make lightning. Not just a single strike, either. I can create the most terrifying storm you've ever imagined. And I can make it rain. Not a sustained rain, but a deluge. I can make the kind of rain that can do damage. Rain the earth can't absorb fast enough."

"Why would you want to do that?"

"I don't know. Why do people want to paint pictures? Why do people want to design skyscrapers? It's just what you do. It's what's in your head. I tried to get Brytlin to fund my research, but they thought I was a nut. All they wanted was a better magnetometer."

"What about Eugene Scanlon?"

"Eugene was okay. He saw what I was doing with the new antennae grid design and the miniaturization. He's the one who started all this in the Barrens. He had some land here, and since the Barrens are filled with nutcases, he figured we wouldn't be bothered by anyone. The problem was, we didn't have any money. All I could do was computer-generated stuff. We did a couple tests with the little rockets, but then we were broke."

"That's where Wulf comes in, right?"

"Yeah. He's got money coming out of his ears. I don't know where he gets it. It's like he makes it in the basement or something."

"Why did he kill Eugene Scanlon?"

"Eugene wanted Wulf's money, but he didn't want Wulf involved. Eugene wanted to be the boss. And then Eugene got all in a snit and said he wanted Wulf to buy him out. Eugene wanted fifty million dollars or he was going public with my research. So Wulf killed him. Wulf doesn't mess around. He's got four BlueBecs on pads for me. You know what they cost? About two million apiece. Not that it's a big loss. He'll get all that money back and more. Once I'm up to speed, I'll be able to destroy every power grid in the country. They'll pay us whatever we want."

"You'd blackmail cities?"

"Yeah. How awesome is that?"

"If Wulf has so much money, why did you steal the transmitter?"

"It was going to take too long to order one. We have a generator that we're using now, but it doesn't give enough power. The radio station had a monster."

"Where's Gail Scanlon?"

"She's at the main facility. She's part of a side experiment I started. Turns out the human brain operates on low frequencies of electromagnetic energy. When you're in active thought, it's maybe at like fourteen cycles per second. When you're sleeping, it's more like four cycles. I can alter that with my machine. Only problem is, I needed to put the helmet on my test subjects so their brain waves would match the resonant frequencies I chose to generate. I can't really control thoughts yet, but I can make monkeys fall asleep or get depressed or enraged. Human trials are my next phase."

Seemed to me that monkeys spent a lot of time sleeping anyway. And as for depressed and enraged, I'd feel that way, too, if I was forced to wear a helmet while Munch conducted experiments on me.

Chapter

TWENTY-TWO

Munch picked the scissors up from the table. "I should start working on your clothes before my time is up."

"These are the only clothes I have with me," I said. "If you cut them up, I won't have anything."

"Yeah, but you won't need anything. I figure you'll just go naked all the time."

"That feels sort of icky."

"You'll get used to it. You'll be like my sex slave. Besides, once I perfect my mind-control device, I'll be able to control your mood, if you know what I mean."

"Wouldn't you rather have a girlfriend?"

"Are you kidding?" Munch said, looking for a place to start with the scissors. "What man wouldn't rather have a sex slave?"

"Lots of men."

"They're lying. Sex slave is the way to go. You could do anything you want to a sex slave."

I was wearing jeans and Diesel's sweatshirt. The sweatshirt was thick and didn't have a front zipper. Munch started cutting at the bottom of the sweatshirt.

"Ow!" I said.

"What?"

"You stuck me."

"I did not. Stop squirming."

"What do you mean, you can do anything you want to a sex slave? You aren't weird, are you?"

"I don't know. I want to try stuff."

"What kind of stuff?"

I really didn't want to hear any of this, but he only had twenty minutes left. If I kept him talking, I could considerably delay the whole naked thing.

"Everything."

"I don't do everything," I said.

"A sex slave does everything."

"Not this one."

"Jeez," Munch said. "Give me a break. I went to a lot of trouble to get you here. The least you could do is cooperate."

"I could cooperate better if you uncuffed me."

"I don't trust you. Last time, you kicked me in the nuts."

"I wouldn't do that this time."

"Wulf would be mad at me. He told me not to do that."

"How are you going to do *everything* if I'm attached to this chair? A lot of my best parts are inaccessible."

"Wulf already thought of that. He said I should have fun with you like this, and then when I want to do something different, like some of the *everything* stuff, I should get the two men outside to help me."

I felt all the blood drain from my head, and I broke out in a cold sweat.

"That would be rape," I said.

"You could think of it like it's a science experiment," Munch said. "And like those two guys are lab techs."

"If you unlocked the restraints around my ankles,

you could pull my pants off," I said to him. "It would be okay because my hands would still be cuffed behind my back on this chair."

Munch thought about it. "I'd like to pull your pants off," he said. "It's going to be hard to cut through the denim with these scissors."

"I'm wearing a thong," I told him.

"Okay," he said. "But you have to promise not to kick me."

"I promise."

Munch unlocked the ankle cuffs and returned the key to the counter. He reached for the snap on my jeans, and I kicked him in the nuts. He went to his knees, his eyes bulged out of his head, and he crashed onto his face.

"If you so much as squeak, I'll kick you again," I said.

I stood and worked my arms up the chair back. Once I was free of the chair, I took the key off the counter and unlocked the cuffs. Munch was curled into a fetal position, the sweat soaking through his *Star Trek* shirt, his breathing labored.

I needed a place to stash him. The bathroom was no good. I couldn't lock the door from the outside. Broom closet? Wouldn't fit. Coat closet? No lock. Cellar door? Yes! The cellar would be perfect. I grabbed the back of his shirt, dragged him moaning to the cellar door, and shoved him down the stairs. *Bump, bump, bump, bump.* I locked the cellar door and crept around the house looking out windows. The two uniforms were in front of the house, laughing and talking, sitting on leftover cement blocks.

I tiptoed out the back door off the kitchen and quietly disappeared into the woods. My heart was pounding so loud I was afraid the guards might hear it in the front of the house. I had no idea where I was going. The Pine Barrens were huge, and if I walked in the wrong direction, I could walk for days and never see a road or a human being or hut. Problem was, I didn't know the right direction from the wrong direction. I would walk a little and then stop and listen. Sooner or later, Wulf would discover Munch in the cellar, and he'd set out to find me. I walked for an hour and came to an ATV path that turned into a dirt road. I followed the dirt road, and in twenty minutes, I was on a two-lane paved road.

I looked at my cell phone. Still no reception. It was five-thirty P.M. and twilight. I saw a pickup truck in the distance, heading in my direction. I could hear the broken muffler a mile away. The truck was a wreck. Not something I could see Wulf owning. I stepped into the road and flagged the truck down.

"I need a ride," I told the driver. "My car broke down on the dirt road. I need to make a phone call."

"There's a gas station and convenience store at the crossroads," he said. "I could take you there. There's a phone inside the convenience store you could use."

I climbed into the truck. "That would be great. I really appreciate it. I'm Stephanie."

"Elmer."

He was in his late sixties. His hair was gray and thinning on top. He was wearing a plaid shirt, a navy quilted vest, and khakis. There was a thick layer of dust inside and outside the truck. The floor was littered with fast-food wrappers, and the upholstery reeked of smoke. Not that I was going to judge. I was happy to have a ride.

"What road are we on?" I asked him.

"This is Banger Road. The gas station's at the corner of Banger and Marbury. I guess you're not from around here."

"I'm from Trenton. I was visiting a friend, and I got lost."

"Easy to get lost here. The gas station is just up ahead."

He reached the corner of Banger and Marbury, and the gas station and convenience store were closed.

"This here's run by Booger Jackson. I guess Booger had something better to do than keep things open tonight," he said. "That's the way it is in this neck of the woods."

I looked at my phone. Still no reception.

"I'll give you fifty dollars if you'll drive me to Trenton," I said.

"Fifty dollars. That's a lot of money."

I wasn't convinced his truck could make it all the way to Trenton, but I'd go as far as he could take me. If I had to flag down another driver in Cherry Hill, it was better than staying here.

"Okay," he said. "I guess you must be in a bind to get home."

He took Route 206, and I didn't object. I didn't think the truck was Turnpike material. Twenty minutes later, I had cell service, and I called Diesel.

"I'm on my way home," I told him.

"Are you okay?"

"Yes. I'm surprised you're not combing the woods, looking for me."

"I was in the air with Boon all afternoon. He just brought me back to Trenton. Ranger has twenty men on the ground. You need to call him."

"I have a favor to ask. I have no clean clothes. Could you take the laundry basket to my mother's house and ask her to throw everything in the washer?"

"I'm on it."

I dialed Ranger.

"I'm okay," I said.

"Where are you?"

"I'm on my way home."

Lula was next on my list, and then my mother.

"I'm sending Diesel over with laundry," I told my mother. "I'd really appreciate it if you'd throw it all in the washer."

"Where are you? I tried to call. I made lasagna. It's still warm."

"Give some to Diesel when he gets there, and I'll be there in about a half hour."

"Was that your mom?" Elmer asked.

"Yes. She's going to hold dinner for me. You can take me to her house in Chambersburg."

"I haven't been to Trenton in about twenty years. You'll have to give me directions."

It was dark when Elmer finally chugged to the curb and parked behind the Subaru at my parents' house.

I wrenched my door open and jumped from the pickup. "I'll be right back with your money," I said.

"I'll be here."

A black Porsche Turbo slid to a stop behind the truck, and Ranger got out. He closed the distance between us, pulled me to him, and held me tight.

"Are you really okay?" he asked.

"Yeah. It was scary, but I got away before anything bad happened."

His voice softened and dropped to a whisper against my ear. "I had to see for myself."

I allowed myself a moment to relax into Ranger. He was warm and strong, and all the bad, frightening things in life went away when he held me like this.

"How did you know I was here?"

"I have the Subaru tagged."

I could feel Ranger smile. He saw the humor in his obsession to keep me on his radar screen.

"Does Diesel know?"

"Hard to tell what Diesel knows." Ranger pulled back a little and looked at me. "Diesel has superbad enemies, and the people he chases aren't normal. You need to be careful if you partner with Diesel."

"He popped into my apartment, and I can't get rid of him."

"You could move into Rangeman until he leaves."

"That's going from the frying pan into the fire."

The smile was back. "In some ways."

"Anyway, he feels like a brother."

"I'm sure he would love that description," Ranger said.

Grandma Mazur opened the front door and looked out. "Stephanie? Is that Ranger with you? Is that your truck?"

"I have to go," Ranger said. "Try to stay out of trouble." He kissed me on the forehead, jogged back to his car, and took off.

Grandma came to see what was going on with the truck. "Who's this?" she said, looking inside at Elmer.

"This is Elmer," I said. "He was nice enough to bring me home when I got stranded in the Barrens."

"He's a cutie," Grandma said. "He don't look too old, either."

"I got most of my original teeth," Elmer said.

"We got a lot of lasagna," Grandma said to him. "We kept it warm for Stephanie. You're welcome to come have some lasagna with us."

"That would be real nice," Elmer said. "I'm starving."

I looked back at the house and saw Diesel standing in the doorway, waiting for me.

"I had to buy more Pepto-Bismol," he said when I reached him. "You're giving me an ulcer."

"I have a lot to tell you."

"What's with the sweatshirt? It looks like someone took a scissor to the bottom of it."

"Munch was trying to get it off me, but it didn't work out."

Diesel grinned. "You kicked him in the nuts again, didn't you?"

"It's my signature move."

He looked beyond me. "Who's the guy with Grandma?"

"Elmer. I flagged him down after I escaped, and I bribed him to drive me home."

"Elmer? And he's from the Barrens?"

"Yeah."

"Honey, you didn't bring Elmer the Fire Farter home with you, did you?"

I glanced back at Elmer. "He didn't say he was the fire farter."

Diesel hooked an arm around my neck and hugged me to him. "This is why I love you."

"Everyone sit down," my mother said, setting the tray of lasagna in the middle of the dining room table. "Frank," she yelled to my father, "come to the table."

"I already ate," my father said.

"You can eat again. Stephanie is here with guests."

My father heaved himself out of his chair. "The big one isn't a guest. I don't know what he is."

"He's like a member of the family," Grandma said.

My father looked down the table at Diesel. "Heaven help us," he said.

Grandma poured Elmer a glass of wine and gave him a slab of lasagna. "We got red sauce for the lasagna, too," she said, passing the gravy boat to Elmer.

"This looks good," Elmer said, digging in. "I can't remember the last time I had a meal like this."

Diesel ate some lasagna and leaned close to me. "This is filled with cheese and hot sausage. I hope Elmer isn't lactose intolerant. He'll burn his truck down on the way home."

At the other end of the table, Elmer was shoveling the food in.

"He doesn't look lactose intolerant," I said. "He's putting extra grated cheese on his lasagna."

My father was swiveled around in his seat, trying to see the television. He was missing a *Seinfeld* rerun.

"It was real nice of you to bring Stephanie home," Grandma said to Elmer. "Do you live in the Pine Barrens?"

"Yep," Elmer said. "It's the best place on earth. It's filled with interesting people, and you don't hardly ever see any of them."

"I go to Atlantic City once in a while," Grandma said, "but the bus don't stop in the Pine Barrens."

"Too bad," Elmer said. "We got some good things there. Antique stores and such."

Grandma gave him a second helping of lasagna. "Do you have a job?"

"No. I'm retired. It's hard for me to keep a job on account of I have an affliction."

"What kind of affliction?" Grandma wanted to know.

"I can't talk about it," Elmer said. "It's unmentionable."

Diesel and I exchanged looks.

"Oh boy," I said.

"Are we done yet?" my father asked.

"We haven't even had dessert," Grandma said. "Hold your shirt on."

Elmer scraped his chair back. "I might have to use your restroom."

"It's at the top of the stairs," Grandma told him. "I'll get the coffee started."

Elmer climbed the stairs, and moments later . . . *BAROOOOM!*

"What was that?" my mother asked. "It sounded like an explosion."

Diesel pressed his lips together, and his face turned red.

"I appreciate the effort you're making not to laugh," I said to him, "but you're going to burst all the blood vessels in your head if you keep holding it in."

"I can't believe you brought the fire farter home," he said. "Couldn't you have gotten a ride from the Easter Bunny or Sasquatch?"

"You should have been taking better care of me. It's all your fault. I got kidnapped by *your* cousin. I'm lucky Martin Munch doesn't have me pinned to a board like a frog in biology class."

"You're right," Diesel said. "I should have done a better job of protecting you. But that said, I would have thought twice about getting in a truck with the fire farter."

"I wasn't thinking. I forgot about the fire farter. I was stressed."

Elmer came back to the table, and Grandma trotted in with coffee and half an apple pie. She served the coffee and pie, and Elmer reached for the cream and farted.

Broomph!

Flames shot out of Elmer's ass, set his pants on fire, and ignited the upholstered seat on the cherrywood side chair. Elmer jumped up and dropped his pants, drawers and all.

"Holy crap," my father said. "That smells like the slaughterhouse burned down."

My mother downed a glass of wine and poured herself another. And my grandmother leaned forward to get a better view.

"Don't get to see this every day," Grandma said.

Diesel dumped a pitcher of water on the chair and stomped on Elmer's pants.

"Excuse me," Elmer said. "The sausage was spicy."

"That was a pip of a fart," Grandma said. "I've seen people fart fire on YouTube, but I never saw anyone do it that good."

We got Elmer outfitted in one of my father's old work pants, Diesel gave him fifty dollars, and we sent him back to the Barrens.

"Got my money's worth out of that fifty dollars," Diesel said, loading the laundry basket into the back of the Subaru. "I got to see a guy fart fire."

I cut my eyes to him. "You were impressed with that?"

"Hell, yeah. I can't do it. At least, not without a Zippo lighter."

"Maybe Elmer had a Zippo lighter."

"I don't care how he did it. It was an *excellent* fart."

We got in the car, and Morelli called just before we reached my building.

"I've had the strangest feeling all day," he said. "Like something awful was happening. Are you okay?"

"Yes. How about you?"

"I'm better than okay. Anthony gets his stitches out tomorrow, and then he's going home. His wife is taking him back. I'm not sure why."

"She loves him."

"Yeah, well, I love him, too, but I don't want to live with him. Although, I have to say we had fun yesterday. We watched the game, and it was almost like he was human. What did you do?"

"Blew up a fuel depot, stole twelve rockets and made off with them in a stolen van, got kidnapped by a maniac, and had dinner with a guy who farted fire."

"That would be funny, but I'm worried it's all true."

"It's been a long couple days."

"Did he really fart fire?" Morelli asked.

"Yeah. Set his pants on fire and burned my mother's dining room chair to a crisp."

"Wish I'd seen it," Morelli said.

"Men are weird."

"Cupcake, we'd all like to be able to fart fire."

"Gotta go."

"Love you," Morelli said.

"Me, too," I said. And I hung up.

Carl was in the kitchen, feeding cereal to Rex, when we got home. Carl would drop in a Fruit Loop, Rex would rush out of his can, stuff the Fruit Loop into his cheek, and rush back to his can. Carl would repeat the drill.

"Cute," I said. "Carl has a pet."

"Either that or he's fattening him up for the kill."

"Do monkeys eat hamsters?"

Diesel shrugged. "They eat pizza with pepperoni."

Mental note: First thing tomorrow, take Rex to stay at parents' house for duration of monkey visit.

I told Diesel about the cement-block house in the woods, and I repeated my conversation with Munch.

"There's no point looking for the house," Diesel said. "Wulf will move Munch. And we've caused him sufficient aggravation that he's probably in the process of moving the whole operation out of the Barrens."

"He can't do that overnight. Munch said he had four BlueBec rockets sitting on pads."

"A rocket that size can be trucked out fairly easily. Most of its weight is in fuel. I just don't know why we aren't seeing it. I suppose he could camouflage a single rocket if he put it in a stand of pines. And he might even be able to hide an antenna array. What we should be seeing from the air is command central. He needs a place to house his men, track his rocket, plant his transmitter. And he'd need a generator. Why aren't we seeing all that?"

"Maybe you're looking in the wrong part of the Barrens?"

"No. Everything he does is in the same area. I know Banger Road and Marbury Road."

"Apparently, they have everything in place to send up the sounding rocket, except for the barium. They're waiting on the barium."

"I talked to Cuddles. He said it would be in late tomorrow."

Chapter
TWENTY-THREE

I opened my eyes and looked at my alarm clock. It was seven A.M. and the phone was ringing. Diesel reached across me and answered it.

"It's for you," he said, handing me the phone. "It's the Batcave."

"This is Gene in the Rangeman control room," a guy said. "I'm going to patch you through to Hal."

A moment later, Hal came on. "I hope I'm not calling too early," he said, "but a new monkey just showed up, and he's wearing a scarf."

"What kind of scarf?"

"It's a scrap of material tied around his neck. Like decoration. Like you see on a dog sometimes. It's made out of hippie material."

"Tie-dye?"

"Yeah. Real bright colors. Like what you see in the house here."

"Hang on to him. I'm on my way."

I returned the phone to the nightstand. "Hal said a monkey just showed up."

Diesel was already out of bed, getting dressed. "I heard."

"How could you hear?"

"I have good ears."

"I was talking to him on the phone!"

"I can't find my shoes," Diesel said.

I took clean jeans and underwear from the laundry basket and headed for the bathroom. "Under the coffee table. Just like always."

"We've been living together too long," Diesel said. "I'm not the man of mystery anymore. Your mother washes my underwear, and you always know where my shoes are."

"You've never been the man of mystery. Ranger's the man of mystery."

"Then who am I?"

"You're Diesel." And just being Diesel was more than enough.

Diesel and I had breakfast sandwiches and coffee to go. Carl was in the backseat of the Subaru with a breakfast sandwich and a bottle of water. Our hope was that Gail had managed to tie a scrap of her skirt around the monkey's neck and set him free. And that somehow we could get the monkey to lead us back to Gail. We'd brought Carl along as translator.

"This is going to be embarrassing," Diesel said.

"What?"

"Talking to a monkey in front of Ranger's man."

"How about if I tell Hal we need to talk to the monkey in private?"

"I know Carl seems rotten enough to be human sometimes, but I'm not completely convinced he understands anything we say."

"He can play Super Mario," I said to Diesel.

"Yeah, but he can't win. Mario keeps dying."

Carl tapped Diesel on the shoulder. Diesel looked at

Carl in the rearview mirror, and Carl gave Diesel the finger.

"I'm just saying," Diesel said to Carl.

An hour later, we were on the dirt road that led to Gail Scanlon's compound. It was early morning, and the Barrens felt benign. The sun was shining. It was in the midseventies. And there was no sign of the Easter Bunny, Fire Farter, Sasquatch, or the Jersey Devil. Diesel drove into the clearing and parked close to the house, next to a black Rangeman SUV.

Hal came out of the house and met us in the yard. "I've got the new monkey in the cage," he said. "It's still got the scarf around its neck."

We all walked to the cage and peered inside.

"The scarf looks like Gail's skirt," I said. "I saw the monkeys before Carl set them loose, and I can't remember any of them having a neck scarf."

"He doesn't look very smart," Diesel said. "He's not even giving me the finger."

"Can monkeys do that?" Hal asked.

Carl gave him the finger.

"Cool!" Hal said.

"So what do you think?" I said to Carl. "Can you get the monkey to take us to Gail?"

Carl looked at me and shrugged.

Hal opened the door to the enclosure, and Carl went in and sidled up to the monkey with the scarf. Carl picked something off the monkey's head and ate it.

Diesel gave a snort of laughter.

"It's a social ritual," I said. "And you have no room to laugh. You were gobstruck by a guy who farted fire."

"No way," Hal said.

"Swear to God," Diesel told him. "Fire came out of

this guy's ass like a blowtorch. I saw him burn down a chair."

"Jeez," Hal said. "I'd give anything to see that."

"Stop the planet," I said. "I want to get off."

Carl did some *chee chee chee* and some *whoo whoo whoo* with the scarf monkey, and then they scampered out the door and ran away into the pine forest.

"Boy, he sure took off," Hal said.

I nudged Diesel. "Okay, big boy, let's see what you're made of. Smell him out."

Diesel grabbed my hand and pulled me into the woods. "I suspect that was sarcasm, but as it happens, I have a highly developed sense of smell."

"Like a bloodhound?"

"Yeah. Or a werewolf."

"Are you a werewolf?"

"No. I have it on good authority werewolves aren't real."

"What about the Easter Bunny?"

"His name is Bernard Zumwalt, and he's originally from Chicago."

"Santa Claus? Sasquatch?"

"They're real. Sasquatch comes from a big family. They're all over the place. Santa Claus is getting on in years. I don't know how much longer he can keep it going."

"I'm not taking the hook," I said to Diesel.

"You were thinking about it."

True. It was hard not to believe Diesel. He looked trustworthy. And "normal" had a tendency to expand in his universe.

"Are you sure we're following the monkeys?" I asked him after a half hour of walking on pine needles and struggling through underbrush.

"I'm sure we're following them. I'm not sure they're taking us to Gail."

We were on an ATV path, and the next moment, we stumbled into the Easter Bunny's yard. He was back in his chair, wearing the same sad rabbit suit, and he was still smoking.

"Hey, Bernie," Diesel said. "How's it going?"

"It's not Bernie," he said. "It's E. Bunny." He took a long drag, pitched his stub of a cigarette onto the ground, and lit another. "Oh hell, who am I kidding, it's Bernie. The bastards retired me, suit and all."

"You don't have to work anymore," Diesel said. "This is the good life."

Bernie nodded. "It ain't bad. I get to sit here and smoke all day. Toward the end, they came in with all that no-smoking crapola. That was a bitch. You know what it's like trying to sneak a smoke in a rabbit suit? It's the shits."

"Did you see a couple monkeys go past?"

"Yeah. One of them was wearing a scarf."

After an hour, I was thinking everything looked familiar. "Have we been here before?" I asked Diesel.

"Yeah. The stupid monkeys are leading us in a circle. Bernie's homestead is just ahead."

"How did you know his name was Bernie?"

"I Googled Easter Bunny."

"And it told you the Easter Bunny's name was Bernie?"

"Okay, so I asked around."

"Who did you ask?"

"Flash. He has a friend at the DMV, and he looked up the rabbit's license plate." Diesel draped an arm across my shoulders. "Do you believe me?"

"No."

Diesel grinned. "People believe what they want to believe."

We ambled back into Bernie's yard and stopped to watch Bernie blow smoke rings.

"Looks like you're still following the monkeys," Bernie said, squinting through the smoke at us. "You're about three minutes behind them. And watch out for the Jersey Devil. He's been in a real bad mood lately."

We walked about a hundred yards, and ran into Carl. He was sitting back on his haunches, looking dejected.

"Where's the other monkey?" I asked him.

Carl looked up. The monkey was in a tree.

"What's he doing there?"

Carl shrugged.

"This was a stupid idea," I said to Diesel.

"Yeah, but at least you walked off your sausage-and-egg sandwich. It would have gone straight to your ass."

"I'm going back to Gail's house, and then I'm going home. I don't care about Munch. I don't care about Wulf. I don't care about their wicked weather machine. I don't care if it rains rhinoceroses."

"What about Gail Scanlon?"

"She's on her own." I looked around. "Which way do I go?"

"Wait," Diesel said. "Do you hear something rumbling?"

I stopped and listened. "It sounds like Elmer's truck with the broken muffler."

We walked through the woods, following the sound. Carl tagged along, but the scarf monkey stayed in the tree. The truck cut out, but we kept walking in the general direction. The trees thinned, and we came to a large patch of scorched earth. A small, egg-shaped Airstream travel trailer sat on the edge of the clearing. Elmer's truck was parked next to the trailer.

Diesel knocked on the trailer door, and Elmer answered.

"Holy cow," Elmer said. "What a surprise. Nobody ever visits me. Do you want to come in?"

I gnawed on my lip. I didn't want to be rude, but there was only one door. If Elmer farted and the trailer went up in flames, I'd die a horrible death.

"No thanks," I said. "We were just out for a walk."

"We're looking for Gail Scanlon," Diesel said.

"That's the monkey lady," Elmer said. "I met her once. She was real nice. I heard she was missing, and all her monkeys got loose."

Elmer looked past me at Carl.

"Is that one of her monkeys?"

Carl gave Elmer the finger.

"Yep," I said. "That's her monkey."

"Do you have any neighbors?" Diesel asked.

"The Easter Bunny is a couple miles through the woods. And one of the Sasquatch boys lives down the road a ways. Used to be a young couple living in a little house at the end of Junior Sasquatch's road, but they moved out, and then the house burned down. I swear, it wasn't my fault."

"Anyone else?"

"Not in this little patch of the Barrens," Elmer said. "There's some businesses on Marbury Road. A couple antique shops, the Flying Donkey Mine, a bed-and-breakfast that don't serve breakfast."

"Is it a real mine?" I asked him.

"I suppose years ago it might have been. I don't know what kind of mine, though. Then it was a tourist attraction. Only thing, there was hardly any tourists. It closed almost as soon as it opened, and it's been closed since. And, of course, there's the Devil, except he isn't much of a neighbor."

"Do you know the Devil?" I asked him.

"Not personal. I hear him flying over the trailer at night sometimes. Lately, he's been flyin' a lot. I tell you, the Barrens are strange and getting stranger."

"Have you ever been in the mine?" Diesel asked Elmer.

"Nope. I thought about it, but it got closed before I got around to visiting. I thought it might have been interesting."

"I think we should take a look at it," Diesel said.

"You can't go in. It's all boarded up."

"Then we'll look at it from the outside," Diesel said to Elmer. "You feel like driving us over there?"

"Sure," Elmer said. "I'll get my keys."

I glanced over at Diesel. "I thought you said it was a bad idea to get in a truck with the fire farter."

"He's what we've got. If we don't go with Elmer, we walk two hours through the woods to Gail's house. That's two hours less to find Munch and Wulf."

"Yeah, but what if we're in the truck and he farts?"

"If he farts, we'll jump out of the truck and run like hell."

Elmer came out with the keys. I got in front with Elmer. Diesel and Carl climbed into the back.

"Do you ever explore around in the woods?" I asked Elmer.

"Hardly ever. I got a creaky knee. Makes it hard to walk in the pine needles. And the truck's gotta have a road. I hear them ATVs riding around behind me, going in the woods, but I haven't got one of them."

It took twenty minutes to get to the mine, and Elmer was right about it being closed. A large, weather-beaten sign advertised tours of the Flying Donkey, but the sign was more of a tombstone than anything else. The Donkey's gift shop windows were covered with crudely nailed-on sheets of plywood. The plywood was warped and water-stained. The shop door was boarded shut. The parking lot was large, made to accommodate tour buses that never came. Weeds struggled to grow in the cracks in the blacktop. The mine itself was several yards behind the gift shop. A path led from the parking lot to the mine.

Elmer parked close to the gift shop. We left Carl in the truck, and Diesel, Elmer, and I got out and took the path. Another sign was posted at the mine's entrance. CLOSED was spray-painted over the tour times. A half-assed chain-link fence was propped across an entrance that looked more like the approach to a cave than a mine.

A dirt path continued past the mine entrance. A smaller, barely legible sign announced that this was a NATURE WALK.

"I'm feeling in the mood for nature," Diesel said, setting off on the path.

Elmer and I walked along with him, and it occurred to me that this was a maintained path. It should have been overgrown by now, but the brush had been weed-whacked away. Diesel stopped after a couple hundred feet and then quietly walked several yards into the woods. We followed him and stared down at an air shaft. We returned to the trail and found six more air shafts at regular intervals. We stood over the last air shaft, and muffled voices carried up to us. Diesel motioned for silence, and we quietly walked back to the trail.

"This is why we couldn't see it from the air," Diesel said to me. "These underground caves can be huge and wind around for miles. Everyone walk in a different direction. Go two hundred feet and come back. Look for any disturbance in the undergrowth."

I walked about fifty feet in and saw a wire running

pine tree to pine tree, even with the top of my head. The pines were straight and tall and most of the lower branches had been trimmed. An antenna stretched along the trunk of the pine tree, disappearing into the upper branches. There were wires crisscrossing the stand of trees, and I counted twenty-six antennae joined by the wires.

I returned to the path and waited for Diesel.

"I found the grid of antennae," I said to Diesel. "They're hidden by the pines."

"And I found a hatch that's probably the roof over a rocket silo."

"I didn't find nothin'," Elmer said.

Chapter
TWENTY-FOUR

We walked back to the mine entrance and pulled the gate away. A walkway led into the mine interior.

"This is convenient for them," Diesel said. "You can pull a truck into the lot, off-load materials, and move everything along an underground path. They probably have a couple heavy-duty carts. And probably there's another entrance to this cave. Maybe several. I'm guessing if we go back to the fuel depot and the two houses where Munch was living, we'll find they all hook up with this cave system. And there has to be another house or business where they can park cars."

"Now that we've found them, what's next?" I asked. "Police? Homeland Security?"

"That would ruin my chances of containing Wulf. I need to get into the mine and look around." He turned to Elmer. "I want you to go to Gail's house. You know where it is, right?"

"Yep. I know exactly where."

"There's a guy staying there. His name is Hal. He'll be dressed in black, and he works for a company called Rangeman. Tell him about the mine, and tell him Stephanie and I are inside. Ask him to tell all that to Ranger."

"Okay. I got it."

Diesel took my hand and tugged me into the mine entrance.

"I hate this," I said to him. "I'm claustrophobic. And I can't see in the dark like you can."

"Walk where I walk, and you'll be fine."

Daylight faded away behind us, and smothering blackness closed in around us. The path under our feet was smooth and level. I was close to Diesel, my hand flat against his back in an effort to absorb some courage.

We walked a short distance and came to a fork. Diesel went right and stopped.

"What's wrong?" I whispered.

"Door."

I felt Diesel put his hand to the door and push it open. Path lights dimly illuminated the corridor in front of us. We were in a rock tube, a Habitrail for spelunkers. Fuel-storage tanks lined the side of the tube, and electric lines ran overhead. A narrow tunnel went off to the right, but we could hear voices ahead, and we followed the voices. We reached what appeared to be the end of the tunnel and peeked around the edge of the rock wall into a cavernous room that looked like it belonged in a low-budget James Bond film. Monitors sat on collapsible rectangular tables. Bundles of wires snaked across the floor. A couple monster computers were housed in a makeshift cubicle. I could see the openings to two more tunnels on the other side of the room. Three men in khaki uniforms were helping Munch pack boxes.

Wulf was moving his operation out of the Barrens.

Diesel backed us out, retreated down the corridor, and took the narrow side tunnel. We came to another large cavern, where cots were stacked triple-decker and a kitchen of sorts had been built into a wall. Dormitory,

I thought, but no one was in it, and the beds had been stripped of linens.

The cave smelled musty, the walls were damp, and there was the constant whoosh of air getting pumped through the tunnels.

The tunnel widened, and more fuel tanks were stacked against the rock. There was another door ahead, on the tunnel wall, and beyond the door, the tunnel narrowed and slanted downhill. Diesel listened at the door, put his hand to the lock, and pushed the door open.

It was a small, cell-like room with a sink and toilet at one end and a chair and cot at the other. A single overhead bulb lit the room. Gail sat on the cot, her eyes dead in her face, her shoulders slumped. She was wearing a khaki jumpsuit and sneakers.

"Gail?"

She looked at me and sighed. No expression.

Diesel scooped her up, carried her out of the room, and closed the door. We hustled down the corridor, retracing our steps. Diesel opened the door to the tunnel entrance, and Elmer and Carl walked through and squinted down the long corridor. Carl stood back, not sure he wanted to go further.

"Look at this," he said. "Isn't this something?"

"What are you doing here?"

"I got to the end of the parking lot, and I had one of them freak accidents, and next thing, my truck was on fire. So I thought I'd come see what you were doing here, but I couldn't get through the door."

I looked at Elmer's pants and realized the seat was burned out and black around the edges.

Two uniformed guys stepped into the tunnel at the far end. One raised his rifle and fired.

"Oh crap!" Elmer said.

I couldn't hear over the rifle fire if he farted, but the packing boxes lining the wall went up like tinder, and flames enveloped the first of the fuel tanks.

"Eep!" Carl said, and he turned tail and disappeared down the tunnel toward the entrance.

Diesel pushed everyone through the door, closed it, and we all ran blind in the dark until we saw the light at the end of the tunnel. Behind me, I heard *POW POW POW,* and I suspected it was the string of tanks exploding. We burst out of the tunnel and didn't stop running until we were in the middle of the parking lot.

Four fireballs rose out of the pines into the sky. There were more explosions, and a wall of fire roared out of the mouth of the cave. Black smoke blanketed the forest and parking lot, blocking the sun, stinging my eyes. I heard wings flapping close overhead, but I couldn't see through the smoke. A load of road apples dropped from the sky and splattered on the blacktop, missing me by inches. The sound of flapping wings faded.

"I guess what with all the explosions, we woke the Devil up," Elmer said.

There was a lot of lightning, and the sky opened up and dumped water on the forest. The rain turned to hail and then back to rain. We walked to the road, past Elmer's truck carcass, and looked back at the pines. There was still a lot of smoke, but not a lot of fire.

"Where's the closest ride?" Diesel said to Elmer.

"There's a bed-and-breakfast a couple miles down the road."

"Mallory Eden's place," Gail said.

It was the first she'd spoken, and we all turned to her.

"Are you okay?" I asked her.

She shook her head. "I'm so depressed." Tears spilled down her cheeks. "My poor monkeys. I couldn't tell you

about Martin Munch and his partner. They had my
monkeys."

"Your monkeys are okay," I said. "We took their helmets off." Most of them, anyway.

"I want to go home," Gail said. "I want to see my
monkeys." She looked down at Carl. "Who's this little
guy?"

"This is Carl," I said. "He's sort of mine."

We walked down the road in the rain. I expected to
hear sirens and see fire trucks barreling down on us, but
the road was deserted. Maybe they came from the other
direction.

"I was scared," Gail said. "I thought they were going to kill me."

"Sorry it took us so long to find you. We didn't know
where to begin looking."

"I should have realized they'd eventually take me to
the mine," Gail said. "The mine was Eugene's big
dream project. He was going to make his fortune with
it, but it turned out to be a bust."

"We couldn't find any record of Eugene owning
property in south Jersey."

"It wouldn't be under his name. He had a partner,
and they bought it under a holding company. They had
a fight over how the business should be run, and the
partner disappeared and was never seen again. I try not
to think about that too much. Eugene didn't have a will
that we know of, so I suppose I own his share of the
mine with my sister now."

It had stopped raining by the time we reached the
bed-and-breakfast. Gail knocked on the door and ex-
plained that we needed a ride to her house. Moments
later, a van pulled out of the garage, and we all piled in.

Gail was the first out when we stopped in her yard.
She ran to the monkey cage and counted them.

"They escaped," I told Gail, "but they almost all came back."

Hal ambled over to us. "The monkey with the scarf came back," he said to me. "I put it in the cage."

"Did you send the monkey with the scarf to get help?" I asked Gail.

"No," she said. "She just likes to wear a scarf. She's always worn it. You probably just didn't notice."

Diesel gave me a poke in the side, and I poked him back.

"I told you it was stupid," he said.

"I'm sure the others will return," I said to Gail.

"The truth is, they've escaped before, and they always come back. They're really clever when it comes to locks and doors."

Hal looked relieved to see Gail Scanlon. His term as monkey man was almost up. Diesel, Carl, and I got into the Subaru and headed for the Expressway.

"I'm wet again," I said to Diesel. "I feel like I'm always wet."

"I have to say, I'm going to miss sleeping on top of you, but I won't miss the Barrens."

"So you're leaving?"

"I always leave."

"Do you mind always leaving?"

"Sometimes, but it's what I do. I'm the job."

"You'll drive me home first, won't you? You won't just pop out in the middle of the Turnpike?"

"I still have a loose end. Wulf made a deal to get barium, and the barium is supposed to come in tonight."

"Do you think he'll still want the barium now that we've torched his project?"

"Don't know. Probably Wulf will move on to something new. He gets bored. Even as a kid, he was always restless. Still, I have to see it through."

I called Morelli when I finally got cell service.

"I have a sort of disaster to report," I told him.

"I hate when a conversation starts like this."

"It's not a big thing. It's that this mine blew up in the Barrens, and I thought someone should look into it, but I don't know any of the local cops."

"I'm assuming it's best if I don't involve you?"

"Yeah. You could say it was an anonymous phone call. The thing is, there might have been people in the mine."

"Oh shit."

"I'm pretty sure they were bad people."

"That makes all the difference," Morelli said.

"Listen, it was an accident. I think Elmer might have farted, and next thing, some boxes were on fire, and then it was one of those chain-reaction things."

"But you're okay?"

"Yes. And Diesel and Carl are okay, too. And we rescued Gail Scanlon."

"Anthony is gone, and I'm going to be lonely tonight."

"I'll keep that in mind and get back to you."

Diesel was smiling when I hung up.

"What?" I said.

"You're gonna get some."

"And?"

"It would be better if it was me."

"You're leaving."

"I could squeeze you in," Diesel said.

I burst out laughing. "What's so awful about that is you're serious!"

Diesel was laughing, too. "I know. I want you bad."

We were about to get on the Expressway. We stopped for a light, I looked left and realized Martin Munch was alongside us, at the wheel of a scorched and dented black SUV. There were four other guys in the car with him. They were wearing the khaki uniforms, and they were soot-smudged and their hair looked singed.

"That's him!" I said. "It's Munch."

"Hang tight," Diesel said.

The light changed, and Diesel got on the gas and rammed Munch, knocking him off the road, onto the shoulder, pinning the black SUV against the guardrail.

Munch looked over at Diesel and me and raced the engine. He threw the SUV into reverse, but the car couldn't move. Diesel's door was smashed against the passenger-side door of the SUV. I was out of the Subaru, rounding the nose of the SUV, when Munch abandoned ship. He hit the ground running and didn't look back.

I ran him down, tackled him, and punched him in the face. Diesel grabbed Munch by the back of his shirt and dragged him to his feet.

"I could have outrun you," Diesel said to me, "but I didn't want to ruin your fun. I figured your day wasn't complete if you didn't shove some poor slob's nuts half-way up his throat. As it was, you broke his nose instead. I'm pretty damn impressed."

"You guys are in big trouble now," Munch said. "Wulf is going to be really mad. I wouldn't be surprised if he doesn't give you that Dragon's Claw thing."

"Where were you going?" Diesel asked Munch.

"We weren't sure. We were just going anywhere. We wanted to make sure *we* didn't get the Dragon's Claw."

I looked back at the black SUV. It was empty. "What happened to the other guys?"

"Took off like roaches when the lights go on," Diesel said.

Chapter

TWENTY-FIVE

Vinnie was saved, I thought. I'd captured his big-ticket bond. My only outstanding was Gordo Bollo, and I'd go back to the produce warehouse wearing a raincoat tomorrow. I had Munch's body receipt in my bag, my monkey hanging on to my leg, and in three minutes, I'd be in my apartment and headed for a nice hot shower.

"I could make that shower a lot more fun," Diesel said, opening the door to my apartment.

"Stop reading my mind."

He reached around me, flipped the light on, and we stared into the black eyes and eerie pale face of Gerwulf Grimoire. There was a moment where anger flashed white-hot fire in Wulf's eyes, and then it was gone, the transformation so fast and so complete, I wasn't sure I'd actually seen the flare of emotion.

"Hello, cousin," Wulf said, his voice perfectly composed. "Ms. Plum."

"This is risky," Diesel said to Wulf. "If I lay my hand on you, you're mine."

"Ah, but you won't. I've acquired a new skill, as I'm sure you've noticed."

"Why are you here?"

"I thought I'd spare you the task of dealing with

Solomon Cuddles. I no longer need the barium. And I hated to leave without saying good-bye. Having you following me to the ends of the earth is the only real amusement in my life."

"Jeez," Diesel said, "that's pathetic."

"Perhaps, but the stakes in this game are high enough to keep it interesting."

"It's not a game," Diesel said.

"It is to *me*," Wulf said. "Isn't it ironic that I was always the serious child, and now you're burdened with your unpleasant job while I'm free to play?"

"What's next?" Diesel asked him.

"I have a date with a witch," Wulf said. "See you in Salem, cousin."

Wulf did his fire-and-smoke thing, and when the smoke cleared, he was gone.

"Damn," Diesel said. "I wish I knew how he did that."

I fanned the smoke away. "My cousin Jessica lives in Salem. Actually, she's next door in Marblehead. I haven't seen her in a couple years, not since she moved from Trenton."

There was a knock at my door, and for a moment, I thought it might be Wulf returning. Diesel opened the door, and Susan Stitch stood there.

"I've come back for my baby," Susan said. "I knew I could count on you to take good care of him. I hope he was a good boy."

"Yeah, he was an angel," I said. "No problemo."

Carl jumped at Susan and wrapped his arms around her neck.

"Kiss, kiss," Susan said. "Mommy loves Carl!"

Diesel took Carl's leash off the kitchen counter and gave it to Susan.

"Oh, yum," Susan said, eyeballing Diesel. "Are there any more of you on the shelf?"

"How was your honeymoon?" I asked Susan.

"Excellent," she said. "Really excellent."

I closed the door on Susan and rolled my eyes at Diesel. "Yum?"

"Hey, I'm *yum*. Deal with it."

I bent to unlace my wet sneakers. "Can a monkey be, you know, special?"

"Unmentionable?"

"Yeah."

"Good question," Diesel said.

I felt his hand on my ass, and I stood and turned to face him, but he was gone.

VISIONS
OF SUGAR
PLUMS

*This book was Plumtacularly edited
and titled by Jennifer Enderlin.
Yahoo, Jen!*

ONE

My name is Stephanie Plum and I've got a strange man in my kitchen. He appeared out of nowhere. One minute I was sipping coffee, mentally planning out my day. And then the next minute . . . *poof,* there he was.

He was over six feet, with wavy blond hair pulled into a ponytail, deep-set brown eyes, and an athlete's body. He looked to be late twenties, maybe thirty. He was dressed in jeans, boots, a grungy white thermal shirt hanging loose over the jeans, and a beat-up black leather jacket hanging on broad shoulders. He was sporting two days of beard growth, and he didn't look happy.

"Well, isn't this perfect," he said, clearly disgusted, hands on hips, taking me in.

My heart was tap-dancing in my chest. I was at a total loss. I didn't know what to think or what to say. I didn't know who he was or how he got into my kitchen. He was frightening, but even more than that he had me flustered. It was like going to a birthday party and arriving a day early. It was like . . . what the heck's going on?

"How?" I asked. "What?"

"Hey, don't ask me, lady," he said. "I'm as surprised as you are."

"How'd you get into my apartment?"

"Sweet cakes, you wouldn't believe me if I told you." He moved to the refrigerator, opened the door, and helped himself to a beer. He cracked the beer open, took a long pull, and wiped his mouth with the back of his hand. "You know how people get beamed down on *Star Trek*? It's sort of like that."

Okay, so I've got a big slob of a guy drinking beer in my kitchen, and I think he might be crazy. The only other possibility I can come up with is that I'm hallucinating and he isn't real. I smoked some pot in college but that was about it. Don't think I'd get a flashback from wacky tobacky. There were mushrooms on the pizza last night. Could that be it?

Fortunately, I work in bail bond enforcement, and I'm sort of used to scary guys showing up in closets and under beds. I inched my way across the kitchen, stuck my hand into my brown bear cookie jar, and pulled out my .38 five-shot Smith & Wesson.

"Cripes," he said, "what are you gonna do, shoot me? Like that would change anything." He looked more closely at the gun and shook his head in another wave of disgust. "Honey, there aren't any bullets in that gun."

"There might be one," I said. "I might have one chambered."

"Yeah, right." He finished the beer and sauntered out of the kitchen, into the living room. He looked around and moved to the bedroom.

"Hey," I yelled. "Where do you think you're going?" He didn't stop.

"That's it," I told him. "I'm calling the police."

"Give me a break," he said. "I'm having a really

shitty day." He kicked his boots off and flopped onto my bed, scoping out the room from his prone position. "Where's the television?"

"In the living room."

"Oh man, you don't even have a television in your bedroom. How crapola is this?"

I cautiously moved closer to the bed, and I reached out and touched him.

"Yeah, I'm real," he said. "Sort of. And all my equipment works." He smiled for the first time. It was a knock-your-socks-off smile. Dazzling white teeth and good-humored eyes that crinkled at the corners. "In case you're interested."

The smile was good. The news was bad. I didn't know what *sort of real* meant. And I wasn't sure I liked the idea that his equipment worked. All in all, it didn't do a lot to help my heart rate. Truth is, I'm pretty much a chickenshit bounty hunter. Still, while I'm not the world's bravest person, I can bluff with the best of them, so I did an eye roll. "Get a grip."

"You'll come around," he said. "They always do."

"They?"

"Women. Women love me," he said.

Good thing I didn't have a bullet chambered as threatened because I'd definitely shoot this guy. "Do you have a name?"

"Diesel."

"Is that your first name or your last name?"

"That's my whole name. Who are *you*?"

"Stephanie Plum."

"You live here alone?"

"No."

"That's a big fib," he said. "You have *living alone* written all over you."

I narrowed my eyes. "Excuse me?"

"You're not exactly a sex goddess," he said. "Hair from hell. Baggy sweatpants. No makeup. Lousy personality. Not that there isn't some potential. You have an okay shape. What are you, 34B? And you've got a good mouth. Nice pouty lips." He threw me another smile. "A guy could get ideas looking at those lips."

Great. The nutcase who somehow got into my apartment was getting ideas about my lips. Thoughts of serial rapists and sex killings went racing through my mind. My mother's warnings echoed in my ears. *Watch out for strangers. Keep your door locked.* Yes, but it's not my fault, I reasoned. My door *was* locked. What's with that?

I took his boots, carried them to the front door, and threw them into the hall. "Your boots are in the hall," I yelled. "If you don't come get them, I'm pitching them down the trash chute."

My neighbor, Mr. Wolesky, stepped out of the elevator. He was holding a small white bakery bag in his hand. "Look at this," he said, "I'm starting the day with a doughnut. That's what Christmas does to me. It makes me crazy and then I need a doughnut. Four days to Christmas and the stores are picked clean," he said. "And they all say everything's on sale but I know they jack up the prices. They always gotta gouge you at Christmas. There should be a law. Somebody should look into it."

Mr. Wolesky unlocked his door, lurched inside, and slammed the door after himself. The door lock clicked into place, and I heard Mr. Wolesky's television go on.

Diesel elbowed me aside, went into the hall, and retrieved his boots. "You know, you have a real attitude problem," he said.

"Attitude this," I told him, closing my door, locking him out of the apartment.

The bolt shot back, the lock tumbled, and Diesel opened the door, walked to the couch, and sat down to put his boots on.

Hard to pick an emotion here. Confused and astounded would be high on the list. Scared bonkers wasn't far behind. "How'd you do that?" I said, squeaky-voiced and breathless. "How'd you unlock my door?"

"I don't know. It's just one of those things we can do."

Goosebumps prickled on my forearms. "Now I'm really creeped out."

"Relax. I'm not going to hurt you. Hell, I'm supposed to make your life better." He gave a snort and another bark of laughter at that. "Yeah, right," he said.

Deep breath, Stephanie. Not a terrific time to hyperventilate. If I passed out from lack of oxygen God knows what would happen. Suppose he was from outer space, and he conducted an anal probe while I was unconscious? A shiver ripped through me. Yuk! "What are we looking at here?" I asked him. "Ghost? Vampire? Space alien?"

He slouched back onto the couch and zapped the television on. "You're in the ballpark."

I was at a loss. How do you get rid of someone who can unlock locks? You can't even have him arrested by the police. And even if I decided to call the police, what would I say? I have a sort-of-real guy in my apartment?

"Suppose I cuffed you and chained you to something. What then?"

He was channel surfing, concentrating on the television. "I could get loose."

"Suppose I shot you?"

"I'd be pissed off. And it's not smart to piss me off."

"But could I kill you? Could I hurt you?"

"What is this, twenty questions? I'm looking for a game here. What time is it, anyway? And where am I?"

"You're in Trenton, New Jersey. It's eight o'clock in the morning. And you didn't answer my question."

He flipped the television off. "Crud. Trenton. I should have guessed. Eight in the morning. I have a whole day to look forward to. Wonderful. And the answer to your question is . . . a qualified no. It wouldn't be easy to kill me, but I suppose if you put your mind to it you could come up with something."

I went to the kitchen and phoned my next-door neighbor, Mrs. Karwatt. "I was wondering if you could come over for just a second," I said. "There's something I'd like to show you." A moment later, I ushered Mrs. Karwatt into my living room. "What do you see?" I asked her. "Is there anyone sitting on my couch?"

"There's a man on your couch," Mrs. Karwatt said. "He's big, and he has a blond ponytail. Is that the right answer?"

"Just checking," I said to Mrs. Karwatt. "Thanks."

Mrs. Karwatt left but Diesel remained.

"She could see you," I said to him.

"Well, duh."

He'd been in my apartment for almost a half hour now, and he hadn't done a full head rotation or tried to wrestle me down to the ground. That was a good sign, right? My mother's voice returned. *It means nothing. Don't let your guard down. He could be a maniac!* Problem was, the maniac thoughts were banging up against a gut feeling that he was an okay guy. Pushy and arrogant and generally obnoxious, but not criminally in-sane. Of course, it's possible my instincts were swayed by the fact that he was incredibly sexy-looking. And he smelled wonderful.

"What are you doing here?" I asked him, curiosity beginning to override panic.

He stood and stretched and scratched his stomach. "How about if I'm the friggin' Spirit of Christmas."

My mouth dropped open. The friggin' Spirit of Christmas. I must be dreaming. Probably I dreamed I called Mrs. Karwatt, too. The friggin' Spirit of Christmas. That's actually pretty funny. "Here's the thing," I said to him. "I have enough Christmas spirit. I don't need you."

"Not my call, Gracie. Personally, I *hate* Christmas. And I'd prefer to be sitting under a palm tree right now, but hey, here I am. So let's get on with it."

"My name's not Gracie."

"Whatever." He looked around. "Where's your tree? You're supposed to have a stupid Christmas tree."

"I haven't had time to buy a tree. There's this guy I'm trying to find. Sandy Claws. He's wanted for burglary, and now he's failed to appear for his court appearance, so he's in violation of his bond agreement."

"Hah! Good one. That's a prizewinning excuse for not having a Christmas tree. Let me see if I've got the details right. You're a bounty hunter?"

"Yes."

"You don't look like a bounty hunter."

"What's a bounty hunter supposed to look like?"

"Dressed in black, six-shooter strapped to your leg, a cheroot clenched between your teeth."

I did another eye roll.

"And you're after Santa Claus because he skipped."

"Not Santa Claus," I said. "Sandy Claws. *S-a-n-d-y C-l-a-w-s.*"

"Sandy Claws. Cripes, how would you like to have *that* name? What'd he steal, kitty litter?"

This was coming from a guy named for a train engine.

"First, I have a legitimate job. I work for Vincent Plum Bail Bonds as a bond enforcement agent. Second, Claws isn't such a weird name. It was probably Klaus and got screwed up at Ellis Island. It happened a lot. Third, I don't know why I'm explaining this to you. Probably I had a stroke and fell down and hit my head and I'm actually in ICU right now, hallucinating all this."

"You see, this is typical of the problem. Nobody believes in the mystical anymore. Nobody believes in miracles. As it happens, I'm a little supernatural. Why can't you just accept that and go with it? I bet you don't believe in Santa Claus either. Maybe Sandy Claws didn't have his name changed from Klaus. Maybe he had his name changed from Santa Claus. Maybe the old guy got tired of the toys-for-kids routine and just wanted to go hide out somewhere."

"So you think Santa Claus might be living in Trenton under an assumed name?"

Diesel shrugged. "It's possible. Santa's a pretty shifty guy. He has a dark side, you know."

"I didn't know that."

"Not many people know that. So if you could catch this Claws guy, you'd get a Christmas tree?"

"Probably not. I haven't got money for a tree. And I haven't got any ornaments."

"Oh man, I'm stuck with a whiner. No time, no money, no ornaments. Yada, yada, yada."

"Hey, it's my life and I don't have to have a Christmas tree if I don't want one."

Actually, I really did want a Christmas tree. I wanted a big fat tree with bright colored lights and an angel on top. I wanted a wreath on my front door. I wanted red candlesticks on my dining room table. I wanted my closet filled with beautifully wrapped presents for my

family. I wanted Christmas music playing on my ste-
reo. And I wanted a fruitcake in my refrigerator. It was
what every red-blooded Plum was supposed to have at
Christmas, right?

I wanted to wake up in the morning and feel happy
and filled with good cheer and peace on earth and good
will toward men. And I wanted to have a partridge in
my pear tree.

Well, guess what? I didn't have *any* of those things.
No tree? no wreath, no candlesticks, no presents, no
freaking fruitcake, and no goddamn partridge.

Every year I chased after the perfect Christmas
and every year Christmas barely happened. My Christ-
mases were always a mess of badly wrapped last-minute
presents, a chunk of fruitcake sent home in a doggy
bag from my parents' house, and for the last couple
years I haven't had a tree. I just couldn't seem to *get
to* Christmas.

"What do you mean, you don't want a Christmas
tree?" Diesel said. "Everyone wants a Christmas tree.
If you had a Christmas tree, Santa would bring you
stuff . . . like hair curlers and slut shoes."

A sigh escaped. "I appreciate your insight into
Christmas, but you're going to have to leave now. I have
things to do. I have to work on the Claws case and then
later I promised my mother I'd be over to bake Christmas cookies."

"Not a good plan. Baking cookies doesn't do a lot
for me. I have a better plan. How about we find Claws
and then we shop for a tree? And on the way home from
the tree shopping we can see if the Titans are playing
tonight. Maybe we can catch a hockey game."

"How do you know about the Titans?"

"I know everything."

I did yet another eye roll and brushed past him. I

was doing so many eye rolls, they were giving me a headache.

"Okay, so I've been to Trenton before," he said. "You've got to stop doing those eye rolls. You're going to shake something loose in there."

I'd planned to take a shower, but there was no way I was getting into the shower with a strange man sitting in my living room. "I'm changing my clothes, and then I'm going to work. You aren't going to pop into my bedroom, are you?"

"Do you want me to?"

"No!"

"Your loss." He returned to the couch and television. "Let me know if you change your mind."

An hour later we were in my Honda CRV. Me and Supernatural Man. I hadn't invited him to ride along with me. He'd simply unlocked the door and gotten into the car.

"Admit it, you're getting to like me, right?" he asked.

"Wrong, I *don't* like you. But, for some unfathomable reason, I'm not totally freaked out."

"It's because I'm charming."

"You are *not* charming. You're a jerk."

He flashed another one of the killer smiles at me. "Yeah, but I'm a *charming* jerk."

I was driving and Diesel was riding shotgun, flipping through my folder on Claws. "So what do we do here, go to his house and drag him out?"

"He's living with his sister, Elaine Gluck. I stopped by their house yesterday, and his sister said he'd disappeared. I think she knows where he is so I'm going back today to put some pressure on her."

"Seventy-six years old, and this guy broke into Kreider's Hardware at two in the morning and stole fifteen hundred dollars' worth of power tools and a gallon of

Morning Glory yellow paint," Diesel read. "Got caught on a security camera. What an idiot. Everybody knows you've got to wear a ski mask when you pull a job like that. Doesn't he watch television? Doesn't he go to the movies?" Diesel pulled out a file photo. "Hold the phone. Is this the guy?"

"Yes."

Diesel's face brightened and the smile returned. "And you stopped by his house yesterday?"

"Yes."

"Are you any good at what you do? Are you good at tracking down people?"

"No. But I'm lucky."

"Even better," he said.

"You look like you've had a revelation."

"Big time. The pieces are beginning to fit together."

"And?"

"Sorry," he said. "It was one of those personal revelations."

Sandy Claws and his sister, Elaine Gluck, lived in North Trenton in a neighborhood of small houses, big televisions, and American-made cars. Holiday spirit ran high in Sandy's neighborhood. Porches were trimmed in colored lights. Electric candles glowed in windows. Postage-stamp front yards were crammed with reindeer, Frosties, and Santas. Sandy Claws' house was the best, or the worst, depending on your point of view. The house was blanketed in red, green, yellow, and blue Christmas lights, interspersed with waterfalls of tiny white twinkle lights. A lighted sign on the roof blinked the message PEACE ON EARTH. A large plastic Santa and his sleigh were stuffed into the minuscule front yard. And three plastic, five-foot-tall Dickens-era carolers huddled together on the front porch.

"Now this is spirit," Diesel said. "Nice touch with the blinking lights on the roof."

"At the risk of being cynical, probably he stole the lights."

"Not my problem," Diesel said, opening the car door.

"Hold it. Close the door," I said. "*You* stay *here* while I talk to Elaine."

"And miss out on all the fun? No way." He angled out of the CRV, and he stood, hands in pockets, on the sidewalk, waiting for me.

"Okay. Fine. Just don't say anything. Just stand behind me and try to look respectable."

"You think I don't look respectable?"

"You have gravy stains on your shirt."

He looked down at himself. "This is my favorite shirt. It's real comfy. And they're not gravy stains. They're grease stains. I used to work on my bike in this shirt."

"What kind of bike?"

"Customized Harley. I had a big old cruiser with Python pipes." He smiled, remembering. "It was sweet."

"What happened to it?"

"Crashed it."

"Is that how you got the way you are now? Dead, or something?"

"No. The only thing that died was the bike."

It was midmorning and the sun was lost behind cloud cover that was the color and texture of bean curd. I was wearing wool socks, thick-soled CAT boots, black jeans, a red plaid flannel shirt over a T-shirt, and a black leather biker jacket. I looked pretty damn tough, in a very cool way . . . and I was freezing my ass off. Diesel was wearing his jacket unzipped and didn't look the least bit cold.

I crossed the street and rang the doorbell.

Elaine opened the door wide and smiled out at me. She was a couple inches shorter than me and almost as wide as she was tall. She was maybe seventy years old. Her hair was snow white, cut short and curled. She had apple cheeks and bright blue eyes. And she smelled like gingerbread cookies. "Hello, dear," she said, "how nice to see you again." She looked to the side where Diesel was lurking and gasped. "Oh my," she said, red scald rising from her neck to her cheek. "You startled me. I didn't see you standing there at first."

"I'm with Ms. Plum," Diesel said. "I'm her . . . assistant."

"Goodness."

"Is Sandy at home?" I asked.

"I'm afraid not," she said. "He's very busy at this time of year. Sometimes I don't see him for days on end. He owns a toy store, you know. And toy stores are very busy at Christmas."

I knew the toy store. It was a shabby little store in a strip mall in Hamilton Township. "I stopped by the store yesterday," I said. "It was closed."

"Sandy must have been busy running errands. Sometimes he closes down to run errands."

"Elaine, you used this house as collateral to bond out your brother. If Sandy doesn't appear in court, my employer will seize this house."

Elaine continued to smile. "I'm sure your employer wouldn't do a mean thing like that. Sandy and I just moved here, but already we love this house. We wallpapered the bathroom last week. It looks lovely."

Oh boy. This was going to be a disaster. If I don't bring Claws in, I don't get paid and I look like a big failure. If I threaten and intimidate Elaine into ratting on her brother, I feel like a jerk. Better to be after a crazed killer who's hated by everyone, including his mother. Of course, crazed killers tend to shoot at bounty hunters, and getting shot at isn't high on my list of favorite activities.

"I smell gingerbread," Diesel said to Elaine. "I bet you're baking cookies."

"I bake cookies every day," she told him. "Yesterday I made sugar cookies with colored sprinkles and today I'm making gingerbread."

"I love gingerbread," Diesel said. He slid past Elaine and found his way to her kitchen. He selected a cookie from a plate heaped with cookies, took a bite, and smiled. "I bet you add vinegar to your cookie dough."

"It's my secret ingredient," Elaine said.

"So where is the old guy?" Diesel asked. "Where's Sandy?"

"He's probably at his workshop. He makes a lot of his own toys, you know."

Diesel wandered to the back door and looked out. "And where's the workshop?"

"There's a small workshop behind the store. And then there's the main workshop. I don't know exactly where the main workshop is. I've never been there. I'm always too busy with the cookies."

"Is it in Trenton?" Diesel asked.

Elaine looked thoughtful. "Isn't that something?" she said. "I don't know. Sandy talks about the toys and about the labor problem, but I can't remember him ever talking about the workshop."

Diesel took a cookie for the road, thanked Elaine, and we left.

"Want some of my cookie?" Diesel asked, the cookie held between perfect white teeth while he clicked the seat belt into place.

"I do not."

He had a nice voice. Slightly husky and hinting of a

smile. His eyes fit the voice. I really hated that I liked the voice and the eyes. My life is already complicated by two men. One is my mentor and tormentor, a Cuban-American bounty hunter/businessman named Ranger. He was currently out of town. No one knew where he was or when he'd return. This was normal. The other man in my life is a Trenton cop named Joe Morelli. When I was a kid, Morelli lured me into his father's garage and taught me how to play choo-choo. I was the tunnel and Morelli was the train, if you get the picture. When I was a teen working at Tasty Pastry Bakery, Morelli sweet-talked me onto the floor after hours and performed a more adult version of choo-choo behind the éclair case. We've both grown up some since then. The attraction is still there. It's been enhanced by genuine affection . . . maybe even love. We haven't totally mastered trust and the ability to commit. I really didn't need a third *potentially nonhuman* guy in my life.

"I bet you're worried about the way those jeans are fitting, right?" Diesel asked. "Afraid to add cookie calories?"

"Wrong! My jeans fit just fine." I didn't want a cookie with Diesel spit on it. I mean, what do I know about him? And okay, so my jeans actually were a little tight. Yeesh.

He bit off the gingerbread man's head. "What's next? Does Claws have kids we can interrogate? I think I'm getting the hang of this."

"No kids. I ran a check on him, and he has no relatives in the area. Same with Elaine. She's widowed with no children."

"That must be hard on Elaine. A woman gets those urges, you know."

I narrowed my eyes. "Urges?"

"Kids. Procreation. Maternal urges."

"Who *are* you?"

"That's a good question," Diesel said. "I'm not sure I fully know the answer to that. Do any of us truly know who we are?"

Great. Now he's a philosopher.

"Don't you have maternal urges?" he asked. "Don't you hear that biological clock ticking? Tick, tick, tick," he said, smiling again, having some fun with it.

"I have a hamster."

"Hey, you couldn't ask for more than that. Hamsters are cool. Personally, I think kids are overrated."

I was getting an eye twitch. I put my finger to my eye to stop the fluttering. "I'd rather not get into this right now."

Diesel held his hands up. "No problemo. Don't want to make you uncomfortable."

Yeah, right.

"Back to the big manhunt. Have you got a plan here?" he asked.

"I'm going back to the store. I didn't realize there was a workshop attached."

Twenty minutes later we stood at the front door to the store, staring at the small, handwritten cardboard sign in the window. CLOSED. Diesel put his hand to the doorknob and the locks tumbled open.

"Pretty impressive, hunh?" he said.

"Pretty illegal."

He pushed the door open. "You're a real spoilsport, you know that?"

We both squinted into the dark. The only windows were the small panes of glass in the door. The shop was about the size of a two-car garage. Diesel closed the door behind us and flipped a light switch. Two overhead fluorescent fixtures buzzed on and threw a dim, flickering light across the interior.

"Boy, this is cheery," Diesel said. "This would make me want to buy toys. Right after I poked my eye out and slit my throat."

The walls were lined with shelves, but the shelves were empty, and train sets, board games, dolls, action figures, and stuffed animals were all jumbled together on the floor.

"This is strange," I said. "Why are the toys on the floor?"

Diesel looked around the room. "Maybe someone had a temper tantrum." An ancient cash register sat on a small counter. Diesel punched a key and the register opened. "Seven dollars and fifty cents," he said. "Don't think Sandy does much business." He walked the length of the store and tested the back door. The door was unlocked. He opened the door and we both peeked into the back room. "Not much to see here, either," Diesel said.

There were a couple of long, metal folding tables and several metal folding chairs. Crude wood toys in various stages of completion cluttered the tables. Most were clunky carved animals and even clunkier carved trains. The train cars were connected by large hooks and eyes.

"Look around for something that might have the address of the other workshop," I said. "It might be printed on a shipping label or box. Or maybe there's a scrap of paper with a phone number."

We worked both rooms, but we didn't find an address or phone number. The only item in the trash was a crumpled bakery bag from Baldanno's. Sandy Claws had a sweet tooth. The store didn't have a phone. None had been listed on the bond agreement and we didn't see any on site. The bond agreement also didn't list a cell phone. That didn't guarantee that one didn't exist.

We left the store, locking the front door behind us.

We stood beside my CRV in the parking lot and looked back. "Do you notice anything odd about this store?" I asked Diesel.

"No name," Diesel said. "There's just a door with a small cutout of a wooden soldier on it."

"What kind of a toy store doesn't have a name?"

"If you look closely you can see where the sign was torn off," Diesel said. "It used to hang above the door."

"Probably this is a front for a numbers operation."

Diesel shook his head. "It would have phones. It would probably have a computer. There'd be ashtrays and cigarette butts."

I raised my eyebrows at him.

"I watch television," he said.

Okay. Whatever. "I'm going to my parents' now," I told him. "Maybe you want me to drop you someplace. Shopping center, pool hall, loony bin . . ."

"Boy, that really hurts. You don't want me to meet your parents."

"It's not like we're going steady."

"My assignment is to bring you some Christmas cheer, and I take my job *very* seriously."

I gave him disgusted. "You do *not* take your job seriously. You told me you don't even like Christmas."

"I was caught by surprise. It's not usually my gig. But I'm starting to get into it. Can't you tell? Don't I look more cheery?"

"I'm not going to get rid of you, am I?"

He rocked back on his heels, hands in jacket pockets, a large grin firmly in place. "No."

I blew out a sigh, put the car into gear, and pulled out of the lot. It wasn't a far ride to my parents' house in the Burg. The Burg is short for Chambersburg, a small residential community that sits on the edge of Trenton proper. I was born and raised in the Burg and

I'll be a Burger for life. I've tried moving away, but I can't seem to get far enough.

Like most houses in the Burg, my parents' house is a small two-story clapboard built on a small, narrow lot. And like many houses in the Burg, the house shares a common wall with an identical house. Mabel Markowitz owns the house that adjoins my parents' house. She lives there alone, now that her husband has passed on. She keeps her windows clean, she plays bingo twice a week at the senior center, and she squeezes thirteen cents out of every dime.

I parked at the curb and Diesel looked at the two houses. Mrs. Markowitz's house was painted a bilious green. She had a plaster statue of the Virgin Mary in her tiny front yard and she'd put a pot of plastic red poinsettias next to the Virgin. A lone candle had been placed in her front window. My parents' house was painted yellow and brown and was decorated with a string of colored lights across the front of the house. A big old plastic Santa, his red suit sun-bleached to pale pink, had been set up in my parents' front yard, in direct competition with Mrs. Markowitz's Virgin. My mother had electric candles in all the windows and a wreath on the front door.

"Holy crap," Diesel said. "This is a car crash."

I had to agree with him. The houses were fascinating in their awfulness. Even worse, they were a comfort. They'd looked exactly like this for as long as I could remember. I couldn't imagine them looking any other way. When I was fourteen Mrs. Markowitz's Virgin had gotten beaned with a baseball and some of her head had chipped away, but that didn't stop the Virgin from blessing the house. She stood stalwart through wind and rain and sleet and storm with a chipped head. Just as Santa faded and dented but returned each year.

Grandma Mazur was behind my parents' glass storm door, looking out at us. Grandma Mazur lives with my parents now that Grampa Mazur's eating pork rinds and deep-fried peanut butter sandwiches with Elvis. Grandma Mazur's mostly spindle bone and slack skin. She keeps her gray hair curled tight to her head and carries a .45 long barrel in her purse. The concept of growing old gracefully has never taken hold with Grandma.

Grandma opened the door when I approached with Diesel. "Who's this?" she asked, eyeballing Diesel. "I didn't know you were bringing a new man over. Look at me. I'm not even dressed up. And what about Joseph? What happened to him?"

"Who's Joseph?" Diesel wanted to know.

"He's her boyfriend," Grandma Mazur said. "Joseph Morelli. He's a Trenton cop. He's supposed to be coming over later for dinner on account of it's Sunday."

Diesel grinned down at me. "You didn't tell me you had a boyfriend."

I introduced Diesel to my mom, Grandma Mazur, and my dad.

"What's with men and ponytails?" my father said. "Girls are supposed to have long hair. Men are supposed to have short hair."

"What about Jesus?" Grandma asked. "He had long hair."

"This guy isn't Jesus," my father said. He stuck his hand out to Diesel. "Nice to meet you. What are you, one of them wrestlers or something?"

"No sir, I'm not a wrestler," Diesel said, smiling.

"They're sports entertainers," Grandma said. "Only some of them are real good at wrestling, like Kurt Angle and Lance Storm."

"Lance Storm?" my father said. "What kind of a name is that?"

"It's one of those Canadian names," Grandma said. "He's a cutie, too."

Diesel looked at me and the smile widened. "I love your family."

TWO

My sister Valerie came in from the kitchen. Valerie is recently divorced and penniless and has moved herself and her two kids into my old bedroom. Before the divorce and the move back to Jersey, Valerie was living in southern California where she had limited success at cloning herself into Meg Ryan. Valerie's still got the blond shag. The resilient perkiness dropped out of her somewhere over Kansas on the flight home.

"Dang," Valerie said, taking Diesel in.

Grandma agreed. "He's a pip, isn't he?" she said. "He's a real looker."

Diesel elbowed me in the side. "You see? They like me."

I dragged Diesel into the living room. "They think you've got a nice ass. That's different from liking you. Sit in front of the television. Watch cartoons. Try to find a ball game. Don't talk to anybody."

My mother and grandmother and sister were waiting for me in the kitchen.

"Who is he?" Valerie wanted to know. "He's gorgeous."

"Yeah, and I can tell he's a hottie," Grandma said.

"He's got that look in his eye. And I bet he's got a good package."

"He's nobody," I said, trying to push aside thoughts of Diesel's package. "He moved into the building, and he doesn't know anybody, so I've sort of adopted him. He's kind of a charity case."

Valerie got serious. "Is he married?"

"I don't think so, but you don't want him. He's not normal."

"He looks normal."

"Trust me. *He's not your normal guy.*"

"He's gay, right?"

"Yep. That's it. I think he's gay." Better than telling Valerie that Diesel was a supernatural pain in the behind.

"The gorgeous ones are always gay," Valerie said with a sigh. "It's a rule."

Grandma had a big wad of cookie dough on the table. She rolled it out and then she gave me a star-shaped cookie cutter. "You do the sugar cookies," Grandma said. "I'm going to get Valerie working on the drop cookies."

If I take anything with me when I die it'll be the way my mother's kitchen smells. Coffee brewing in the morning, red cabbage and pot roast steaming the kitchen windows on a cold day in February, a hot apple pie on the counter in September. Sounds corny when I think about it, but the smells are real and as much a part of me as my thumb and my heart. I swear I first smelled pineapple upside-down cake when I was in the womb.

Today the air in my mother's kitchen was heavy with butter cookies baking in the oven. My mom used real butter and real vanilla, and the vanilla scent clung to my skin and hung in my hair. The kitchen was warm and cluttered with women, and I was drunk on butter cookies. It would be a perfect moment, if only there wasn't a space alien sitting in the living room, watching television with my dad.

I stuck my head out the kitchen door and looked through the dining room to Diesel and my dad in the living room. Diesel was standing in front of the Christmas tree—a scrawny, five-foot-tall spruce set into a rickety stand. Four days to Christmas and already the tree was dropping needles. My father had placed a green and silver foil star at the balding top of the tree. The rest of the tree was ringed with colored twinkle lights and decorated with an assortment of ornaments collected over the lifetime of my parents' marriage. The rickety stand was wrapped in white cotton batting that was supposed to resemble snow. A village of aging cardboard houses had been assembled on the cotton batting.

Valerie's kids, nine-year-old Angie and seven-year-old Mary Alice, had finished the tree off with gobs of tinsel. Angie is the perfect child and is often mistaken for a very short forty-year-old woman. Mary Alice has had a longstanding identity problem and is usually convinced she's a horse.

"Nice tree," Diesel said.

My father concentrated on the television screen. My father knew a loser tree when he saw one and this was no prizewinner. He'd cheaped out, as usual, and he'd gotten the tree from Andy at the Mobil station. Andy's trees always looked like they were grown next to a nuclear power plant.

Mary Alice and Angie had been watching television with my father. Mary Alice tore her attention away from the screen and looked up at Diesel. "Who are you?" she asked.

"My name's Diesel," he said. "Who are you?"

"I'm Mary Alice, and I'm a beautiful palomino. And that's my sister Angie. She's just a girl."

"You aren't a palomino," Angie said. "Palominos have golden hair, and you have brown hair."

"I can be a palomino if I want to," Mary Alice said.

"Can not."

"Can too."

"Can not."

I closed the kitchen door and returned to the cookie cutting. "There's a toy store in the Price Cutter strip mall in Hamilton Township," I said to my mother and grandmother. "Do either of you know anything about it?"

"I never saw a toy store there," Grandma said, "but I was shopping with Tootie Frick last week, and we saw a store with a toy soldier on the door. I tried the door, but it was locked, and there weren't any lights on inside. I asked someone about it and he said the store was haunted. He said last week there was an electrical storm *inside* the store, with thunder and everything."

I transferred a raw cookie-dough star from the table to the cookie sheet. "I don't know about the haunted part, but the place is supposed to be a toy store. The guy who owns it has failed to appear for a court date, and I haven't been able to find him. Supposedly he makes some of his own toys, and he has a workshop somewhere, but I haven't been able to get an address for the workshop."

When the bail bonds office opened tomorrow morning I'd have Connie, the office manager, run a cyber search on Claws. I could also check to see if Claws was on the books for electric and water at a location other than his house and his store.

"You're gonna have to pick the pace up here,"

Grandma said. "We still got to put the frosting on these cookies. And we got the filled cookies to make yet. And the cream cheese snowballs. I can't be doing this all day because I gotta go to a viewing tonight. Lenny Jelinek is laid out. He was a member of the Moose lodge, and you know what that means."

My mother and I looked at Grandma. We were clueless.

"I give up," my mother said. "What does that mean?"

"There's always a crowd when there's a Moose laid out. Lots of men. Easy pickins, if you're in the market for a studmuffin."

My mother was mixing cookie dough in a big bowl. She looked up, spoon in hand, and a glob of dough slid off the spoon and plopped onto the floor. "Studmuffin?"

"Of course, I've already got my studmuffin all picked out," Grandma said. "I met him at Harry Farfel's viewing, week before last. It was a real romantic meeting. My studmuffin just moved into the area. He was driving around, trying to find a business associate, and he got lost. So he went into Stiva's Funeral Parlor to ask for directions, and he bumped right into me. He said he bumped into me on account of he has vision problems, but I knew it was fate. All the little hairs on my arm stood up the second he knocked me down. Can you imagine? And now we're practically going steady. He's a real honey. He's a good kisser, too. Makes my lips tingle!"

"You never said anything," my mother said.

"I didn't want to make a fuss, what with Christmas on top of us."

I thought it was sort of cool that Grandma had a studmuffin, but I didn't really want a mental image of Grandma and the good kisser. Last time Grandma brought a man home to dinner he took his glass eye out at the table and set it alongside his spoon while he ate.

I had some success at eliminating senior studmuffin thoughts. I was having less success at eliminating thoughts of Diesel. I was worried he was in the living room deciding who in my family should be beamed up to the mothership. Or maybe he wasn't an alien. What then? Maybe he was Satan. Except, he didn't smell like fire and brimstone. His scent was more *yum*. Okay, probably he wasn't Satan. I went to the kitchen door and did another look out.

The kids were on the floor, transfixed by the television. My father was in his chair, sleeping. No Diesel. "Hey," I shouted to Angie. "Where's Diesel?"

Angie shrugged. Mary Alice looked around at me and also shrugged.

"Dad," I shouted. "Where'd Diesel go?"

My dad opened one eye. "Out. He said he'd be back by dinnertime."

Out? As in *out for a walk*? Or out as in *out of body*? I looked up to the ceiling, hoping Diesel wasn't hovering above us like the Ghost of Christmas Past. "Did he say where he was going?"

"Nope. Just said he'd be back." My father's eyes closed. End of conversation.

I suddenly had a scary thought. I ran to the front foyer with the spatula still in my hand. I looked out the front door and my heart momentarily stopped. The CRV was gone. He took my car. "Damn, damn, damn!" I went outside to the sidewalk and looked up and down the street. "Diesel!" I yelled. *"Deeezel!"* No response. Big deal Man of Mysterious Talents can open doors but can't hear me calling him.

"I just got to thinking about today's paper," Grandma

said when I returned to the kitchen. "I was looking at the want ads this morning, thinking I could use a job if the right thing turned up . . . like being a bar singer. Anyway, I didn't see any ads for bar singers, but there was an ad in there for toy makers. It was worded real cute, too. It said they were looking for elves."

The paper was on the floor beside my father's chair. I found the paper and read through the want ads. Sure enough, there was an ad for toy makers. Elves preferred. A phone number was given. Applicants were told to ask for Lester.

I dialed the number and got Lester on the second ring.

"Here's the thing, Lester," I said. "I got this phone number out of the paper. Are you really hiring toy makers?"

"Yes, but we're only taking toy makers of the very highest caliber."

"Elves?"

"Everyone knows, they're the top of the line toy makers."

"Are you taking on anyone other than elves?"

"Are you a non-elf, looking for a job?"

"I'm looking for a toy maker. Sandy Claws."

Click. Disconnect. I redialed and someone other than Lester answered. I asked for Lester and was told Lester wasn't available. I asked for the job seeker interview location and this resulted in another disconnect.

"I didn't know we had elves in Trenton," Grandma said. "Isn't that something? Elves right under our nose."

"I think he was kidding about the elves," I said.

"Too bad," Grandma said. "Elves would be fun."

"You're always working," my mother said to me. "You can't even bake Christmas cookies without making phone calls about criminals. Loretta Krakowski's daughter doesn't do that. Loretta's daughter comes home from the button factory and never thinks about her job. Loretta's daughter handmade all her own Christmas cards." My mother stopped mixing dough and looked at me, wide-eyed and fear-filled. "Did you send out your Christmas cards?"

Omigod, Christmas cards. I forgot all about Christmas cards. "Sure," I said. "I sent them out last week." I hoped God and Santa Claus weren't listening to me fib.

My mother blew out a whoosh of air and made the sign of the cross. "Thank goodness. I was afraid you forgot, again."

Mental note. Buy some Christmas cards.

By five o'clock we were done with the cookies and my mother had a tray of lasagna in the oven. The cookies were in cookie jars and cookie tins and some were stacked high on plates for instant eating. I was at the sink, washing the last of the baking sheets, and I felt the skin prickle at the back of my neck. I turned and bumped into Diesel.

"You took my car," I said, jumping back. "You just drove off with it. You *stole* it!"

"Chill. I *borrowed* it. I didn't want to disturb you. You were busy with the cookie making."

"If you had to go somewhere why didn't you just pop yourself there . . . like you popped into my apartment?"

"I'm keeping a low profile. I save the popping for special occasions."

"You're not really the Spirit of Christmas, are you?"

"I could be if I wanted. I hear the job's up for grabs."

He was wearing the same boots and jeans and jacket, but he'd substituted a brown sweater for the stained thermal.

"Did you go home to change?"

"Home is far away." He playfully twirled a lock of my hair around his finger. "You ask a lot of questions."

"Yeah, but I'm not getting any answers."

"There's a chubby little guy in the living room with your dad. Is that your boyfriend?"

"That's Albert Kloughn. He's Valerie's boyfriend."

I heard the front door open, and seconds later, Morelli sauntered into the kitchen. He looked first to me and then to Diesel. He extended his hand to Diesel. "Joe Morelli," he said.

"Diesel."

They spent a moment measuring. Diesel was an inch taller and had more bulk. Morelli wasn't someone you'd want to meet in a dark alley. Morelli was all lean hard muscle and dark assessing eyes. The moment passed, Morelli smiled at me and dropped a feather-light kiss on the top of my head.

"Diesel is an alien or something," I said to Morelli. "He appeared in my kitchen this morning."

"As long as he didn't spend the night," Morelli said. He reached around me to a cookie tin, removed the lid, and selected a cookie.

I cut my eyes to Diesel and caught him smiling.

Morelli's pager buzzed. He checked the readout and swore to himself. He used the kitchen phone, staring at his shoes while he was talking. Never a good sign. The conversation was short.

"I have to go," Morelli said. "Work."

"Will I see you later?"

Morelli pulled me out to the back stoop and shut the kitchen door behind us. "Stanley Komenski was just found stuffed into an industrial waste barrel. It was sitting in the alley behind that new Thai restaurant on Sumner Street. Apparently it had been sitting there for

days and was attracting flies, not to mention some local dogs and a pack of crows. He was muscle for Lou
Two Toes so this is going to get ugly. And if that isn't
bad enough, there's something screwy going on with the
electric grid. There have been power outages in pockets all over Trenton and they all of a sudden correct
themselves. Not a big deal, but it's making a mess out
of traffic." Morelli turned his head to look through the
glass pane, into the kitchen. "Who's the big guy?"

"I told you. He popped into my kitchen this morning. I think he's an alien. Or maybe he's some kind of
a ghost."

Morelli felt my forehead. "Are you running a fever?
Have you fallen down again?"

"I'm fine. Pay attention. The guy popped into my
kitchen."

"Yeah, but *everyone* pops into your kitchen."

"Not like this. He really popped in. Like he was
beamed down, or something."

"Okay," Morelli said, "I believe you. He's an alien."
Morelli dragged me tight against him, and he kissed
me. And he left.

"So," Diesel said, when I returned to the kitchen.
"How'd that go?"

"I don't think he believed me."

"No kidding. You go around telling people I'm an
alien and they're eventually going to lock you up in the
booby hatch. And just for the record, I'm not an alien.
And I'm not a ghost."

"Vampire?"

"A vampire can't enter a home without an invitation."

"This is too weird."

"It's not that weird," Diesel said. "I can do some
things most people can't do. Don't make more of it than
it is."

"I don't know what it is!"
Diesel's smile returned.

At precisely six o'clock we sat down to the table.

"Isn't this nice," Grandma said. "It feels like a party."

"I'm squished," Mary Alice said. "Horses don't like when they're squished. There's too many people at this table."

"I've got room," Albert Kloughn said. "I can pick my fork up and everything."

My father already had lasagna on his plate. My father always got served first with the hope that he'd be busy eating and wouldn't jump up and strangle Grandma Mazur. "Where's the gravy?" he asked. "Where's the extra sauce?"

Angie carefully passed the bowl with the extra marinara sauce to Mary Alice. Mary Alice had a hard time getting her hooves around the bowl, the bowl wobbled in midair and then crashed onto the table, setting loose a tidal wave of tomato sauce. Grandma reached across the table to grab the bowl, knocked over a candlestick and the tablecloth went up in flames. This wasn't the first time this had happened.

"*Yow!* Fire," Kloughn yelled. "Fire. *Fire!* We're all gonna die!"

My father looked up briefly, shook his head like he couldn't believe this was actually his life, and returned to shoveling in his lasagna. My mother made the sign of the cross. And I dumped a pitcher of ice water into the middle of the table, putting an end to the fire.

Diesel grinned. "I love this family. I just *love* this family."

"I didn't really think we were going to die," Kloughn said.

"Have another slice of lasagna," my mother said to Valerie. "Look at you, you're all skin and bones."

"That's because she throws up when she eats," Grandma said.

"I have a virus," Valerie said. "I get nervous."

"Maybe you're pregnant," Grandma said. "Maybe you got the morning sickness all day long."

Kloughn went white and fell off his chair. *Crash,* onto the floor.

Grandma looked down at him. "They don't make men like they used to."

Valerie clapped her hand to her mouth and ran out of the room, up the stairs to the bathroom.

"Holy Mary Mother of God," my mother said.

Kloughn opened his eyes. "What happened?"

"You fainted," Grandma said. "You went down like a sack of sand."

Diesel got out of his chair and helped Kloughn to his feet. "Way to go, stud," Diesel said.

"Thank you," Kloughn said. "I'm very virile. It runs in the family."

"I'm tired of sitting here," Mary Alice said. "I need to gallop."

"You will not gallop," my mother yelled at Mary Alice. "You're not a horse. You're a little girl, and you'll act like one or you'll go to your room."

We all sat stunned because my mother never yelled. And even more shocking, my mother (having put her time in with me, the original space cadet) never made an issue of the horse thing.

There was a moment of silence and then Mary Alice started bawling. She had her eyes scrunched tight and her mouth wide open. Her face was red and blotchy and tears dripped off her cheeks onto her shirt.

"Christ," my father said. "Somebody do something."

"Hey, kid," Diesel said to Mary Alice, "what do you want for Christmas this year?"

Mary Alice tried to stop crying but her breath was coming in gulps and hiccups. She scrubbed tears off her face and wiped her nose with the back of her hand. "I don't want anything for Christmas. I *hate* Christmas. Christmas is poopy."

"There must be something you want," Grandma said.

Mary Alice pushed her food around on her plate with her fork. "There's nothing. And I know there's no Santa Claus, too. He's just a big fat fake."

No one had an immediate response. She'd caught us by surprise. *There was no Santa Claus.* How crappy is that?

Diesel finally leaned forward on his elbows and looked across the table at Mary Alice. "This is the way I see it, Mary Alice. I can't say for sure if there's really a Santa Claus, but I think it's fun to pretend. The truth is, we all have a choice to make, and we can believe in whatever we want."

"I think you're poopy, too," Mary Alice said to Diesel.

Diesel slid his arm across my shoulders and leaned close, his breath warm against my ear. "You were smart to choose a hamster," he said.

Valerie returned to the dining room in time for dessert. "It's an allergy," she said. "I think I'm lactose-intolerant."

"Boy, that's a shame," Grandma said. "We got pineapple upside-down cake for tonight, and it's got lots of whipped cream on it."

Beads of sweat appeared on Valerie's upper lip and forehead, and Valerie ran back upstairs.

"Funny how these things come on," Grandma said.

"She was never lactose-intolerant before. She must have caught it in California."

"I'm going to get some cookies from the kitchen," my mother said.

I followed after her and found her belting back a tumbler of Four Roses.

She jumped when she saw me. "You startled me," she said.

"I came to help with the cookies."

"I was just taking a nip." A shudder raced through my mother. "It's Christmas, you know."

This was a nip the size of a Big Gulp. "Probably Valerie isn't pregnant," I said.

My mother drained the Big Gulp, crossed herself, and went back into the dining room with the cookies.

"So," Grandma said to Kloughn, "do you make Christmas cookies at your house? Is your tree up yet?"

"We don't actually have a tree," Kloughn said. "We're Jewish."

Everyone stopped eating, even my father.

"You don't look Jewish," Grandma said. "You don't wear one of them beanies."

Kloughn rolled his eyes up as if looking for his missing beanie, clearly at a loss for words, probably still not getting total oxygen to his brain after fainting.

"How great is this?" Grandma said. "If you marry Valerie we can celebrate some of those Jewish holidays. And we can get a set of the candlesticks. I always wanted one of those Jewish candlestick things. Isn't this something," Grandma said. "Wait until I tell the girls at the beauty parlor that we might get a Jew in our family. Everyone's going to be jealous."

My father was still sitting lost in thought. His daughter might marry a Jewish guy. This wasn't a great thing to happen, in my father's view. Not that he had anything against Jewish guys. It was that chances were slim to nonexistent that Kloughn was Italian. In my father's scheme of things, there were Italians and then there was the rest of the world. "You wouldn't be of Italian descent, would you?" my father asked Kloughn.

"My grandparents were German," Kloughn said.

My father sighed and went back to concentrating on his lasagna. Yet another fuckup in the family.

My mother was white-faced. Bad enough her daughters didn't attend church. The possibility of non-Catholic grandchildren was a disaster right up there with nuclear annihilation. "Maybe I need to put a couple more cookies on the plate," my mother said, pushing back from the table.

One more cookie run and my mother was going to be passed out on the kitchen floor.

At nine o'clock Angie and Mary Alice were tucked into bed. My grandmother was somewhere with her studmuffin, and my mother and father were in front of the television. Valerie and Albert Kloughn were *discussing* things in the kitchen. And Diesel and I were standing outside on the sidewalk in front of the CRV. It was cold and our breath made frost clouds.

"So what happens now?" I asked. "Do you get beamed back up?"

"Not tonight. Couldn't get a flight."

My eyebrows raised a quarter of an inch.

"I'm kidding," he said. "Boy, you'll believe anything."

Apparently. "Well, it's been a real treat," I said, "but I've got to go now."

"Sure. See you around."

I got into the CRV, cranked the engine over, and took off. When I got to the corner I swiveled in my seat and looked back. Diesel was still standing exactly where

I'd left him. I drove around the block, and when I returned to my parents' house the sidewalk was empty. Diesel had vanished without a trace.

He didn't pop into my car when I was halfway home. He didn't appear in my apartment building hallway. He wasn't in my kitchen, bedroom, or bathroom.

I dropped a piece of butter cookie into the hamster cage on my kitchen counter and watched Rex jump off his wheel and rush at the cookie. "We got rid of the alien," I said to Rex. "Good deal, hunh?"

Rex looked like he was thinking, *alien schmalien*. I guess when you live in a glass cage you don't care a lot about aliens in the kitchen. When you're a woman alone in an apartment, aliens are pretty damn frightening. Except for Diesel. Diesel was inconvenient and confusing, and as much as I hate to admit it, Diesel was annoyingly likeable. Frightening had dropped low on the list. "So," I said to Rex, "why do you suppose I'm not afraid of Diesel? Probably some kind of alien magic, right?"

Rex was working at getting the cookie into his cheek pouch.

"And while we're having this discussion," I said to Rex, "I want to reassure you that I haven't forgotten about Christmas. I know it's only four days away, but I made cookies today. That's a good start, right?"

Truth is, there wasn't a trace of Christmas in my apartment. Counting down four days and I didn't have a red bow or twinkle light in sight. Plus, I didn't have presents for anyone.

"How did this happen?" I asked Rex. "It seemed like just yesterday that Christmas was months away."

I opened my eyes and shrieked. Diesel was standing beside my bed, staring down at me. I grabbed the sheet and pulled it up to my chin.

"What? How?" I asked.

He handed me a large-size take-out coffee. "Didn't we do this bit yesterday?"

"I thought you were gone."

"Yeah, but now I'm back. This is the part where you say, good morning, nice to see you, thanks for the coffee."

I pried the plastic lid off and examined the coffee. It looked like coffee. It smelled like coffee.

"Cripes," he said. "It's just coffee."

"A girl can never be too careful."

Diesel took the coffee back and drank it. "Rise and shine, gorgeous. We have things to do. We need to find Sandy Claws."

"I know why *I* need to find Sandy Claws. I don't know why *you* need to find Sandy Claws."

"Just being a good guy. I thought I'd come back and help you out."

Uh-hunh.

"Are you going to get up, or what?" he said.

"I'm not getting up with you standing there. And I'm not taking a shower with you in my apartment, either. Go out and wait for me in the hall."

He shook his head. "You are *so* untrusting."

"Go!"

I waited until I heard the front door open and close and then I slid out of bed and crept to the living room. Empty. I padded barefoot to the front door, opened the door, and looked out. Diesel was leaning against the opposite wall, arms crossed over his chest, looking bored.

"Just checking," I said. "You're not going to pop into my bathroom when I'm in there, are you?"

"No."

"Promise?"

"Honey, I don't need a thrill that bad."

I closed and locked the door, ran into the bathroom, took the fastest shower in the history of Plum, rushed back to my bedroom, and got dressed in my usual uniform of jeans, boots, and T-shirt. I refilled Rex's water bottle and gave him some hamster crunches, a raisin, and a corn chip for breakfast. He rushed out of his soup can, stuffed the raisin and the corn chip into his cheek pouch, and returned to his soup can.

I'd had a brilliant idea while I was in the shower. I knew a guy who might help me find Claws. His name was Randy Briggs. Briggs wasn't an elf, but he *was* only three feet tall. Maybe that was good enough.

I thumbed through my address book and found Briggs' phone number. Briggs was a self-employed computer geek. He usually worked at home. And he usually needed money.

"Hey," I said to him. "I have a job for you. I need an undercover elf."

"I'm not an elf."

"Yes, but you're short."

"Christ," Briggs said. And he hung up.

Probably best to talk to Briggs in person. Unfortunately, I now had a dilemma. I thought there was a possibility that Diesel might go away if I never opened the door and let him in. Problem was, I needed to go out.

I opened the door and looked at Diesel.

"Yeah, I'm still here," he said.

"I need to go someplace."

"No kidding."

"Alone."

"It's the supernatural thing, isn't it? It's still got you weirded out, right?"

"Um . . ."

He slung an arm around my shoulders. "I bet you

think Spider-Man is a real cute guy. I bet you think it'd be fun to be friends with a guy like that."

"Maybe . . ."

"So just pretend I'm Spidey."

I looked at him sideways. "Are you Spidey?"

"No. He's a lot shorter."

I grabbed my bag and my keys and shrugged into my fleece-lined jacket. I locked my front door and took the stairs to the parking lot.

Diesel was right behind me. "We can take my car," he said.

"You have a car?"

There was a black Jaguar parked a few feet from the back entrance to my apartment building. Diesel beeped the Jag open with the remote.

"Wow," I said, "you do okay for an alien."

"I'm not an alien."

"Yeah, you keep saying that, but I don't know what else to call you."

"Call me Diesel."

I angled onto the passenger side seat and buckled in. "It's stolen, right?"

Diesel looked over at me and smiled.

Damn. "We're going to Cloverleaf Apartments on Grand. It's about a mile from here, off Hamilton."

The Cloverleaf apartment building looked a lot like mine. It was a big redbrick cube and strictly utilitarian. Three stories. A front and a back entrance. Parking lot in the rear.

Randy Briggs lived on the second floor. I'd met him a while back in a professional capacity. He'd been accused of carrying a concealed weapon and had failed to appear for a court appearance. I'd dragged him kicking and screaming back into the system. The charge had actually been borderline bogus, and Briggs was ultimately released without penalty.

"And why are we doing this?" Diesel asked, climbing the stairs to the second floor.

"There was a want ad in the paper for toy makers. When I called and inquired about Sandy Claws I got disconnected."

"And in your mind, this indicates that Claws is part of the toy maker operation."

"I think it's suspicious and warrants further investigation. I'm going to ask this guy I know to help infiltrate the operation."

"Is he a toy maker?"

"No. He has other talents."

We were in the stairwell and all of a sudden we were plunged into total darkness. I felt Diesel step closer, felt his hand protectively settle at my waist.

"Power blackout," I said. "Morelli told me they were happening all over Trenton."

"Great," Diesel said. "Just what I need. Power blackouts."

"Not a big deal," I told him. "Morelli said they last long enough to snarl traffic and then disappear."

"Sunshine, it's a bigger deal than you could possibly imagine."

I had no idea what he meant by that, but it didn't sound good. I was about to ask him when the lights popped back on, and we took the rest of the stairs to the second floor. I rapped on the door to 2B and there was no response. I put my ear to the door and listened.

"Hear anything?" Diesel asked.

"Television."

I rapped again. "Open the door, Randy. I know you're in there."

"Go away," Randy called. "I'm working."

"You're not working. You're watching television."

The door was wrenched open, and Randy glared out at me. "What?"

Diesel looked down at Randy. "You're a midget."

"No shit, Sherlock," Randy said. "And, just for the record, midget is no longer politically correct."

"So, what do you like?" Diesel asked. "How about 'little dude'?"

Randy was holding a soup ladle, and he whacked Diesel in the knee with it. "Don't mess with me, wiseass."

Diesel reached down, grabbed Briggs by the front of his shirt, and lifted him three feet off the floor so they were eye level. "You need to get a sense of humor," Diesel said. "And you want to lose the soup ladle."

The soup ladle slid through Randy's fingers and clattered onto the parquet floor.

"So you don't want to be called a little dude," Diesel said. "What *do* you want to be called?"

"I'm a little *person*," Randy said, feet dangling in the air.

Diesel grinned at Randy. "Little person? That's the best you can do?"

Diesel set Randy back down on the floor, and Randy gave himself a shake, looking a lot like a bird settling its feathers.

"So," I said, "now that we have that straightened out . . ."

Briggs looked at me. "Here it comes."

"Have I ever asked for a favor?"

"Yes."

"Okay, but I saved your life."

"My life wouldn't have been in danger in the first place if it wasn't for you!"

"All I want is for you to pose as an elf."

Diesel gave a snort of laughter.

I cut my eyes to him, and he squelched the laughter down to a grin.

"I am *not* an elf," Briggs said. "Do I have pointy ears? No. Do I wear shoes that turn up on the ends? No. Do I enjoy this humiliation? No, no, no."

"I'll pay you for your time."

"Oh," Briggs said. "That's different."

I handed the ad over to Briggs. "All you have to do is answer this ad. Probably you don't even have to say you're an elf. Probably you could just tell him you're . . . qualified. And then when you go for the job interview, keep your eyes open for a guy named Sandy Claws. He's FTA."

"Give me a break. Santa Claus is FTA. How about the Easter Bunny? Is the Easter Bunny FTA, too?"

I flashed the photo of Sandy Claws at Briggs, and I spelled the name for him. I gave Briggs my card with my cell phone and pager number. And I left, not wanting to overstay my welcome, not wanting to give him time to change his mind.

I looked over at Diesel's knee when we were in the car. "Are you okay?"

"Yeah. He hits like a girl. Someone needs to show him how to swing a soup ladle."

THREE

Connie Rosolli manages my cousin Vinnie's bail bonds office. Connie is a couple years older than me. She has big hair, big boobs, and a short fuse. And she could probably kick my butt from here to downtown Trenton. Good thing for me, Connie never feels compelled to kick my butt since Connie and I are friends.

I called Connie and asked her to check on water and electric accounts for Claws. Between semiclandestine computer searches and the tight-knit network of Burg women who love to dish, there isn't a lot of information Connie and I can't access.

I'd barely disconnected with Connie when my cell phone chirped.

It was my mother. "Help," she said.

I could hear a lot of hysterical shouting going on in the background. "What's happening?"

"Valerie took one of those home pregnancy tests, and now she's got herself locked in the bathroom."

"Don't worry about it. She'll come out when she gets hungry."

"It's our only bathroom! I've got two kids home from school for the holidays, an old lady with a bad bladder, and your father. Everybody needs to use the bathroom."

"And?"

"Do something! Shoot the lock off."

Now if I was any kind of a good sister and loving daughter I'd have sympathy for Valerie. I'd be worried about her physical and emotional health. The ugly truth is, Valerie was always the perfect child. And I was the kid who had the skinned knee, consistently flunked spelling, and lived in Lala Land. My entire childhood was an out-of-body experience. Even as adults, Valerie had the great marriage and gave birth to two grandchildren. I had the marriage from hell that ended before my father got the wedding reception paid off. So, I love my sister and wish her well, but it's hard not to smile once in a while now that her life is in the toilet.

"Uh-oh," Diesel said. "I'm not sure I like that smile."

"It sort of slipped out. Actually, I need you to help me with a domestic problem. I need a lock opened."

"Someday I should show you some of my other skills."

Oh boy. It's never good when a man starts talking about his skills. Before you know it you're in the garage watching a power tool demonstration. And after all the power tools are revved, there's only one tool left to haul out of the box. Someday a study should be done on the effect of testosterone production in the presence of a band saw.

Everyone was huddled outside the bathroom when I got to my parents' house. Mary Alice was galloping in circles and the rest of my family was alternately pacing and yelling and banging on the door.

"Pretty amazing," Diesel said to me. "I'm always knocked out by the way a family can be at the upper end of dysfunction and insanity and still work so well as a unit. Do you want me to open the door?"

"No." I was afraid they'd all rush in and someone

would get trampled in the stampede. I went downstairs to the kitchen and out the back door. There was a small roof over the back stoop, and the roof butted up to the bathroom window. When I was a kid I used to sneak out the bathroom window to hang with my friends. "Give me a boost up," I said to Diesel. "I'll bring her out through the window. Then you can open the door."

Diesel laced his fingers together, I put my foot in his hands, and he lifted me to roof level. I scrambled onto the roof and glanced down at him. He was impressively strong.

"Could you stop a runaway freight train?" I asked.

"Probably not a freight train. That would be Superman."

I looked in the window at Valerie. She was sitting on the toilet lid, staring at the little test strip. She looked up when I knocked.

"Open up," I said. "It's cold out here."

She pressed her nose to the window and looked out. "Are you alone?"

"I'm with Diesel."

She looked down to the ground, and Diesel waved to her. It was a goofy little finger wave.

Valerie opened the window, and I climbed inside.

"What's going on?" I asked.

"Look at my test strip!"

"Maybe it made a mistake."

"It's the fifth time I've taken the test. They keep coming out positive. I'm pregnant. I'm goddamn pregnant. Albert Kloughn got me pregnant."

"Didn't you take precautions?"

"No, I didn't take precautions. Look at him! He looks like a loaf of yeast bread just before you bake it. He's soft and white and totally without substance. Who would have thought he'd have sperm? Do you know what this poor kid will look like?" Valerie wailed. "It'll look like a dinner roll."

"Maybe this isn't so bad. I thought you were all anxious to get married."

"I was anxious to get married, not to get pregnant. And I don't want to marry Kloughn. He lives with his *mother,* for God's sake. And he makes *no* money."

"He's a lawyer."

"He chases ambulances down the street. He might as well be a German shepherd."

It was true. Kloughn was having a difficult time getting his practice established and had resorted to listening to the police band.

"A woman has choices these days," I said.

"Not in this family!" Valerie was pacing and waving her arms. "We're Catholic, for crissake."

"Yeah, but you never go to church. It isn't like you have religion."

"You know what's left when the religion goes away? Guilt! Guilt *never* goes away. I'm stuck with the goddamn guilt for the rest of my life. And what about Mom? I even mention abortion, and she'll be crossing herself until her arm falls off."

"Don't tell her. Tell her the strip was negative."

Valerie stopped pacing and looked at me. "Would you get an abortion?"

Whoa. Me? I took a beat to think about it. "I don't know," I said. "I'm having a hard time relating. The closest I've come to childbirth is buying a hamster."

"Fine," Valerie said. "Suppose Rex was never born. Suppose the mommy hamster had an abortion and Rex was bagged up along with the dirty kennel bedding in the breeder hamster cage."

Sharp pain to the heart. "When you put it that way . . ."

"It's all his fault," Valerie said. "I'm going to find him. I'm going to track him down, and I'm going to maim him."

"Kloughn?"

"No. My dog turd ex-husband. If he hadn't run off with the babysitter this never would have happened. We were so happy. I don't know what went wrong. One minute we were a family and then next thing I know he's in the coat closet with the babysitter."

"Open up!" Grandma yelled from the other side of the door. "I gotta go. Lock yourself in some other room."

"Just because you have the baby doesn't mean you have to marry Kloughn," I said. Although I actually thought Valerie could do a lot worse than Albert Kloughn. I liked Kloughn. He wasn't a big, handsome, supercool guy, but he tried hard at everything, he was nice to Valerie and the girls, and there seemed to be genuine affection between them all. I wasn't sure anymore what made a good marriage. There had to be love, of course, but there were so many different kinds of love. And clearly, some love was more enduring than others. Valerie and I thought we'd found the loves of our lives, and look where that took us.

"Shoes," I said to Valerie. "When in doubt, I find it always helps if I buy a new pair of shoes. You should go shopping."

Valerie looked over at the door. "I could use a new pair of shoes, but I don't want to go out there."

"Use the window."

Valerie climbed out the window, got to the edge of the roof and hesitated. "This is scary."

"It's not a big deal," Diesel said. "Just hang your ass over the edge, and I'll bring you down."

Valerie looked back at me.

"Trust him," I said. Trust Superman, Spider-Man, E.T., the Ghost of Christmas Present . . . whoever the hell.

"I don't know," Valerie said. "This feels kind of high. I don't like the way this feels. Maybe I need to go back into the house." Valerie turned toward the window, and her foot slipped on the shingle roof. "Eeeeee," she shrieked, flailing out with her arms, grabbing me by my jacket. "Help! *Help!*"

She yanked me forward, and we both lost balance, slammed onto the roof, and rolled off the edge, clinging together. We crashed into Diesel, and the three of us went to the ground.

Diesel was flat on his back, I was on top of him, and Val was on top of me. The whole family came running out the back door and crowded around us.

"What's going on?" Grandma wanted to know. "Is this some new sex thing?"

"If she jumps on the pile, I'm out of here," Diesel said.

"Call 911!" my mother said. "Don't anybody move . . . your backs might be broken." She looked down at Valerie. "Can you wiggle your toes?"

"You didn't unlock the bathroom," my father said to Valerie. "Someone's gotta go back up and unlock the bathroom."

"Frank! I told you to call 911."

"We don't need 911," I said. "We just need for Valerie to get off me."

My mother pulled Valerie to her feet. "Is the baby okay? Did you hurt yourself? I can't believe you went out through the window."

"What about me?" I said. "I fell, too."

"You're always falling," my mother said. "You jumped off the garage roof when you were seven years old. And now people shoot at you." She shook her finger at me. "You're a bad influence on your sister. She never used to do things like this."

I was still lying on top of Diesel, and I was sort of enjoying it.

"I knew you'd come around," Diesel said to me.

I narrowed my eyes. "I have *not* come around."

My pager buzzed at my waist. I rolled off Diesel and checked the readout. It was Randy Briggs. I got to my feet and went into the house to use the phone while Diesel went upstairs to unlock the bathroom door.

My father followed Diesel to the bathroom. "Women," my father said. "There's gotta be a better way."

I was waiting at the door when Diesel came down. "Randy's got a job interview," I said. "He's on the road. I have the address."

"What about the shopping?" Valerie asked.

"You have to shop by yourself," I said. "I have to find Sandy Claws. And why aren't you working?"

"I don't want to see Albert. I don't know what to say to him."

"I'm lost," Diesel said. "What's Albert got to do with working?"

"He's Valerie's boss."

"This is like watching daytime television," Diesel said.

"Look at you," my mother said to me. "It's almost Christmas and you're not wearing anything red." She took a Christmas tree pin off her shirt and attached it to my jacket. "Have you bought your tree yet?" she asked.

"I haven't had time to get a tree."

"You have to make time," my mother said. "Before

you know it your life will be over and you'll be dead and then what?"

"You have a tree," I said. "Why can't I use yours?"

"Boy, you don't know much," my grandmother said.

Diesel was standing back on his heels, hands in his pockets, smiling, again.

"Go to the car," I said to Diesel. "And stop smiling."

"It's Christmastime," Diesel said. "Everybody smiles at Christmastime."

"Wait right here," my mother said. "Let me pack you a bag for lunch."

"No time," I said to my mother. "I need to get moving."

"It'll only take a minute!" She was already in the kitchen, and I could hear the refrigerator open and close and drawers open and close. And my mother returned with a bag of food.

"Thanks," I said.

Diesel looked in the bag and extracted a cookie. "Chocolate chip. My favorite."

I had a feeling *every* cookie was Diesel's favorite.

When we were both in the car, I turned to Diesel. "I want to know about you."

"There isn't a lot to tell. If I hadn't gotten dropped into your kitchen we wouldn't be having this conversation. If you met me on the street you'd think I was just another guy."

"So you're strong and can open locks. Anything else you're especially good at?"

Diesel smiled at me.

"All men think that," I said.

Diesel pulled onto Hamilton Avenue and turned left. "What happens when you find Claws?"

"I hand him over to the police. Then my cousin

Vinnie probably goes to the lockup and bails Claws out a second time."

"Why would Vinnie do that?"

"He gets paid more money. Claws has a local business, and he's signed his house over for security, so it's a good risk for Vinnie."

"And what if Claws doesn't want to be handed over to the police? Do you shoot him?"

"I hardly ever shoot people."

"This should be fun," Diesel said.

I cut my eyes to him. "Is there something you're not telling me?"

"Lots of things."

I put my finger to my lower lid.

"You have a problem?" he asked.

"Eye twitch."

"I bet that would go away if you got a Christmas tree."

"All right. Okay! I'll get a Christmas tree."

"When?"

"When I have time. And you're driving too slow. Where'd you learn how to drive, Florida?"

Diesel stopped the car in the middle of the road. "Take a deep breath."

"What are you doing? Are you nuts? You can't just stop in the middle of the road!"

"Take a deep breath. Count to ten."

I took a breath, and I counted to ten.

"Count slower," Diesel said.

The guy behind us honked his horn, and I cracked my knuckles. My eye was twitching like mad. "This isn't working," I said. "You're giving me heart palpitations. People in Jersey don't do *slow down*."

"We're sitting in traffic," Diesel said. "Notice that the car in front of us is less than a car length away and not moving. The only way to drive faster would be to drive on the sidewalk."

"What's your point?"

"I can't fit on the sidewalk."

"So do something supernatural," I said. "Can't you tip the car sideways or something? They do that in the movies all the time."

"Sorry, I flunked levitation."

My luck, I get a guy who flunked levitation.

Twenty minutes later, we parked across from a hole-in-the-wall storefront office. The makeshift sign in the window advertised IMMEDIATE OPENINGS FOR MASTER TOY MAKERS. I wanted to take a closer look, so we left the car and crossed the street.

We stood on the sidewalk and looked through the dusty plate-glass window. Inside, the place was wall-to-wall little people.

"Are they elves?" I asked Diesel. "I don't see any pointy ears."

"Hard to tell at this distance, and I heard somewhere that elves don't necessarily have pointy ears."

"So elves could be walking around in our midst, disguised as normal, everyday, vertically challenged citizens."

Diesel looked at me and grimaced. "You don't really believe in elves, do you?"

"Of course not," I said. But the truth was that I didn't know *what* I believed in anymore. I mean, what the hell was Diesel? And if I believed in Diesel . . . why not believe in elves? "Do you see Briggs?" I asked him.

"He's at the back, talking to a big guy with a clip-board. And I don't see Claws."

We watched for a moment longer and then retreated to the Jag and worked our way through my mother's food bag. After a while Randy Briggs came out, walked halfway down the block, and got into the passenger side of a waiting car. The car pulled away, and we followed. Before we'd gone two blocks my cell phone buzzed in my bag.

"Cripes, is that you behind me in the Jag?" Briggs asked. "You bounty hunters must do okay to be riding around in a Jag."

"Diesel isn't a bounty hunter. He's an alien or something."

"Yeah, whatever. Man, I've never seen so many little people in one place. It was like they came out of the woodwork. I thought I knew everyone in the area, but I didn't know *any* of these guys."

"Did you get hired?"

"Yeah, but I'm not going to make toys. I got a job in the office, setting up a Web site."

"What about Claws?"

"Didn't see him. No one said anything to me about anyone named Claws. I start work tomorrow. Maybe I'll see him at the factory."

"Factory?"

"Yeah, that's what this is . . . a small toy factory. They're going to make handmade toys and advertise that they were made by elves. Pretty cool, hunh?"

"Do you suppose some of these little people today actually were elves?"

There was a pause where I could imagine Briggs staring open-mouthed at the phone. "What are you, nuts?" he finally said.

"So, where is this factory?" I asked Briggs.

"It's in a light industrial complex off Route 1. You aren't going to screw up this job for me, are you? This is a dream job. The pay is good and the guy who hired me said the toilets are all made for little people. I won't have to climb up on a stool to take a crap."

"I'm not going to screw it up for you. What's the address?"

"I'm not telling you. I don't want to lose the job." And he hung up.

I looked over at Diesel. "When the car in front of us stops and Briggs gets out, I want you to run over him."

"I'd really like to do that, but then he'd probably be dead and we couldn't follow him to work tomorrow."

I glanced at the almost empty bag of food sitting between my feet, and I had an idea.

"What does Elaine do with all her cookies?" I asked Diesel.

"Is this a trick question?"

"She said she bakes cookies every day. Lots of cookies, if yesterday's batch was any indicator. So what does she do with them? They don't have family in the area. Sandy wasn't at home. Does she eat them all herself?"

"Maybe she gives them away."

"Turn around," I said. "Go back to the employment place."

It took less than five minutes for us to get back to the storefront office. "Wait here," I said. "I'll only be a minute." I jumped out of the car, ran across the street and into the office. It was still wall-to-wall little people but now the little people were all wearing fake elf ears. I was about ten feet into the fake elves when I realized the room had gone dead silent.

"Hi," I said brightly. "I saw the sign in the window, and I'd like to apply for a job."

"You're too big," someone said behind me. "These jobs are for elves."

"That's not fair," I said. "I could report you for height discrimination." I wasn't sure exactly who was in charge of height discrimination, but it seemed like there should be *some* agency *somewhere* that would address the issue. I mean, where are the protections for the masses? Where are the protections for people who are average?

"We don't want your kind here," someone else said. "Get out."

"My kind?"

"Big and stupid."

"Hey! Listen to me, shorty—"

A cookie came flying through the air and hit me in the back of the head. I looked down at the cookie. Gingerbread!

"Where'd this cookie come from?" I asked. "Do you have any more? Did Sandy's sister, Elaine, make this cookie?"

"Get her!" someone yelled, and I was hit with a barrage of cookies. They were coming from everywhere. Gingerbread, peanut butter, chocolate macaroons. The elves were berserk, yelling and swarming around me. I was hit in the forehead with an iced butter cookie, and someone bit me in the back of the leg. I had elves hanging on me like ticks on a dog.

I felt Diesel come up hard to my back. He wrapped his arm around me, holding me tight against him, and he hauled me out of there with my feet two inches off the ground. He was kicking elves out of the way as he went, occasionally grabbing one by the shirt and throwing him across the room. He got to the sidewalk, rammed the office door closed, and did his magical locking thing, trapping the elves inside.

Contorted little elf faces smushed up against the large glass windows, glaring out at us, yelling elf threats, their pudgy little elf middle fingers extended. Inside, the room was a wreck. Tables and chairs were overturned, and cookies were smashed everywhere.

Diesel set me on my feet, took me by the hand, and

yanked me to the car. "What the hell was that about?" he asked. "I've never seen anything like it. A whole room filled with pissed-off little people. It was fucking frightening."

"I think they were elves. Did you see their ears?"

"Their ears were fake," Diesel said.

I slid onto the passenger seat and a sigh escaped. "I know. I just don't want to have to tell anyone I was attacked by a horde of angry little people. A horde of angry elves sounds better, somehow."

A fake elf smashed through the plate-glass door with a fire ax, and Diesel took off.

"Did you see the cookies?" I asked him. "They looked just like Elaine's cookies."

"Honey, all cookies look alike."

"Yes, but they *might* have been Elaine's cookies."

My cell phone chirped. "I'm at the mall," Valerie said, "and I need help. I can't remember everything that was on Mary Alice's list. I got her the Barbie, the television, the game, and the ice skates. I have the train and the computer at home. Do you remember what else she wanted?"

"How are you going to pay for all that?"

"MasterCard."

"It'll take you five years to pay it off."

"I don't care. It's Christmas. You have to do these things at Christmas."

Oh yeah. I kept forgetting. "Mary Alice had about fifty things on that list. The only one I remember is the pony."

"Omigod," Valerie cried. "The pony! How could I forget the pony?"

"Val, you can't get her a pony. This isn't *Little House on the Prairie*. We live in Trenton. Kids in Trenton don't get ponies."

"But she wants one. She'll hate me if I don't get her a pony. It'll ruin her Christmas."

Boy, I was really glad I had a hamster. I was planning on giving Rex a raisin for Christmas.

I hung up on Valerie, and I turned to Diesel. "Do you have any kids?"

"No."

"How do you feel about kids?"

"The same way I feel about fake elves. I think they're cute from a distance."

"Suppose you wanted to have kids . . . could you reproduce?"

Diesel looked over at me. "Could I reproduce? Yeah, I guess I could." He gave his head a shake. "I have to tell you, I am *never* again going to let anyone pop me in on someone. It's too weird. Not that this was my idea in the first place." He reached across me, into the bag my mother gave us, and found a leftover brownie. "Usually women are asking me to buy them a beer. Not you. You're asking me if I can reproduce."

"Make a turn at Clinton," I told him. "I want to have another chat with Elaine."

It was midafternoon and unusually gloomy when Diesel drove down Grape Street. Dark clouds swirled in the sky, and an eerie green light streaked through them. The air felt heavy and ominously charged. Doomsday air.

Lights were on in houses, and Elaine had her roof lights blazing, blinking out her season's greetings. Diesel parked in front of the house, and we both got out. The wind had picked up, and I pulled my chin in and walked head down to Sandy Claws' front porch.

"I'm very busy," Elaine said when she answered the door.

Diesel brushed past her, into the house. "It smells like you're still baking cookies."

Elaine followed Diesel into the kitchen, half running to keep up with Diesel's stride. "Pecan shortbread for tomorrow," she said. "And big cookies with M&Ms in them."

"I'm curious," Diesel said. "Who eats all these cookies?"

"The elves, of course."

Diesel and I exchanged glances.

"They're not really elves," Elaine said. "Sandy just likes to call them that. His little elves. Sandy is so clever. He has a whole scheme worked out to sell toys. It's because of his name, Sandy Claws. Have you noticed how it sounds like Santa Claus?"

"How many elves are you feeding?" Diesel asked Elaine.

"Goodness, I don't know, but there must be a lot of them. I make dozens of cookies every day."

"And they go where?"

"I don't know, exactly. Lester stops around and picks them up. Lester is Sandy's production manager."

"About five-foot-ten? Gray hair, slim, dark-rimmed glasses?" Diesel asked.

"Yes. That's him," Elaine said.

The guy who was interviewing elves.

"I don't mean to be rude," Elaine said, "but you're going to have to leave now. I have to finish my baking."

"You don't mind if I look around, do you?" Diesel asked.

Elaine nervously picked at her apron. "I don't see why you would want to do that. Sandy isn't here."

Diesel opened the door to a small downstairs powder room and looked inside. "Are you sure you don't know where Sandy is?"

"Stop that!" Elaine said. "Stop snooping in my house. I'm going to call the police."

"We have a legal right to search this house," Diesel said. "Isn't that right, Steph?"

"Yep. We received that right when your brother signed his bond agreement."

"This whole thing is so silly," Elaine said. "All over a couple power tools and some paint. And Sandy wouldn't have had to steal anything if the store had been open. You can't stop a whole production line just because you run out of Morning Glory paint. And everyone knows elves work at night. My goodness, Sandy has enough labor problems without having a whole crew sit out until the stores open at nine A.M."

"I thought they weren't actually elves."

"Real elves, fake elves . . . what's the difference? They all get time and a half after five o'clock."

Diesel leaned against the kitchen counter, arms crossed over his chest. "When was the last time you talked to Sandy?"

"He called me at lunchtime." Elaine pressed her lips together.

"Did you tell him I was looking for him?"

"Yes." Elaine glanced at me and then looked back at Diesel. "I've been trying to be discreet in front of Ms. Plum."

"Too late for that," Diesel said. "I was dropped into her kitchen."

Elaine looked horrified. "How did that happen?"

Diesel did a palms up and an *I don't know* shrug. "It would have to be a team effort. I'm not easy to move."

Elaine wiped her hands on her apron. "I'm sorry, but Sandy doesn't want to talk to you. He wants to be left alone."

"I'm curious," Diesel said. "Why the name Sandy Claws?"

Elaine took a tray of cookies from the oven and set them on top of the stove. "His birth name was Sandor Clausen. We thought it was appropriate that he return to his birth name now that he's retired. Sandy Claws seemed like a natural derivative."

"Sandor Clausen," Diesel said. "I didn't read that far back in the file."

Hold on here. File? What the heck are they talking about? Okay, now I'm really confused. Clearly, Elaine and Diesel know each other. It sounds like they recognized each other from the very beginning, and Diesel kept that tidbit of information secret from me. This was presenting me with the opportunity to practice some anger management.

"Sandor wants to make toys. He should be able to do what he wants in retirement," Elaine said.

"No one cares if he makes toys in his retirement," Diesel said. "I'm here because Ring followed him out."

The surprise was obvious. "Ring!"

Diesel pushed off the counter, took a cookie, and turned to leave. "You have to persuade Sandor to cooperate with me," he said to Elaine. "I'm trying to protect him."

Elaine nodded. "I didn't know about Ring."

Ring? Am I understanding this correctly? There's someone or *something* named Ring involved in this mess?

I didn't say a word until we were back in the Jag. I was trying to look casual, but I was fuming inside. I felt like demon Stephanie with glowing red eyeballs and snarling gargoyle mouth. Fortunately, the image was all internal. Or at least I *hoped* it was all internal. "What the hell was that all about?" I asked Diesel, making an effort to squelch the demon thing, going with steely eyes and tight lips, instead.

Diesel turned in his seat and looked at me. Thinking. Making silent assessments.

"Trying to decide what to tell me?" I asked, still sticking with the steely eyes.

"Yeah." He was Mr. Serious. Not smiling.

I waited him out.

"Some human beings have the ability to operate beyond what are considered to be normal limitations," Diesel finally said. "Most of these people tend to have rogue personalities and work pretty much alone, playing by their own rules. Sandor was one of the best. Very powerful and very good. Unfortunately, he's old, and he's lost his power. So he's retired. Usually retirees go into an assisted living complex in Lakewood. Sandor tried it and decided he wanted out."

"And Ring?"

"Ring's a bad guy. Old, like Sandor. The story I was told is that Ring and Sandor were best friends when they were kids. I guess they both knew they were different, and this was a secret they shared. As they got older the differences in their personalities drove a wedge between them. Ring was using his power to dominate people and to amuse himself. And Sandor was using his power mostly to clean up after Ring. When they reached full power in their early twenties, some of Ring's peers got together and Ring was told to stop all superpower activity.

"Ring refused to stop, of course. Ring loved causing chaos. And Ring was drunk on his own power. Unfortunately, Ring was so powerful and so clever, there were only a few people who could control him. And it was virtually impossible to contain him.

"Sandor was one of the few who had matching power. Much of Sandor's life was spent battling Ring, trying to eliminate him."

"Eliminate?"

Diesel did a slash across the throat and a looking-dead face. "Anyway, Sandor never succeeded, but he did manage to cripple Ring from time to time, making Ring ineffective for years or months, sending Ring into hiding."

"And now Ring's lost his power, too?"

"Pretty much. He was in the locked ward at Lakewood. They have a special area for villains and Alzheimer's. Somehow, he managed to get out. I guess he has power left that no one knew about."

So here I am having a conversation about what? Superheroes! And I'm having it with the guy who rolled his eyes because I suggested the possible reality of elves.

"Where do you fit into this?" I asked.

"I'm kind of like you. I track people down who've strayed from the system. And I go after bad guys."

FOUR

Okay. I'm sitting in a car with a guy who thinks he's part of a supersociety. And the weird thing is . . . I'm half believing him. Truth is, I kind of like the idea that there are some superheroes out there, trying to save us from ourselves. I'm not sure how I feel about Diesel being one of them.

"Let me get this straight," I said to Diesel. "You're after Ring, right? You want to get him back to Lakewood. And in the meantime, you're worried Sandor is in danger."

Diesel pulled away from the curb, cruised down the street, and turned at the corner. "When Ring was in his prime he worked with electricity."

"What, like with PSE&G?"

That cracked Diesel up. "No. Like he was Electrical Man. He could make lightning. I don't know how he did it. I always thought it was kind of show-off, but hell, he could do a lot of damage. I don't know how dangerous he is now. I have a feeling he tried to destroy the toy store but only could get up enough juice to knock boxes off the shelves. And then I'm guessing he got pissed off and tore the sign off the front of the store. A few of the boxes in the store were singed, so it seemed like he was able to throw some electricity, but maybe not accurately and probably of short duration. Nothing to lose sleep over. The power outages are different. If he's responsible for the power outages it means he's gaining power somehow. And I don't like the way the air feels around Sandor's house."

"Do you think Sandor will get in touch with you?" I asked Diesel.

"No. He's always worked alone. I can't see him asking for help now."

My phone buzzed in my handbag.

"You were right about the horse," Valerie said. "I don't know what I was thinking. It's impossible to get a horse at this late date. It isn't like they sell them in Sears. So I got Mary Alice a book about horses, and I got her a sleeping bag with horses on it. I have to get something for Mom now. Do you have any ideas?"

"I thought you got Mom a robe."

"Yes, but that doesn't seem like enough. It's only one box to open. What do you think about perfume? Or a blouse? And I can get a nightgown to go with the robe. And then some slippers."

"Maybe you've shopped enough for one day, Val. Maybe you're sort of . . . carried away with shopping."

"I can't stop now. I hardly have anything! And there are only three shopping days left."

"How much coffee have you had today, Val? You might want to think about cutting back on the coffee."

"Gotta go," Valerie said. And she disconnected.

"So, where were we?" I asked Diesel.

"We were saving the world."

"Oh yeah." Personally, I'd be happy just to collect my finder's fee on Sandy Claws so I could make the minimum payment on my credit card.

"Do you think Connie has the water and electric information on Claws yet?"

I called Connie, but the information wasn't helpful. No additional accounts for Sandy Claws. I had her try Sandor Clausen. Big zero there, too.

Diesel stopped for a light, and I saw his eyes cut to the rearview mirror and the line of his mouth tighten. "I'm getting a real bad feeling."

Diesel made a U-turn and suddenly there was a flash of light in the sky in front of us. The light was followed by a low rumbling, and then there was another flash and smoke billowed over the rooftops.

Diesel stared at the smoke. "Ring."

It took us less than a minute to return to Claws' house. Diesel parked the Jag, and we joined the small group of people who'd collected in the street, eyes wide, mouths open in astonishment. Not often you see lightning at this time of the year. Not often you see the sort of carnage that resulted from the strike.

The Claws house was perfectly intact, but the life-size plastic Santa that had been strapped to the next-door neighbors' chimney had been blasted off the roof and lay in a smoking, melted red blob on the sidewalk. And the neighbors' garage was on fire.

"He melted Santa," I said to Diesel. "This is serious stuff."

Diesel gave his head a disbelieving shake. "He hit the wrong house. All those years of inciting terror and this is what it comes down to—frying some molded plastic. And not even the *right* molded plastic."

"I saw the whole thing," a woman said. "I was on the porch, checking my lights, and a ball of fire swooped out of the sky and hit the Patersons' garage. And then a second ball came in and knocked the Santa Claus off the roof. I've never seen anything like it. Santa just flew off the roof!"

"Did anyone else see the fireballs?" Diesel asked.

"There was a man on the sidewalk, across the street from Sandy and Elaine's house, but he's gone now. He was an older gentleman, and he seemed pretty upset."

A police car arrived, lights flashing. A fire truck followed close behind and hoses were run to the garage.

Elaine was on her porch. She had a heavy wool coat pulled around her dumpling body, and she had a belligerent set to her mouth.

Diesel draped an arm across my shoulders. "Okay, partner, let's talk to Elaine."

Elaine drew the jacket tighter when we got closer. "Crazy old fool," she said. "Doesn't know when to stop."

"Did you see him?" Diesel asked.

"No. I heard the crackle of electricity, and I knew he was out there. By the time I got to the porch, he was gone. It's just like him to attack at Christmas, too. The man is pure evil."

"It's not a good idea for you to stay here," Diesel said. "Do you have someplace else to go? Would you like me to find a safe house for you?"

Elaine tipped her chin up a fraction of an inch. "I'm not leaving my home. I have cookies to make. And someone has to keep the bird feeders filled in the backyard. The birds count on it. I've been taking care of Sandor ever since my husband died, fifteen years ago, and I've never once had to resort to a safe house."

"Sandor was always able to protect you. Now that his power is failing you need to be more careful," Diesel said.

Elaine bit her lower lip. "You'll have to excuse me. I have to get back to my baking."

Elaine retreated into her house, and Diesel and I were left on the porch. The garage fire was almost extinguished, and someone, who I suspected was Mrs. Paterson, was attempting to pry Santa off the sidewalk with a barbecue spatula.

My phone chirped from my bag.

"If that's your sister again, I'm throwing your phone in the river," Diesel said.

I pulled the phone out of my bag and pressed the off button. I *knew* it was my sister. And there was an outside chance Diesel was serious about throwing the phone in the river.

"Now what?" I asked Diesel.

"Lester knows where the factory is."

"Forget it. I'm not going back to the employment office."

Diesel smiled down at me. "What's the matter? Is the big bad bounty hunter afraid of the little people?"

"Those fake elves were crazy. And they were mean!"

Diesel ruffled my hair. "Don't worry. I won't let them be mean to you."

Swell.

Diesel parked half a block from the employment office and we sat wordlessly staring at the emergency vehicles in front of us. A fire truck, an EMT truck, and four police cars. The windows and the front door to the office were shattered, and a charred chair had been dragged out to the sidewalk.

We left the car and walked over to a couple cops I recognized. Carl Costanza and Big Dog. They were standing back on their heels, hands resting on their utility belts, surveying the damage with the sort of enthusiasm usually reserved for watching grass grow.

"What happened?" I asked.

"Fire. Riot. The usual. It's pretty ugly in there," Carl said.

"Bodies?"

"Cookies. Smashed cookies all over the place."

Big Dog had an elf ear in his hand. He held it up and looked at it. "And these things."

"It's an elf ear," I said.

"Yeah. These ears are all that's left of the little buggers."

"Did they burn?" I asked.

"No. They ran," Carl said. "Who would have thought the little guys could run that fast? Couldn't catch a single one of them. We arrived on the scene, and they took off like roaches when the light goes on."

"How did the fire get started?"

Carl shrugged and looked up at Diesel. "Who's he?"

"Diesel."

"Does Joe know about him?"

"Diesel is from out of town." Way out. "We're working a skip together."

There wasn't anything more to be learned from the employment office, so we left Carl and Big Dog and returned to the car. The sun was shining someplace other than Trenton. Streetlights were on. And the temperature had dropped by ten degrees. My feet were wet from slogging through two fire scenes and my nose was numb, frozen like a popsicle.

"Take me home," I said to Diesel. "I'm done."

"What? No shopping? No Christmas cheer? Are you going to let your sister beat you out in the present race?"

"I'll shop tomorrow. I swear I will."

* * *

Diesel parked the Jag in my apartment building parking lot and got out of the car.

"It's not necessary to see me to the door," I said. "I imagine you want to get back to the Ring search."

"Nope. I'm done for the day. I thought we'd have something to eat and then chill in front of the TV."

I was momentarily speechless. That wasn't the evening I had planned out in my mind. I was going to stand in a scalding hot shower until I was all wrinkly. Then I was going to make myself a peanut butter and Marshmallow Fluff sandwich. I like peanut butter and Fluff because it combines the main course with the dessert and it doesn't involve pots. Maybe I'd watch some television after dinner. And if I was lucky I'd be watching it with Morelli.

"That sounds great," I said, "but I have plans for tonight. Maybe some other time."

"What are your plans?"

"I'm seeing Morelli."

"Are you sure?"

"Yes." No. I wasn't sure. I figured the possibility was about fifty percent. "And I wanted to take a shower."

"Hey, you can take a shower while I make dinner."

"You can cook?"

"No," he said. "I can dial."

"Okay, so here's the thing, I don't feel entirely comfortable with you in my apartment."

"I thought you were getting used to the Super Diesel thing."

Old Mr. Feinstein shuffled past us on his way to his car. "Hey, chicky," he said to me. "How's it going? You need any help here? This guy looks shifty."

"I'm fine," I told Mr. Feinstein. "Thanks for the offer, though."

"See that," I said to Diesel. "You look shifty."

"I'm a pussycat," Diesel said. "I haven't even come on to you. Okay, maybe a little teasing, but nothing serious. I haven't grabbed you . . . like this." He wrapped his fingers around my jacket lapels and pulled me to him. "And I haven't kissed you . . . like this." And he kissed me.

My toes curled in my shoes. And heat slashed through my stomach and headed south.

Damn.

He broke from the kiss and smiled down at me. "It isn't as if I've done anything like that, right?"

I gave him a two-handed shot to the chest, but he didn't budge, so I took a step back. "There will be no kissing, no fooling around, no *anything*."

"Sure."

I did an *I give up* gesture, turned, and went into the building. Diesel followed after me, and we waited in silence for the elevator. The doors opened, and Mrs. Bestler smiled out at me. Mrs. Bestler is just about the oldest person I've ever seen. She lives alone on the third floor, and she likes to play elevator operator when she gets bored.

"Going up," she called out.

"Second floor," I said.

The elevator doors closed, and Mrs. Bestler chanted, "Ladies' handbags, Santa's workshop, better dresses." She looked at me and shook her finger. "Only three shopping days left."

"I know. I know!" I said. "I'll go shopping tomorrow. I swear, I will."

Diesel and I stepped out of the elevator, and Mrs. Bestler sang, *"It's beginning to look a lot like Christmas,"* as we walked down the hall.

"I'm laying odds she's eighty proof," Diesel said, opening my door.

My apartment was dark, lit only by the blue digital clock on my microwave and the single, red, blinking diode on my answering machine.

Rex ran on his wheel in the kitchen. The soft whir of his wheel reassured me that Rex was safe and probably there weren't any bridge trolls hiding in my closet tonight. I flipped the light, and Rex immediately stopped running and blinked out at me. I dropped a couple Froot Loops into his cage from the box on the counter, and Rex was a happy camper.

I hit the play button on the answering machine and unbuttoned my jacket.

First message. "It's Joe. Give me a call."

Next message. "Stephanie? It's your mother. You don't have your cell phone on. Is something wrong? Where are you?"

Third message. "It's Joe again. I'm stuck on this job, and I won't make it over tonight. And don't call me. I can't always talk. I'll call back when I can."

Fourth message. "Christ," Morelli said.

"Guess it's just you and me," Diesel said, grinning. "Good thing I'm here. You'd be lonely."

And the terrible part was that he was right. I had one foot on the slippery slope of Christmas depression. Christmas was sliding away from me. Five days, four days, three days . . . and before my eyes, Christmas would come and go without me. And I'd have to wait an entire year to take another crack at a ribbons and bows, candy canes, and eggnog Christmas.

"Christmas isn't ribbons and bows and presents," I said to Diesel. "Christmas is about good will, right?"

"Wrong. Christmas is about presents. And Christmas trees. And office parties. Boy, you don't know much, do you?"

"Do you really believe that?"

"Aside from all the religious blah, blah, blah, which we won't get into . . . I think Christmas is whatever turns you on. That's what I really believe. Everyone decides what they want out of Christmas. Then everyone gets a shot at making it happen."

"Suppose every year you blow it? Suppose every year you screw up Christmas?"

He crooked his arm around my neck. "Are you screwing up Christmas, kiddo?"

"I can't seem to get to it."

Diesel looked around. "I noticed. No garlands of green shit. No angels, no Rudolphs, no kerplunkers or tartoofers."

"I used to have some tartoofers but my apartment got firebombed and they all went up in smoke."

Diesel shook his head. "Don't you hate when that happens?"

I woke up in a sweat. I was having a nightmare. There were only two days left until Christmas, and I still hadn't bought a single present. I gave myself a mental head smack. It wasn't a nightmare. It was true. Two days until Christmas.

I jumped out of bed and scurried into the bathroom. I took a fast shower and power-dried my hair. Yikes. I tamed it with some gel, got dressed in my usual jeans, boots, and T-shirt, and went to the kitchen.

Diesel lounged against the sink, coffee cup in hand. There was a white bakery bag on the counter, and Rex was awake in his cage, leisurely working his way to the heart of a jelly doughnut.

"Morning, sunshine," Diesel said.

"There are only two days left until Christmas," I said. "Two days! And I wish you would stop letting yourself into my apartment."

"Yeah, right, that's gonna happen. Have you given Santa your list? Have you been naughty?"

It was early in the morning for an eye roll, but I managed one anyway. I poured myself coffee and took a doughnut.

"It was nice of you to bring doughnuts," I said. "But Rex will get a cavity in his fang if he eats that whole thing."

"We're making progress," Diesel said. "You didn't shriek when you saw me here. And you didn't check the coffee and doughnuts for alien poison."

I looked down at the coffee and had a rush of panic. "I wasn't thinking," I said.

Half an hour later we were on a side street with a good view of Briggs' apartment building. Briggs was going to work today. And we were going to follow him. He'd lead us to the toy factory, I'd locate Sandy Claws, I'd snap the cuffs on him, and *then* I could have Christmas.

At exactly eight-fifteen, Randy Briggs strutted out of his building and got into a specially equipped car. He cranked the engine over and drove out of the lot, heading for Route 1. We followed a couple cars back, keeping Briggs in sight.

"Okay," I said to Diesel. "You flunked levitation and obviously you can't do the lightning thing. What's your specialty? What tools have you got on your utility belt?"

"I told you, I'm good at finding people. I have heightened sensory perception." He cut his eyes to me. "Bet you didn't think I knew big words like that."

"Anything else? Can you fly?"

Diesel blew out a sigh. "No. I can't fly."

Briggs stayed on Route 1 for a little over a mile and then exited. He left-turned at the corner and entered a light industrial complex. He drove past three businesses before pulling into a parking lot, adjacent to a one-story redbrick building that was maybe five thousand square feet. There were no signs announcing the name or the nature of the business. A toy soldier on the door was the only ornamentation.

We gave Briggs a half hour to get into the building and settle himself. Then we crossed the lot and pushed through the double glass doors, into the small reception area. The walls were brightly colored in yellow and blue. There were several chairs lined up against one wall. Half the chairs were big and half were small. The boundary to the reception area was set by a desk. Behind the desk were a couple cubbies. Briggs was sitting in one of them.

The woman behind the desk looked at Diesel and me and smiled. "Can I help you?"

"We're looking for Sandy Claws," Diesel said.

"Mr. Claws isn't in this morning," the woman said. "Perhaps I can help you."

Briggs' head snapped up at the sound of Diesel's voice. He looked over at us and worry lines creased his high forehead.

"Do you expect him in later today?" I asked.

"It's hard to say. He keeps his own schedule."

We left the building, and I called and asked for Briggs.

"Don't call me here," Briggs said. "This is a great job. I don't want it screwed up. And I'm not going to inform for you, either." And he hung up.

"I guess we could stake out the building," I said to Diesel. I wanted to do this just behind poke out my eye with a burning stick.

Diesel pushed his seat back and stretched his legs. "I'm beat," he said. "I worked the night shift. How about if you take the first watch."

"The night shift?"

"Sandor and Ring have a long history in Trenton. I made the rounds of some of Ring's old haunts after I left you last night, but I didn't turn anything up."

He crossed his arms over his chest and almost instantly seemed to be asleep. At ten-thirty my cell phone rang.

"Hey, girlfriend," Lula said. "What's up?"

Lula does filing for the bonds office. She was a ho' in a previous life but has since amended her ways. Her wardrobe has pretty much stayed the same. Lula's a big woman who likes the challenge of buying clothes that are two sizes too small.

"Not much is up," I said. "What's up with you?"

"I'm going shopping. Two days to Christmas and I don't have nothing. I'm heading for Quakerbridge Mall. You want to ride shotgun?"

"Yes!"

Lula checked her rearview mirror for one last look at Diesel before leaving the toy factory parking lot. "That man is *fine*. I don't know where you find these guys, but it isn't fair. You got the market cornered on *hot*."

"He's actually a superhero, sort of."

"Don't I know it. I bet he got superhero *boys,* too."

Lula was sounding a lot like Grandma. I didn't want to think about Diesel's *boys,* so I put the radio on. "I have to be back to relieve him at three o'clock," I said.

"Dang," Lula said, pulling into Quakerbridge. "Look here at this parking lot. It's full. This mother is *full*. Where am I supposed to park? I only got two days to shop. I can't deal with this parking thing. And what's with all the best spots going to the handicapped? You see any handicap cars in all these handicap places? How many handicap people they think we got in Jersey?"

Lula rode around the lot for twenty minutes, but she didn't find a parking space. "Look at this itty bitty Sentra nosed up to a wreck of a Pinto," Lula said, wheeling around so she had the front bumper of her Firebird inches from the back bumper of the Sentra. "Uh-oh," she said, easing forward, "look how that Sentra's moving forward all by itself. Before you know it, there's gonna be a parking space available on account of that Pinto is rolling into the driving lane."

"You can't just push a car out of its space!" I said.

"Sure I can," Lula said. "See? I already did it." Lula had her handbag over her shoulder, and she was out of the Firebird, booking toward the mall entrance. "I got a lot to do," Lula said. "I'll meet you back at the car at two-thirty."

I glanced down at my watch. It was two-thirty. And I only had one present. I'd gotten a pair of gloves for my dad. That was a no-brainer. I got him gloves every year. He counted on it. I was at a loss for everyone else. I'd given Valerie all my good gift ideas. And the mall was a mob scene. Too many shoppers. Not enough clerks at registers. Picked-over merchandise. Why did I let this go to the last minute? Why do I go through this *every* year? Next year I'm getting my Christmas presents in July. I swear, I am.

Lula and I reached the car simultaneously. I had my little bag with the gloves, and Lula had four huge shopping bags filled to bursting.

"Wow," I said, "you're good. I only got gloves."

"Hell, I don't even know what's in these bags," Lula said. "I just started grabbing stuff that was close to a register. I figure I'll sort it out later. Everybody always takes their shit back anyway, so it don't really matter what you buy the first time around."

Lula cruised toward the exit and her eyes lit when she came to the edge of the lot. "Do you believe this?" she said. "They set up a Christmas tree lot here. I *need* a Christmas tree. I'm gonna stop. I'll only be a minute. I'm gonna get myself a Christmas tree."

Fifteen minutes later we had two six-foot Christmas trees stuffed into Lula's four-foot trunk. One tree for Lula. And one tree for me. We secured the trunk lid with a bungee cord, and we were on our way.

"Good thing we saw that tree lot so you could get a tree, too," Lula said. "You can't have Christmas without a Christmas tree. Boy, I *love* Christmas."

Lula was dressed in knee-high, white fake-fur boots that made her look like Sasquatch. She had her bottom half stuffed into skin-tight red spandex pants that magically had gold glitter embedded in them. She was wearing a red sweater with a green felt Christmas tree appliqué. And she had it topped off with a yellow-dyed rabbit-fur jacket. Every time Lula moved, yellow rabbit hairs escaped from the jacket and floated on the air like dandelion fluff. Behind us, the tree lot was lost in a yellow haze.

"Okay," Lula said, stopping for a light. "We got Christmas knocked. We're on our way to Christmas." The light turned and the guy in front of us hesitated. Lula leaned on the horn and gave him the finger. "Move it," she yelled. "You think we got all day? It's Christmas, for chrissake. We got things to do." She reached the highway and took off, ripping into "Jingle Bells" at the top of her lungs. *"Jingle bells, jingle bells, jingle all the wa-a-a-ay,"* she sang.

I put my finger to my eye.

"Hey, you got that eye twitch again?" she asked. "You should do something about that eye twitch. You should see a doctor."

Lula was on the third chorus of "Silent Night" when she parked next to the black Jag. I got out of the Firebird and bent to talk to Diesel.

"Lula and I can take the next watch," I told him. "If anything happens, I'll call you."

"Sounds good," Diesel said. "I could use a break. It's been quiet all day, and that's the way I like it. If there aren't any more disturbances, Sandor will eventually come back to his workshop."

"Don't you worry, Diesel honey," Lula said from behind me. "We'll watch the heck out of this place. *Peace and Quiet*'s my middle name."

Diesel checked Lula out and smiled.

"So what's the deal?" Lula wanted to know when Diesel left.

"I'm after an FTA named Sandy Claws. He owns this toy factory."

"And what's with the car next to us? It's got a big booster seat behind the wheel. And what are those levers on the steering column?"

"Most of the employees here are little people."

Sometimes when Lula got excited her eyes opened wide and popped out like big white duck eggs. This was one of those duck-egg-eye times. "Are you shitting me? Midgets? A whole building full of midgets? I love midgets. I've had this thing for midgets ever since I saw *The Wizard of Oz*. Except for that guy, Randy Briggs. He was a nasty little bugger."

"Briggs is here, too," I said. "He's working in the office."

"Hunh. I wouldn't mind kicking his ass."

"No ass kicking!"

Lula stuck her lower lip out and pulled her eyes back into their sockets. "I know that. You think I don't know that? I got a sense of decorum. Hell, *Decorum*'s my middle name."

"Anyway, you won't see him," I said, "because we're just going to sit here."

"I don't want to sit here," Lula said. "I want to see the midgets."

"They're little people now. Midget is politically incorrect."

"Cripes, I can't keep up on this political correct shit. I don't even know what to call *myself*. One minute I'm black. Then I'm African American. Then I'm a person of color. Who the hell makes these rules up, anyhow?"

"Well, whoever they are, little people, elves, or whatever, you'll see them when the shift changes, and they go home."

"How do you know this Claws guy didn't come in through a back door? I bet this factory's got a big ol' back door. It's probably got a loading dock. I think we should go ask if Claws has come in yet."

Lula had a point. There was for sure a back door.

"All right," I said, "I guess it won't do any harm to try the woman at the desk one more time."

Briggs went pale when we entered the reception area. And the woman at the desk looked apologetic. "I'm afraid he's still not here," she said to me.

"Where are the toys made?" Lula asked, walking toward the door to the factory. "I bet they're made in here. Boy, I'd really like to see the toys getting made."

The woman behind the desk was on her feet. "Mr. Claws prefers not to have visitors in the workshop."

"I'll just take a quick peek," Lula said. And she opened the door. "Holy cats," she said, walking into the warehouse. "Will you look at this! It's a bunch of freaking elves."

Briggs rounded the reception desk, and we both ran after Lula.

"They're not really elves," Briggs said, skidding to a stop in front of her.

Lula was hands on hips. "The hell they aren't! I guess I know an elf when I see one. Look at those ears. They all got elf ears."

"They're fake ears, stupid," Briggs said to Lula. "It's a marketing ploy."

"Don't go calling me stupid," Lula said to Briggs.

"Stupid, stupid, stupid," Briggs said.

"Listen up, you moron," Lula said. "I could squash you like a bug if I wanted. You gotta be more careful who you disrespect."

"It's her," one of the elves yelled, pointing his finger at me. "She's the one who started the fire in the employment office."

"Fire?" Lula asked. "What's he talking about?"

"She started the riot," someone else yelled. "Get her!"

The elves all jumped up from their workstations and rushed at me on their little elf legs.

"Get her. Get her!" they were all yelling. "Get the big stupid troublemaker."

"Hey!" Lula said. "Hold on here. What the—"

I grabbed Lula by the back of her jacket and yanked her toward the door. "Run! And don't look back."

FIVE

We barreled through the workroom door to the reception area, pushed through the front door, sprinted across the lot and jumped into the car. Lula popped the doors locked, and the elves swarmed around us.

"These aren't elves," Lula said. "I know elves. Elves are cute. These are evil gremlins. Look at their pointy teeth. Look at their red, glowing eyes."

"I don't know about gremlins," I said. "I think the guy with the red eyes is just a little person with bad teeth and a hangover."

"Hey, what's that noise? What are they doing to the back of my Firebird?"

We turned and looked out the back window, and we were horrified to find that the elves had dragged the trees out of the trunk.

"That's my Christmas tree!" Lula yelled. "Get away. Leave that tree alone."

No one was listening to Lula. The elves were in a frenzy, tearing the trees limb from limb, jumping up and down on the branches.

Suddenly there was an elf on the hood. And then a second elf scrambled up after the first.

"Holy crap," Lula said. "This here's a horror movie."

She shoved the key into the ignition, put her foot to the floor, and rocketed across the lot. One elf flew off instantly. The second elf had his hands wrapped around the windshield wipers, his snarling face pressed to the windshield. Lula made a fast right turn, one of the windshield wipers snapped, and the elf sailed away like a Frisbee, windshield wiper still clutched in his little elf hand.

"Fuck youuuuuuuu," the elf sang as he sailed away.

We went a mile down Route 1 before either of us said a word.

"I don't know what those nasty-assed little things were," Lula finally said. "But they need to learn some people skills."

"That was sort of embarrassing," I said.

"Fuckin' A."

And I still didn't have a Christmas tree.

It was a little after five when I waved goodbye to Lula and trudged into my building. My apartment was quiet. No Diesel. I said a silent *thank goodness,* but the truth is, I was disappointed. I hung my jacket on a hook in the hall and listened to my messages.

"Stephanie? It's your mother. Mrs. Krienski said she didn't get a Christmas card from you. You *did* mail them, didn't you? And, I'm making a nice pot roast for supper tonight if you want to come over. And your father got a tree for you at the service station. They were having a close-out sale. He said he got a good deal."

Omigod. A close-out tree from the service station. Does it get any worse than that?

Mary Alice and Angie were in front of the television when I got to my parents' house. My father was sleeping in his chair. My sister was upstairs, throwing up. And my mom and grandmother were in the kitchen.

"I didn't misplace them," Grandma said to my mother. "Someone *took* them."

"Who would take them?" my mother asked. "That's ridiculous."

I knew I was going to regret asking, but I couldn't help myself. "What's missing?"

"My teeth," Grandma said. "Someone took my teeth. I had them setting out in a glass with one of them whitening tablets and next thing they were gone."

"How was your day?" my mother asked me.

"Average. Got attacked for the second time by a horde of angry elves, but aside from that it was okay."

"That's nice," my mother said. "Could you stir the gravy?"

Valerie came in and clapped a hand over her mouth at the sight of the pot roast, sitting on a platter.

"What's new?" I asked Valerie.

"I've decided I'm going to have the baby. And I'm not getting married right away."

My mother made the sign of the cross, and her eyes wistfully drifted to the cupboard where she kept her Four Roses. The moment passed, and she took the pot roast into the dining room. "Let's eat," she said.

"How am I supposed to eat pot roast without teeth?" Grandma said. "If those teeth aren't returned by tomorrow morning, I'm calling the cops. I got a date for Christmas Eve. I invited my new boyfriend over for dinner."

We all froze. The studmuffin was coming to Christmas Eve dinner.

"Christ," my father said.

After dinner my mother gave me a bag filled with food. "I know you don't have time to cook," she said. It was part of the ritual. And someday, if I was lucky, I'd carry the tradition to a new generation. Except the bag to *my* daughter would probably be filled with takeout.

My father was outside, attaching the tree to my CRV. He was tying it to the roof rack, and every time he tightened the rope there was a shower of pine needles. "It might be a little dry," he said. "You should probably put it in water when you get home."

Halfway home I saw the lights behind me. Low-slung sporty car lights. I checked the rearview mirror. Hard to see at night, but I was pretty sure it was a black Jag. I parked in the lot, and Diesel parked beside me. We both got out and looked at the tree. There was no moonlight, thank God.

"Can't hardly see it in the dark," Diesel said.

"It's better that way."

"How'd the stake-out go?"

"Like you said—quiet."

Diesel smiled when I told him the stake-out was quiet.

"I guess you know about the stake-out," I said with a sigh.

"Yup."

"How?"

"I know everything."

"Do not."

"Do so."

"Do not!"

There was a rush of wind, the air crackled, and Diesel grabbed me and threw me to the ground, covering me with his body. Light flashed and heat rippled over me for a moment. I heard Diesel swear and roll off. When I looked up I realized the tree was on fire. Sparks jumped against the black sky and the fire spread to the car.

Diesel pulled me to my feet, and we backed away from the flames. I was bummed about the car, but I wasn't all that unhappy to be rid of the tree.

"So, what do you think?" I asked Diesel. "Meteor?"

"Sorry, sunshine. That was meant for me."

I was standing facing my car, and behind me, I could hear windows being thrown open in my apartment building. It was Lorraine in her nightie and Mo in his cap. They'd just settled their brains for a long winter's nap in front of the television. When out in the lot there arose such a clatter, they sprang from their recliners to see what was the matter. Away to the window they flew like a flash, tore open the blinds and threw up the sash. And what to their wondering eyes should appear, but Stephanie Plum and yet another of her cars burning front to rear.

"Hey," Mo Kleinschmidt yelled. "Are you okay?"

I waved back at him.

"Nice touch with the tree," he yelled. "You never torched a tree before."

I glanced sideways at Diesel. "This isn't the first time one of my cars has been exploded, burned, or bombed."

"Gee, that's a big surprise," Diesel said.

Fire trucks screamed in the distance. Two patrol cars rolled into the lot, keeping a safe distance from the smoke and flames. Morelli pulled in behind the second patrol car. He got out of his truck and sauntered over. He looked at me, and then he looked at the toasted CRV. He gave his head a shake and a sigh escaped. Resignation. His girlfriend was a trial.

"I heard the call go out on the scanner, and I knew it had to be you," Morelli said. "Are you okay?"

"Yep. I'm fine. I figured this was the only way I'd get to see you."

"Funny," Morelli said. He checked Diesel out. "Do I have to worry about him?"

"No."

Morelli gave me a kiss on the top of the head. "I have to get back to the job."

Diesel and I watched him drive off.

"I like him," Diesel said. "I like the way he kisses you on the top of your head."

"Maybe you want to take your jacket off," I said to Diesel. "It's smoking."

Next morning, Diesel was on the couch, watching television, when I got out of the shower. His presence was unexpected, and I had a brief moment of terror until my brain connected the dots between *big, uninvited man on couch* and *Diesel*.

"Jeez," I said. "Why don't you try using the doorbell? I wasn't expecting to find a man on my couch."

"Sounds like a personal problem," Diesel said. "What's the plan for the day?"

"I don't have a plan. I thought you'd have a plan."

"My plan is pretty much to follow you around. I figure there was a reason I was dropped here. So I'm waiting for it all to shake out."

Oh boy.

"There's some stuff for you in the kitchen," Diesel said. "The kerplunkers were picked over, but I got you a poinsettia and a Christmas tree. Seemed like I owed you a tree."

I went into the kitchen to investigate and found a nice big red poinsettia sitting on my counter. And a five-foot, fully decorated Christmas tree stood square in the middle of my kitchen floor. It was a live tree trimmed in gold and white, its base planted in a plastic tub swaddled in gold foil, the perfectly formed top of the tree capped with a star. It was gorgeous, but vaguely familiar. And then I remembered where I'd seen the tree.

Quakerbridge Mall. The trees were strung along the entire ground floor of the shopping center.

"I'm afraid to ask where you got this tree," I said.

Diesel clicked the television off and ambled into the kitchen. "Yeah, some things are better left unknown."

"It's a nice tree. And it's all decorated."

"Hey, I deliver."

I was standing there admiring the tree, wondering if I could get jail time for being an accomplice to grand theft spruce, and Randy Briggs called.

"I just got in to work, and something strange is going on here. Your pal Sandy Claws showed up and sent everyone home. He shut down the whole production line."

"It's Christmas Eve day. He probably was just being nice."

"You don't get it. He shut down permanently."

"I thought you weren't going to rat for me."

"I just lost my job. You're the only thing between me and welfare."

"Are you still there?"

"I'm in the parking lot. It's just Claws and Lester inside."

"I'm on my way. Stick with Claws and Lester."

I hung up, grabbed my jacket and bag, and Diesel and I ran for the stairs. I paused for a moment when I pushed through the lobby doors and saw the charred spot on the pavement. No more CRV. Just some heat-scorched blacktop and a couple patches of ice where water had frozen.

Diesel snagged me by the sleeve and yanked me forward. "It was a car," he said. "It can be replaced."

I belted myself into the Jag. "It's not that simple. It takes time and money. And then there's the insurance." I didn't even want to *think* about the insurance. I was an insurance joke.

Diesel took off, flying low, heading for Route 1. "No problemo. What kind of car would you like? Another CRV? A truck? How about a Z3? I could see you in a Z3."

"No! I'll get my own car."

Diesel sailed through a red light and hit the on ramp to Route 1 south. "I bet you thought I was going to steal a car for you. In fact, I bet you thought I stole your Christmas tree."

"Well?"

"It's complicated," Diesel said, cutting into the far left lane, foot to the floor, looking far too calm for a guy going ninety.

I closed my eyes and tried to relax into my seat. If I was going to die in a fiery crash I didn't want to see it coming. "These superpowers you're supposed to have . . . they include driving, right?"

Diesel smiled and gave me a sideways glance. "Sure."

Damn. Not an answer that gave me confidence.

He took a corner with tires screaming, I opened my eyes and we were in the toy factory lot. Briggs was still there. And two other cars were parked close to the building entrance.

Diesel killed the engine and was out of the car. "Wait here."

"No way!" But my door was locked. *All* the car doors were locked. So I leaned on the horn.

Diesel wheeled around halfway to the factory entrance and sent me a warning glare, fists on hips. I kept my hand on the horn, and he did a disbelieving headshake. He walked back to the car, opened my door, and pulled me out. "You know, you're a real pain in the ass."

"Hey, without me, you'd be nowhere on this case."

He sighed and draped an arm across my shoulders. "Honey, I'm nowhere *with* you."

Another car door opened and closed, and Briggs joined us. "I'll come along in case you need muscle," Briggs said.

"If I get any more help I'll need a permit for a parade," Diesel said.

The reception area and front office cubbies were deserted. We found Sandy Claws and Lester, alone, in the back room where the toys were made. Lester and Claws were sitting together at one of the workstations. They looked over at us when we entered the room, but they didn't get up. There was a small block of wood in front of Claws, some shavings, and a couple woodworking tools. The corners had been shaved off the block of wood.

We walked over to the two men, and Diesel looked down at the wood. "What are you making?" he asked.

Claws smiled and ran his hand over the wood. "A special toy."

Diesel nodded as if he knew what that meant.

"Have you come to take me back?" Claws asked.

Diesel shook his head. "No. You're free to do whatever you want. I'm after Ring. Unfortunately, Ring is after *you*."

"Ring," Claws said with a sigh. "Who would have thought he had power left?"

"Looks to me like his aim is off," Diesel said.

"Cataracts. The old fool can't see."

Diesel scanned the room. Toys were scattered around, in various stages of completion. "You shut down the factory."

"He's out there," Claws said. "I can feel the electricity in the air. I couldn't take a chance on endangering the workers, so I sent them away."

"Good riddance," Lester said. "Nasty little slackards. They were more trouble than they were worth."

"The elves?" I asked.

Claws made a derisive sound. "We trucked them in from Newark. I rented this space sight unseen and then found out it used to be a daycare facility. Everything is sized for kids. I thought it would be cheaper to hire little people than to change out all the toilets and sinks. Problem was, we got a bunch of crazies. Half of them actually claimed to be elves. And you know how unmanageable elves can be."

We all nodded. "Yeah," we said in half-assed unison, "elves are flighty. You can't count on an elf."

"What will you do now?" Diesel asked.

Claws shrugged. "I'll make the occasional special toy. It's what I most enjoy, anyway."

"I'd like to put you and Elaine in a safer place until I get Ring under control," Diesel said.

"As long as Ring is at large, no place is safe," Claws said.

I cleared my throat and cracked my knuckles. "I sort of hate to bring this up right now, but I'm supposed to apprehend you." I reached into my bag and dragged out a pair of cuffs.

"Jeez," Briggs said.

"It's my job, remember?"

"Yeah, but it's Christmas Eve day. Cut the guy some slack."

"You don't get paid until I get paid," I told Briggs.

"Good point," Briggs said. "Cuff him."

I looked over at Diesel.

"It's your job," Diesel said.

I looked at the cuffs dangling from my hand. This was my last shot at Christmas present money. And bringing Claws in was the right thing to do. He'd broken the law and failed to appear for his court hearing. Problem was, it was Christmas Eve, and there was no guarantee I'd be able to get Claws bonded out again and released before everything shut down for the holiday. I thought about his house, bursting with baked goods and Christmas spirit, decorated with twinkle lights, blinking out best wishes to the world.

"I can't do it," I said. "It's Christmas Eve. Elaine would be alone with all those cookies."

Claws and Lester let out a whoosh of relief. Briggs looked conflicted. And Diesel grinned at me.

"Now what?" I asked.

"Now we hunt down Ring," Diesel said.

I didn't have to look at my watch to know it was midmorning. Time was oozing away from me. I had half a day to make Christmas happen. And some or all of that time was going to be spent hunting Ring. I could feel the panic sitting thick in my throat. I didn't even have the gloves I'd gotten for my dad. They'd gone up in smoke with the CRV.

"You could bail," Diesel said to me, reading my thoughts. "We'd understand."

Before I could make a decision there was a clap of thunder, the building shook, and a crack angled across the ceiling. We started for the door, but we were stopped midway by another *boom*. Plaster rained down from above, and we dove under a large butcher-block workstation. A couple large chunks of ceiling broke loose and crashed to the floor. More ceiling followed. The light blinked out, and demolition dust swirled around us. The workstation table had saved our lives, but we were buried under debris from the roof.

We did a head count and concluded we were all okay.

"I could dig my way through this mess," Diesel said, "but I'm afraid it's unstable. It needs to be cleared from the top."

We all tried our cell phones, but we had no reception.

"I don't get it," Briggs said. "What was that? It felt like an earthquake, but we don't get earthquakes in Jersey."

"I guess it was a . . . phenomenon," I said.

We sat there for a half hour, waiting for the sound of fire trucks and emergency equipment.

"No one knows we're trapped here," Claws finally said. "We're separated from the other businesses by parking lots and roadways. And most of the businesses here are storage facilities with minimum traffic."

"And it's possible the ceiling collapsed but the walls are still standing," Lester said. "If someone doesn't look closely they might not see the damage."

I inched closer to Diesel. He felt big and safe and solid.

He playfully tugged at a strand of my hair. "You aren't scared, are you?" he asked me, his lips skimming across my ear.

"Not me. Nope. I'm cool."

Liar, liar, pants on fire. I was scared beyond all reason. I was trapped under a ton of rubble with four men and no bathroom. My heart was beating with a sickening thud in my chest, and I was cold to the bone with fear and claustrophobia. If I got out alive I'd probably have a few uncomfortable moments remembering the way Diesel's mouth had felt on my ear. Right now, I was trying to keep my teeth from chattering in panic.

"Someone needs to go for help," Claws said.

"I guess that would be me," Diesel said. "Don't anyone freak."

There was a sound like a soap bubble bursting. *Plink*. And I no longer felt Diesel beside me.

"Holy crap," Briggs said, "what was that?"

"Uh, I don't know," I said.

"We're all still here, right?" Briggs asked.

"I'm here," I said.

"I didn't hear anything," Lester said.

"Yeah, me either," Briggs said. "I didn't hear anything."

We sat and waited in the eerie quiet.

"Hello," Briggs called after a while, but no one answered, and we all fell silent again.

There was no way to assess time in the pitch-black cave. Minutes dragged by, and then suddenly there was a faraway sound. Scraping and clunking. And muffled voices carried in to us. We heard sirens, but they were faint, the sound deadened by the debris.

Two hours later, after I'd made a lot of deals with God, a large piece of ceiling was hauled off our table, and we saw daylight and faces peering in at us. Another piece was removed, and Diesel dropped through the opening.

"I'm thinking that I just imagined you were trapped under the ceiling with us," Briggs said. "You were actually on the outside all the time, right?"

"Right," Diesel said, reaching for me.

He gave me a boost, a couple firemen pulled me through the hole, and a cheer went up. Briggs came next, then Lester, then Claws, and finally Diesel emerged.

Pretty much the entire roof had collapsed, but as Lester had suggested, the walls were still standing. The lot was filled with emergency vehicles and the curious. I stood in the lot and shook my head and plaster dust flew off. My clothes were caked with it, and I could still taste the dust in the back of my throat.

I looked over at Claws and realized for the first time that he'd taken his toy-in-progress with him when the building started to collapse. He had it cradled in his arm, held close to his chest. It was a small, half-carved block of wood, covered in dust, just like the rest of us. Too early for me to tell what sort of toy he was making. I watched him slip past the first line of rescue workers and quietly get into his car and drive off. Smart move, since he was wanted for failing to appear.

I looked around the lot. And then I looked into the sky.

"He isn't here," Diesel said to me. "He doesn't hang around after he strikes."

"What does he look like?" In my mind I was envisioning the Green Goblin.

"Just a normal, little old guy with cataracts."

"No utility belt? No lightning bolt embroidered on his shirt?"

"Sorry."

An EMT draped a blanket around my shoulders and tried to guide me to a truck. I looked at my watch and dug my heels in. "Can't get checked out right now," I said. "Gotta shop."

"You don't look that great," the guy said. "You're kind of pale."

"Of course I'm pale. There are only four shopping hours left before I'm due at my parents' house for Christmas Eve dinner. You'd look pale too if you were in my shoes." I turned to Diesel. "I had time to do some serious thinking while I was trapped under the table, and things became very clear to me. My mother is more of a threat to me right now than Ring. Take me to Macy's!"

It was midafternoon and the roads were relatively empty. Businesses had shut down early. Kids were on vacation. Shoppers were retiring their credit cards. Jersey was at home, preparing the holiday beast for Christmas Day dinner, gearing up for an evening of toy assembly and package wrapping. In eight hours, when the stores are all closed, the entire population of the state will be in desperate search for batteries, wrapping paper, and tape.

In eight hours, children statewide will be listening for reindeer hooves on the roof. Except for Mary Alice, who no longer believed in Christmas.

Anticipation hung in the air over the mall, the highway, the Burg, and every house in every town that mashed together to form the megalopolis. Christmas was almost here. Like it, or not.

Diesel swung into the lot and got a space close to the mall entrance. No problem with parking now. Inside the mall, the silence was oppressive. Shell-shocked salesclerks stood motionless, waiting for the closing bell. A few customers staggered from rack to rack. Men, mostly. Looking lost.

"Cripes," Diesel said. "This is frightening. This is like being with the living dead."

"What about you?" I asked. "Is your Christmas shopping all done?"

"I don't do a lot of Christmas shopping."

"Wife, girlfriend, mother?"

"I'm currently without."

"I'm sorry."

He tweaked my nose and smiled. "It's okay. I've got *you*."

"Did you get me a present?"

Our eyes locked, and his expression warmed a couple notches. He raised his eyebrows ever so slightly in question, and I felt my temperature rise.

"Do you *want* a present?" he asked. Both of us understanding what he was offering.

"No. Nope." I sucked in some air and busied myself, brushing some dust off my jacket. "Thanks, anyway."

"Let me know if you change your mind," he said, his voice back to playful.

Ordinarily, two people walking through Quaker-bridge covered in construction dust would attract some attention. At four o'clock on Christmas Eve, no one would have noticed if we'd been naked. I didn't waste time on details such as the right size or color. I went with Lula's method. Fill your bag with stuff close to the register. I finished up at five-thirty, and I wrapped the presents on the way to my parents' house.

Diesel jerked to a stop at the curb, and we tumbled out of the car with our arms full of boxes and bags.

Grandma was at the door. "She's here," she called to the rest of the family. "And she's got that hunky sissy boy with her again."

"Sissy boy?" Diesel asked.

"It's complicated," I said.

"Omigod," my mother said when she saw us. "What happened? You're filthy."

"It's nothing," I said. "A building fell down on us, and we didn't have time to change."

"A couple years ago I would have thought that was unusual," my mother said.

"You've gotta help me," Grandma said. "My stud-muffin is coming to dinner, and I still haven't got my teeth."

"We've looked everywhere," my mother said. "We even looked through the garbage."

"Someone stole them," Grandma said. "I bet a good set of teeth would bring a pretty penny on the black market."

There was a knock at the door, and Morelli let himself in.

"Just the person I want to see," Grandma said. "I want to report a crime. Someone stole my teeth."

Morelli looked over at me. The first look said, *help.*
And the second look said *what the hell happened to
you?*

"A ceiling sort of fell in on us," I told Morelli. "But
we're fine."

A muscle worked in Morelli's jaw. He was trying to
stay calm.

"Where were your teeth when you saw them last?" I
asked Grandma.

"In a glass, getting cleaned."

"Did you lose just the teeth? Or is the glass gone,
too?"

"The lousy rotten robber took everything, glass and
all."

Mary Alice and Angie were in front of the television.

"Hey," I said to them. "Either of you see Grandma's
teeth? They were in a glass in the kitchen and now
they're missing."

"I thought Grammy was throwing them away, so I
took them for Charlotte," Mary Alice said.

Charlotte is a big lavender dinosaur that lives in
Grandma's bedroom. Grandma won Charlotte at the
Point Pleasant boardwalk two years ago. Grandma put
four quarters down on number thirty-one, red. The guy
spun the game wheel. And Grandma won Charlotte.
Charlotte had originally been intended for Mary Alice, but Grandma got attached to Charlotte and kept
her. Some of the stuffing has shifted in Charlotte's big
dino body, so she has lumpy spots now . . . kind of like
Grandma.

Mary Alice ran upstairs and retrieved Charlotte. And
sure enough, the teeth were nicely set into Charlotte's
gaping mouth.

"Charlotte's teeth had lost their stuffing," Mary

Alice said. "And Charlotte was having trouble eating, so I gave her Grandma's teeth."

"Isn't that something," Grandma said. "I never noticed."

We all looked more closely at the teeth. They were decorated with flowers and tiny rainbows and colorful stars.

"I made the teeth more pretty with my markers," Mary Alice said. "I used the waterproof ones so they wouldn't wash off."

"That's nice, honey," Grandma said, "but I need my choppers on account of I've got a hot date tonight. I'll get Charlotte some teeth of her own."

Grandma took the teeth from Charlotte and put them into her mouth. Grandma smiled, and we all tried to stifle ourselves. Except for my father.

"Holy crap," my father said, staring transfixed at Grandma's decorated teeth.

The phone rang and Grandma ran to answer it. "It was my studmuffin," Grandma said when she hung up. "He said he had a hard day, and he needs to take a nap and recharge his battery. So we're going to meet up at Stiva's after dinner. There's going to be a special Christmas Eve viewing for Betty Schlimmer."

We always had baked ham for Christmas. The ham was hot on Christmas Eve, and for Christmas Day my mom would set out a big buffet with cold sliced ham and macaroni and about a billion other dishes.

Kloughn arrived just as we were sitting down to the table. "Am I late?" he asked. "I hope I'm not late. I tried not to be late, but there was an accident on Hamilton Avenue. A really good one. Legitimate neck injuries and everything. I think they might hire me." He kissed Valerie on the cheek and blushed bright red. "Are you okay?" he asked. "Did you throw up a lot today? Are you feeling any better? Boy, I sure wish you'd feel better."

Grandma passed Kloughn the mashed potatoes. "I hear those neck injuries can be worth a lot of money," Grandma said.

Kloughn looked at Grandma's teeth, and the potato spoon dropped out of his hand and clattered onto his plate. "Ulk," Kloughn said.

"You're probably wondering about my teeth," Grandma said to Kloughn. "Mary Alice decorated them for me."

"I've never seen decorated teeth before. I've seen decorated nails. And people get tattoos all over the place, right? So I guess decorated teeth could be the next big thing," Kloughn said. "Maybe I should get my teeth decorated. I wonder if I could get fish painted on them. What do you think about fish?"

"Rainbow trout would be good," Grandma said. "That way you could have lots of colors."

Mary Alice was fidgeting in her chair. She was softly talking to herself, twisting her hair around and around her index finger, wriggling on her seat.

"What's the matter?" Grandma asked. "Do you need to gallop?"

Mary Alice looked to my mother.

"Go for it," my mother said. "It's been too quiet around here. I think we need a horse to liven things up."

"I know there isn't any Santa Claus," Mary Alice said, "but if there *was,* do you think he'd give presents to a horse?"

We all jumped right in.

"Absolutely."

"Of course."

"You bet."

"Darn tootin', he'd give presents to a horse."

Mary Alice stopped fidgeting and looked thoughtful. "I was just wondering," she said.

Angie watched Mary Alice. "There *might* be a Santa," Angie said, very seriously.

Mary Alice stared at her plate. There were weighty decisions to be made here.

Mary Alice wasn't the only one caught between a rock and a hard place. I had Diesel on one side of me and Morelli on the other, and I could feel the pull of their personalities. They weren't competing. Diesel was in an entirely different place from Morelli. It was more that their energy fields were intersecting over my airspace.

Grandma jumped up halfway through dessert. "Look at the time," she said. "I gotta go. Bitsy Greenfield's picking me up, and she'll go without me if I'm not ready. We gotta get there early for this one. It's a special ceremony. It'll be standing room only."

"Maybe you shouldn't do too much talking," I said to Grandma. "People might not understand about the artwork on your teeth."

"No problem," she said. "Nobody in that crowd can see good enough to know anything's different. What with everyone having macular degeneration and cataracts, I don't have to even wear makeup. Being old has a lot of advantages. Everybody looks good when you got cataracts."

"Okay, so tell me again why this guy is your new best friend," Morelli said. We were outside on the small back porch, flapping our arms to keep warm. It was the only place to have a private conversation.

"He's looking for a guy named Ring. And he thinks Ring is somehow connected to me. But we don't know how. So he's staying close to me until we figure it out."

"How close?"

"Not that close."

Inside the house my parents and sister were dragging presents out from hiding places and arranging them under the tree. Angie and Mary Alice were sound asleep. Grandma was off somewhere, presumably with her studmuffin. And Diesel had been sent in search of batteries.

"I have a present for you," Morelli said, curling his fingers into my coat collar, pulling me to him.

"Is it a big present?"

"No. It's a small present."

So that eliminated the first item on my Christmas wish list.

Morelli gave me a little box, wrapped in red foil. I opened the box and found a ring. It was composed of slim intertwined gold and platinum bands. Set into the bands were three small deep blue sapphires. "It's a friendship ring," Morelli said. "We tried the engagement thing, and that didn't work."

"Not yet, anyway," I told him.

"Yeah, not yet," he said, sliding the ring onto my finger.

Sound carried crystal clear on the cold air. I heard a car pull up to the curb. A door opened and closed. And then a second.

"Aren't you the one," Grandma said.

The deeper male voice didn't carry back to us as clearly.

"It's Grandma and the studmuffin!" I whispered to Morelli.

"Listen," Morelli said, "I'd really like to stay but I've got this assignment . . ."

I opened the kitchen door. "Forget it. You're staying. I'm not facing the studmuffin alone."

"Look who I've got," Grandma announced to everyone. "This here's my friend John."

He was about five-foot-nine, with white hair, a ruddy complexion, and a slim build. He wore thick-lensed glasses and was dressed for the occasion in neatly pressed gray slacks, casual rubber-soled shoes, and a red blazer. Truth is, Grandma had dragged home a lot worse. If John had artificial parts, he was keeping them to himself. Fine by me.

Grandma didn't look nearly so well groomed. Her lipstick was smeared, and her hair was standing on end.

"Yikes," Morelli whispered to me.

I extended my hand to the studmuffin. "I'm Stephanie," I said.

He shook my hand and my scalp tingled and a tiny spark passed between us. "I'm John Ring," he said.

Oh boy. So this is the connection. This is the reason Diesel was dropped into my kitchen.

"He's just full of static electricity tonight," Grandma said. "We're gonna have to rub him down with one of them fabric softener sheets."

"I'm sorry I couldn't make dinner," Ring said. "I had a stressful day." He stepped closer, adjusted his glasses, and squinted at me. "Do I know you? You seem familiar, somehow."

"She's a bounty hunter," Grandma said. "She tracks down bad guys."

Zzzzzt. A series of sparks crackled off Ring's head.

"Isn't that something the way he can do that?" Grandma said. "He's been doing that all night."

My mother slyly made the sign of the cross and took a step backward. Morelli moved closer to me, pressing himself against my back, his hand at the nape of my neck.

"Look at the hair on my arm," Kloughn said. "It's

all standing up. Why do you suppose it's doing that? Boy, I'm kind of creeped out. Do you suppose it means something? What do you suppose it means?"

"The air's real dry," I said. "Sometimes hair doesn't lie down when the air's real dry."

Here I was, face to face with Ring, Diesel was off hunting batteries, and I hadn't a clue what to do. My heart was skipping beats, and I was humming from head to toe. I could feel vibrations coming through the soles of my shoes.

"I feel like a Slurpee," I said to Grandma and Ring. "How about we all go to 7-Eleven and get a Slurpee?"

"Now?" Grandma said. "We just got here."

"Yep. *Now.* I really need a Slurpee."

What I needed was to get Ring out of my parents' house. I didn't want him near Angie and Mary Alice. I didn't want him near my mom and dad.

"Maybe you could stay here and help wrap presents," I said to Grandma. "And Mr. Ring could give me a ride to 7-Eleven. It would give us a chance to get acquainted."

Zzzzt. Zzzzzt. Mr. Ring didn't seem to like that idea.

"Just a suggestion," I said.

Morelli's hand was steady at my neck, and Ring took a couple deep breaths.

"Are you okay?" Grandma asked Ring. "You don't look too good."

"I'm . . . excited," he said. "M-m-meeting your family." *Zzzt.*

It looked to me like Ring was having a control problem. He was leaking electricity. And he seemed as uncomfortable with his position as I was.

"Well," he said, forcing a smile, "this is a typical fun family Christmas, isn't it?" *Zzzzt.* He wiped a bead of sweat from his forehead. *Zzzt. Zzzt.* "And this is your lovely Christmas tree."

"I paid fifteen bucks for it," my father said.

Zzzt.

The tree had about twelve needles left on it and was tinder dry. My father diligently watered it every day, but this tree died in July.

Ring reached out, tentatively touched the tree, and it burst into flames.

"Holy shit," Kloughn yelped. "Fire. *Fire!* Get the kids out of the house. Get the dog. Get the ham."

The fire spread to the cotton batting wrapped around the base of the tree and then to the presents. A streak of fire raced up a nearby curtain.

"Call 911," my mother said. "Call the fire company. Frank, get the fire extinguisher from the kitchen!"

My dad turned to the kitchen, but Morelli already had the extinguisher in hand. Moments later, we all stood dazed, mouths agape, staring at the mess. The tree was gone. The presents were gone. The curtain was in tatters.

John Ring was gone.

And Diesel hadn't returned.

There was a loud series of explosions outside and through the window we saw the sky light up, bright as day. And then all was dark and quiet.

"Cripes," my dad said.

Grandma looked around. "Where's John? Where's my studmuffin?"

"You mean Sparky," Kloughn said. "Get it? Sparky?"

"Looks like he left," I said.

"Hunh, just like a man," Grandma said. "Burn down your Christmas tree and then up and leave."

Morelli set the fire extinguisher aside and crooked his arm around my neck. "Is there anything you want to tell me?"

"I don't think so."

"I didn't see any of this," Morelli said. "I didn't see the sparks coming off his head. And I didn't see him set the tree on fire."

"Me either," I told him. "I didn't see any of that stuff, either."

We all stood there for some more long moments with nothing to say. There were no words. Just shock. And maybe some denial.

A small, sleepy voice broke the silence.

"What happened?" Mary Alice asked.

She was on the stairs in her jammies. Angie was behind her.

"We had a fire," my mom said.

Mary Alice and Angie approached the tree. Mary Alice studied the charred boxes. She looked up at my mom. "Were these presents from the family?"

"Yes."

Mary Alice was sober. Thinking. She looked at Angie. And she looked at Grandma.

"That's good," she finally said, "because I'd hate to have Santa's presents get burned." Mary Alice climbed onto the couch and sat with her hands folded in her lap. "I'm going to wait for Santa," she said.

"I thought you didn't believe in Santa," Grandma said.

"Diesel said it's important to believe in things that make you happy. He was in my room just now, and he said he was going away, but Santa Claus would come to visit tonight."

"Did he have a horse with him?" Grandma asked. "Or a reindeer?"

Mary Alice shook her head. "It was just Diesel."

Angie climbed next to Mary Alice. "I'll wait, too."

"We should clean this mess up," Grandma said.

"Tomorrow," my mother told her, taking a dining

room chair into the living room, sitting across from Mary Alice and Angie. "I'm going to wait for Santa."

So we all sat and waited for Santa. We put the television on but we weren't really watching. We were listening for footsteps on the roof. Hoping to catch a glimpse of reindeer flying past the window. Waiting for something magical to happen.

The clock struck twelve and I heard cars drive up and doors open and close. And I heard voices, babbling in hushed excitement. There was a knock on the front door and we all jumped to our feet. I answered the door and wasn't too surprised to see Sandy Claws. He was dressed in a snappy red suit with a red Christmas tie. He held a box, all wrapped up in shiny paper and tied with a golden bow. Behind him squirmed a legion of elves. (Who was I to say if they were fake or real?) All bearing presents. Randy Briggs was among them.

"Diesel said you needed some help with Christmas," Claws said to me.

"Is he okay?"

"He's fine. Diesel is always fine. He's returning Ring to the Home."

"How can he do that? How can he get around the electricity stuff?"

"Diesel has ways."

"I bet you get harassed, right?" Kloughn said to a couple of the elves. "I bet you could use a good lawyer. Let me give you my card."

My mother rushed to the kitchen and returned with platters of cookies and fruitcake. My father cracked out some beer. Grandma eyed Claws.

"He's a cutie," she said to me. "Do you know if he's taken?"

The party lasted until all the presents were opened, the last cookie was eaten, the last beer swilled. The elves said their good-byes and packed off in their cars. Sandy Claws and Briggs remained with one last box. It was the box with the golden bow, and Claws gave the box to Mary Alice.

"I made this myself," he said. "Just for you. Keep it always. It's a special present for a very special person."

Mary Alice opened the box and looked inside. "It's beautiful," she said.

It was a horse. Carved from curly cherrywood.

Mary Alice held it in her hand. "It's warm," she said.

I felt the horse. It was cool to my touch. I raised eyebrows in question to Sandor.

"A special present for a special person," he said to me.

"A special person with special abilities?"

He smiled. "There are signs."

I smiled back at him.

"See you in court," he said.

I awoke at dawn and gently slid away from Morelli. I padded through my dark apartment to the kitchen. The mall tree was lit with tiny twinkle lights, and Diesel was leaning against the counter.

"Is this good-bye?" I asked him.

"Until next time." He took my hand and kissed my palm. "It was a good Christmas," he said. "See you around, sunshine."

"See you around," I said, but he was already gone.

And he was dead-on right, I thought. It was a *very* good Christmas.